JIM SHEPARD

LOVE AND HYDROGEN

Jim Shepard is the author of five previous novels, the story collection *Batting Against Castro*, and *Project X*, a novel to be published in hardcover simultaneously with this collection. He teaches at Williams College and lives with his wife, two sons, worrisome dog, and tiny, tiny daughter in Williamstown, Massachusetts.

ALSO BY JIM SHEPARD

Flights

Paper Doll

Lights Out in the Reptile House

Kiss of the Wolf

Nosferatu

Batting Against Castro: Stories

Project X

AS EDITOR

You've Got to Read This
(with Ron Hansen)

Unleashed: Poems by Writers' Dogs
(with Amy Hempel)

Writers at the Movies

LOVE & HYDROGEN

LOVE & HYDROGEN

NEW AND SELECTED STORIES

JIM SHEPARD

VINTAGE CONTEMPORARIES

VINTAGE BOOKS · A DIVISION OF RANDOM HOUSE, INC. · NEW YORK

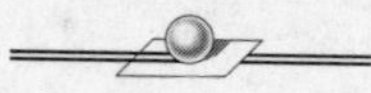

A VINTAGE CONTEMPORARIES ORIGINAL, JANUARY 2004

"The Gun Lobby" and "Eustace" appeared originally in *The Atlantic Monthly*; "Love and Hydrogen," "Runway," and "Ajax Is All About Attack" in *Harper's*; "Alicia and Emmett with the 17th Lancers at Balaclava" and "John Ashcroft: More Important Things Than Me" in *Tin House*; "Glut Your Soul on My Accursed Ugliness" in *DoubleTake*; "The Creature from the Black Lagoon" and "Won't Get Fooled Again" in *Playboy*; "Batting Against Castro" and "Climb Aboard the Mighty Flea" in *The Paris Review*; "Astounding Stories" in *McSweeney's*; "Messiah" in *GQ*; "Reach for the Sky" in *The New Yorker*; "Descent into Perpetual Night" in *SEED*; and "The Assassination of Reinhard Heydrich" in *Fiction*.

"Mars Attacks," "Spending the Night with the Poor," and "Krakatau" originally appeared in the collection *Batting Against Castro*, copyright © 1996 by Jim Shepard (Alfred A. Knopf, a division of Random House, Inc., New York).

"Piano Starts Here" originally appeared in the anthology *You Don't Know What Love Is: Contemporary American Love Stories*, edited by Ron Hansen (Ontario Review Books, 1987) and subsequently appeared in the collection *Batting Against Castro* (Alfred A. Knopf, a division of Random House, Inc., New York, 1996).

Library of Congress Cataloging-in-Publication Data
Shepard, Jim.
Love and hydrogen : new and selected stories / Jim Shepard.
p. cm.—(Vintage contemporaries original)
ISBN 1-4000-3349-7
I. Title.
PS3569.H39384L68 2004
813'.54—dc22 2003057554

Book design by Suvi Asch

www.vintagebooks.com

Printed in the United States of America
10 9 8 7 6 5 4 3 2 1

For Karen—again—

Acknowledgments

Without the contributions from the following sources, many of the stories in this book would have existed in a much paltrier form: Mano Ziegler's *Rocket Fighter*; William Beebe's *Half Mile Down*; Tom Simkin and Richard Fiske's *Krakatau 1883*; Mireille Majoor and Ken Marschall's *Inside the Hindenburg*; Cecil Woodham-Smith's *The Reason Why*; Jan Weiner's *The Assassination of Heydrich*; David Winner's *Brilliant Orange*; The *Congressional Record*; and John Ashcroft and Gary Thomas's *Lessons from a Father to His Son.* I'm also grateful for the expertise provided by James Wood, David Dethier, and Grant Farred. And I particularly want to cite the invaluable, tireless, and long-term contributions of Steve Wright, Geoff Sanborn, Gary Zebrun, Mike Tanaka, Sandy Leong, Ron Hansen, and—as always—Karen Shepard.

Contents

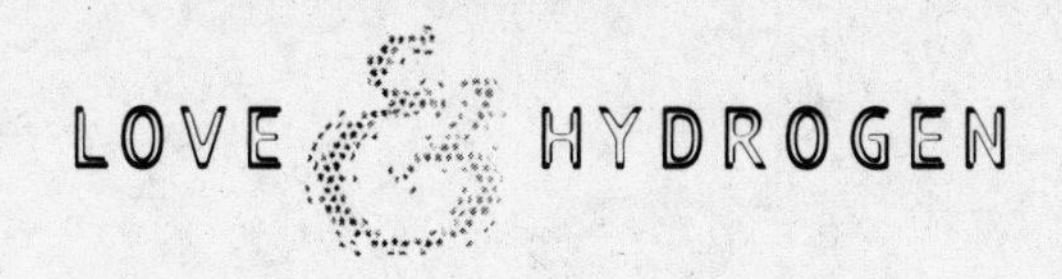
LOVE & HYDROGEN

THE GUN LOBBY

My old friend Chick sells guns out of a hamper he keeps in his basement. He sells them at gun fairs and uses the money to buy more guns that he sells at other gun fairs. It's a living, he says.

I give him some mild grief about the hamper and he puts up with it, like a little rain on a nice day. The hamper's got straw flowers on it and a little wicker clasp. He could have phased it out by now, certainly, and it hasn't been close to big enough since what he calls The Early Years, but he keeps it in service. He says, "My reasons cluster in the What Do *You* Care? category." As in, when you ask, that's what you're told. His attachment to the hamper feels to me like nostalgia. But Chick is a puzzle, and I may be wrong.

Chick says that a sentence about selling whatever you want to whoever you want is in the Bill of Rights and never gets talked about. He says that in our history books, every paragraph and a half, someone's reaching for a gun.

He gets no arguments from me. I grew up on all those snub-nosed pioneer kids sitting around on their little woven rugs, learning their long division with coal on the backs of shovels while they listened to stories about Daniel Boone's Old Bess, Bess Boone's Little Danny, Betsy Ross's Philadelphia derringer, or Carrie Nation's homemade zipgun. Sgt. York from the hills of West Virginia, who could peg a squirrel's retina at nine thousand yards. Slow Tick Billy, last to draw but first to let fly once things were unholstered. We just knew as kids that everybody, tiny tots to tall Texans, sat around dreaming about potting the next Mohawk to cut through the back garden.

As far as Chick's concerned, guns pay for braces, trips, and pretty soon, colleges. He has two big girls, Amanda and Astra, and two little boys, Emmett and Jasper. Before bed the girls kneel side by side and pass along to God prayers for Mommy and Daddy and their brothers and the gun lobby.

Chick sells Colts, Walthers, Glocks, Uzis, and Ingrams. He services the Colts and Ingrams himself, with one hand on the manual. He dabbles in Kalashnikovs. His big score was a Schmeiser with the original firing pin which he turned around in two days for triple profit. He's had poison-tipped darts from the Amazon and a box of curved rubber truncheons said to be favored by the Albanian police. He has squirreled away in his little root-cellar-y sub-basement some high-end contraband laser sights, a crate of phased-out NATO flash grenades (with the rounder bodies, before they went to the narrow design), and a drop tank from an F-18. In the sub-sub-basement in a beer cooler he's stashed an old scorched liquid nitrogen canister wrapped in gummy and tenacious biohazard tape. The kids call the sub-sub-basement Daddy's secret secret room. He's mum on what's inside the canister, which is part of the mystery of Chick.

He also stockpiled some Claymores for a buddy moving them upstate. He gave the buddy thirty-six hours to pick them up. They had to be primed and set to blow, but even so, you don't want the kids poking around the antipersonnel mines. He kept everything locked up tight, but still, how many parents have said that before?

He sold my wife everything she wanted when she stopped by his basement, without fully consulting me. She went the better-safe-than-sorry route when it came to quantity. He sold her a Glock, an Uzi, an Ingram M-10, and a nifty little Travis Bickle .25 caliber on a sliding brace arrangement that fits around the forearm and allows the wearer to squeeze off a clip even after massive arm trauma. It looked like overkill to me, and now he admits that he may have gone, as he puts it, a gun too far. Stephanie paid in cash—Chick doesn't take Visa—and I have to assume the total was a stiff piece of change, especially with holsters and ammo thrown in.

Stephanie kept her family name when she married me, so our mailbox says Home of Roger Chanute and Stephanie von Watzdorf. I tell her I'm sorry she's never been happy here and she tells me she's always thought the place was fine; it's me she's never been happy with.

"Here" is Waterbury, Connecticut, which is right now the main show in terms of the cutaway news, because of the standoff. You can see Stephanie or me, the Hostage, at the windows every so often on TV. We watch ourselves.

The house is always on. My rake's still in the leaves in the front yard. You can see frost on the ground.

Stephanie's turned off the heat, to get serious, she says, so she's usually in her outgrown Brearley blazer. In the mornings we can see our breath. I asked about the heat the first morning, but I'm not going to press it. She goes around the house with a semiautomatic in each hand. She's originally from Manhattan.

"They're lining me up right now," she cackled yesterday when she passed a window. "Some SWAT guy's shouting into his radio, 'I could take her now.'"

I reminded her of all the hostage movies we've seen that have turned out badly. *Dog Day Afternoon*. I ran out of titles.

"*Rebel Without a Cause,*" I added.

"They weren't hostages," Stephanie said contemptuously.

"He was waving a gun around," I told her.

She was sitting at the kitchen table flipping a quarter in one hand like George Raft.

"My point was, it was a tragedy that could easily have been averted," I murmured.

"You're a pig," she said. "You respect nothing. You have the integrity of a grease trap."

I asked her whatever happened to divorce in such situations. Flak-jacketed sharpshooters for the state were peeking out here and there around the cop cars and TV vans. She gave me a look to let me know that the whole standoff could have come to an end right then.

I'm not going to provide a whole Ring trilogy of what she's been mad at. I will say that she's right in that I'm not much good when it comes to empathy, my share of the day-to-day work, sobriety, monogamy, fiscal responsibility, or periodontal hygiene. We'd had two trial separations and she'd gotten skinned both times on support. She had her Manhattan lawyers but they had to deal with good old-fashioned Waterbury judges. She didn't need the money, but, you know. It's humiliating.

Chick's been the only one allowed in to negotiate, maybe because he sold her the guns. Maybe because he's a mystery. She won't talk to the police directly even on the phone. They drove Kurt and Lucille, her father and mother, all the way up from the East Side and she didn't bother to come to the line. Lucille's way of easing into the situation was to open with, "Stephanie, *pick up the phone.*" This over the bullhorn. I could've told her how that was going to go over.

Every so often I ask her what she thinks she's going to get out of this situation. I can tell it's not the right question to ask.

Negotiations have been on hold since one of the troopers took a round in the shoulder while passing out coffee. "What was *that* all about?" I asked her after I ran into the room. She didn't answer.

Chick, when he came, came unarmed, which was lucky for him. You'd think she'd been frisking people with the business end of an Ingram her whole life. He gave the pantry a glance to see how our food was holding out. Between calls from the police, he talked to us about how the neighborhood was taking it.

When he got the chance he gave me a look as if to say, Sorry, Buddy. I gave him back the I'm-looking-through-you thing. I call it The Stephanie.

For those who think Chick would be a different man had he had some personal connection to what can happen when handguns proliferate, let me report that his uncle in Florida was shot four times in the head with a Saturday night special in a disagreement over a game of gin rummy. Apparently it was the fourth shot that killed him. The guy who shot him was a real mutt. The guy bought the gun that day, drunk, at a gun fair in Orlando. After his purchase, he threw up in the aisle and got thrown out of the mall. A simple background check would have saved the uncle's life. Chick says a saliva test would have weeded the guy out. And has that changed his mind about guns? "Hey, I didn't stop eating ham sandwiches after Mama Cass choked to death," he says.

Nobody's even tried to negotiate with us for the last day and a half. We've been pretty much staying in the kitchen. Every so often I toast a little something in the oven with the door open, to warm up.

Stephanie's been keeping to herself, across the room. After Chick's last visit, she magic-markered an orange-and-white target and cut it out and pinned it to her Agnès b. blouse. She hung the blouse in the front window. It's a weird effect on TV.

The gun lobby's not really a "lobby," in the sense of a pleasant little room with chairs and some nice light, or in the sense of a group of concerned citizens trying to get their point of view a hearing. It's more a lobby the way the Stasi was a lobby. If the gun lobby were a famous athlete, ESPN's Kenny Mayne would have it shout, like after a three-run jack in the ninth, "I am the *lord* of *all* I *survey*!" Dan Patrick would say, "You can't stop The Gun Lobby. You can't even hope to slow it down."

The gun lobby's not pernicious or evil or embattled or heroic; it just is. It's like the Samarian Gorge, or German efficiency, or beans in the soup, or the death of the Sun. What does it mean to "stand up" to the gun lobby? How do you solve a problem like Maria? How do you catch a cloud and pin it down?

There're all sorts of things about this country I never liked, and I'm a guy who believes in making a difference. My way of doing that is by not taking part in any political activity whatsoever. When we were courting, Stephanie used to say that it was all of a piece: when there was a problem, if she brought it up, we talked about it—at least for a few minutes—and if she didn't, we didn't. I'm a big sins of omission kind of guy, apparently. I just go through life not doing anything to anyone, wreaking havoc left and right.

"Here're my options with you," Stephanie would say, lying in bed next to me, her eyes wet. "Either my lifemate-soulmate-husband is too stupid and self-involved to know what he's doing to me, which isn't good news, or he *does* know, and he's being disingenuous about it. Which is even worse news."

Then of course I'd catch grief for not having any comeback to that. And what exactly is an acceptable comeback for that?

The truth is, in most of my regrettable recent moves it's like I'm throwing a sheet over a sawhorse: I'm just trying to give some shape to all the disappointment.

I've been a problem baby, a lousy son, a distant brother, an off-putting neighbor, a piss-poor student, a worrisome seatmate, an unreliable employee, a bewildering lover, a frustrating confidant, and a crappy husband. Among the things I do pretty well at this point I'd have to list darts, reclosing Stay-Fresh boxes, and staying out of the way.

Stephanie's been pretty hemmed in the last few years, between me—The Lump—her mother, whom she calls Ilsa Koch Without the Charm, and this whole cervical problem that's allowed us to go to meeting after meeting and watch doctors scratch their heads. Doctors find Stephanie's condition an interesting puzzle, something meaty to mull over. We see a lot of pursing of lips and nodding while we recite our tale of woe, and then we're told what it isn't, and then we all decide to Wait and See how things develop, and then on the way out Stephanie or I pay what the insurance doesn't cover. It's not clear whether we can have kids, but they do make it clear that I should have been doing more hand-wringing about it. Instead of screwing around with one of the checkout girls at an auto-parts store.

Add to that Roger's old friend Chick, handling the entrepreneurial training and emotional counseling. He and Stephanie hit it off, in a cobra-mongoose sort of way, right from the beginning. I used to think they competed to see who could put up with more from me.

"You see that look?" he said to me, right in front of her, after he first met her. "That's the 'Now I see where my husband gets it from' look."

"Does he seem like a bad influence?" I asked Stephanie after he left.

"In every way possible," she said.

FOR YEARS CHICK has been disappointed in my politics, my education, my general deportment, and my lack of overall curiosity about the way things work. He's always seen a residue of potential, though.

The last few years we've been like the Collier Brothers. I was over there most nights nine to one. His wife went to bed at nine. He counseled me against involvement with Stephanie, though it was a little late in the day for that. At the same time, he had dry mounted and pinned to his worktable in the sub-sub-basement an infrared photo of her that he'd taken with a nightscope. It looked like a cross between a pinup and a black-light poster. I mentioned it to Stephanie. She didn't give me a lot of reaction. "The mystery of Chick," she said to herself every so often when I'd be heading out the door.

A few months ago he dropped by to show off a set of Finnish Puukko knives and invited himself for dinner. Stephanie gave me a look and I let it go by. So she said, "Allrighty, then," and stretched the fish by poaching it in a can of minestrone soup. Chick waded right in next to her. He started pitching spices into the saucepan and promising to get the dish up on its feet.

"Not that he'll notice," he said, indicating me.

"I could blindfold him and feed him an onion, he'd think it was an apple," Stephanie said.

They went on like that all through dinner. They commiserated about how my eyelids tended to droop when I was trying to concentrate.

"He lies all the time," Chick complained to her. "He tells you one thing and he's thinking another."

"Did you used to think he was kind?" she asked him. "I used to think he was kind. Or wanted to be kind. Or something."

"Sometimes I think he's a good man, and sometimes I'm not so sure," Chick told her.

"Exactly," she told him back. "Exactly."

I played with the knives and sat there. I told them I felt like a guy in a glass booth and they were two Israelis haggling over a verdict.

"That's perfect," Stephanie said. "The banality of evil."

"Oh, man," Chick said.

"You and Chick hit it off this evening," I told Stephanie later that night.

"When are you going to talk to me?" she said. "Are you ever going to talk to me?"

"What're we doing right now?" I wanted to know. But that was it, end of discussion. She whacked her bedside lamp switch and shut down for the night.

She called him once or twice that I knew about and tried to talk to him about me. She even flirted with him once, a month or two after that dinner, when I was keeping to my bed. She went over there and hung out in the sub-sub-basement, with the wife asleep upstairs. She told me the next morning that she got a look at the canister. She still refers to the whole thing as her Low Point.

For a while she drew lines on the inside of her arm with my Gillette. I didn't say anything. I broke it off with the auto-parts woman.

Like I said before, she's right. I have the integrity of a four-dollar tent.

Last night I gave it one last shot. I appealed to the Old Us. Remember when I used to listen? I asked. Remember when we respected me a little bit? Remember when there was something worth saving here? Meaning me. She just lay there, her palm spread over the Glock, her eyes wet.

Chick remembered. On the way out after his last negotiation attempt, he said to me, "Hang in there, buddy. Don't forget Orchard Street." He was talking about the morning junior year when a woman sat down in the grass in front of us and her grocery bag tipped over. He ran to call the ambulance and I sat with her. She was gray and sweaty and hung on to my shoulder and started telling me about how she met her husband. How it was because he went back for his sweater and how for a while she worried she didn't deserve to be so happy. Every so often whatever it was would grab her and she'd clench my shirt in her hands. The ambulance went to Orchard Drive instead of Orchard Street, so it was twenty minutes getting there. I laid her down and she kept my shirt in her hands. Chick stayed half a backyard away, watching. I had my hands on both sides of her head. When the ambulance finally came they went about getting her ready to load in. When they tried to separate my shirt from her fist and I saw her face, I said I'd ride with her. She nodded to them over and over again and they figured I was family.

I sat with her the whole day and night. I called my parents to tell them I'd be late. Her husband never showed up. The nurses called and then I called a few times. I found out her name was Anne DiCicco. She had no kids. She was in a lot of pain and slept on and off. She told me again about her husband's sweater.

I told Stephanie about it on one of our dates. She especially liked the part about my going to see the bereaved husband afterward, and my asking to see the sweater. She touched my fingers, on the tablecloth.

A little while later, before we got married, we were lying around in a bed-and-breakfast in Winsted one morning and she started volunteering what she liked about me. I had a sense of humor, I handled instruction well, and I had a good heart. She mentioned the woman in the hospital, and the sweater.

I told Chick how much the story meant to her. That's also what he meant when he said, "Don't forget Orchard Street."

I fall asleep seeing him climb a balloon, with Stephanie not far behind. Their faces are peaceful.

In the morning when I come out of my doze, I'm alone.

I lie still, listening. The bedroom window's right there: all I have to do is climb out on the garage roof.

The whole house is quiet. It's quiet outside.

When I come downstairs, she's at the kitchen table leafing through the little notebook she kept the first time we tried to get pregnant.

"I made tea," she says, like her heart's going to break.

We can tell that the sunlight's amazing even with the shades pulled. On the street, things are stirring. The sound's off on the TV but lots of vehicles are backing up and moving out. We've been Breaking News for a full four and a half days, and the forces of order are probably getting antsy.

On the next channel, the SkyView Eye on Connecticut shows a lot of activity in the rear echelons. Stephanie and I are quiet about it, just watching.

"I think this may be it," she says, like my corn muffin's ready. She throws the bolt on the Uzi.

From the helicopter view someone who looks like Chick is squatting near a hydrant. Guys fan out from dark blue vans. Then the coverage switches to something suspiciously bland, a little stretch around our front door. You can see in the blurry foreground our mailbox, all shot to pieces when she hamstrung the mailman. The next channel's showing only talking heads.

Around us outside we can hear the thumping on the lawn of big heavy guys trying to be catlike. There're leaves all over the ground, too, so the whole surprise thing is really out the window.

"Hey, Roger," Stephanie says: a nice hello.

Glass shatters and there's a white, chest-thumping concussion of flash grenades and the sound of all three doors caving in, like four or five breakfronts being cannonaded. We're propelled out of our seats, spinning, moles in sunlight. The Ingram sounds like a portable jackhammer and the Uzi like manic static.

I have a hold of Stephanie's ankle. For the longest time I'm not hurt. Her rate of fire is spectacular. The ordnance coming back at us sets everything in the kitchen into electric life. Our overhead fixture's doing a tarantella.

There are events in which every second can be taken out of line, examined this way and that, and then allowed to move along. This is one of them. What I think are hits are shell casings cascading down my head and shoulders. A flash grenade bumps and hisses and teeters on the floor by my cheek. Two guys are down in the hallway and one seems to be napping on the sofa. A second concussion separates us, and then there's the gift of resumed fire everywhere, and my foot and leg are grated and chopped. The house is a festival of small-arms fire. Stephanie's on her side, under the kitchen table. The .25 caliber's come down her forearm mount but isn't firing. The linoleum deforms and sprouts. This is my way of finding her, and her way of finding me. I have the time to think, and in that time I think that we failed not because of what we didn't have but because of what we wanted: one more look into those old hearts, the ones we turned our backs on, the ones we owed everything to.

LOVE AND HYDROGEN

Imagine five or six city blocks could lift, with a bump, and float away. The impression the 804-foot-long *Hindenburg* gives on the ground is that of an airship built by giants and excessive even to their purposes. The fabric hull and mainframe curve upward sixteen stories high.

Meinert and Gnüss are out on the gangway ladder down to the starboard #1 engine car. They're helping out the machinists, in a pinch. Gnüss is afraid of heights, which amuses everyone. It's an open aluminum ladder with a single handrail extending eighteen feet down into the car's hatchway. They're at 2,000 feet. The clouds below strand by and dissipate. It's early in a mild May in 1937.

Their leather caps are buckled around their chins, but they have no goggles. The air buffets by at eighty-five miles per hour. Meinert shows him how to hook his arm around the leading edge of the ladder to keep from being blown off as he leaves the hull. Even through the sheepskin gloves the metal is shockingly cold from the slipstream. The outer suede of the grip doesn't provide quite the purchase they would wish when hanging their keisters out over the open Atlantic. Every raised foot is wrenched from the rung and flung into space.

Servicing the engines inside the cupola, they're out of the blast, but not the cold. Raising a head out of the shielded area is like being cuffed by a bear. It's a pusher arrangement, thank God. The back ends of the cupolas are open to facilitate maintenance on the blocks and engine mounts. The engines are 1,100-horsepower diesels four feet high. The propellers are twenty-two feet long. When they're down on their hands and knees adjusting the vibration dampers, those props are a foot and a half away. The sound is like God losing his temper, kettledrums in the sinuses, fists in the face.

MEINERT AND GNÜSS are both Regensburgers. Meinert was in his twenties and Gnüss a child during the absolute worst years of the inflation. They lived on mustard sandwiches, boiled kale, and turnip mash. Gnüss's most cherished toy for a year and a half was a clothespin on which his father had painted a face. They're ecstatic to have found positions like this. Their work fills them with elation, and the kind of spuriously proprietary pride that mortal tour guides might feel on Olympus. Meals that seem giddily baronial—plates crowded with sausages, tureens of soups, platters of venison or trout or buttered potatoes—appear daily, once the passengers have been served, courtesy of Luftschiffbau Zeppelin. Their sleeping berths, aboard and ashore, are more luxurious than any other place they've previously laid their heads.

Meinert and Gnüss are in love. This complicates just about everything. They steal moments when they can—on the last Frankfurt to Rio run, they exchanged an intense and acrobatic series of caresses 135 feet up inside the superstructure, when Meinert was supposed to have been checking a seam on one of the gasbags for wear, their glue pots clacking and clocking together—but mostly their ardor is channeled so smoothly into underground streams that even their siblings, watching them work, would be satisfied with their rectitude.

Meinert loves Gnüss's fussiness with detail, his loving solicitude with all schedules and plans, the way he seems to husband good feeling and pass it around among his shipmates. He loves the celebratory delight Gnüss takes in all meals, and watches him with the anticipatory excitement that an enthusiast might bring to a sublime stretch of *Aïda.* Gnüss has a shy and diffident sense of humor that's particularly effective in groups. At the base of his neck, so it's hidden by a collar, he has a tattoo of a figure eight of rope: an infinity sign. He's exceedingly well proportioned.

Gnüss loves Meinert's shoulders, his way of making every physical act worthy of a Johnny Weissmuller, and the way he can play the irresponsible daredevil and still erode others' disapproval or righteous indignation. He's openmouthed at the way Meinert flaunts the sort of insidious and disreputable charm that all mothers warn against. In his bunk at night, Gnüss sometimes thinks, *I refuse to list all his other qualities,* for fear of agitating himself too completely. He calls Meinert *Old Shatterhand.* They joke about the age difference.

It goes without saying that the penalty for exposed homosexuality in this case would begin at the loss of one's position. Captain Pruss, a fair man and an excellent captain, a month ago remarked in Gnüss's presence that he'd throw any fairy he came across bodily out of the control car.

Meinert bunks with Egk; Gnüss with Thoolen. It couldn't be helped. Gnüss had wanted to petition for their reassignment as bunkmates—what was so untoward about friends wanting to spend more time together?—but Meinert the daredevil had refused to risk it. Each night Meinert lies in his bunk wishing they'd risked it. As a consolation, he passed along to Gnüss his grandfather's antique silver pocket watch. It had already been engraved *To My Dearest Boy.*

Egk is a fat little man with boils. Meinert considers him to have been well named. He whistles the same thirteen-note motif each night before lights out.

How much happiness is someone entitled to? This is the question that Gnüss turns this way and that in his aluminum bunk in the darkness. The ship betrays no tremor or sense of movement as it slips through the sky like a fish.

He is proud of his feelings for Meinert. He can count on one hand the number of people he's known he believes to be capable of feelings as exalted as his.

Meinert, meanwhile, has developed a flirtation with one of the passengers: perhaps the only relationship possible that would be more forbidden than his relationship with Gnüss. The flirtation alternately irritates and frightens Gnüss.

The passenger is one of those languid teenagers who own the world. She has a boy's haircut. She has a boy's chest. She paints her lips but otherwise wears no makeup. Her parents are briskly polite with the crew and clearly excited by their first adventure on an airship; she is not. She has an Eastern name: Tereska.

Gnüss had to endure their exchange of looks when the girl's family first came aboard. Passengers had formed a docile line at the base of the main gangway. Gnüss and Meinert had been shanghaied to help the chief steward inspect luggage and personal valises for matches, lighters, camera flashbulbs, flashlights, even a child's sparking toy pistol: anything that might mix apocalyptically with their ship's seven million cubic feet of hydrogen. Two hundred stevedores in the ground crew were arrayed every ten feet or so around their perimeter, dragging slightly back and forth on their ropes with each shift in the wind. Meinert made a joke about drones pulling a queen. The late afternoon was blue with rain and fog. A small, soaked Hitler Youth contingent with two bedraggled Party pennants stood at attention to see them off.

Meinert was handed Tereska's valise, and Tereska wrestled it back, rummaging through it shoulder to shoulder with him. They'd given one another playful bumps.

The two friends finished their inspections and waited at attention until all the passengers were up the gangway. "Isn't she the charming little rogue," Gnüss remarked.

"Don't scold, Auntie," Meinert answered.

The first signal bell sounded. Loved ones who came to see the travelers off waved and shouted. A passenger unbuckled his wristwatch and tossed it from one of the observation windows as a farewell present. Meinert and Gnüss were the last ones aboard and secured the gangway. Two thousand pounds of water ballast was dropped. The splash routed the ranks of the Hitler Youth contingent. At 150 feet the signal bells of the engine telegraphs jangled, and the engines one by one roared to life. At 300 feet the bells rang again, calling for higher revolutions.

On the way to their subsequent duties, the two friends took a moment at a free spot at an observation window, watching the ground recede. The passengers were oohing and aahing the mountains of Switzerland and Austria as they fell away to the south, inverted in the mirrorlike expanse of the lake. The ship lifted with the smoothness of planetary motion.

ALOFT, their lives had really become a pair of stupefying narratives. Frankfurt to Rio in three and a half days. Frankfurt to New York in two. The twenty-five passenger cabins on A deck slept two in stateroom comfort and featured featherlight and whisper-quiet sliding doors. On B deck passengers could lather up in the world's first airborne shower. The smoking room, off the bar and double-sealed all the way round, stayed open until the last guests said good night. The fabric-covered walls in the lounge and public areas were decorated with hand-painted artwork. Each room had its own theme: the main salon, a map of the world crosshatched by the routes of famous explorers; the reading room, scenes of the history of postal delivery. An aluminum bust of General von Hindenburg sat in a halo of light on an ebony base in a niche at the top of the main gangway. A place setting for two for dinner involved fifty-eight pieces of Dresden china and silver. The butter knives' handles were themselves minizeppelins. Complementary sleeping caps were bordered with the legend *An Bord Des Luftschiffes Hindenburg.* Luggage tags were stamped *Im Zeppelin Über Den Ozean* and featured an image of the *Hindenburg* bearing down, midocean, on what looked like the Santa Maria.

WHEN HE CAN put Tereska out of his head, Gnüss is giddy with the danger and improbability of it all. The axial catwalk is 10 inches wide at its base and 782 feet long and 110 feet above the passenger and crew compartments below. Crew members require the nimbleness of structural steelworkers. The top of the gas cells can only be inspected from the vertical ringed ladders running along the inflation pipes: sixteen stories up into the radial and spiraling bracing wires and mainframe. Up that high, the airship's interior seems to have its own weather. Mists form. The vast cell walls holding the seven million cubic feet of hydrogen billow and flex.

At the very top of Ladder #4 on the second morning out, Meinert hangs from one hand. He spins slowly above Gnüss, down below with the glue pots, like a high-wire act seen at such a distance that all the spectacle is gone. He sings one of his songs from the war, when as a seventeen-year-old he served on the LZ-98 and bombed London when the winds let them reach it. His voice is a floating echo from above:

In Paris people shake all over
In terror as they wait.
The Count prefers to come at night,
Expect us at half past eight!

Gnüss nestles in and listens. On either side of the catwalk, great tanks carry 143,000 pounds of diesel oil and water. Alongside the tanks, bays hold food supplies, freight, and mail. This is one of his favorite places to steal time. They sometimes linger here for the privacy and the ready excuses—inspection or errands—that all this storage space affords.

Good news: Meinert signals that he's located a worn patch, necessitating help. Gnüss climbs to him with another glue pot and a pot of the gelatin latex used to render the heavy-duty sailmaker's cotton gas-tight. His erection grows as he climbs.

THEIR REPAIRS COMPLETE, they're both strapped in on the ladder near the top, mostly hidden in the gloom and curtaining folds of the gas cell. Gnüss, in a reverie after their lovemaking, asks Meinert if he can locate the most ecstatic feeling he's ever experienced. Meinert can. It was when he'd served as an observer on a night attack on Calais.

Gnüss still has Meinert's warm sex in his hand. This had been the LZ-98, captained by Lehmann, Meinert reminds him. They'd gotten nowhere on a hunt for fogbound targets in England, but conditions over Calais had been ideal for the observation basket: thick cloud at 4,000 feet, but the air beneath crystalline. The big airships were much safer when operating above cloud. But then: how to see their targets?

The solution was exhilarating: on their approach they throttled the motors as far back as they could while retaining the power to maneuver. The zeppelin was leveled out at 500 feet above the cloud layer, and then, with a winch and a cable, Meinert, as Air Observer, was lowered 2,000 feet in the observation basket, a hollow metal capsule scalloped open at the top. He had a clear view downward, and his gondola, so relatively tiny, was invisible from the ground.

Dropping into space in that little bucket had been the most

frightening and electric thing he'd ever done. He'd been swept along alone under the cloud ceiling and over the lights of the city, like the messenger of the gods.

The garrison of the fort had heard the sound of their motors, and the light artillery had begun firing in that direction. But only once had a salvo come close enough to have startled him with its crash.

His cable extended above his head into the darkness and murk. It bowed forward. The capsule canted from the pull. The wind streamed past him. The lights rolled by below. From his wicker seat he directed the immense invisible ship above by telephone, and set and reset their courses by eye and by compass. He crisscrossed them over the fort for forty-five minutes, signaling when to drop their small bombs and phosphorus incendiaries. The experience was that of a sorcerer's, hurling thunderbolts on his own. That night he'd been a regular Regensburg Zeus. The bombs and incendiaries detonated on the railroad station, the warehouses, and the munitions dumps. When they fell they spiraled silently out of the darkness above and plummeted past his capsule, the explosions carried away behind him. Every so often luminous ovals from the fort's searchlights rippled the bottoms of the clouds like a hand lamp beneath a tablecloth.

Gnüss, still hanging in his harness, is disconcerted by the story. He tucks Meinert's sex back into the opened pants.

"That feeling comes back to me when I'm my happiest: hiking or alone," Meinert muses. "And when I'm with you, as well," he adds, after having seen Gnüss's face.

Gnüss buckles his own pants, unhooks his harness, and begins his careful descent. "I don't think I make you feel like Zeus," he says, a little sadly.

"Well, like Pan, anyway," Meinert calls out from above him.

• • •

THAT EVENING darkness falls on the ocean below while the sun is still a glare on the frames of the observation windows. Meinert and Gnüss have their evening duties, as waiters. Their stations are across the room from one another. The dining room is the very picture of a fine hotel restaurant, without the candles. After dinner, they continue to ferry drinks from the bar on B deck to thirsty guests in the lounge and reading rooms. Through the windows, the upper surfaces of the clouds in the moonlight are as brilliant as breaking surf. Tereska is nowhere to be found.

Upon retiring, passengers leave their shoes in the corridor, as on shipboard. Newspaper correspondents stay up late in the salon, typing bulletins to send by wireless ahead to America. In the darkness and quiet before they themselves turn in, Gnüss leads Meinert halfway up Ladder #4 yet again, to reward him for having had no contact whatsoever with that teenager. Their continuing recklessness feels like Love itself.

Like their airship, their new home when not flying is Friedrichshafen, beside the flatly placid Lake Constance. The Company's presence has transformed the little town. In gratitude the town fathers have erected a Zeppelin fountain in the courtyard of the Rathaus, the centerpiece of which is the Count bestride a globe, holding a log-sized airship in his arms.

Friedrichshafen is on the north side of the lake, with the Swiss mountains across the water to the south, including the snowcapped Säntis, rising some 8,000 feet. Meinert has tutored Gnüss in mountain hiking, and Gnüss has tutored Meinert in oral sex above the tree line. They've taken chances as though cultivating a death wish: in a lift in the famous Insel Hotel, in rented rooms in the woodcarving town of Überlingen and Meersburg with its old castle dating back to the seventh century. In vineyards on the southern exposures of hillsides. Even, once, in a lavatory in the Maybach engine plant, near the gear manufacturing works.

When not perversely risking everything they had for no real reason, they lived like the locals, with their coffee and cake on Sunday afternoon and their raw smoked ham as the ubiquitous appetizer for every meal. They maintained their privacy as weekend hikers and developed the southerner's endless capacity for arguing the merits of various mountain trails. By their third year in Friedrichshafen their motto was "A mountain each weekend." They spent nights in mountain huts, and in winter they might go entire days skiing without seeing other adventurers. If Meinert had asked his friend which experience had been the most ecstatic of *his* young life, Gnüss would have cited the week they spent alone in a hut over one Christmas holiday.

NEITHER HAS BEEN BACK to Regensburg for years. Gnüss's most vivid memory of it, for reasons he can't locate, is of the scrape and desolation of his dentist's tooth-cleaning instruments one rainy March morning. Meinert usually refers to their hometown as Vitality's Graveyard. His younger brother still writes to him twice a week. Gnüss still sends a portion of his pay home to his parents and sisters.

Gnüss knows that he's being the young and foolish one but nevertheless can't resist comparing the invincible intensity of his feelings for Meinert with his pride at serving on this airship—this machine that conquers two oceans at once, the one above and the one below—this machine that brought their country supremacy in passenger, mail, and freight service to the North and South American continents only seventeen years after the Treaty of Versailles.

Even calm, cold, practical minds that worked on logarithms or carburetors felt the strange joy, the uncanny fascination, the radiance of atmospheric and gravitational freedom. They'd watched the *Graf Zeppelin,* their sister ship, take off one beautiful morning, the sun dazzling on its aluminum dope as if it were levitating on light, and it was like watching Juggernaut float free of the earth. One night they'd gone down almost to touch the waves and scared a fishing boat in the fog, and had joked afterward about what the boat's crew must have experienced: looking back to see a great dark, whirring thing rise like a monster upon them out of the murky air.

THEY'RE BOTH PARTY MEMBERS. They were over Aachen during the national referendum on the annexation of the Rhineland, and helped the chief steward rig up a polling booth on the port promenade deck. The Yes vote had carried among the passengers and crew by a count of 103 to 1.

MEALS IN FLIGHT are so relaxed that some guests arrive for breakfast in their pajamas. Tereska is one such guest, and Gnüss from his station watches Meinert chatting and flirting with her. *She's only an annoyance,* he reminds himself, but his brain seizes and charges around enough to make him dizzy.

The great mass of the airship is off-limits to passengers except for those on guided tours. Soon after the breakfast service is cleared, Meinert informs him, with insufficient contrition, that Tereska's family has requested him as their guide. An hour later, when it's time for the tour to begin, there's Tereska alone, in her boyish shirt and sailor pants. She jokes with Meinert and lays a hand on his forearm. He jokes with her.

Gnüss, beside himself, contrives to approach her parents, sunning themselves by a port observation window. He asks if they'd missed the tour. It transpires that the bitch has forewarned them that it would involve a good deal of uncomfortable climbing and claustrophobic poking about.

He stumbles about below decks, only half-remembering his current task. What's happened to his autonomy? What's happened to his ability to generate contentment for himself independent of Meinert's behavior? Before all this he saw himself in the long term as First Officer, or at least Chief Sailmaker: a solitary and much admired figure of cool judgments and sober self-mastery. Instead, now he feels overheated and coursed through with kineticism, like an agitated and kenneled dog.

He delivers the status report on the ongoing inspection of the gas cells. "Why are you *weeping*?" Sauter, the Chief Engineer, asks.

RESPONSIBILITY HAS FLOWN out the window. He takes to carrying Meinert's grandfather's watch inside his pants. His briefs barely hold the weight. It bumps and sidles against his genitals. Does it show? Who cares?

HE SEES MEINERT only once all afternoon, and then from a distance. He searches for him as much as he dares during free moments. During lunch the Chief Steward slaps him on the back of the head for gathering wool.

Three hours are spent in a solitary and melancholy inspection of the rearmost gas cell. In the end he can't say for sure what he's seen. If the cell had disappeared entirely, it's not clear he would have noticed.

RHINE SALMON for the final dinner. Fresh trout from the Black Forest. There's an all-night party among the passengers to celebrate their arrival in America. At the bar the man who'd thrown away his wristwatch on departure amuses himself by balancing a fountain pen on its flat end.

They continue to be separated for most of the evening, which creeps along glacially. Gnüss sorts glassware for storage upon landing, and Meinert lends a hand back at the engine gondolas, helping record fuel consumption. The time seems out of joint, and Gnüss finally figures out why: a prankster has set the clock in the bar back, to extend the length of the celebration.

On third watch he takes a break. He goes below and stops by the crew's quarters. No luck. He listens in on a discussion of suitable first names for children conceived aloft in a zeppelin. The consensus favors Shelium, if a girl.

Someone asks if he's seen Meinert. Startled, he eyes the questioner. Apparently the captain's looking for him. Two machinists exchange looks.

Has Gnüss seen him or not? the questioner wants to know. He realizes he hasn't answered. The whole room has taken note of his paralysis. He says he hasn't, and excuses himself.

He finds Meinert on the catwalk heading aft. Relief and anger and frustration swarm the cockleshell of his head. His frontal lobe is in tumult. Before he can speak Meinert tells him to keep his voice down, and that the party may be over. What does *that* mean? Gnüss wants to know. His friend doesn't answer.

They go hunting for privacy without success. A crossbrace near the bottom of the tail supports a card game.

On the way back forward, they're confronted by their two roommates, Egk and Thoolen, who block the catwalk as though they've formed an alliance. Perhaps they feel neglected. "Do you two *ever* separate?" Egk asks. "Night and day I see you together." Thoolen nods unpleasantly. One is Hamburg at its most insolent, the other Bremerhaven at its foggiest. "Shut up, you fat bellhop," Meinert says.

They roughly squeeze past, and Egk and Thoolen watch them go. *"I'm so in love!"* Egk sings out. Thoolen laughs.

Gnüss follows his friend in silence until they reach the ladder down to B deck. It's a busy hub. Crew members come and go briskly. Meinert hesitates. He seems absorbed in a recessed light fixture. It breaks Gnüss's heart to see that much sadness in the contours of his preoccupation.

"What do you mean: the party may be over?" Gnüss demands quietly.

"Pruss wants to see me. He says for disciplinary matters. After that, you know as much as I," Meinert says.

The radio officer and the ship's doctor pass through the corridor at the bottom of the stairs, glancing up as they go, without stopping their quiet conversation.

When Gnüss is unable to respond, Meinert adds, "Maybe he just wants me to police up my uniform."

At a loss, Gnüss finally puts a hand on Meinert's arm. Meinert smiles, and whispers, *"You are the most important thing in the world right now."*

The unexpectedness of it brings tears to Gnüss's eyes. Meinert murmurs that he needs to get into his dining room whites. It's nearly time to serve the third breakfast. They've served two luncheons, two dinners, and now three breakfasts.

They descend the stairs together. Gnüss is already dressed and so gives his friend another squeeze on the arm and tells him not to worry, and then goes straight to the galley. His eyes still bleary with tears, he loads linen napkins into the dumbwaiter. Anxiety is like a whirling pillar in his chest. He remembers another of Meinert's war stories, one whispered to him in the early morning after they'd first spent the night together. They'd soaked each other and the bed linens with love and then had collapsed. He woke to words in his ear, and at first thought his bedmate was talking in his sleep. The story concerned Meinert's captain after a disastrous raid one moonless night over the Channel. Meinert had been at his post in the control car. The captain had started talking to himself. He'd said that both radios were smashed, not that it mattered, both radiomen being dead. And that both outboard engines were beyond repair, not that *that* mattered, since they had no fuel.

AROUND FOUR A.M., the passengers start exclaiming at the lights of Long Island. The all-night party has petered out into knots of people waiting and chatting along the promenade. Gnüss and Meinert set out the china, sick with worry. Once the place settings are all correct, they allow themselves a look out an open window. They see below that they've overtaken the liner *Staatendam,* coming into New York Harbor. She salutes them with blasts of her siren. Passengers crowd her decks waving handkerchiefs.

They're diverted north to avoid a front of thunderstorms. All morning, they drift over New England, gradually working their way back to Long Island Sound.

At lunch Captain Pruss appears in the doorway for a moment, and then is gone. They bus tables. The passengers all abandon their seats to look out on New York City. From the exclamations they make, it's apparently some sight. Steam whistles sound from boats on the Hudson and East Rivers. Someone at the window points out the *Bremen* just before it bellows a greeting. The *Hindenburg*'s passengers wave back with a kind of patriotic madness.

The tables cleared, the waiters drift back to the windows. Gnüss puts an arm around Meinert's shoulders, despair making him courageous. Through patchy cloud they can see shoal water, or tide-rips, beneath them.

Pelicans flock in their wake. What looks like a whale races to keep pace with their shadow.

In New Jersey they circle over miles of stunted pines and bogs, their shadow running along the ground like a big fish on the surface.

It's time for them to take their landing stations.

Sauter passes them on their way to the catwalk and says that they should give the bracing wires near Ladder #4 another check and that he'd noticed a bit of hum.

By the time they reach the base of #4, it's more than a bit of a hum. Gnüss volunteers to go, anxious to do something concrete for his disconsolate beloved. He wipes his eyes and climbs swiftly while Meinert waits below on the catwalk.

Meinert's grandfather's pocket watch bumps and tumbles about his testicles while he climbs. Once or twice he has to stop to rearrange himself. The hum is near the top, hard to locate. At their favorite perch, he stops and hooks on his harness. His weight supported, he turns his head slightly to try and make his ears direction finders. He runs a thumb and forefinger along nearby cables to test for vibration. The cables are covered in graphite to suppress sparks. The slickness seems sexual to him. He's dismayed by his single-mindedness.

On impulse, he takes the watch, pleasingly warm, from his pants. He loops it around one of the cable bolts just so he can look at it. The short chain keeps slipping from the weight. He wraps it once around the nut on the other side of the beam. The nut feels loose to him. He removes and pockets the watch, finds the spanner on his tool belt, fits it snugly over the nut, and tightens it, and then, uncertain, tightens it again. There's a short, high-pitched sound of metal under stress or tearing.

BELOW HIM, his lover, tremendously resourceful in all sorts of chameleon-like self-renovations, and suffused with what he understands to be an unprecedented feeling for his young young boy, has been thinking to himself, *Imagine instead that you were perfectly happy.* Shivering, with his coat collar turned up as though he was sitting around a big cold aerodrome, he leans against a cradle of wires and stays and reexperiences unimaginable views, unearthly lightness, the hull starlit at altitude, electrical storms and the incandescence of clouds, and Gnüss's lips on his throat. He remembers his younger brother's iridescent fingers after having blown soap bubbles as a child.

Below the ship, frightened horses spook like flying fish discharged from seas of yellow grass. Miles away, necklaces of lightning drop and fork.

Inside the hangarlike hull, they can feel the gravitational forces as Captain Pruss brings the ship up to the docking mast in a tight turn. The sharpness of the turn overstresses the after-hull structure, and the bracing wire bolt that Gnüss overtightened snaps like a rifle shot. The recoiling wire slashes open the gas cell opposite. Seven or eight feet above Gnüss's alarmed head, the escaping hydrogen encounters the prevailing St. Elmo's fire playing atop the ship.

From the ground, in Lakehurst, New Jersey, the *Hindenburg* malingers in a last wide circle, uneasy in the uneasy air.

The fireball explodes outward and upward, annihilating Gnüss at its center. More than 100 feet below on the axial catwalk, as the blinding light envelops everything below it, Meinert knows that whatever time has come is theirs, and won't be like anything else.

Four hundred and eighty feet away, loitering on the windblown and sandy flats weedy with dune grass, Gerhard Fichte, chief American representative of Luftschiffbau Zeppelin and senior liaison to Goodyear, hears a sound like surf in a cavern and sees the hull interior blooming orange, lit from within like a Japanese lantern, and understands the catastrophe to his company even before the ship fully explodes. He thinks: *Life, motion, everything was untrammeled and without limitation, pathless, ours.*

MARS ATTACKS

#1: The Invasion Begins

A bubble-helmeted Martian in the left foreground stares out at us and points at the saucer, which is silvery white and spotted along its outside rim with the black ovals of windows. The saucer stands on four narrow poles, like a tent at a wedding. A column of Martians in green spacesuits with red scuba tanks on their backs extends to a prosaic ladder leading to an open hatch. Another saucer is on the ground behind the first. An easy diagonal of saucers swoops by in the background. The sky is a deep blue, fading to an ominous yellow on the horizon. Jagged orange peaks rise in the distance on the right. The Martian's pupils are red. His whites are huge. His nose and teeth are a skull's. His brain is oversized and exposed. The back of the card is a caramel brown. On it we learn why they're doing this: buildup of atomic pressures beneath the surface of Mars with an explosion only weeks or months away, no choice, and a reckless overconfidence in the power of their weapons. We're told to *See Card #2: Martians Approaching.*

#2: Martians Approaching

Again a face looking out from the left foreground, with an excited, sheepish grin. Behind him, two other Martians, one working controls, one pointing out the window. The Martians clearly point a lot. Behind them, saucers, extending to Earth. Earth's continents are emerald green and its oceans a pale bathroom-tile color. Eastern Canada seems oversized.

#3: Attacking an Army Base

One GI, the only one not on fire, shoots up at the closest saucer. The yellow line of the bullet looks feeble, the squirt of a water pistol. All around him, his pals in agony. The saucers crowd in, jostling one another, blocking out sky. In one corner, a few bodies lying around, incinerated. On the back: *A quiet Sunday afternoon was turned to tragedy as flying saucers launched their first attack against Earth.*

#55: Mars Attacks! A Short Synopsis of the Story

Planning to conquer the Earth, Mars sends flying saucers through space carrying deadly weapons. Burning the cities, the Martians destroy much of Earth's population. The enemy then enlarges insects to over 500 times their normal size and releases them on the helpless planet. People go into hiding, knowing that death is the consequence if they are discovered by the creatures. Despite its losses, Earth launches a counterattack that shatters the Martians on their home planet, Mars. I was eight years old. Martian Cards, we called them. I filled in each box on the checklist in pencil, in case one was lost or traded. As a collector of Martian Cards, I was a figure to be reckoned with. I carried doubles to and from school wrapped in a rubber band. The nuns hated them. For a full year, they were everything. My brother and I were constantly deciding: should we pool what we had, or compete for cards? Did my parents have an opinion? What sort of gum came with them? *Did* gum come with them?

#4: Saucers Blast Our Jets

One saucer; nine jets. The saucer tilted in a lazy diagonal, like Maurice Chevalier's straw hat. A jet alongside it explodes in a V shape.

Flying outward with the rest of the debris, a human figure. (*One of the pilots tried to get a look at the inside of a spaceship. Seeing this, the saucer smashed itself into the jet without any damage to itself.*) Delta-wing fighters chug toward the saucer from the foreground and background. Another, below, exploded by the heat ray. Its nose cone, interestingly, popping off from the impact. Another on the far right doing a fiery corkscrew to Earth. Two others streaking by below, presumably part of a different, fatal, attack. *See Card #5: Washington in Flames.*

#5: Washington in Flames

On the back: *The Martians did not spare anyone from their vicious death rays, and fear for the president's welfare continued to grow by the hour.* What happens to him? We never find out.

#6: Burning Navy Ships

The sky in the background is brilliant purple. Two men manning the machine gun are on fire, one showing his back, head down, as if submitting. Behind them, a white-hatted officer, raising an elbow to deflect a saucer's heat ray, squinting at its brightness. My brother calls long distance to ask if I know what these cards are worth. He was at one of the conventions; he saw a full set on one of the tables. Fifteen hundred dollars, he says. He's calling from New Orleans. He's crisscrossing the country. He stays in youth hostels, rooming houses. He's forty-two. My father wires him money—a hundred dollars, two hundred dollars—every few weeks. He rarely works, and when he does he loses the job quickly. He calls me, his only brother, the younger brother, when he's at his most despairing. His calls are monologues of defeat. I fancy myself always busy, and listen for one or two hours at a stretch, aggrieved. The only safe subject is our old collecting days: what's implicit between us is his belief that that's the only thing in his life that has panned out.

#7: Destroying the Bridge

Finally a good view into the top of a saucer: tiny figures in the green suits and scuba tanks facing inward, sitting in pairs around a large round table. More death rays. The sky canary yellow. The Golden Gate Bridge in scarlet. The suspension cables falling away like noodles. Tumbling cars. Below, a ship flying an American flag from the bow is halved by the falling debris. *Cars plunged into the icy waters bringing death to the helpless passengers within. Screaming hysterically, the people had no way of escaping their steel coffins.* My brother, later institutionalized, was then just beginning to "act up," as my father put it. I'd recently killed my dog by running her across the street into a car. I retreated to my room for long stretches to lay the cards out and give my parents more to worry about. Did I think of the cards as a Refuge? I did not.

#10: The Skyscraper Tumbles

The Empire State Building breaking like a cookie, its top third tumbling off at a thirty-degree angle. The saucer responsible is out of proportion and half the building's length. The sky an electric red. Other buildings, other saucers, other fires. *New York was burning down and no one could do anything to help.* On good days I would tap the cards on my palm to line them up. Hold them under my nose to reexperience their smell: faint, musty, dry, sugary. Fan them out before me while I drank Tom Collins mix with ice and pretended it was a cocktail.

#11: Destroy the City

A rampart of burning bodies and skeletal remains. Vacant mouths, gaping eye sockets, tumbled rib cages. Flames issuing from a stomach cavity. In the middle ground, on a perfectly featureless street, four Martians: one erect and pointing, three charging off in the direction he indicates. They carry short, speargun-sized weapons wired to their suits. Behind them, more bodies. A factory resembling Sikorsky Aircraft, where my father worked. A smashed car. A black figure writhing in the yellow heart of a fireball. My brother would walk home from school in the middle of the day, two miles, without notifying anyone. He refused to cut his hair. He refused to sing the national anthem. During an assembly the principal brought him to the microphone and had him sing it alone. Nothing was glamorous about these rebellions; his misery with his own behavior was too transparent. He lost cards; gave them away; stopped buying. I began to pull ahead.

#13: Watching from Mars

A circular room, not well lighted, with a polished floor. Immense curved windows and a lunar landscape beyond with moonlight (or earthlight) and another home in the distance. It has the overall shape of the plastic dome shielding doughnuts in a diner. In the foreground a sober Martian face considering a panel of magenta dials. Another barefoot and half-naked Martian in a curved seat offering little back support. The large head and skinny limbs give the impression of early childhood. One hand holds a champagne glass full of cranberry juice. One points at a huge screen. On the screen, the Capitol Building, flanked by saucers against a blood-red sky. *Their advanced civilization had developed TV cameras which were capable of sending pictures millions of miles through space.*

#14: Charred by Martians

A generic tomato red sixties convertible up on two wheels, its back end bursting into flame. The driver's arms up and head back in a Victorian tableau of distress. The saucer only a few feet overhead. Two Martians visible peeping down, like skeletal Kilroys. *The young doctor was driving home after visiting a patient when he heard a humming noise overhead. . . .*

#16: Panic in Parliament

Outside, a mild blue day and flying saucers. The sketchy outlines of a stately hall with the roof torn away. A large Martian grinning and firing in, suspended impossibly in the air. Panic. One man jumping down from his desk, arms spread wide. *Ironically, the topic being discussed at the time was about military plans to beat back the space invaders.* Confiscated by Sister Justine, who held it before me like an illustration of sin. Was this what I wanted for myself? she wanted to know. Was this what I aspired to? I had no idea what she meant. Later I realized they were frightened for my brother, worried that they hadn't caught whatever was happening to him in time, and anxious to avoid the same mistake with me.

#19: Burning Flesh

Too gross to talk about. A crouching Martian on the left, a little vacant-eyed, his death ray blooming in the belly of a man with a matinee idol's face: blue eyes, Rock Hudson hair. The man's hands cup themselves around the white light. The flesh below his shoulders and above his knees is shearing off the bone. At his feet, another skeleton with the face intact, and behind him another Martian tilting forward hesitantly, weapon raised and expression apprehensive. As if he's thinking, Whoa. Do we want to keep doing this?

#20: Crushed to Death

Three Martians looking down with sadistic absorption from their saucer at three men and four women being crushed between what looks like an outlandishly large snow shovel and the wall of a building. The shovel is operated by a metal arm from the saucer. The brick wall is crumbling and tumbling down, as if the bricks had never been mortared. The man closest to the wall resembles Joe E. Brown. How slow *were* these people? How'd they get caught in front of a shovel like this? *The terror caused by the flying saucers was endless. It seemed as if the Martians always had a new form of horror to inflict upon the people of Earth.* During one of my brother's recent calls I made a mark on a scratch pad for every word I contributed to the conversation. The call went fifty-five minutes and I put eleven marks on the pad. When I'm sitting down listening to him, my knee bounces like I'm keeping rhythm in a zydeco band. Among the things I volunteer occasionally when he calls: You need to see somebody professional. You need to find out how much of this is biochemical. You're not getting anywhere wandering all over the country. Among the things I never volunteer: Whenever you need or want to, call.

#21: Prize Captive

A horror-stricken blonde in the wraparound embrace of a Martian who's all smiles and eyes at his good fortune. She's wearing a cravat. The first bit of good news in twenty-one cards: *The girl kicked and screamed at the touch of the alien. The Martian was so startled by the woman's antics that he released her. Taking the opportunity, the girl fled. See Card #22: Burning Cattle.*

#22: Burning Cattle

#23: The Frost Ray

A red sun in a red sky, and six men frozen in supplicating poses. *The rays of the sun had no thawing effect at all.* In my brother's mind, I have a successful life: a home, a job, some status. Talking with me is a humiliation. The card conjures up a memory: my mother on the phone to my aunt, elaborating on my performance in the diocesan spelling bee. My cards spread in front of me on the living room rug in rows of five, with gaps for the ones still missing. My brother staring at the television set, rigid with shame.

#24: The Shrinking Ray

One GI charges while another, the size of his foot, shrinks. His helmet, flying off, threatens to cover him, as in a shell game. Another handheld Martian ray, this one looking like an insecticide spray. *His buddy watched horrified as the six-foot-tall man was reduced to inches, before vanishing from sight.* So was his buddy watching or charging? Do we believe our eyes or the narration? What else are we not being told?

#25: Capturing a Martian

The second bit of good news. A netted Martian in the foreground, his hand in a soldier's face, drawing blood. A few other soldiers stand around helpfully with their ends of the net. *A quick jab with the bayonet quieted the alien and he was carried off to Earth's military headquarters. There, trained specialists would attempt to break the language barrier and communicate with the captured Martian.*

#26: The Tidal Wave

A disappointment: I'd heard about the card, loved the idea. The wave was a nonmonumental swirl of blue and white, tumbling toylike ocean liners around indifferently rendered skyscrapers. Saucers in the foreground. Crumbling buildings. *The saucers' powers seemed unlimited.*

#27: The Giant Flies

A beetle-shaped blue thing resembling no fly we've ever seen, clutching and contemplating a helpless policeman waving a tiny gun. Two large compound eyes and curved mandibles, like tusks. Eleven other flies tumble from an overhead saucer. Humans run panicked in all directions. The sky is a lemon yellow. *The normally annoying pests were now transformed into deadly menaces, attack-*

ing any slow-footed human around. I fought, with Gary Holter, over this card. He broke his tooth. I cut my hand. My father said, "I wouldn't be throwing those friends away. There aren't that many to go around, sport."

#29: Death in the Shelter

The victim Italian-looking, a cross between my uncle Guido and Richard Conte, with Latin features and curly black hair. Families cowering behind him. Beside him, inexplicably, a dead ringer for Lon Chaney in *The Phantom of the Opera,* a movie I'd already seen at that age. An *homage?* Even I wondered.

#30: Trapped!!

The huge spiders were perhaps the ugliest and most frightening of all the giant insects. The woman, dressed in white, entangled head to foot, has one arm above her head as if wanting to answer a question. Her head is turned away but her eyes look back at the spider. The spider, tiger-striped in red and black, holds her with three legs and has bright white pedipalps, like teeth. My father bought me the pack that contained this card and I forget which others. This I remember because of the teasing noise he made when he saw it, knowing I was afraid of spiders.

#31: The Monster Reaches In

Lost. What I remember: Another blonde wrapped in an embrace, the double green tarsus of an insect reaching through a window. A leg reaches farther in for a soldier, whose bayonet opens a lawn sprinkler of blood along its length.

#32: Robot Terror

A greenish robot like a squat peppermill with arms. Three arms: one with a vacuumlike attachment that's already sucked up half a human; two with pincerlike claws, one of which is driven deep into the center of a swooning young woman in a sundress. It rolls along on low, spiked wheels. On its side, rivets. In its head, a Martian, who looks genuinely sympathetic.

#33: Removing the Victims

By some means the aliens had found a way to communicate with the giant insects they had created. The bugs followed any instruction given to them by the spacemen. Did the bugs want anything in return? Could humans hear their talk? Were the negotiations difficult? More mysteries.

#8: *Terror in Times Square.* #9: *The Human Torch.* #12: *Death in the Cockpit.* #15: *Saucers Invade China.* #17: *Beast and the Beauty.* #18: *A Soldier Fights Back.* #35: *The Flame Throwers.* #38: *Victims of the Bug.* #40: *High Voltage Execution.* #41: *Horror in Paris.* #42: *Hairy Fiend.* One afternoon Sister Justine confiscated eleven cards from Milton Dietz. For three days she had them in her desk. On the fourth day while I watched from the boys' bathroom she pitched them into the Dumpster. That night I got them back with a flashlight, one leg sunk into someone's applesauce from lunch. Milton was crushed at the loss, but I didn't return them. Worse: I didn't confess it to Father Hogan. Who knew how closely he worked with the nuns?

#34: Terror in the Railroad

A gigantic ant, fire-engine red, filling a curved rail shed, embracing, with three of its six legs, a lighted green railway car, and crushing the top of it in its jaws. My parents worry that when they're dead I'll inherit their job as my brother's keeper. My brother has no one else. That leaves them unhappy when he's in contact with me and unhappy when he's not. I maintain the disingenuous position of the good son, offering to do more and deferring to the wisdom of their greater caution. Bodies tumble out of the connecting railway cars. One is outlined with ragged and filigreed white light, suggesting the third rail. *The entire station was thrown into a panic as they watched the fascinated insect crush several cars the way a child might crush a toy he had grown tired of.*

#36: Destroying a Dog

The boy shrieks as he runs to prevent it, both fists raised in protest like a figure on a left-wing poster. The dog, a cross between a German shepherd and a golden retriever. The dog's coat flies to pieces under the force of the ray, separating like autumn leaves off a pile in the wind. The little mail flag on the mailbox is down.

#37: Creeping Menace

Two men sprinting past demolished rural buildings. One man carrying a small boy in a red shirt and white socks. The boy seems to want to tell him something. The giant insect right behind them is indigo with cherry-red eyes.

#39: Army of Giant Insects

An entomological Guadalcanal: in the foreground, GIs armed with cannons, bazookas, machine guns, and rifles, the NCO exhorting them to hold the line; in the background, an oncoming storm of insects as far as the eye can see. Air Force jets overhead offer support. One bug flies up into the air backward out of the mass. One of the hardest cards to find, and it had to be replaced, at the cost of three months: my brother held it up in front of me early one morning, when I was still in bed, and tore it into eighths.

#43: Blasting the Bug

The bug's leg resting with a casual friendliness on the front of a tank that blasts its compound eye at point-blank range. Two soldiers hurl grenades. One holds out his palm as if to reason with everyone. Everything floats on an undifferentiated red background. We all went out for lunch the day of my brother's institutionalization, before he was to be dropped off. He answered questions monosyllabically. It was the worst day of my parents' lives. At some point my father went to pay the check. My mother went to help. I didn't blame her. My brother and I sat around the ruins of our chili dogs. "I put all my cards and stuff in boxes upstairs," he told me. "Don't let them screw around with them."

I nodded. That night my mother cried her way around the house and ended up in his room. She was rearranging things, packing things. Was she messing up what he'd organized? I couldn't go up to find out. At dawn I crept into his room and found his shoeboxes arranged on the floor of his closet. Was that the way he'd left them? Were they all there? I looked at his Martian cards: Eleven I already owned. One I didn't—#28: *Helpless Victim.* A perverse love scene: a giant insect and young boy lying alongside one another, a mandible poised at the jugular, the boy trying to avert his head, his mouth open in protest. I took the card and closed the box. I'd return it when—or if, I thought, crouching on the floor of his closet—my brother came back.

#44: Battle in the Air

A red Sikorsky helicopter, an old S-58, and a fat, ludicrous flying bug the same color. Below, monochromatic suburban homes. An attempt at stylization? Saving on colors? A shot from a rifleman onboard deflects something issuing from the bug: A tongue of some sort? A stream of fire?

#45: Fighting Giant Insects

Better production values. The soldiers' helmets look German. A bazooka in one place draws thick black blood. A bayonet in another draws white. The insect has a body of black fur. How much research was done for this series? Were there things like this in the Amazon?

#46: Blastoff for Mars

Without explanation, Earth takes the offensive. In a forest of Cape Canaverals, whole formations of men and tanks clamber up ramps directly into the exhaust cones of liquid-fueled rockets. Other rockets streak by on a diagonal. White smoke billows out in various directions. What are the Martians doing while all this is happening? Where are the giant insects? *Men from the ages of 16 to 45 were given quick physical examinations and enlisted into the Earth Army.*

#47: Earth Bombs Mars

The bombardier's fingers bring back a photo of a family vacation in Montauk. Who took the picture? My mother slung in a low sand chair, squinting grimly out to sea. My father demonstrating how to add a tower to a rambling sand castle. Behind him, my brother and I squatting over something on our scratchy old army blanket: cards, two new packages each, that my father bought us at the drugstore near the beach.

#48: Earthmen Land on Mars

Another purple sky. Parachutists coming down, a huge Earth behind them. The horizon curves sharply. The ground is arid and broken by palisades. Martians are running toward us. One who's being shot in the head from behind is tilting delicately toward the shot. He's wearing a close-fitting shirt with pointed padded shoulders and bikini briefs. Another, about to run out of the frame, is all brain and bulging eyes. Don't the Martians have radar? Is this all a trap?

#49: The Earthmen Charge

Soldiers with red standard-issue helmets under glass mill around a tank porcelain-white like a Frigidaire. Otherwise they wear regular khakis. Why aren't they cold? Or hot? How does the glass form a seal? On their backs, the same red scuba tanks the Martians wore, but no regulators, and no air hoses. In the distance, a domed city out of the Jetsons, with air taxis and floating platforms. A monorail toots out toward them. Are the Martian commuters puzzled as to what's going on? *The leader of the troop gave his orders and the soldiers continued toward the dome, with revenge in their hearts.*

#50: Smashing the Enemy

A soldier whose helmet reads US on the front drives the butt of his rifle into a charging Martian's brain. A buddy at his side sporting a Norwegian flag drives his bayonet into another Martian's eye. All of this takes place on an immense flight of stairs. One Martian attacks with what appears to be a vegetable peeler. Where are the heat rays? Where are the forces in reserve? Where is the Martian National Guard?

#51: Crushing the Martians

A Martian in the foreground losing all his dentition. Another dead in the middle ground and leaking a winding stream of blood. A small boy's notion of the ultimate tank, bristling with cannons pointed in all directions, breaks through the aquarium wall of the dome and fires. At my brother's confirmation I sat in the car after the ceremony and traded for this card, with a cousin I rarely saw. My brother was wildly unhappy. The scrutiny was excruciating to him. Waiting in line for the bishop's blessing, he pawed at his suit, his haircut, his eyes. He spent the ceremony crying and enraged at himself for doing so. My parents were frozen with mortification.

Afterward they dispensed with the photos in front of the church. They couldn't get my brother to come back to the car. My mother found me in the backseat and told me she didn't know what they were going to do. My cousin was embarrassed for us. My mother wanted me to help however I could, and I knew it. I could see my brother yank his arm away from my father across the parking lot. I had no idea what I could or couldn't accomplish. I was too frightened to find out. Meanwhile, here was my cousin: he lived nowhere near me, so I knew he'd have different cards.

#52: Giant Robot

Silly. Buttons for eyes, transformers for antennae, wrench-grip pliers for hands. No one's even wearing helmets or oxygen tanks anymore. *An Army bazooka hit its mark, and the robot crumbled disabled to the ground.*

#53: Martian City in Ruins

Martian victims were sprawled across the desert sands, many badly wounded and others beyond repair. The advanced civilization had been beaten into the dust under the force of Earth's violent counterattack. The dangerous atomic pressures were rapidly building to the climactic point and it was now only hours before the explosion which would destroy Mars. See Card #54: Mars Explodes.

#54: Mars Explodes

The end of the series. Collecting took a year. What was the first card? *Death in the Shelter.* I pored over it at night under the covers, cupped it in my hands at Mass, laid it on my thigh, school days, in the boys' bathroom. What did it connect to? What was the rest of the story? I had no synopsis and had seen no other cards. Everything lay ahead of me. I was hooked when I saw the first one. A giant bug, eating a guy: that was for me. My parents did what they could. They were attentive; they were flexible. Who knows if they trace their disappointment with me back that far?

What was the last card? *Watching from Mars.* Months of searching, and it was my brother who finally found it. A few weeks after the doctors let him come home, he left it on my desk, with a note: *For your collection.* In the meantime, I'd lost *The Monster Reaches In.* When he calls now, and tells me what the set's going for, I tell him I don't have the set; I lost one. And he says, Yeah, you have the set. Remember? I found the last one. *Watching from Mars.*

And it kills me that he remembers the title. It kills me that I can't bring myself to keep talking to him, to tell him, No, I don't have the whole set.

Now I'm trying to remember: Did I ever have them all or not? Did they further separate me from my family, or allow me a place within it? Did I know then how much they affected what I could imagine? Do I know now? But that was how I learned to see, and that was what I saw.

GLUT YOUR SOUL ON MY ACCURSED UGLINESS

Anson started signing his seventh grade worksheets *The Fist* because of his ugliness. Mrs. Ackley asked him what was up. She recognized his handwriting.

"Is this a joke?" she asked from her desk. She graded the math worksheets while the class worked on social studies.

"The joke's my face," Anson answered.

It got a laugh. Still, his classmates were wary.

"Who's 'The Fist'?" she asked them. She was always complaining about never recognizing the newest trend. "A superhero?"

The class looked at her.

The kids who owned recess misunderstood. They thought she'd caught him bragging. One kid kicked him in the tailbone. "Hey, I'm 'The Foot,'" the kid said.

Anson walked around crying and holding his butt. The nicer kids seemed to think that what was going on was sad. A girl he liked looked mystified. Games went on around him.

After recess Ackley announced that he was getting all zeros on his assignments. She said she was getting perfectly good assignments from someone named "The Fist," but Anson had apparently stopped doing his work.

The class looked to see how he was taking the news.

"I suck," Anson said. He meant it. There was a week's detention, right there.

On the way to the first detention, after school, he went to the nurse about his tailbone. She was sympathetic.

She gave him a pillow for his chair. The pillow turned out to be a bad move, in terms of the other kids in detention.

The next day Mrs. Ackley lost her patience. "Anson," she said when she got to his worksheet.

His butt was killing him. The hair on the side of his head over his ears looked like somebody's armpit. His nose felt like the bill of a cap. "Feast your eyes," he said, to whoever was looking. "Glut your soul on my accursed ugliness."

He'd seen Lon Chaney's *The Phantom of the Opera* on video fourteen times.

"Beware: the Strangler's noose is quick," he reminded Ackley. The class hooted.

"What is your *dam*age?" Ackley asked. She seemed to really want to know.

Part of his damage was that his dad was moving out. His dad was head over heels for one of the veterinarians at the animal hospital. The veterinarian's name was Jeanne and she looked like a shorter Christina Ricci. He'd seen them making out at the movies. He'd lost his gloves and they'd had to go back and help him look. They never found them.

His mom spent her time trying to figure out how to hook the DVD, the laser disc player, and the VCR into the back of the same monitor. The monitor had only two inputs. She sat at the kitchen table with the manuals spread out around her after dinner. "Nobody talk to me," she said.

His dad when he was home after dinner listened to gospel albums. He liked to fake a German accent and say things like, "*Listen* to zem. Zey are animals. But zey sing zo *beau*tifully . . ."

They kept on him about his homework. The afternoon after the first detention he watched his man Lon on the old suitcase-sized VCR in the finished basement. That night he wandered around the house wanting to get out, nowhere to go. He toured the upstairs and ended up in the living room with his dad, in front of whatever movie was on. It was always something like a spoiled teenager having an affair with her plastic surgeon. Sometimes it wasn't so clear because his dad liked to play with the mute.

"I'm gonna throw this monitor right out the window," his mother said. She was cross-checking the Sony manual with the JVC. "I'm gonna pitch it out the window and watch it smash."

His father had the mute going so he could listen to the Golden Gate Quartet. "Massa's in the Cold, Cold Ground." "Stalin Wasn't Stallin'."

A torn woofer in one speaker fuzzed the deeper tones. They had the right glue to fix it somewhere. His father was not the *You want something done right, do it yourself* type. He was more the *The only way this'll be done right is if* I *do it, but I'm* still *not gonna do it* type.

His father paused the Golden Gate Quartet to take the call from Mrs. Ackley.

"Well, I heard of The Chin," he said when he got off. "But not The Fist. I'm surprised it wasn't The Nose."

"Very nice," Anson's mother said.

"Shut up," Anson said, not to her. His dad unpaused the music.

They sat around listening. His mom looked at him, thoughtfully.

"I was thinking about plastic surgery," he said.

"That's a good idea," his dad said. "You being twelve years old and all."

His dog, Shitface, was at the deck door in the snow, scratching to be let in. His real name was Johnny, after Johnny Depp, but his father called him Shitface because he was always eating his own poop. The dog lowered his head and threw up a greenish mess. You couldn't hear it through the glass.

"Why not?" Anson said. "Why can't I?"

"The Fist," his dad said. He filled his cheeks with air and swallowed it. "You're not The Fist anymore," he said. "You got it? You're not The Torso, The Bicep, or The Tower of Power."

"*You* don't have to go to school like this," Anson told him.

"Join the circus," his dad said. "Exploit your deformity."

"You look fine," his mother said. "Your face is still growing."

"I look like a ferret," Anson said.

"You're not The Ferret, either," his dad said.

HIS MOM went to bed around nine. At eleven, he heard his dad turn in. He got up and pushed open the door to their room.

"I'm serious," he said.

"I don't think your face calls for radical intervention," his dad said from under the covers.

"You think I'm good-looking?" Anson said.

"I'm really attracted to a whole different look," his father said.

"You're a pig," his mother said from the other side of the bed.

"Sorry," his father said.

He went back to his bed. He watched car headlights on the ceiling. It was supposed to go below zero tonight but he couldn't hear the wind. He got up and walked back down the hall to his parents' room.

"Ah, morning already," his father said.

"I'm not going to school like this," Anson told them.

"What way you gonna go?" his father asked.

He stood there for a while. He didn't have anything else to say. His head was a balloon that filled the house and had nothing inside it.

Shitface came up to see what the discussion was about. Anson led him back to his room. The dog curled up at the foot of the bed. An hour later, his mom started crying. His parents talked. He couldn't hear what they said.

He gave it as long as he could and then he trooped back down the hall again, hating himself. They were still lying in the dark, but they were each up on one elbow. "You think I'm bringing this up because of what's going on with you guys, but I'm not," he said.

They looked at him together. "We're kind of in the middle of something here," his father said.

"Sorry," Anson said.

"Your father's explaining why he's better off without us," his mother said.

"That's productive," his father said. "That should help."

"Would you go back to your room?" his mother asked. "I'll come tuck you in in a minute."

On his way back down the hall he stopped in the bathroom. He stood over the toilet in the dark but couldn't pee. "Go to bed," his father said.

In bed his covers came off the foot of the mattress, and his toes stuck out. He tried to kickbox the sheets back into place.

There was a sound on the floor like a stick in gravel. "The dog threw up again," he called.

He heard his mother padding down the hall. "Oh, jeez," she said, from the doorway.

She turned on the light, and he had to roll his face into the pillow. "Oh, Geoff," she called.

His father came quickly down the hall. Anson tried to rush getting his eyes used to the light so he could look. He hung over the bed. Shitface was on his side. Ropy saliva and blood looped over his nose and whiskers. More was soaking the rug under his chin.

His father moved his mother's hands away from the dog's mouth and put his hand on the rib cage, feeling for something. "Get me a blanket," he said. She got up off her knees and went down the stairs.

"What's wrong with him?" Anson asked.

"He's not doin' too good," his father said. "You're not doin' too good, are you, pal?" he said to the dog.

The dog sounded like he was clearing his throat, and gave a little shake. Anson's mother came back upstairs with an old wool blanket, and his father took it and laid it on the rug behind the dog. Then he got ahold of the skin of the dog's neck and butt and slid him over onto the blanket. The dog barely seemed to notice. His father flapped the two ends of the blanket over, dug his arms underneath, and lifted.

"Comin' through," he said, and carried him downstairs.

They heard him open the back door with one hand and shut it behind him with his foot. They heard the car doors open and close, and the car start up and drive away.

His mother stood where she was. She rubbed her eyes.

"I wasn't happy with the way *I* looked in school," she said.

He started to get teary. He was the biggest pussy who ever lived.

"What do you think Grandma would've said if I'd said I wasn't going because I didn't like the way I looked?" she asked.

He looked at his hands. If he didn't stop crying at the count of three, he was going to punch himself so hard he'd cave his face in. "Grandma told me looks aren't everything," he finally said.

His mother turned out his light and stood at the top of the stairs. "So isn't that true?" she said.

"We hadn't been talking about looks," Anson said. "She just brought it up out of nowhere."

His mother laughed. She came back to his bed and gave him a kiss. She kissed him again on the mouth. "I think you're the beautiful one," she whispered.

He snorted, so happy she'd said that.

"Good night," she said. At the bottom of the stairs, she turned off the light in the stairway.

He listened. The furnace kicked on. Someday his cheeks and chin would catch up, he thought. Maybe his nose and bug eyes were just adult-sized, and the rest of his face would catch up.

He went downstairs without making noise, though he wasn't trying to be quiet. His mother was on the sofa in the dark, facing the TV. The TV was off.

"Hey," he said.

"Hey hey," his mother answered.

His pajama bottoms didn't have any pockets. He put his hands on his thighs. "I cleaned the rug," he said. "Good as I could."

She nodded.

He turned on the lamp near the TV table so he could look through the videos. The babysitter had messed them all up.

"You worried about Shitface?" he asked.

"Yeah," his mother said.

"Put on your movie," she said. "Put on Lon Chaney."

"You wanna see it?" he asked.

"Yeah," she said.

Here she was worrying about him. He hunted around, throwing things aside, and found it. He slid it out of its box and into the VCR. He hit Fast Forward.

"She may not be the one there," he said. "She may not be the one who comes in."

"On call," his mother said.

"On call," he said. "She may not be the one on call tonight."

"No, she may not," his mother said. She sounded okay.

He stopped the tape and hit Play at the forty-five-minute mark. But it wasn't *The Phantom of the Opera*. The babysitter had put things in the wrong boxes. Instead it was something he didn't recognize: guys were trying to rope black horses in a corral and the horses were bucking and rearing. It was in black-and-white and the horses' eyes were huge.

His mother made a noise. He went to hit Stop, but she said, "Leave it on."

"What is this?" he said, but she didn't hear.

Even at this point, he wasn't trying to help as much as show off how sad he was. He spent all his free time striking poses, whining and complaining.

"What happens when you really hate who you are?" he asked.

"It's a problem," his mother said.

His father had left the mute on. In the movie, a little truck was driving along a desert road.

Sunday afternoons Anson and his father went to the movies. Jeanne had started showing up. His dad had asked him not to tell. Now whenever he was with his mother he imagined LIAR painted across his face. A week ago, she'd said something about the movies and he'd thought: She already knows. She knows all about me.

The cellular rang. His mother picked it off the arm of the sofa, hit the Talk button with her thumb, and held it to her ear. She listened.

"Should we come down?" she said. Anson stopped the movie and ejected it. He looked around for the *Phantom* and found it without its box in the back of the cabinet.

"Shouldn't we come down, then?" she said again.

LIAR, he thought to himself. LI—AR.

"Sssh," his mother said. She went back to listening.

"All right," she said. She hit the Talk button again and tossed the phone onto the cushions.

"Did you really clean up upstairs?" she asked.

"I will," Anson said.

She sniffled. She cleared her throat.

"How's Johnny?" Anson said.

"Your father doesn't think he should leave," she said. "You know how he loves that dog."

He couldn't tell if she was being sarcastic. "Is he dying?" he asked.

"He might be. They'll know in a little while," she said.

"Is that what the vet said?" he asked.

His mother shrugged. She put her chin in her palm and slapped her cheek a few times with her fingers. "You find it?" she asked, gesturing at the videotape.

He loaded it in and hit Play and then Fast Forward so he could watch it fly by. He passed the Phantom's shadow against the wall while he's listening to the beautiful Christine. He passed his bringing the chandelier down on everybody's heads. He passed Christine's telling her boyfriend that the Phantom had a voice like an angel. The shock when they realize that the way to the Phantom's lair is through the mirror. He hit Play when Christine got to the other side, the secret side, of the opera house.

They watched the Phantom escorting her on horseback, farther and farther down through aqueduct-like tunnels, and then by gondola, her white veil trailing in the water.

"If we get a digital receiver we could run all three of the inputs through it," his mother said.

She chuckled at the Phantom standing at the end of the gondola and leaning over the black water, poling them along.

"It could just be me and you if it had to be," Anson told her.

"I've done everything I know to keep him around," his mother answered. "It doesn't seem to be working."

The Phantom was following Christine around the bedchamber he'd made for her. The intertitle read, *So that which is good within me, aroused by your purity, might plead for your love.* They must've missed something.

When his father called again his mother didn't say hello, but said "Okay," before she hung up. "Johnny might die," she said. "They think he ate something like antifreeze. They said we should go see him."

Getting dressed in his room, Anson thought, Could my dog die? He remembered the times the dog had just stood around him, wanting to be with him. The mess on the rug smelled.

"C'mon," his mother called.

"He would've told me," she said to herself, during the drive to the animal hospital.

But when his father came to the lighted front doors, they could see Jeanne behind him in the examining room.

His mother said something he couldn't hear. "Don't start," his father said.

He led them both into the examining room. "I'm sorry," Jeanne said to Anson's mother. The dog was strapped to the table with two flat elastic straps. He was panting and seemed to recognize them. Nobody said anything.

"Hi, Anson," Jeanne said.

"What's wrong with him?" Anson asked.

"We think he was poisoned," Jeanne said. "Poisoned himself."

His dad was over by the sink. His mom was close to the table, facing her. "He's gonna die?" he asked.

"I'm worried he might," Jeanne said. "I thought you'd want to say good-bye."

His father blew out air. He was looking at the dog.

But the dog didn't die. They waited, and he panted, and hung on. He didn't get any worse.

His mother was getting teary and looking at the table.

"Why don't you all go back," Jeanne finally said. "I'll call if there's a change."

It smelled like wet dog even though Shitface was dry. There was a syringe filled with something on the counter but it didn't have a needle screwed onto it. His hands were cold.

"You lose your gloves again?" Jeanne asked.

His mother turned to him. She left the table.

How was he going to explain? How was he going to explain? He followed her past the reception counter and out the main doors. He didn't have to run, but he had to walk fast. "Mom," he called.

She got in her side of the car and he got in his. She backed it out and bumped over the frozen ruts to the main road. How was he going to explain? She looked both ways and pulled out after a fish-tailing truck.

He started crying. "I shoulda told you," he said. He was whining. His mom was like there was nobody else in the car.

"I'm sorry," he said. He'd seen a picture of himself crying once. Crooked teeth, everything scrunched: the worst thing he'd ever seen.

"Please," he said.

"Nothing to be sorry about," his mother said.

"Yes there is," he said.

She didn't say anything else until they got home. Then she said, "Take your boots off." She dropped her coat on the table and went into the TV room. One of the bows was a knot and he wrestled with it before he could get it off and follow her.

She had the *Phantom* back on. She was reading the intertitle: *If you turn the Scorpion—you have said "Yes" and spared de Chagny.* The Phantom pointed into a wooden chest. *Turn the Grasshopper—and the opera house is blown to a thousand bits!*

"I need a drink," his mother said. She didn't get up.

They heard his father's car in the garage.

"Tell her you feel bad," Anson cried when he heard the back door shut.

"Can I get my coat off here?" his father called.

"Tell her you feel bad," Anson said.

"I feel bad," his father said.

There was some clinking and then his dad came in with two drinks and gave his mom one. He wedged himself on the sofa between her and Anson.

They watched the movie go by. The Phantom on the roof of the opera house, his cape billowing in the wind. His escape in the carriage, the horses' too-sharp turn, the carriage going over. His holding off the mob by pretending to have a bomb, and then his opening his hand, voluntarily, to show that he didn't.

"Look at that," his father said.

He was looking out the deck doors at a shape in the yard. It was black and the snow was blue. It was the Airedale that played with Shitface. The wind was blowing the snow around, but the Airedale's fur was barely moving.

"It's gotta be twenty below," his father said.

The dog lowered itself to the snow. It took the sphinx position.

Anson slapped himself. He slapped himself again. His father grabbed his hand.

"Geoff," his mother said. She was crying. He stopped trying to twist his hand out of his dad's grip. What they didn't get was this: He didn't blame himself for what happened. He blamed himself for who he was. He blamed himself for who he'd be. Someday he'd take himself into the woods and run his head into a tree. He wasn't going to make things harder. He was going to make things work. And that was the most selfish thing of all.

THE CREATURE FROM THE BLACK LAGOON

Before they came, I went about my business in pond muck, slurry, roiling soups and thermoclines of particulate matter and anaerobiotic nits and scooters. I'd been alone for somewhere between 250 and 260 million years. I'd forgotten the exact date. Our prime had been the Devonian, and we'd been old news by the Permian. We'd become a joke by the Triassic and fish food by the Cretaceous. The Cenozoic had dragged by like the eon it was. At some point I'd looked around and everyone else was gone. I was still there, the spirit of a fish in the shape of a man. I breaststroked back and forth, parting underwater meadows with taloned mitts. I watched species come and go. I glided a lot, vain about my swimming, and not as fluid with my stroking as I would have liked to have been. I suffered from negative buoyancy. I was out of my element.

Out of the water, I gaped. In the hundred percent humidity it felt like I should be able to breathe. My mouth moved like I was testing a broken jaw. My gills flexed and extended, to pull what I needed out of the impossible thinness of the air. The air felt elastic and warm at the entrance to my throat, as though it had breath behind it that never got through. The air was strands of warmth pulling apart, dissipating at my mouth.

My mouth was razored with shallow triangular teeth. I lived on fish that I was poorly equipped to catch. I killed a tapir out of boredom or curiosity but it tasted of dirt and parasites and dung. For regularity I ate the occasional water cabbage. I'd evolved to crack open ammonites and rake the meat from trilobites. Instead I flopped around after schools of fish that moved like light on leaves. They slipped away like memories. Every so often a lucky swipe left one taloned.

How long had it been since I'd seen one of my own? We hadn't done well where we'd been, and our attempt at a diaspora had been a washout.

I'd gotten pitying looks from the plesiosaurs.

Was I so unique? In the rain forest, the common was rare and the rare was common.

The lagoon changed over the years. It snaked out in various directions and receded in others. Most recently it had become about nine times as long as it was wide. The northern end was not so deep and the southern end fell away farther than I'd ever needed to go. Something with bug eyes and fanlike dorsals had swum up out of there once seventy-five hundred years ago, and hadn't been seen since.

Every so often the water tasted brackish or salty.

There was one crescent of sandy beach that came or went by the decade, depending on storms, a wearying expanse of reedy shoreline that flooded every spring (silver fish glided between the buttress-roots, gathering seeds), and a shallow-bottomed plateau of thickly cloaking sawgrass that turned out to be perfect for watching swimmers from concealment. There was a minor amphitheater of a rocky outcrop suitable for setting oneself off against when being probed for at night with searchlights (stagger up out of the waist-deep water, perform your blindness in the aggravating glare, swipe ineffectually at the beams). There were two seasonally roving schools of piranha with poor self-control, a swarm of unforgiving parasitic worms in a still water cul-de-sac, five or six uninviting channels that led to danger and mystery, one occasionally blocked main artery in from the bend of the Amazon, one secret underwater passageway which led to an oddly capacious and echoey chamber of stone, and a gargantuan fallen stilt palm which seemed to be still growing despite its submarine status. From below, the water was the color of tea. From above, even on sunny days, the deeper levels looked black.

During the day, the air was humid and blood-warm. In the morning, orchid-smelling mists surrounded columns buttressed with creepers. Lines of small hunting vireos moved like waves through the trees. Wrens sang antiphonally, alternating the opening notes and completing phrases with their mates.

Night fell in minutes. Bats replaced birds, moths replaced butterflies. In the close darkness, howler monkeys roared defiance. Nectar-gathering bats sideslipped through the clearings. Fishing bats gaffed pickerel and ate them in flight.

I didn't go far. I entertained dim memories of thickets of stinging insects, poisonous snakes and spiders, and the yellow-eyed gleams of jaguars. Away from the water, all trees looked the same and there were no clues to help with orientation. Everything considered me with a diffident neutrality: the bushmaster in the leaf-litter, the army ants in the hollow tree, the millipede spiraled into its defensive position. I chewed leguminous beans and certain fungi for the visions their hallucinogens provided. The visions stood in for insights.

One afternoon after 470 million years of quiet, a boat chug-chugged into the lagoon. Old rubber tires hung over its side. It leaked black oil and something more pungent that spread small rainbows over the water. It made a lot of unnecessary and fish-scaring noise. Once it settled into quiet, I fingered its bottom from below with a talon, scraping lines in the soft slime.

Later, across the lagoon, I hovered in the black water, invisible in the sun's glare. The figures on the boat had my shape. Naturally, I was curious.

They spoke over one another in headlong squabbles and seemed to have divided their tasks in obscure ways. Just what they were doing was something I could not untangle. Had I found Companions? Was I no longer completely alone? Had the universe singled me out for good fortune? My heart boomed terror.

I had not one single illusion about this group. Spears were unpacked. Nets. Other ominous-looking instruments. Nothing about any of this suggested diffident neutrality.

A smaller boat steadily brought minor hills of junk ashore. A canvas tent went up. Floating off by myself, savoring that moment of illusory coolness when I'd rise from the water in the early, early morning, I watched a bare-chested native lead a hurrying scientist in a Panama hat to an exposed bank of rock. They arrived to confront a conspicuous claw waving menacingly from the shale.

I paddled over for a listen.

What was it, Doctor? the native asked.

The Doctor admitted he didn't know. He was fumbling with a cumbersome flash camera. He said he'd never seen anything like it before.

Was it important? the native wondered.

The Doctor took pictures, his flash redundant in the sunlight. He said he thought it was. Very important. He set the camera aside and pickaxed the fossil arm right out of the rock. So much for the preciousness of the find.

He announced he was going to take it to the Institute. Luis and his friend were to wait here for his return.

First, he said, he had to make some Measurements. Then he fussed about for days.

There were four men: a figure with a hat who remained on the boat, and Luis, Andujar, and the Doctor on the shore, their sagging tent beside that still water cul-de-sac with the swarm of parasitic worms.

The foreclaw that they kept in the center of the tent in a box had some sentimental value for me. In the middle of the night at times I stood beside the open tent flaps, dripping, ruminating on whether or not to go in for it. The Doctor's breathing was clogged and he sounded like a marine toad.

In the morning they made their waste down the end of a trail leading to a stand of young palms that turned from orange to green as they matured.

One day the foreclaw was gone; I could feel it. The Doctor was gone with it. The boat was gone.

LUIS AND ANDUJAR SANG as they worked. They didn't work often. They played a game with a sharp knife they used to hack down plants.

I watched them and learned their idiosyncrasies. I learned about camp stools and toilet paper. I learned about rifles. They enjoyed disassembling and oiling rifles. The procedure for loading rifles and killing animals with rifles was patiently walked through every morning, as though for the benefit of those creatures like myself watching interestedly from the bush. I was impressed with the rifles.

THAT NIGHT BESIDE THEIR CAMP I rose so slowly from the water that the surface meniscus distended before giving way. With my mouth still submerged, my eyes negotiated the glow of their lanterns. The tent canvas blocking the light was the color of embers. On a nearby hibiscus, the light refracted through an insect disguised as a water droplet.

I stood beside their tent in the darkness. One of them looked out and then withdrew his head.

Even with my scales glimmering moonlight and water seeping from my algae, I had a talent for invisibility, for sudden disappearance, the way blue butterflies in the canopy vanished when entering shade.

On the other side of the canvas Luis and Andujar nattered and thumped about. I waited as quietly as an upright bone. My chest was stirred by an obscurely homicidal restlessness.

They fell silent. This was more annoying than their noise. I stood before the closed flaps of the tent's entrance, spread a taloned claw, and extended it slowly into the light. No response.

I pulled the flap aside. Luis gaped, goggled, brandished one of the lanterns; threw it. Andujar sprang from his cot swinging the big sharp knife. They weren't as much exercise as the tapir.

I ENJOYED THROWING THEM about. I raked meat off the bone, lathed, splintered, and shredded; wrung, wrenched, rooted, and uprooted. I noted my lack of restraint. I opened them to the jungles. I unearthed their wet centers.

I sat outside the tent, not ready to return to the water. I held my claws away from my body. Space in the upper canopy turned blue and paled. Two tiny scarlet frogs wrestled beside me. Leaf-litter beneath them slipped and scattered. Along the water, one set of noisemakers retired and the next took its place.

I swam off my murderousness. I floated on my back in the center of the lagoon. Fish nipped at my feet. I had even less appetite than usual.

Days passed. Luis and Andujar, slung across shredded cots and canvas, became festive gathering places. In the evenings, even a jaguarundi stopped by. In the opened chest cavities, beetles swarmed and tumbled over one another. Compact clouds of emerald-eyed flies lifted off and resettled.

The big boat came chug-chugging back into the lagoon.

I watched it come from out of the east. My head ached. The sunrise spiked my vision.

I dove to the bottom, corkscrewed around in the muck, and startled some giant catfish.

I resurfaced. Once again, the boat stopped and settled into quiet. Once again there was oblique activity back and forth on deck. Once again the smaller boat was loaded and sent to shore.

The Doctor stood in the front. Three other men spread themselves across the back. They centered their attention on a slender figure between them that I could smell all the way across the water. She smelled like the center of bromeliads torn open, mixed with anteater musk and clay. Anteater musk for years had made me pace certain feeding trails, obscurely excited.

Female scent tented through the membranes in my skull. I gawped. I sounded. I hooted, their nightmare owl.

The group looked off in my direction, startled by the local color. The Doctor called for Luis and Andujar. Luis and Andujar weren't answering. The boat rocked and pitched and scuffed up onto the same muddy bank it had left. The Doctor clambered out and marched off toward his tent. The men called the female Kay and helped her out and followed.

I cruised over, a lazy trail of bubbles.

They made their discovery. I hovered nearby in the deeper water, stroking every so often to remain upright. A few of them picked up shattered objects and examined them. There were a number of urgent motions and decisive gestures. Kay was trundled back to the small boat and the entire group returned to the bigger one. On its deck, crates were wrenched open and still more rifles passed around. Rifles were exchanged and admired.

The sun toiled across the sky. Above the wavelets the steamy air was thick enough to bite. I dozed, watching them bustle.

The water cooled. The moon rose. Frogs made their early evening chucking noises. A giant damselfly pulled a big spider out of its web and bit it in half, dropping the head and legs and devouring the rest.

BY THE NEXT DAY the visitors were again anxiety-free. In the morning they putt-putted back ashore in their small boat, and scooped and chipped away at the bank of rock. Fragments piled up and were sifted. The sifters complained.

Kay, reclining in the shade with her back to the work, looked entranced. "And I thought the Mississippi was something," she mused to her companions, who kept working, pouring sweat. In the afternoon, everyone returned to the bigger boat and slept like lizards on the deck in the heat, heads or arms sprawled over one another.

I decided to spend more time on the bottom of the lagoon. I was alternately appalled and bemused by my need to spy. I got the sulks. I kept my distance.

Over the years I'd been continuously taken aback by the ingenuity with which I could disappoint myself.

I heard a splash.

Kay swam on her back away from the boat in my direction, cutting widening wake-lines into the sunlight above her. I watched her cruise by. I left the bottom, and swam on *my* back beneath her for a stretch, as if her reflection.

When she stopped, I sank lower into the murk. She turned, did somersaults; played, in some obscure way. Resting, she treaded water.

I ascended and drifted a talon into one of her kicking legs, which jerked upward. I dove. She dove. Vegetative murk billowed up around us. She surfaced and swam back to the boat. Suddenly ferocious, I followed. It was an exciting race, which I lost. She climbed a ladder out just ahead of my arrival.

Braced on the bottom in the ooze, I took the keel and uprooted it with both arms. Tons of displaced water surged and rocked. On the deck above, boxes slid and smashed and shinbones barked against wheelhouses.

I climbed up a convenient rope to give them a look. They each produced individualized noises of consternation. I made my peccary snarl and backhanded a lantern hanging on the rail into the water. Everyone held up their favorite rifle and I dove back in.

I surfaced on the other side of the boat. "The lantern must have frightened him," Kay said. In the middle of the afternoon.

Within minutes, two men came after me, with little masks on their faces and breathing tubes in their mouths. Bubbles bubbled from their heads. Back in the deep reeds, I watched them churn by overhead, a body's length away, and then swam the other direction. I backstroked through the weeds. They seemed to have trouble following. I did an underwater plié. They spotted me. Their legs thrashed and pounded inefficiently. More bubbles bubbled. This went on for some time.

AND AGAIN THE NEXT DAY they went about their business.

I kept being *drawn* to them and their leaking hippo-belly of a boat.

This whole thing had affected me. My eye glands were secreting. I rubbed my face on tree bark. I urinated on my feet.

Normally for me the geologic periods came and went, and normally I had the tender melancholic patience of a floodplain, but with them in the lagoon I found myself foolish and hopeful, carp-toothed. I was a creature of two minds, one of them as unteachable as the swamp. I wanted to make this signal event a signal event. I wanted to *become* something.

• • •

TO THEM I WAS the unknown Amazon embodied—*who knew what lay undiscovered in those hidden backwaters?*—and *still* they lounged and chatted. They flirted. They acted as if they were home.

At midday, one wilted crewmember stood guard. He exchanged vacant stares with a cotton-topped tamarin eating its stew of bugs and tree gum on a shoreline branch. The rest of the group squabbled below deck.

I hauled myself back up the rope—why didn't they just *pull up* the rope?—and schlumped past the porthole while they argued. I was dripping all over the planking. I grabbed the crewmember by both sides of his head and toppled us over the rail.

His internal workings ran down on shore later that night. I sat with him with my elbows on my knees. Every so often he got his breath back. A yellow tree boa angled forward from a branch but I waved it away. He called out to the boat. They called back.

They built a cage. Bamboo.

THEY ROWED AROUND in their smaller boat dumping powder all over their section of the lagoon. It paralyzed the fish, which floated to the surface. A few eyed me dazedly on the way up.

While they worked, I waited under their larger boat. It seemed safer there.

That night they lined the deck stem to stern under their lanterns, their rifles nosed out toward the darkness. I bobbed under the curve of the bow. Off in the distance, a giant tree fell, shearing its way through canyons of canopy, opening up new opportunities.

"Do you suppose he remembers being chased and intends to take revenge?" Kay asked.

"I've got a hunch this creature remembers the past and more," her favorite male answered. He watched his own arms whenever he moved so I named him Baby Sloth.

I floated and listened while they tried to get under the rock of my primitive reasons. How sly was it possible I was? How instinctual? "Just what do you think we're dealing with here, Doctor?" I heard Baby Sloth ask.

I cleared my throat. I cleaned bone bits from my talons. Hours passed. I listened to the quiet crunch of beetle larvae chewing through the boat's hull. One by one, the talkers above me ran out of words and announced they were going to sleep. There were dull, resonant sounds of them settling in below. I sank, my neck back, only my face above the dark water. For some reason I thought of scorpions, those brainless aggravations who went back as far as I did.

Back up into the night air tiptoed Kay, with Baby Sloth. They whispered. The sound carried. "How much more time do you think you'll need?" I heard her tease. "From where I'm sitting, a lifetime," I heard him answer. One more time, I hauled myself up the rope.

I slipped and tumbled over the railing, sending the shock of my greeting across the deck. Kay shrieked. She was within arm's reach. Baby Sloth swung, whonking me with his rifle butt. I knocked him overboard. Others came stumbling up from below. They ringed me as if everyone was ready to charge but no one harbored any unreasonable expectations.

I grabbed Kay and tilted us over the rope and into the water.

I surfaced to let her fill her lungs. There was splashing behind me. I dove and towed her through my secret underwater passageway. Particles of their powder were suspended in the water even at this depth and I could feel them befuddling me.

In my hidden cavern, I rose from the water and lugged her around. "Kay!" Baby Sloth called, hoarse from held breath. I splotched along in the shallow water puddling the rocks. "Kay!" he called again. I bellowed some response.

I had no stamina. Everything was too much work. I laid her out on a shelf and then, once he knelt next to her, surfaced from a convenient nearby pool. I approached him woozily, planning mayhem. He bounced a head-sized rock off my face. He stabbed at my chest. I lifted him up and started working my talons into his ribs. Gunshots, from all those rifles, made little fire tunnels through my back and shoulders. The others had found the land entrance to my lair. A headache came on. I put him down.

I turned from him. Kay gave another shriek, for someone's benefit. They all fired again. I staggered past them to the land entrance and out into the warmer air. "That's enough," I heard Baby Sloth tell the others. "Let him go."

Lianas patted and dabbed at my face. Day or night? I couldn't tell. I walked along bleeding and gaping. The path was greasy with mud. My feet were scuffling buckets filling with stones. I hallucinated friends. I could hear them all cautiously following. I headed for the lagoon.

What was less saddening, finally, than a narcissist's solitude? I'd been drawn to Kay the way insects singled out the younger shoots or leaves not yet toughened or toxic. I'd added nothing but judgment and violence to the world. If their law, like the lagoon's, was grim and casual, they at least took what they found and tried to make the best of it.

So they liked to disassemble their surroundings and tinker with them. Was it such a shame that they didn't save all the parts?

Once in the water I sank to my knees down a slope, the muck giving way in clouds. I was happy they'd turned me out. I was rooting against me. I was less their shadow side than an oafish variant on a theme. Extinction was pouring over me like a warm flood, history swirling and eddying one last time before moving on, and I was like the pain of a needle frond in the foot: I filled the moment entirely, and then vanished.

RUNWAY

He often wondered, sitting at the window watching Billy and Theophilus play in the street, what he would do if one of them were hit by a car. Billy sat against the telephone pole, where he always did, near the end of the driveway, throwing a chewed-up tennis ball off the tire of a parked car. The ball perpetually fooled Theophilus with its change of direction. Depending on how Billy threw it, the ball would ricochet or arc softly back, and the dog, sprinting at the first motion of his arm, was endlessly surprised by all trajectories. One ricochet caught the dog squarely in the forehead, and it wobbled comically and flopped over onto the pavement.

WITH A SON LIKE BILLY you don't wonder things like that, Jay would find himself saying while shaving. He would peer at his image in the mirror.

And in the living room, nights, watching television with Billy on the floor in front of him, he'd think, Has the boy ever come close to doing anything reckless? Has the boy been anything less than all he should be?

He sat before the TV and clasped and unclasped the arms of his chair. He nudged his son with his foot.

"Quit it," Billy said.

"This is a good show," Jay said. "In case you didn't notice."

Billy made a small dismissive noise.

"By the way," Jay said. "Has anyone ever given you high praise? Anybody ever tell you you were the greatest?"

"You did," Billy said. "Yesterday."

Their eyes went back to the TV, and Jay drummed his fingers on his knee.

"Oh," Anne said, on the sofa. It was her terminal boredom voice. She had a film book, a big coffee table thing, on her lap. She'd gotten it on a good deal from a publisher's clearinghouse. He could see Garbo upside down, regarding them.

David Janssen was squinting at the street through some venetian blinds. Jay had lost the story for a second. What was he doing inside the house?

"So where do you go on these walks of yours?" Anne asked.

"I'm watching," Jay said.

"He won't tell you," Billy said.

Anne flipped a few more pages in her film book. She closed it with a thump.

There was a commercial and Jay stood up. He saw Anne looking at him and crossed to her and leaned over, his hands on his thighs, as if examining her face microscopically.

"You didn't answer my question," Anne finally said.

"You're very beautiful," Jay said. He said it as if after much debate as to how to put it.

"I know," Anne said. "I'm gorgeous. Where're you going?"

He kissed her, and held the kiss longer than she expected. Then he straightened up.

"Where are you *go*ing?" she said.

"You sound tired," he said.

"I *am* tired." She switched off the lamp and looked back at the television. She was eighteen in its light. "This is over. I'll turn it off."

"No, it's all right. I'll be back in a little while." He touched his wife's ear, for a good-bye, and slipped away.

THEOPHILUS HAD almost been hit once, by an old Le Sabre. Jay heard the screech but no body sound and no horn, and he reacted, he remembered later, like he was underwater, swimming futilely toward the front door and the yard in time to see Anne already crouching over the dog, making sure it was all right, with another arm on Billy's shoulder. Billy was lifting and dropping Theo's front paw in a rudimentary medical exam and the driver was waiting for Jay to get there to exchange apologies before leaving. Jay hadn't had anything to say and the guy had gotten into his Le Sabre and waved like he'd enjoyed the visit. Anne had said on the way back to the house, What were you, asleep? and he hadn't been able to shake the feeling of being underwater until hours later, watching television.

BEHIND HIM ANNE SURFED channels in frustration with her remote, and Billy said, "Ma. Leave it on one." Jay eased past the dog asleep on the floor in the kitchen. He opened the door softly. The dog was immediately on its feet but too late to get to the door. It stood with its front paws on the windowsill, backlit by the kitchen light. Jay stretched in the driveway, rubbing his forearms against the chill. August, and the nights were already cool. He left the dog panting silently behind the glass and crossed the yard to the street, conjuring up Anne's face in the light of the television. He was away from the lights of his house quickly, and then he left the streetlights, off-white and quiet, behind him as well.

The lights receded and the darkness and quiet increased. His street was a dead end. He was heading for the fence on the grassy bluff beyond the pavement, and for the airport beyond the fence.

• • •

THEY HAD AN ARRANGEMENT for Thursday nights: he got to see his shows, Anne got to see hers, and Billy got to see his. The times lined up. They had a VCR but only used it for rental movies. On other nights when shows competed, Jay sometimes stuck it out and sometimes didn't. When he didn't he sat by the window in the kitchen with the lights out. Anne would say to Billy, "Your father's in there communing with the darkness."

THE SIEBERTS' DOG, an Irish setter/beagle mix, barked at the rattle of the chain link every time Jay reached the fence, and kept barking until he slid underneath it and got down to the base of the bluffs. He tried not to let the dog hurry him, picking his way through the brambles and fallen birches in the moonlight. He was off his usual path—here was some splintered and ragged sumac, where he expected a small clearing—but it was no problem; he knew his way around.

BILLY WAS NINE and Theophilus was four and Anne was thirty-five, and Jay spent as much time as he could with them, watching. They were all happy. When he thought of his family he thought of the dog snuffing under the azalea, sprinting in bursts after squirrels and birds, barking and leaping splay-legged at the tennis ball. Anne was happy. She loved her job and concentrated on it at home in a knit-browed, serious way that he admired; she loved her books, her cooking, her landscaping. Billy was happy. He had his father and mother and Theo. Theo was happy. Everybody was happy.

• • •

AS HE EXPECTED, once on the bottom, at runway level, he had no problems. He headed for the four red threshold lights spanning diagonally away from him. He kept an eye out for security vehicles. He moved through the high groundcover the way he moved through his own darkened house. He found the huge chevrons of the overrun area, and then his feet were on the landing threshold and the hard surface of the runway itself.

He stood between the central red lights. They seemed attentive, obedient and waiting. He crossed to one and held his hand over it, the red glowing up through his skin and between his fingers, creating a pleasing, instant X-ray. He held on to the thick, warm glass and leaned back, squeezing, staring out into the darkness and stars in the direction of the approach pattern of the planes.

He pulled away from the lights, finally, moving toward the center of the runway, the circling beam of the tower in the distance calming him. He crossed the nonprecision approach markings, great, white parallel squares, and stood over the sweeping number of the runway designation. The number was twenty-eight. It was probably the compass bearing, as well. He sat down. He turned back to the four red lights, still silent and waiting. Then he lay back, spread-eagle, and looked up into the darkness.

It wasn't long before he heard the first plane. It was a light, far-off buzzing, starting out beyond his left arm and circling quietly, slowly, around him until it was coming, harder and louder, from below his heels. He told himself he wouldn't look, he'd keep his eyes straight up, but when it got so loud it seemed already on him he jerked his head up, his chin hitting his chest, and caught the landing lights full in the face. They passed over him in an instant, streaking up the runway far ahead of the plane, leaving him momentarily blinded, but everything reappeared immediately, and right overhead swinging toward him like a great pendulum were the red and white running lights, spread out unevenly in a line and gleaming on the smooth underside of the wings and fuselage, the wheels swaying low beneath them. He rolled, face pressed against the pavement, as the noise rushed over him in a wave, shaking him, and was gone.

He rose to his elbows and lay on his belly, watching the plane skirt into the darkness, the lights slowly joining the concentration of lights around the tower.

He marked the spot in his mind and computed how far into the runway the next spot should be. Then he left, heading for the bluff at a good speed, because the airport security wasn't that bad.

THERE WAS NO PATTERN to the runway visits. He varied their frequency to baffle airport security. He was certainly reported each time by the incoming pilot. Sometimes he waited as much as three months to go out, watching the security jeeps on their rounds through the chain-link fence at the end of the street. Sometimes he went as often as once a week. This week he was going twice: Thursday and Saturday.

SATURDAY NIGHT he heard a twin-engine, it sounded like, even before he'd found his spot. He went to his knees and scuttled forward, approximating, and turned around. The lights were banking, slowly coming around to level, parallel now to the threshold lights beyond the runway's edge. The noise increased, and he picked up the landing lights slipping slowly along the ground, suddenly speeding up and flashing over him as the roar grew louder and the lights sank closer, and at the last moment he flattened out as much as he could on the surface of the tarmac, turning his face as his ears filled with sound and his clothing shook and he felt it touch down hard behind him, the shock traveling through him, and he knew, as he got up, running for the bluff, that the next time, farther out onto the runway, might be the last time.

He remembered a movie he'd seen some years ago called *The Magnificent Seven.* In it, Steve McQueen, one of a group of gunfighters who have banded together for no apparent reason to protect a poor Mexican town from bandits, is asked by the bandit chief why they stay and fight against insurmountable odds for no reward. He replies, "Well, it's like a guy I once knew in Waco. Took off all his clothes one day and jumped into a cactus. I asked him why he did it."

And the bandit chief says impatiently, "Well? What did he say?"

And McQueen replies, "He said it seemed like a good idea at the time."

WHEN HE GOT BACK Billy and Theo were in the sunroom, Theo still nose to the window. Had the dog been like that the whole time? Billy was sitting in the lawn chair they kept inside and was shelling peanuts on his lap. Billy said, "So where'd you go, Dad?"

He realized he was still wired and flushed and he put his hand over the top of Billy's head and mussed his hair, though he never did that. He said, "I went for a walk. What're you, a cop?"

But Billy held his ground, staring up at him, and he was forced to turn to Anne, who came around the corner from the kitchen, the phone to her ear and the cord stretched taut. She nodded hello and said, "Moth*er.* He just came in."

She gave him a stern look and he kissed her until she had to pull away to say, "Yes, Mother, yes, I'm listening."

"Mr. Mystery," Billy said behind him. Jay crossed the kitchen, ducking while Anne held the cord up, and dropped onto the sofa in the living room, casting around for the remote. Billy had left it turned around atop the TV, the electric eye facing him.

• • •

SOMETIMES HE THOUGHT, You're a responsible young man, you need to consider this, but nothing coherent or plausible came to him when he did. Nothing made him do it, he realized, mowing the first summer grass or piling clippings into the trunk to take to the dump. Part of the reason, he knew, was the way it felt that first split second when he heard a Cessna or an Allegheny or something make that distant turn, start that faint buzz way off in the night.

HE'D BEEN OUT nine times. He was six-one and each time he went out he moved six feet and an inch farther down the runway, each time coming closer to the touchdown point of most aircraft. Of course, there'd always been the chance that someone would touch down early, as well.

HE BUSTLED AROUND the house after supper for a week, cleaning, fixing, storing, and straightening, and Anne watched him happily and took him aside and said, smiling, "You're a real dynamo this week, know it?" When he started to pull away, hedge clippers in hand, she got serious and added, "You're wonderful, you know that?"

He settled his affairs at work, getting the last shipments of the week out two days early and working with such efficiency even for him that his fellow workers were sure something was up. He made sure before he left on Friday that someone could cover for him Monday if he was late or couldn't make it.

The guys at Sikorsky knew he was a good worker. And they knew he was crazy.

He wasn't inclined to believe them.

He didn't feel wild or out of control when he did the things he did.

When he was five, every Sunday night for a week he jumped off the roof of the porch of the old house on Spruce Street. He was practicing landing and rolling.

When he was seventeen he and a friend raced twin Kawasakis off a dock and into the Housatonic River. The Kawasakis had taken two weeks to clean and get back into shape. When he was twenty-five, ten years ago, he climbed the roof of the main hangar at Sikorsky on his lunch break. It was his first year on the job.

Two years after that he'd found himself on his belly behind the forklift in Hangar 6, out of reach of the light drizzle slicking the helicopter pad, thirty-three yards away from him, and the HH-52 warming up on it.

He'd measured the thirty-three yards. He'd measured everything, including the time it would take to cross them and the time from the first revving of its turbines that it would take the HH-52 to get airborne and out of reach. He'd figured out the best day (Saturday), the best weather conditions (rainy), and the best copter (the 52, with its massive pods surrounding the landing gear) for what he planned. The landing gear would be his handholds, and the pods would shield him initially from the tower's view.

The turbines went into their high metallic rush and the blades of the big ship pitched and he counted one, two, three, and broke for the copter, spattering across the gleaming blacktop and into the rotor wash, approaching from the rear diagonally to avoid pilot detection and the tail rotor, and he jumped as the landing gear was lifting up and swaying away from him. He caught one arm around the inside strut and pulled himself up and around, banging his head on the undercarriage. There was no hesitation in the climb so he knew he was okay, and the copter immediately banked out over the Housatonic, and with his head throbbing he swung his legs down, looking past them to the water spinning away below, and then let go, the noise of the rotors filling his ears all the way down.

SOMEWHERE ALONG THE LINE he decided to go back to the runway Sunday night. He asked Anne if she wanted to go out to dinner Saturday. Get a sitter for Billy. She loved the idea. When she left the bathroom Saturday night, ready to go, he thought her beauty must increase in some way proportionate to her happiness.

HE'D FIRST THOUGHT of the runway on a Christmas Day. It came to him as a visual image while he was stuffing scattered wrapping paper into a brown grocery bag. Billy was confusing Theo with an orange Nerf basketball by compressing it and hiding it in his fist. Anne was on the phone, in her blue nightgown with the tiny embroidery on the shoulders. He got up, got dressed, kissed her on the cheek, and headed out into the snow. It was very cold. It occurred to him before he reached the airport that they wouldn't have had time to plow yet, but he kept going. Out over the runway the snow had drifted into little ridges that reminded him of the roof of a dog's mouth. There was a bright glare over everything from the morning light. He crossed to where he judged the center of the runway must be, and lay down, sinking and looking up at the sky.

SUNDAY MORNING he bought the papers. He played catch with Billy down the length of the driveway, enjoying the feel of the old Rawlings. He threw Billy grounders, soft line drives, pop-ups.

He had drinks in the backyard with Anne. He helped her with the pork chops for supper. He helped Billy with his homework.

When that was over they joined Anne in the den. She was catching the end of *Moby Dick.* Gregory Peck was nailing a gold coin to the masthead and making speeches.

Anne looked over at him and gave him a smile. He was starting to get fidgety. He said he was going to take a look around. He poured some cranberry juice from the refrigerator and drank it. He washed out the glass in the sink. He took Theo out to let him take a leak, jingling change in his pockets while the dog decided on a bush. Then he let it back in, closed the door behind it, and went down the driveway, enjoying the summer smells and heading down the street at a jog.

ANNE NEVER FOUND OUT about the copter ride, though it had been in the papers (a UPI photographer there to cover another test flight had happened to get a shot of him on the way down, a tiny figure, grainy and blurred; it had caused a minor sensation at Sikorsky security). She knew about other things, including the hangar roof, and when he did things like that she told him she wanted to understand. She also asked if he ever thought about her and Billy. Things like that she expected more from the kind of kids she hoped to keep Billy away from.

He didn't answer because he loved her and wanted to protect her, and also because he didn't know how to explain it without sounding as if he were refusing to explain it.

HE TOOK HIS TIME on the bluffs. The Sieberts' dog kicked up a racket. He imagined he heard another dog answering. He ran his fingers over the chain link of the fence before slipping under it, sliding through the damp smooth hole scuffed in the dirt. Halfway down he stopped and surveyed the runway. Then he leaned out over the slope and cantered down, every step sure, digging his heels in the gravel and slaloming around the bushes and larger stones.

At the bottom he heard the rumble of something big, and a four-engine Allegheny came thundering over the bluffs to his right, close enough that he could see heads in the windows. It swept over the runway, its rear wheels slamming down with a tremendous, murderous screech, right, he estimated as he hurried toward the overrun area in its wake, where he would momentarily be lying.

He stopped at the markings and crouched, looking for security activity, and then crossed to the middle. He found his old mark, measured out from it, and set his new one. He lay back on his elbows, made one last check of the runway around him, and settled in, looking up at the stars. Something rustled in the high grass. He waited.

Far off he could hear cars moving, beyond the tower on the other side of the airport. From that grew another sound.

He looked back for the tower and caught in the gleam of one of its circling beams a Pilgrim Airlines twin-engine banking slowly around toward his strip.

He lay back, trying to keep still, the plane circling gradually in the darkness off to the left, disappearing beyond the bluff as it made its final gliding bank into its approach, its engines still audible. He could feel them getting higher in pitch. He watched the section of bluff visible over his feet, waiting for the red and white lights to explode over it toward him, but felt vibration coming from the opposite direction as well, and twisted around and there were the headlights of the security jeep down by the tower, bouncing along the shoulder of the runway. He got up in a crouch but then hesitated, and turned to face the bluff, the Pilgrim's engines roaring behind it now, and lay back down.

Then he saw Theo.

He picked up movement in his peripheral vision and turned as the dog reached the runway. He shouted something as Billy piled out of the darkness onto the tarmac, too, slipping to his knees. He shot a look back at the jeep while trying to push the dog away, and Billy was shouting something and running toward them, and then the dog cringed and there was a roar as the Pilgrim twin-engine burst over the bluffs. Billy froze looking up at the huge lighted dark shape swinging down toward him, screaming, maybe; Jay couldn't hear. He grabbed Theo by the skin and hair of his neck and dove at Billy, throwing the dog as far as he could, sending him sprawling and skidding off the runway, and hitting Billy in the midsection and driving him hard onto his back as the twin-engine hit beside them, the wing sweeping over, and was gone.

Billy was crying and twisting around in his arms as the jeep pulled up alongside, becoming audible only as the plane taxied farther down the runway. Men in blue vinyl jackets grabbed them. One was chasing Theo around the scrub nearby. Even then and there they were asking questions, which he waved off, trying to indicate he'd answer everything soon. His voice was coming back to him with his hearing. Someone shook him, and he nodded, yes. He was watching Theo, who was all right. He was concentrating on Anne, and on not letting go of Billy.

AJAX IS ALL ABOUT ATTACK

The acoustics of empty stadiums were very beautiful. When a single bird called out, you heard it from wherever you were. In the early morning, or after matches, when the lights were out and the sky was black, from the bench, you heard the wind in the grass. In the Dutch leagues then, the stadium superstructures were skeletal and intimate. The advertising panels were like old friends and smelled of wet wood. The empty balconies overhung the stands so that stray papers blown from above were snared by seat-backs below.

When you took a ball out to the middle of the pitch and struck it once, the thump filled the entire space. The thump seized something in your chest.

My name is Velibor Vasovic and for eleven years I played football, first for Partizan Belgrade and my national team, and then for Ajax. For eleven years I played for money, I should say; football I played my entire life. My brother played with his friends, and when I was old enough to stand I started joining in. I began in goal but could never stay there, and was always running after the ball and upsetting everyone and ruining the game, and eventually they made someone else goalie. We played every day. This was just after the war. When it rained, we played in the cowshed. The cow stood in the rain and watched. Six or so kids in three square meters: you learned precise passing.

We played with anything that was round. Mostly tennis balls; one boy's family had an old box of tennis balls. You developed great technique trying to dribble tennis balls.

At the 1954 World Cup in Switzerland in the group matches my brother played against the immortal Hungarians with their bright red shirts—Puskas, Kocsis, Hidegkuti—the team that had humiliated England 6–3 and 7–1 just months before.

"What was it like?" we asked upon his return. We had followed the match on the radio but the announcer had been at a loss to describe what he was seeing. Crowded around the countertop of the local bar, we'd been informed that Kocsis had entered the penalty area, and stopped, and turned. Then God had been invoked, at a high volume. Followed by a tinny roar. So when my brother returned, one of the heroes of our 2–8 loss, it was as if we had and hadn't been there; as if we did and didn't know what brilliant football was truly like.

After the game, he'd traded shirts with Puskas. He showed the shirt around the bar. It passed from person to person like Achilles' shield. An old man wiped his hands before taking it.

We had to ask my brother our questions many times. Everyone had their own theories as to the secret of the Hungarians' game. Was it their skills? Their tactics? Their size? Their speed? And what was it like in the West?

I thought about his answers when I first came to Amsterdam and saw Johan Cruyff play a thirty-yard cross on a dead run so that the trajectory bent away from the stunned goalie's attempt at a deflection and dropped the ball lightly in front of the right-winger's boot. The right-winger put it in the back of the net as though he'd just happened by. This was in 1966. Ajax's coach and club president both had seen me score our only goal in Partizan's loss to Real

Madrid in that May's European Cup final. I was to be the rock around which Ajax would build its defense.

Understand: it was quite a change from Zagubica to Amsterdam in 1966. What was rebelliousness in Zagubica then? Old farmers fondling their donkeys in public. Civil disobedience was refusing to roll out of the lane once you fell over drunk. I arrived in Amsterdam soon after their Liberation Day and thought on the ride in from the airport that there'd been a coup. A revolution. An invasion from space. Thousands of young people were surging about the center of town, arm in arm, singing and shouting something. My interpreter, the Yugoslav wife of a Dutchman, explained that they were shouting, "We want our Bolletjes!" Bolletjes turned out to be a breakfast snack. It was an advertising slogan. Why were they shouting this? They were bored, she told me. Thousands of young people chanting this absurdity! Groups shouted it back and forth to one another. The police stood by, polite, their hands clasped in front of them.

We were imprisoned by the sheer numbers in a large plaza called the Leidseplein. My interpreter apologized for not having anticipated this, but seemed serene about the delay. The taxi driver rested his forearms on the wheel and every so often shouted something good-naturedly to those who stood on his car's bonnet. When our taxi was stopped, young girls pressed their cheeks to my window glass as if the car were an infant relative. Atop a statue of a civic leader, a man dressed as a shaman performed antismoking rituals—he crushed packs of cigarettes, or put cigarettes in his mouth and then broke them and threw them away with wild gestures—while the crowd chanted, "Bram bram! Ugga ugga! Bram bram!"

What did "Bram bram! Ugga ugga!" mean? I wanted to know.

My interpreter shrugged. "Bram bram. Ugga ugga," she said.

She identified a small man atop a flagpole as Johnny the Selfkicker, who talked himself into a trance and threw himself from high places. Many of the people in white, she explained, were the Provos, anarchists who looked upon playfulness as the key to a better world.

"Playfulness," I repeated, and she answered, with some defensiveness, "Well, you needn't say it like *that*."

Understand: I am not political. Everywhere I've gone, people have nodded when those words have emerged from my mouth, as though they understood. And then they've gone right on with plebiscite this and student movement that. "Vasovic doesn't give a rat's ass about anything," Michels, Ajax's coach, used to say to the reporters and my teammates. It was his highest praise. He meant other than football.

My interpreter that day had been proud of her adopted country. Her face suggested that I was like a visit from a backward relative. She asked about my hometown: what was life like in those hills? It all seemed so wild and remote.

"That was a quiet shithole," I told her. "This is a noisy shithole."

The taxi driver asked her a question and she answered with the word for "Welcome," in my language. "Welcome," he said to me.

"He's speaking to you," my interpreter told me. I lit a cigarette. I don't like being scolded.

"This is a time of great change in Holland," she told me, as if that should affect my smoking.

"Is the currency stable?" I asked.

After that she gave up on me. After a few minutes of silence, the taxi driver made a remark, and she answered in a way which evidently made him sad.

JOHAN CRUYFF *WAS* political. The same day I was introduced to Dutch politics, I was introduced to Dutch football. I sat between the club president and my interpreter and watched an Ajax home game against PSV Eindhoven. I drank many beers. I noticed their left-winger, a blank-faced beanpole with endless stamina. He ran for ninety minutes and looked at the end as if he could have run to Maastricht and back. And he ran with *purpose:* he continually set up Ajax's offense, flew down the wing, touched off chaos in PSV's penalty area, created space for himself and his teammates. He was envisioning whole geometries while his opponents scurried about like moles. He was a Pythagoras in shorts. I was told he was nineteen. Then I was told I needn't worry about him, because left wing was the position of the club's best player, who wasn't playing at the moment. I stood and started to leave. I told the interpreter, "Tell the president that if they have anyone better than this guy, they don't need me." They caught up to me halfway up the aisle and returned me to my seat. I met with Cruyff after the game.

He had the same blank expression while he toweled off. His teammates were showering. His towel was the size of a facecloth. At that point the players still had to wash their own kits and provide their own towels and shampoo.

I heard the interpreter mention Partizan Belgrade. Cruyff nodded. He led me back out to the pitch, intercepted a ball boy heading in with a net full of balls, and lined them up at the eighteen-yard mark from the goal. There were nine of them. The interpreter and club president trailed along behind us, making remarks that he chose not to answer. While I watched, he tucked his hair behind his ears and struck each of the first five balls in line precisely against the crossbar. Then he stepped away. In my street shoes, I did the same with the four that were left. Blank-faced Cruyff smiled and the interpreter and club president burst into applause.

When they stopped, Cruyff turned his attention to the club president. They talked, and I felt the need for more beer. The interpreter explained that Johan was always agitating for something.

"What's he want?" I asked.

"Oh, you know," she said, embarrassed. "It's always something."

Cruyff spoke to her in a low voice. They looked at one another.

"He wants me to tell you what they're talking about," she said miserably.

It turned out he was asking why officials were insured on foreign trips and players weren't. Why coaches got meal money and players didn't. She seemed aware that this was a poor strategy for attracting me to change teams. He had what he called his List of Grievances, she confided.

His willingness to be a pain in the ass appealed to me. And only the Dutch had a short transfer period in those years, so they were my ticket to the West.

The club president knew that, as well, so after sitting around a rented room for three days, I signed a contract for half the sum for which I'd been asking.

The Dutch carried on like the Sermon on the Mount but their hearts were ledger books. Merchants squeezed each guilder while giving change. *Does it make you nostalgic?* my brother wrote. *It makes me feel like I'm home,* I wrote back.

He worked twelve-hour days on one of the recently consolidated collective farms to the south. His career had been destroyed by a clumsy tackle.

That first morning out on the practice pitch with the rest of Ajax, long-haired boys nodded greetings and included me in their warm-up drills. The sun warmed the little canals and cows in the distance. When the coach arrived and blew his whistle, the long-haired boys formed two lines and proclaimed their objective with a little poem:

Open game, open game
You can't afford to neglect the wing.

And then went back to what they were doing. A handprinted translation was provided for me on an index card. I was introduced. Practice began.

Few remember that before Ajax became Ajax, Holland's football record in internationals had been the equal of Luxembourg's. It took all of us—coach, communist, and long-haired boys—all of thirty minutes that first day to realize that what we'd collected was a group of people who *thought* about space. The ultra-aggressive football in which players switched positions and rained attacks from every angle was worked through and worked out on that pitch over the next three years. It was a collective. During rest breaks we all talked. We all listened. Suppose we tried this? What happened when we tried that? We started letting midfielders and defenders join in attacks, and saw the ways in which forwards would have to support such flexibility by flowing back to cover. Position-shifting came easily and provided opponents, once we started playing matches, with a chaos of movement and change with which to deal. The first Dutch word I really learned to speak was *switch*.

We built our moves from the back; the goalkeeper only rarely kicked the ball long, instead clearing it to our defenders, and the team moved in set and improvisational patterns from there: if someone came back for a pass, someone else broke downfield. In possession we made the pitch as large as possible, spreading play to the wings and seeing everything as a way to increase and exploit space. If we lost the ball, the same thinking was used in reverse. We talked about space in a practical way. How could you play for ninety minutes and remain strong? If you were the left back and you ran seventy meters up the wing, it wasn't so good if you then had to run back to your starting position. If the midfielder took your place, it shortened the distances. Even then I could see that it was very Dutch to look for the simple solution. And to find the biggest thrill in the even simpler solution.

Cruyff was the genius at this. Good players always found ways of receiving the ball in space, but Cruyff *while playing* saw where *everyone* should be, or go. He was three moves ahead and the moves were all about shaping space. From above—from up in the press box—it was a lesson in architecture.

When we spaced ourselves properly, it suddenly became very quiet. No noise. You heard only the wind. And the ball: the sound it made on the foot, the sound that made clear where it was going, how hard, how low, and how fast.

Suddenly football was not about kicking each other's legs anymore. Fans at our matches came away feeling they'd seen something they could see nowhere else on earth. *You guys really have something going,* my brother wrote back, after I wrote him about what was happening.

MY PARENTS: *they* were political. Their Partisan unit during the war had both an antitank rifle and a mimeograph machine, and my mother had lost two frostbitten fingers dragging it over some ridgelines in heavy snow to keep it from German hands. God forbid. The whole tide might have turned. They each produced for me a wry little smile when I came home, a wildly excited seventeen-year-old, to announce I'd be playing for Belgrade. I hadn't understood why until I realized that they were smiling at the *Partizan* on my shirt.

When I was ten, I asked to be included in the confirmation classes which my uncle, a pastor, was going to conduct for my brother and two cousins. I think I believed that that, at last, would make me a part of the family, or at least a part of a common cause. My uncle agreed to interview me, to measure my suitability. The interview was held in the presence of my grandmother. I failed to answer a single question. My collapse caused my uncle and brother considerable amusement, and my grandmother none at all.

When the Germans came my parents enlisted in the first Slovene brigade to be named after a poet, in their case, Cankar. *("The people will write their destiny alone / Without tuxedoes, or the beads of priests.")* They fought illiteracy by giving begging children pencils and paper instead of money or candy. They disseminated periodicals like *Death to Death!* and *Today's Woman.* They lectured on the relation between spontaneity and ideology. They used doors for blackboards. They stayed frozen and hungry. They stopped at doorways from Stajerska to Koruska and sang the old Slovene songs to pry some bread out of the shuttered homesteads. Sometimes they were allowed to sleep in the barn.

My grandmother was my mother's mother. Her father had been a minor railway official and had died of typhus. Her mother had been widowed with six children, my grandmother the last of the six. By the time I knew her, she had her little bit of jam each morning in a spoon that had to be cleaned just so the night before.

She described her son-in-law as someone with a good memory, but no depth. Our father always smiled when she said so. It was hard for us to imagine him as having shot Germans. He was pleasant and gentle, if not always direct.

Before the war, he'd worked late into the night, under a feeble lamp, to enable imprisoned comrades to mull over the most recent literature and prepare themselves for the battle outside. My mother had made lists and tea and helped him with the phrasing. They saw themselves as in battle with the medieval darkness and fury in the souls of our backward peasants. They believed the Party and the movement were very special, and that people within the Party and the movement were very special. They were convinced that they had a scientific ideology. Misery and despair were all around them, and the more unbearable life became, the closer they were to the new world. Implementing decisions was not sufficient. Anyone could do that. They had to transform themselves so that at any time all of their actions could be measured in terms of the interests of the revolution. The role of history's observers had seemed undignified once history had pointed the way to final freedom and brotherhood among men.

• • •

A PERSON ABOUT TO LEAVE prison suddenly becomes loved by everyone. And he feels the same about those he is leaving behind. Quarrels and hatreds are forgotten and forgiven, and he says goodbye warmly and directly, as if nothing had ever happened.

The night before my departure for the West I wept and waited for the dawn. While I made tea and watched the sun rise, my mother and father brought my belongings—a suit and a few other things, packed and creased and smelling of mothballs—to the door. My lawyer came with me to get a big shot to sign the necessary final papers. In the corridor where we waited there were several frantic young men. I registered little of the train trip to the airport. Willows and alders along clear streams.

Colors and smells overwhelmed me when I stepped off the plane at Schiphol. Women in spring coats and hats, strange fashions. My translator met me with a hug, though she was a pretty young woman. I rode to the city in a stupor. A far-off bridge, suspended on an invisible thread. A university. A square in front of it.

I was left in my new flat to tidy up after my trip. I wandered to the back garden. A branch full of purple blossoms hung over the wall, and from the window of the house next door a young woman was shaking rugs. In my own language, I told her I was a persecuted student. I asked if she would lend me a rug to lie on. She smiled.

My eyes filled with tears for my father. What hadn't he thrown underfoot and sacrificed? He'd built himself a life which, for the sake of an idea, had buried itself. A life surrounded by spite in a godforsaken, frightened little town. They thought they were doing it for us, and for our children. But this was the world of their imagination, and they'd pictured it falsely to us, and we at first hadn't wanted to believe things to be different.

• • •

MICHELS WAS THE PERFECT COACH for me. He required fantastic discipline. Even with the assistant coaches he was like an animal trainer. He told me I was his favorite player because I couldn't ask him questions. He told us all that when we came to the stadium, we were the numbers on our backs. When we left, we became people and he could talk to us.

Each night I went home satisfied to my flat with its one chair. I never understood why you'd play a game in which you lost four kilos of your body weight for nothing. When you put on the shirt and laced up the boots, you had to win. Otherwise you might as well stay at home and watch the television.

With such an attitude I was very helpful to the Dutch, who were not naturally ferocious. If there was an art to defending, they were blind to it. They prized Technique and Tactics. Courage, will to win, speed, size: none of that aroused much interest.

So during training sessions Michels did all he could to develop aggression. We played games in which he acted as the referee from hell, calling the fouls with such enraging one-sidedness that our nickname for the matches became the Bloodbaths. He made sure we lived only football: he got our salaries raised, so that Cruyff could leave the printing works, Keizer the tobacco shop, Swart his haberdashery.

Understand, though: he never scored the goals. He did his part, and we did ours.

We couldn't believe, ourselves, what we held in our palms. Against MVV Maastricht in our first game we won 9–3 and I scored five goals. A defender! We scored 122 goals in the League season.

Johan Cruyff, Piet Keizer, Barry Hulshoff, Ruud Krol, Gerrie Mühren: they were all unleashed, with me, on Liverpool in the fog in the second round of the European Champions' Cup on the 7th of

December, 1966. Together we remade the football globe. Liverpool barely deigned to look over at us during the warm-ups; the side was stuffed with demigods from their World Cup Champion team of the previous summer. While we stretched, the fog rolled in, and the game was played in such a murk that the scoreboard operator, who sat near our bench, needed runners to let him know what was happening down the ends of the field. He demanded confirmation when told we'd scored the first goal, and then confirmation when told we'd scored the second, and then, when the third went in, less than ten minutes into the match, he shouted at his runners, "Come on, boys, don't make up stories!" His words were reprinted in all the Dutch newspapers the next day. One front page, in letters large enough that there was room for nothing else, proclaimed: AJAX 5–1! Everywhere we went—shops, cinemas, schools, restaurants—those two numbers appeared.

When we traveled to Liverpool for the second leg, everyone said that now we had their attention. Their coach predicted they'd win 7–0. We drew, 2–2. An Amsterdam headline read AJAX WINS, 2–2.

Was there a connection between cultural and football revolutions? Reporters wanted our opinions. Keizer said no. Hulshoff said no. Krol said no. Mühren said no. I said no. Michels refused to answer. Cruyff said it was an intriguing idea. He spent postgame interviews talking about the Provos' White Plans. What did he think of Luud Schimmelpeninck's plan for free bikes, all over the city? Poor Michels sat in his office, his elbows on his desk and his hair in his fists.

He came out every so often to throw a Provo out of the locker room. They were easy to spot, all in white. And they loved Cruyff, who attracted reporters.

"What's he on about?" Michels would ask someone standing nearby, jabbing a thumb toward a Provo.

"He's saying that under New Babylonic circumstances, the lust for aggression will be sublimated into the lust for playfulness," Cruyff would explain.

"Oh, for Christ's sake," Michels would say.

Cruyff didn't spout such stuff, but you could see he believed in parts of it, kept an eye on it. He was intrigued by his own uniqueness. Whenever we set foot on a pitch, he was interested in revolutionizing the game. The rest of us were happy to settle for winning it.

And yet at night, lying in my bed and hearing my neighbor still shaking her rugs, I'd envision my parents' faces and wonder if this were in some strange way their gift to me: Partisan tactics, Partisan strategies. In their war, there'd been no front lines or rear, and encirclements had emerged and dissolved fluidly on both sides; superiority had been achieved not by numerical strength, but by tactical resourcefulness. Survival as a Partisan had meant being creative about space.

"Fascinating," Michels had said when I mentioned this to him. I'd brought it up on a bus when he'd complained to me about Cruyff. My Dutch was by that point sufficient for semicomic conversation.

But all was well as long as we kept winning. We were becoming something majestic and invincible. One moment we'd be marked by two defenders, the next, completely free. One moment the pitch before us was crowded and narrow, the next, huge and wide. The brilliance of our passing was unassuming: the white and black of the ball against the blue of the sky. Against the green. Beautiful in its precision, and quiet and modest. No one danced or took off their shirts after such passes.

Bad weather or rotten pitches meant different kinds of advantage. Keizer in a swamp of a pitch produced a goal by lobbing a high ball into the thickest mud where Turkish defenders, expecting a bounce, found themselves wrong-footed when the ball stuck. A Kuwaiti Emir in the stands was so moved that after the match he gave Keizer the gold watch from his wrist. Against Panathinaikos in a downpour we spent the match playing passes into the areas of poorest drainage, knowing the balls would stop while the Greek defenders continued to overrun them.

Following Cruyff's lead, we built castles in the air, while he appeared where most needed, always pointing, pointing, pointing: *you go there; you belong here.* He would have been happy on a pitch two kilometers long with no goals, and nothing but beautiful waves of movement, streaming up and streaming down.

Our perfection seemed to be automatic. Our instincts intimidating. We brought to bear on our opponents calm minds, immaculate technique, and visionary passing. The beauty of Ajax at its peak was like the beauty of thought.

Cruyff became the young Amsterdammers' hero. "Our John Lennon," Keizer told me after a match.

"Who's John Lennon?" I asked him back.

I got furniture for my apartment. I sent money home. My brother was twice denied permission to visit.

Cruyff's opinion was consulted on every conceivable subject: science, culture, technology. The present, the future, even the past. Modern youth needed to know what he thought of the past. Two months before I'd arrived, Holland's princess had married a German who'd served in the Wehrmacht. All of Amsterdam had found this the end of the world. One afternoon I found Cruyff giving an interview about that. Who knows with whom. Should the protestors have carried out their threat to put LSD into the water supply? he was asked.

He turned to me. "What about it, Vasovic?" he asked.

The reporter, bushy-haired with thick black glasses, turned with him, pen poised. "Should they have put LSD in the water supply?"

"No speak," I told him, and dropped my shorts to change.

The protests went on for much of the summer. You could watch on the television the Provos and student demonstrators, all in white, carrying their banners. And the police, all in black, waiting to beat them up.

Help me, my brother wrote. *Your brother's in need of help,* my father wrote. My brother had developed a romantic rivalry with a lawyer named Tasa who'd turned out to be UDBA. *That's your brother,* my father wrote. *Cuckolding the Civil Secret Police.* In a bar, drunk, he had railed against Yugoslavia's silence in the face of the invasion of Hungary. It had been ten years ago, his nervous friends had counseled. He should let it rest. But my brother had mounted a table and balanced with his bad knee. The immortal Hungarians! Puskas in prison!

I was able to arrange a return trip only at the end of the season. I spent the night in Belgrade and walked to the train station during the following dawn. Mist hovered above the woods and in the golden treetops. I needed clean air. I snorted like a horse and felt the freshness.

I found my brother in hiding in a town not far from our own. He was staying in a room with a metalworker from Bosnia, a poverty-stricken Moslem who'd moved in the hope of survival. The room was clean, with two beds, a wood stove, a small fir table, and a wash-stand. An alder shadowed the tiny back window.

The metalworker set out tea for us and then disappeared. We embraced. Everyone liked my brother. He was an open, emotional man, so handsome that women turned to look at him on the street.

He told me he'd read about the Liverpool match. We smiled and talked about the old days and the cowshed.

He asked me to get him out. I wanted to know his financial picture. He had no financial picture. Our parents were in a terrible state, he confided. He was testing their faith in the Party's infallibility. It caused him pain to be doing this. Could I get him out?

I told him I would try. Of course, I would try. We were silent, the fir table between us. He looked into my expression. It was as if I had said, What can I do?

I'd brought money, hidden, as well as other gifts. He accepted them all with a combination of apathy and good-natured fear. He'd never refused financial assistance.

At the airport check-through, a commissioner asked why I was not playing in my homeland. I told him I was spreading the glory of Yugoslav football to the West. While he looked over my paperwork, he said, "And your father's an honest man."

"What makes you think I'm not?" I asked. Everyone around us looked up.

He was unembarrassed. "I was talking about your father," he said mildly, holding out my passport. "I don't even know you."

I wrote my brother upon my return to tell him how my attempts were proceeding. I heard nothing back. My father wrote a week or so later and mentioned nothing about it. He described instead how he'd felt during the Liberation: the muddle inside. The enormous happiness all around him—everyone on the street dancing and jumping—and he himself just walking through it all, feeling only a sort of heaviness.

THE DUTCH MEANWHILE, as always, went ahead drawing their straight lines into the future. They were unsatisfied to simply win; they were determined, as well, to proselytize their beauty and goodness to the world. Their football was to be like their foreign policy: a light unto all nations. The Provos unveiled a poster with Cruyff at its center and the motto *Better Long-haired Than Shortsighted*.

I felt accused by it. I avoided it. I avoided Cruyff. Then, before an exhibition, the trainer ran out of tape with the two of us still barefoot. He disappeared into the bowels of the stadium to search for more. Cruyff and I sat on facing tables, bobbing our feet at one another.

His hair was longer than ever. He picked at an ear. He studied me like someone else's chess problem. He asked, "What's happening to your country, Vasovic?"

"I don't know," I finally said, when able to speak.

"You just went back," he said.

"Yes," I said.

"To see your brother," he said.

"Yes," I said.

"He was in some sort of trouble," he said.

"Michels told you this?" I asked.

"He didn't return with you," he said.

"Is he here?" I asked. "Do you see him?"

He looked around. He resumed with his ear.

"He was a great player," he eventually remarked.

"What's wrong with you?" the trainer asked me, when he finally returned.

"He's been like that the whole time," Cruyff informed him.

I played the worst match of my life. Afterward I just lay on the pitch. Someone asked for my jersey.

Everything became less pleasurable for me. I had football intelligence, which had nothing to do with normal intelligence. The most difficult things in life were choices, as our trainer used to say. I tore a muscle in my thigh which would not heal. Running was now an application of fire. As the Saint said, Pain was a holy angel, who showed treasures to men which otherwise remained forever hidden.

My parents had stopped writing. My brother had stopped writing. It happened to be the case that certain things remained unsaid in their country, while they were expressed in this one. There was no point in discussing which was the "right" way. Each involved different people who acted as they had been inwardly conditioned to act.

One sunny Sunday, soon after Queen's Day, which had been marked by mobs selling things on the street and drinking to excess,

I took a throw-in in an exhibition against Glasgow and caught the eye of a blonde girl with an overbite and tears in her eyes, and I stepped away from the ball and never kicked one again.

What had she conjured for me? The young woman with the rug. My father. My brother. The overbite of a boy who'd played with us in the cowshed. Who is it that goes free when those he loves are not?

Michels tried to work with me and reason with me for a week or so and then gave up.

"Let him go," Cruyff said, witness to his final attempt.

I got a job sweeping the new Café Het Station, which seemed chilly and fantastical. The huge bleak spaces of the adjacent bus station rose out of the mist beyond every morning as I pushed my broom.

On one occasion I even stepped away from a ball that rolled toward me from a nearby boys' game.

Wasn't it so that even when we were laughing, we were sad. In the last letter I received from my brother, he wrote that he was writing from the saddest of all prisons: his heart.

Good thoughts, bad thoughts, perfect headers, crooked, dipping volleys from impossible angles, and envisioned geometries. Placid-faced neighbors and beer: all these become part of a great invisible sphere in which one lived and about whose reality there was no doubt. Those spheres keep us cosseted from pain. We used to sing in one of our children's songs about the angels, *"Two to cover me, two to wake me,"* and guardianship by the invisible powers was something grown-ups needed no less than children.

Therefore, I wrote my parents, one last time, *you must not think me unhappy. What is happiness and unhappiness? It depends on what happens inside. I am grateful every day for those spheres inside—that I have them—that I have you—and that,* all *of that, makes me happy.*

EUSTACE

Against the glass, Sister Emelia's face looked surprising, Biddy realized. Like the blowfish in the encyclopedia. She was yelling something, her eyes wide and her face red, but he couldn't make it out through the double doors. He was scared at first, because she looked like the Flahertys' dog, who always had to be chained up and when he jumped at you was all pink gums and yellow teeth, but that passed. After a while she wasn't funny anymore. She yelled something again, shaking the handles on the doors, and he examined her teeth.

Biddy wasn't his real name; it was Eustace Lee, named for some uncle his father always remembered as sharp, as in "Old Eustace Lee was sharp, boy." He didn't like the name Biddy and he didn't like the way strangers would screw up their faces and repeat it when they heard it, but then, he always thought it fit him for some reason, and Eustace Lee was no bargain, either. He never knew where the name came from. His mother claimed it came from his being a little "biddy" baby, but he didn't think even she believed that. It was his from as far back as he could remember. Even Sister Emelia called him Biddy, except when she got mad.

Although later the doctor kept telling everyone how well planned it was, Biddy hadn't decided to do anything until right before recess, and after Sister Emelia had come in for Question Time. He'd interrupted Janie Hilgenberg (everybody did), who'd been asking something stupid about when the new bathrooms would be finished and had asked the same question for the third day in a row about the old drunk and Father Hogan, and the whole class had swallowed together, and it had gotten quiet. Sister Emelia had put her chalk down and had looked over at him and had gotten red (though not as red as later, against the glass) and then had stood up just as the recess bell rang. Biddy had managed to get outside with the pack. She hadn't followed him out onto the playground. He wasn't fooled. He knew where he was headed after recess and he knew that while yelling had been enough the first two times, it wouldn't be anymore.

—ALL RIGHT NOW, Biddy, let's try it again. Why'd you lock everybody out?

—Answer the doctor, Biddy.

—Please, Mr. Siebert. It's a little more helpful if you're less of a . . . presence. Biddy?

—C'mon, Biddy. We talked about this. The doctor can't help unless you want to help yourself. Right?

—Biddy?

—I didn't want to get hit.

—Who was going to hit you?

—Sister Emelia.

—Why was Sister Emelia going to hit you?

—You must've done *some*thing, Biddy. Tell the man.

—Mr. Siebert, this really isn't working out. Would you please take your wife and leave us now? We'll see what we can do on our own.

—Look—you said we could stay the first time.

—I know, but I think we need to be one-on-one here. Please.

Walk around. Do some shopping. Come back around three. We'll still be here. Biddy doesn't mind if you go, do you Biddy?

—No.

—Biddy, you're gonna be all right?

—Yeah.

—You gonna remember what we talked about and not waste everybody's time?

—Yeah, you guys go do something.

—We'll be back in a little while. Okay?

—Okay.

—Shut the door all the way. Thanks. Thanks. Okay. Now. Do you want to sit somewhere else? Is that good?

—This is good.

—You ready to talk some more?

—If you want.

—Okay. So. Why was she going to hit you?

—Because I asked about the old drunk again.

—What?

—I asked her about this old drunk, and Father Hogan. It's a long story. It was a stupid question.

—I don't understand.

—It's okay. Nobody does.

—She was going to hit you for asking a question?

—I asked it before. She'd told me to stop asking it. It was like I knew it was going to start trouble.

—How'd you know she was going to hit you?

—She gets this look.

—Has she hit you before?

—Sure. Otherwise why would I be worried?

—And that's when the recess bell rang? What'd you do then?

—I went back in. Everybody was out except the two old secretaries in the office and Mrs. Krenning—

—Mrs. Krenning?

—The fifth-grade teacher, so I told the secretaries that Sister Emelia wanted them, and Mrs. Krenning that Greg—that's her kid—got hurt on the monkey bars. When they left I locked the doors.

—But . . . let me get this . . . how did you *lock* the doors?

—I had time enough. Sister Emelia left her keys on the desk and I went around and locked them.

—It was that easy? *All* the doors?

—There're only three, not counting the main ones.

—Amazing. And the other sisters didn't have keys?

—Only to the main doors, I think. I remember being early one morning and Sister Theresa saying we had to go around to the front because her keys didn't open the other doors.

—So what about the main doors, then?

—I got Chuck's push broom—the janitor's—and slid it through the things on the doors. I just jammed it in there.

SISTER EMELIA hadn't figured out what was going on; nobody had, until they noticed the push broom through the glass and Biddy on the stairs.

He thought, while they pounded and stared in at him, The door's a force field. The planet outside has no air.

He went up to the second floor to follow the nuns' progress around the building. He could hear the far-off rattle when they tried each door. He stayed near a window with a good view of the street, and some of his classmates found him and stood around below, looking up and pointing. After about twenty minutes his parents came. They were led to the main doors. He stayed where he was. A little bit after that Chuck came and started fooling with the office door in the back, so Biddy went down and stuffed a doorstop under it and then slid the heavy office desks over in front of it end to end until three together just about reached the opposite wall.

He walked up and down the halls before settling into a ground-floor classroom. He hadn't planned on this. However much time he had left was his.

He jumped about three feet when Michael Graham tapped at the window and asked if he could come in, too. There were unlocked windows on both sides of the one Michael was tapping on, and Biddy hurried over, trying to look like nothing was wrong, and locked them, and then ran from the room to check the other windows. Across the hall a seventh grader was trying to get in with a boost from Sister Veronica, and Biddy ran over and tried to pry him loose but he wouldn't let go so Biddy bit his hand and he yelled and fell back onto Sister's head and Biddy shut the window. There were more noises, in the fifth- and first-grade rooms, and he got rid of one quick but the other kept him away by slapping at him with his free hand until he got some erasers from the chalkboard and clapped at the kid's face until his hair was all white and he was choking and gagging and he let go, too.

He was coughing himself from the dust, still holding the erasers. He could see the kid he bit outside with the nuns, showing off the hand to the other kids.

There was a crash down the hall and he took off, and in the boys' bathroom there was Sister Theresa, trying to wiggle through the frosted window. She said to him, "Biddy—don't you make it worse, Biddy, don't you *move*," and he took a stack of tiles from the corner from under the new toilet seats and, just out of her reach, slid the frame down tight on her, wedged the tiles in, and left her hanging there yelling his name.

• • •

—WHAT DO YOU THINK of me asking all these questions?

—I ask questions, too.

—Uh—that other sister—how'd you trap her in the window like that?

—I don't know how she got up that high. Someone must've given her a boost. I got a stack of tiles and stuck them in the top, you know, like this, so she couldn't move either way.

—Why do you think she tried to climb in, instead of the janitor?

—Chuck's kind of old for things like that.

—But why her, do you think?

—She probably figured she was the skinniest.

—You don't think it was because she was especially worried about you?

—No.

—Is she pretty much your favorite sister?

—I don't know.

—Do you have a favorite sister?

—I guess so.

—Who's your favorite sister?

—She is.

—You know how long she hung there?

—No. I heard her yelling. Then I didn't. I guess they got her when they got me.

—Didn't you worry about her hanging there?

—No. She couldn't move.

—No, I meant . . . why didn't you push her back out, instead of trapping her?

—I didn't think she'd let go.

—Did you try?

—No.

—Why didn't you bite her hand, too?

—I didn't want to. I couldn't.

—Ah. Why not?

—Her fingers are like . . . cold. Like worms. I couldn't.

HE SAT ON THE STEPS of the second-floor landing, watching everyone running around below. His parents were talking to Sister Emelia. The teachers were trying to keep the kids together and quiet on the playground and weren't doing too good a job. Sister Veronica was chasing a kid who'd crossed the street. It was windy and her habit was slowing her up.

He wondered if he'd stay all night. He wondered if he'd find something to eat. He wondered if they'd break something to get at him. Then the nuns all ran down to the street and a big black Oldsmobile pulled up—Father Hogan's car—and he knew he wouldn't be staying all night.

—YOU NEVER THOUGHT that all they'd have to do is get ahold of Father Hogan?

—No. I forgot about him.

—You didn't think all along that he'd come and let them in?

—No. That's a dumb question.

—Why?

—Because. It's dumb.

—Why is it dumb?

—Because! If I knew they'd get back in, why would I lock them out?

—What did you think when he drove up?

—I don't know.

—What did you do?

—I ran down and tried to jam up the last doors.

—And you couldn't.

—There was nothing around, and I heard them coming.

—So what did you do?

—I ran. I ran up to the top. I ran into a room but it was stupid to try and hide and I knew it, so I came back out to the stairs.

—Who was the first person you saw?

—Sister Emelia.

HE CROUCHED AT THE TOP of the stairs, rolling back and forth on the balls of his feet. Sister Emelia came up slowly, one hand gripping the rail. He saw what he should do—what he should've done long ago—sail down those stairs he'd walked down so much. And he was out, arms outstretched, and Sister Emelia's open mouth was rushing up at him and there was a shock, first soft, then hard as they tumbled down the stairs, the loud *ka-thumping* mixing weirdly with Sister Emelia's shrieks. Then they weren't moving, at the bottom, and Sister Emelia's leg was over his chest and everyone was running and shouting.

—DO YOU REMEMBER anything lying there?

—No.

—Do you remember it hurting?

—No. There was a lot of crying and screaming.

—That's because they saw the blood from your head.

—I guess they thought I was dead.

ABOUT SEVEN DOCTORS in a row asked him what happened, and his parents kept asking, too. He got impatient with the question. Sister Veronica had seen what had happened, along with everybody behind her on the stairs. They asked if he liked the food. They asked if he was warm enough. They played with his feet and asked if he could feel it. They asked if he wanted anything to read or anything from home, and when he couldn't think of anything to say, his mother cried.

—YOU SAID SOMETHING a few sessions ago about an old drunk.

—Uh-huh.

—Tell me about the old drunk. Where did you see him?

—McDonald's.

—What was special about him? Why'd you notice him?

—Nothing was special about him.

—Then why'd you notice him?

—I don't know. It's stupid.

—I may not think so.

—It's stupid.

HE DIDN'T LIKE MCDONALD'S any more than his father did. But his mother was refusing to cook again, so there they were. It was empty except for some old men in a booth by the bathrooms. One of the guys had the sleeve torn off his jacket. Biddy's father said, Meeting of the Board, and nodded at them. Biddy watched them until his father told him to stop staring and finish his shake. The one with the missing sleeve had amazing eyes. They locked onto something and then shot over and locked onto something else. He talked like soon he wasn't going to be allowed to talk again, and he'd sweated through his shirt in the middle. The other old men were losing interest in him. The booth got into a fight over somebody's fries, and the manager had to go over. Biddy's father shook his head and Biddy felt terrible and wasn't sure why. He didn't finish his shake and when they got up to go his father gave him that look and told him he'd better start eating.

. . .

—YOU MIND YOUR PARENTS not being here when we talk?

—No.

—Why not?

—They were sorta a pain, I guess.

—Ah. Why do you feel that way?

—I mean to you.

—Oh. Are they ever a pain to you?

—No.

—Never?

—No.

—Do they understand lots of things, you think?

—No.

—Do they understand most things?

—No.

—Does that bother you?

—No.

—Do you think they try to understand?

—I don't know.

HE TRIED TO EXPLAIN about the old man in the car on the way back, but he couldn't figure it out himself. His father listened for a while and then told him he should've spent more time eating and less trying to make eye contact with the homeless. Some of those guys looked pretty belligerent, his father said. And he wasn't eating enough, that was problem number one. Mr. Skin and Bones.

Sister Theresa wasn't too interested in the old man either. The more Biddy thought about it the more he figured somebody should know, somebody should help. What bothered him was that *he* didn't want to help. So he went to Sister Theresa. He asked her:

Maybe it was crazy, but couldn't Father Hogan be a sort of missionary? Didn't priests want to be missionaries? He recognized the lameness of his good deed: *couldn't someone take care of this for me?* Wasn't there something—it didn't have to be that big—that someone could do?

At the conference with his mother and Sister Theresa he tried to explain that all they had to do was go down there and see the guy, but Sister Theresa kept asking the wrong questions, and his mother cried.

—WHY DON'T YOU TALK about things with your mother?

—Who said I didn't?

—Do you talk about things with your mother?

—No.

—Uh-huh. Why not?

—I don't know. Are we almost finished for today?

—Almost. Do you tell your mother things that happen during the day?

—I don't know.

—Do you tell her what you like and don't like?

—No.

—Why not?

—Because. I don't know. She knows, I guess. We don't fight.

BIDDY DIDN'T LIKE Froot Loops. He didn't like the way they got so sweet after a few mouthfuls or how they turned the milk pink. There was a time when he would eat things he didn't like, but he didn't see any reason to anymore. And he didn't like Froot Loops. So they sat together patiently, Biddy and the Froot Loops, waiting for his mother to give in and throw the dish into the sink, spilling milk and soggy Froot Loops across the counter, and to say again, "And your father yells at me because you're not eating."

He would feel bad when she did, but, after all, Froot Loops were Froot Loops.

—DIDN'T YOUR MOTHER say you had some pets? A turtle, or something?

—No.

—You never had a pet?

—I had a canary once.

—Did your parents give it to you?

—I got it at Woolworth's.

—What was his name?

—Nero.

—Why Nero, do you think?

—I don't know. I like Roman stuff.

—So what happened to Nero?

—My mother gave him away. He was pretty sick, too.

—Why'd she do that?

—I didn't take care of him.

—What didn't you do? Did you not feed him or something?

—I didn't take care of him.

—Were you mad at your mother for that?

—Maybe wherever he went, he got better.

—Do you ever miss him?

—No.

—Do you think he ever misses you?

—I don't think so.

—Why not?

—He was a canary.

• • •

HE HAD NO IDEA they'd been waiting three days for him to ask about Sister Emelia. They were mad. His mother said, "Biddy, don't you even care?" in such a way that he was scared that some part of himself he needed for that was missing. The doctor said he was sure it had just slipped his mind, and his mother after talking about it for a while felt better. His father stared at him. He tried to watch TV. He wondered if he should ask about Sister Emelia.

—LET'S TALK about Sister Emelia. . . . You don't mind, do you?

—No.

—When did you find out she was hurt?

—When they told me.

—Did you feel bad for her?

—I guess.

—You guess?

—I guess.

—Was she your least favorite teacher?

—I guess.

—Why was that?

—She hit people.

—Is that the only reason?

—She yelled a lot. She hit people and she yelled a lot.

HE NEVER GOT AS UPSET as other kids after he got slapped. Michael Graham and Luis were always getting slapped and their mothers were always coming in and getting mad at Sister Emelia sometimes and at Michael and Luis sometimes, and neither did any good. He never thought it would.

He didn't mind the bandages on his head. Everybody in the hospital thought he did and asked about it, but he didn't. For a while he wished they were over his mouth, too. It would look good, nothing showing but his eyes. He wouldn't have to talk, either. Still, the bandages and everything made his mother cry more easily, and she cried a lot before.

After his parents fought nobody talked and that was okay with him. A lot of times after supper his mother would go into the den and turn the TV up and cry. He wasn't big on TV so he would go upstairs. Then the next meal would be quiet, and they'd tell him to stop playing with his food, but they'd only say it once. His mother would cry during meals if it was a bad fight. He tried to eat everything so they wouldn't argue about why he wasn't eating. Mostly he liked breakfast, because he ate breakfast alone.

His mother kept asking if he was excited about going home and he didn't feel like making her cry, so he said he was and she seemed better. His father told him he should "go easy" but he didn't really know what that meant. His last night in the hospital when his parents were getting ready to go, his mother told him everything was going to be all right, and he knew she was going to start crying again. She started in the hall and he wished the fall had made him deaf instead of breaking his head.

—YOU LOOKING FORWARD to going back to school tomorrow?

—I guess.

—Are you worried about it?

—I don't know.

—Are you worried you'll get into trouble again?

—No.

—Why not?

—I won't get into trouble.

—Why not?

—I won't.

—This is our last session for a while, Biddy. What do you think? Did we learn anything?

—Mmm.

—Do you feel better?

—Mmm.

—Do you?

—Absolutely.

—Well, if you start to have trouble again, you can come back, right? And we can talk about it, right?

—Mmm.

NO ONE SPOKE to him except Luis, who wanted the rest of his Yodel. He played kickball out front and everybody got quiet when he came up. He tripled and it was like the sound was turned off. No one looked at him until it was Question Time and Sister Emelia came in with her neck brace. She asked if there were any questions. There weren't.

THE ASSASSINATION OF REINHARD HEYDRICH

We flew in a Halifax. We flew on Christmas Eve. Each group had expected to travel alone. But we had all trained together, so we were surprised, but not by strangers. Our mission officer had walked us to the plane and then ordered us at the hatch to talk to no one during the flight. But once inside, we slapped backs and shook one another's shoulders and shouted, "Good luck!" over the noise. There was no harm in that.

Bartos, Potuchek, and Valchik sat together. Valchik grinning as always. Potuchek had what looked like a breadbox strapped to his chest, and his auxiliary chute over that. Gabchik and I exchanged looks. Gabchik's eyes said: *How'd you like to jump with that?*

Farther down, nearer the front, Hruby and Bublik kept to themselves after their initial surprise and greetings.

NATURALLY WE WONDERED about the others' assignments. But the Halifax on takeoff and at altitude was relentlessly noisy. The four engines shook your jaw when you opened your mouth. The roar drove you into isolation.

Gabchik made an O with his mouth and raised an arm and

scratched under his armpit. For the last two days he'd been making wearying jokes about our code name, which was "Anthropoid."

Our night's assignment was to survive the jump. In the morning we'd worry about getting into Prague.

Bublik ran his index finger and thumb over his nose. Hruby patted each of his equipment pockets in clockwise order. Who knew where they were going?

Far from us, we hoped, without saying so to each other. Let them stir up the Germans somewhere else.

Someone smelled like urine. A Christmas angel hung on the canvas of the cargo net.

Under our jumpsuits it was Old Home Week. Our clothes were Czech. Our equipment, down to the chocolate and razor blades, was Czech.

We were Czechs all over again, parachuting out over a Czech field to strike a blow for Czech pride. Gabchik had gone without a look back, pitching forward with his legs together into the slipstream and the darkness. I looked down the length of the fuselage at Bartos, Potuchek, and Valchik, at Hruby and Bublik, all with the bland expressions of someone watching a customer order in a café, before I went too. I spiraled and tumbled into the moonless darkness. The relief from the noise was a sharp pleasure. The wind whooped. My chin strap flexed and bucked. My boots floundered in the blast and I tucked and tried to stay aimed at the black rag of my falling teammate.

He had the disassembled Sten gun, I had the disassembled bomb. We were ribboning downward to a farmer's field at sixty meters a second filled with animal joy, filled with excitement, letting our guilt stream out behind us. I could hear Gabchik's joyous shrieks, far ahead, far below. If we didn't shatter our legs or impale ourselves on a pine tree we would soon—within weeks, or at least months—be turning our disassembled parcels on the hangman

Heydrich, the newest Reichsprotector of Bohemia and Moravia. Starlight showed little of what was below. My face was already frozen from the fall. Perhaps we would die in the attempt. Perhaps hundreds would die in reprisals. Our families were far from Prague. Our hearts were full of brutality.

The Crown of St. Wenceslas, the Sokol, Moravian apples, Radnoti Ice. Sledny Peas. A girl on the Park trolley car in the late spring, rubbing lotion into her elbow with her fingertip. Up went my boots. Down went my head.

WE WORKED OUR WAY into Prague, walking through the woods, hitching a ride on a cart. We split up at daybreak a kilometer or two from the outskirts. Professor Jan Zelenka, No. 6, Staromestské. Professor Jan Zelenka, No. 6, Staromestské. Gabchik amused himself by pretending he'd memorized a different address.

I arrived first and waited on the Professor's back garden stoop with the milk. I imagined big-eyed children, helpless before the Germans' guns. We had no notion of how barbaric the reprisals would be. It did nothing to deter me.

SOMEWHERE, AT SOME POINT, the German Heydrich would appear before us. I saw Gabchik throwing the bolt on his Sten. I saw my briefcase flying end over end. What followed was always kaleidoscopic and abstract. Vehicles disintegrated. Bits of uniform confettied.

WE'D HEARD DURING TRAINING in Scotland about the stupidities of Pavelka. Before he'd left, he had tormented us all with his renditions of Grieg. He hadn't been sent to assassinate anyone, just to reestablish radio contact, and he'd been warned that the Germans had discovered the identities and therefore the relatives of those who'd gotten out to England. He'd sworn up and down to contact no one but those who'd be hiding him. He'd made his first transmission and then visited his family, where he was arrested, interrogated, and executed. His equipment was captured and his code key rendered useless.

That and bad weather put us back two months.

Gabchik worked the delay by stuffing himself with English cream and shooting wooden targets to pieces.

I practiced pitching leather briefcases loaded with stones.

This Heydrich was someone to throw a bomb at. His first week in office 163 Czechs were executed and 718 sent to concentration camps from courts in Prague and Brno. The following week Gabchik and I were invited to a special meeting of the Ministry of National Defense in Exile. They needed paratroopers. We were both volunteers from General Palecheck's Special Forces group. We'd volunteered for Special Tasks. We were asked if we would like to take part in an action that would enter history.

Who wouldn't want to take part in an action that would enter history? Gabchik answered.

You're not going to have second thoughts about the effects of your actions, are you? the British officer wanted to know.

Fine soldiers we'd be if we had second thoughts about the effects of anything, Gabchik answered.

Won't get cold feet thinking about civilians rounded up? one officer persisted. A little squeamish, with women and children in the balance?

Gabchik answered with an old saying that didn't translate well into English.

What about you? the officer asked me.

What about me? I asked. We all looked around the room. We all laughed.

• • •

ZELENKA HAD A ROUND, mournful face and a meticulously trimmed walrus mustache. I was to be his second cousin, in from the country to look for winter work. Gabchik would stay across town.

This was the war of nerves. The natural tendency was to rush. Rushing was to be resisted. It would take weeks to cement the target's schedule and guarantee the partridge shoot. Rushing was lethal. And waiting too long was lethal. Even in Prague, new faces and unattached young men were the subject of interest. Informers drifted about throwing you solicitous looks. Newcomers were supposed to have registered; were always subject to forced labor deportation; were rounded up arbitrarily for questioning. Gabchik's motto was: Don't rush; don't dawdle. He compared it to potting cats on the moors.

FROM ZELENKA'S FRONT WINDOW that first morning I peered out at the winter sun in the city with its long, low shadows. Groups of soldiers lounged in a café and threw paper napkins. Police chatted with passersby and thumbed through identity papers. Too excited to sleep, we set to work. A tourist's visit to St. Vitus's Cathedral, inside Hradcany Castle, which was the home—office, to be exact—of the Ogre. We spent the day making certain what a fortress it was. We spent the next two days discovering his villa in the country was equally well guarded.

That left his route to and from work. Heydrich traveled by car. When was he escorted? When was he not? Where were the pinch points where traffic slowed? Mornings and evenings we worked the route. Each day, noting variables. His Mercedes was forest green. With the top up, it was impossible to see who was inside. So there it was: we were waiting until spring.

This was nerve-wracking for Zelenka and his superior, Vanek.

Day after day we seemed to do nothing. They assumed we were here to assassinate Heydrich, or perhaps the quisling Moravec. They gave us everything we wanted the way one might hand over family china to hooligans. Finally Vanek without comment showed us the text of a message he was sending to London:

From preparations made by Anthropoid and from the place these preparations are made, we judge, despite their continuous silence on the matter, that they intend to kill Heydrich. His assassination probably would not help the Allies in any way and would have the most far-reaching consequences for our nation. It will doom our hostages and political prisoners, cost thousands of additional lives, and expose the nation to unheard-of terror. At the same time, the last vestiges of our Organization would be destroyed. It would thus be impossible for us to do anything for the Allies in the future. We ask you to give orders to call off this action via Silver 3. Delay is dangerous. Answer immediately.

JUST ONCE, cooped in, I wandered down the Alchemists' Lane near the cathedral: a small risk, with no tactical objective in mind. In each direction, children flew down narrow passages and called and hung from balconied houses. At night the peace inside me at being home was explosive, tumultuous; it dynamited the British superstructure erected by exile.

Gabchik had worked his way up from nothing—a shirtless refugee floated over on a boat—through his own efforts, and as a result had absolute faith in his own opinions. I had no particular faith in my own opinions but found others' opinions to be daft, crazy, senseless, abnormal. So we worked smoothly together.

For part of training we stayed in some big shot's summer home in the middle of nowhere. We had a wing to ourselves. When a room became filled with ration cans and meat-stained butcher's paper and Gabchik's cigar butts, we moved on to the next.

Gabchik had never been hurt, not even in training. For the past three years I'd played ducks and drakes with my life.

IN THE MORNINGS we reconnoitered. We pinned down the precise route. We found the right spot: a sharp bend in a street in Holesovice. Being German, he always passed within the same few minutes, and at the same speed. Police protection varied. Escape routes were good.

Afternoons we kept to our rooms and practiced. Gabchik had been trained for two months to assemble his Sten very rapidly and with one hand. I had trained to do the same with the timer and detonator on my device. I called my device "Ottla," after my little sister. It gave Zelenka the willies.

MARCH COLLAPSED into April, April into May. Potato soup and kale and beets gave way to fresh asparagus. Had we really been playacting as killers for four months? Gabchik had even taken a lover: Rela Fafek, a teenager with a beautiful painted mouth whom Zelenka had apparently pined for for years. She worked as courier for the organization. He told me he sat her on a bench across from Zelenka's front windows and put his hand inside her blouse.

SHE HAD MULTIPLE USES, Gabchik confided. It was he who came up with the final plan. With the warm weather it was now Heydrich's custom to motor to work with the top down. Since sometimes he traveled with police escort and sometimes without, Rela would on the appointed day travel ahead of him in a rented car, and make the bend in the road at Holesovice before he did. If he had his escort, she'd wear her summer hat. If not, she would be bareheaded.

The day this was decided Zelenka and Vanek arranged a meeting, very excited. A watchmaker, summoned to fix a clock, had taken advantage of the emptiness of Heydrich's office to read the typed personal schedule for the week on his desk. According to the schedule, Heydrich was to leave Prague permanently in two days. Zelenka and Vanek were delighted; they now hoped the whole business could be abandoned. Gabchik and I listened to their arguments with the openhearted faces of reasonable men.

The next morning it was bright and clear: top-down weather. We each took our positions with our bicycles and our battered briefcases. Rela had already been dispatched. And there, posted right at the bend itself like a loitering farm boy, was Valchik, still grinning. If Rela went by hatless, he'd signal the Mercedes' turn with a hand mirror.

I stood about; walked my bicycle back and forth. Gabchik slumped on steps across the road and seemed to be snoozing, with his hand inside his briefcase.

Rela drove slowly around the corner with her rented car, bareheaded. I could see Gabchik's hand going inside the briefcase. Inside mine I screwed the detonator wires onto the terminals and moved the minute hand on the clock's face to the 1. Valchik's mirror flashed. I let the minute hand go. Gabchik dropped his briefcase and stepped into the street. The open Mercedes took the curve carefully. Gabchik pulled the trigger. The Sten jammed. The Mercedes jolted to a stop. Gabchik gazed openmouthed upon the spectacle of himself and the Mercedes. The chauffeur and Heydrich stood and drew pistols. I threw my briefcase. I threw it high to make sure, but it still planed downward too quickly. There was a flash of white light and I saw the passenger door shatter upward and an eagle tore my eye and scalp.

I was facing the wrong way, on my knees. Someone had poured hot fluid down half of my head. I was trying to catch it all with my hands together at my chin. I was making a repetitive sound.

There was shooting. I turned around and Heydrich's chauffeur fell into the street in front of the car's headlights. Gabchik was already turning a corner, still firing like a Red Indian.

Heydrich was standing upright in the back seat, empty-handed. His uniform was torn and flapped slightly over his chest.

I reeled back, found my bicycle, pulled myself onto it, and started pedaling, seeing as though through a bath, keening at our stupidity and ineptitude.

I FOUND THE PREARRANGED safehouse. A woman there did what she could with my wounds. An organization doctor did what he could for my eye. I asked after the examination if it was much damaged. He said it had been jellied by a metal fragment. I got a hold of myself and congratulated him on the vividness of his language.

IN OUR SEPARATE hiding places, there was nothing to do but listen to the radio, set to the faintest volume possible, switched off at the slightest sound. I had nothing for the pain, and the bandages over my eye were continually soaking through. All exits from Prague were blocked. Martial law was proclaimed. Anyone leaving their homes after nine or before six would be shot. With all movement stilled, a building-to-building, room-to-room search had been initiated. Ten thousand—ten thousand!—hostages had been arrested. On the second day there was a burst of martial music and the announcement that one hundred of the ten thousand had been shot. All guests had to be registered. Failure to do so was punishable by death for the entire family. Until the attackers were apprehended, red posters would be hung on kiosks daily, listing the executed.

Heydrich had not been killed. He had barely been touched. For a week, according to the radio, he got better and better, and then he died.

The radio announced that the entire Protectorate was guilty of sheltering the assassins. Then it was silent. For the rest of the day, requiem music played.

The next morning there was the shaking of armored vehicles in the streets.

The day after that was the news of Lidice—a mining village fifteen miles out of town—all the men shot—all the women and children sent to the camps. The buildings set afire and razed to the ground. Topsoil was to be spread over the site. Grass was to be planted.

IN A HIDDEN CRYPT of the sub-basement of a Greek Orthodox church we wailed and pounded the stone and slapped our own faces.

"Two hundred men," Gabchik cried. He was still unhurt. He was talking about Lidice alone. Valchik was there, with Hruby and Bublik. Two others.

"Three hundred women and children," Gabchik cried.

"Shut up," Valchik said, his hands on his ears. "Shut up shut up shut up."

The priests brought us food. For water we had a small cistern.

We didn't need light. We had our self-hatred.

Children with neutral expressions stood around in my imagination. I wanted to put my thumb in my bad eye and find my brain.

We passed right from bitter harangues into sleep. In my dreams I was the Prince of Evil. Father appeared over me and told me to use the big spoon and to not fool around.

Valchik had stopped grinning. Vanek asked to see us. Zelenka asked to see us. We let no one in. We hung on the iron ring of the slab when they tried to lift it. We clamored to give ourselves up to stop the killings. There were shouting matches through the stone.

Gabchik had long since gone silent in his sleeping-niche in the wall. We'd dragged and dumped the coffins into the middle of the chamber. Valchik and Hruby still argued and strategized and speculated in bitter whispers. For twelve-hour stretches we sat. We kept to ourselves with our heads bowed, our backs to the stone. We were lacerated by pictures. We contemplated the faces of dead children. We relieved ourselves in a grate. The last two words Gabchik had said had been Rela Fafek's name.

Then, as we had expected and prayed, the Germans found us.

They came for us before dawn. We'd come to recognize the very early morning by the additional dampness. Someone must have betrayed our hiding place. We heard first the deployment of heavy trucks; then the treads of half-tracks. We had plenty of time to prepare. Being German, they spent an hour boxing in the square, eradicating escape routes. Valchik and Hruby began attacking a corner of the crypt wall facing the street. They used their pistol butts and part of a metal balustrade. Their plan was to escape into the sewer system.

I gathered up two automatic pistols and four or five ammunition magazines. Hruby asked what I thought I was doing. I told him I was going to go kill Germans.

Two others collected pistols and came with me: Opalka and Schwartz. Valchik and Hruby continued their work on the wall. Bublik looked on from where he sat, as if watching a chess match in the park. Gabchik lay in his niche.

I put a hand on his shoulder. "Come with me," I urged him.

"Gabchik," I said. "They're coming."

"Kubish," he said. He spoke slowly and distinctly. "I do not want to be mistaken for a hero," he said.

We ensured everyone had a pistol and a few rounds before we

left. I set one beside Gabchik in his niche. I climbed the steps weeping, and after listening carefully we pushed open the slab.

Opalka and Schwartz made their way to the choir loft while I replaced the carpet over the slab and pulled a metal lectern over the carpet.

In the loft we listened. Soon we heard the Germans tiptoeing about like clumsy children in their big brothers' rainboots. Schwartz continually wiped his eyes and Opalka prayed or whispered imprecations to himself.

In came our friends along the north wall, a little shock troop of Gestapo and SS, led by the sexton. They held an automatic rifle to his neck. We waited until we were sure he would give away the others. When the German officer stooped and raised the carpet, I fired and missed. With one eye my depth perception was off. All three of us fired and missed. We fired again. One of the Germans threw up his hands and tumbled to the floor.

The clerestory windows shattered inward all together. Glass showered us like a rain of gravel. Machine gunners from the outside chipped and filed the stonework. From the chancel the shock troops had taken cover and were also firing small arms. More soldiers rushed in. We had a clear field of fire to the entrance to the crypt, and there was only one way up to us. Thousands of rounds ricocheted harmlessly through the air.

Schwartz was clopped on the head by a tossed grenade. It made a sound on his skull like a wooden block. He tossed it back and it exploded below. Two, three, four came after it. We tossed them back. One we missed blew us off our feet. The cathedral's vault was a bowl of water, jolted and righting itself. Opalka stood, bleeding from the ear. A force like hornets tore into his shoulders and he tilted and tumbled down the stairs. He still held his pistol and we could still hear him firing. Schwartz's legs were smashed and he pulled himself into the corner. Greasy blood smeared in a broad S behind him. He fumbled with his pistol. More grenades bounced and clattered into our little space. I addressed myself to Churchill, who crouched beside me in a black frock coat. I asked if he knew that we called our shortwave radios "churchillkys." He said that he did, and that he was honored. He gave a little bow. He asked where Gabchik was. I told him Gabchik was too wise and clear-sighted to cope with life.

Blood from a wound on my hand had marbled and hung in the air. The instant itself was a large hallway, airy with corridors, worthy of observation. A grenade an arm's length away in mid-ignition showed the light of the sun.

"The Germans are at the top of the stairs," Churchill remarked. He leaned close but seemed awkward about touching me. He smelled of cigars.

I nodded.

"I do, at intervals, stand in awe before the unfurling scroll of human destiny," he said ruefully.

"I would not have foreseen this," I agreed.

"The iron demands of war. Duty inescapable," he said sadly.

"We've killed thousands with our heroics," I shouted. "A whole village paved under."

He told me that Rela had died, as well. And my parents. "The pain ahead is so extreme," he said. "Perhaps it'll come this morning. Perhaps in a week. Perhaps never. The trick is to bear the sudden violent shock or, if need be, the prolonged vigil."

"Tell the world these Czechs fought for all the wrong reasons," I cried.

"I'll tell the world the Czechs are still in the field, sword in hand," he answered. His voice carried great kindness. The light of the grenade expanded like a tent in all directions.

He said not to cumber our thoughts with reproaches. We fought to serve an unfolding purpose. More misfortunes and shortcomings lay ahead. We fought *by* ourselves alone, but not *for* ourselves alone. I told him that as Czechs we moved along a circle whose perimeter was closed. The circle belonged to us only as long as we kept moving; the moment we stepped aside or hesitated, through forgetfulness, fright, astonishment, or fatigue, it spun off from beneath us, leaving us in free fall. We were outside the law; no one knew this, but everyone treated us accordingly. He took my hand. I spat in his. The expanding light lifted itself through me. I told him we would yield in such a way as to shame the victors.

REACH FOR THE SKY

Guy comes into the shelter this last Thursday, a kid, really, maybe doing it for his dad, with a female golden/Labrador cross, two or three years old. He's embarrassed, not ready for forms and questions, but we get dogs like this all the time, and I'm not letting him off the hook, not letting him out of here before I know he knows that we have to kill a lot of these dogs, dogs like his. Her name is Rita, and he says, "Rita, sit!" like being here is part of her ongoing training. Rita sits halfway and then stands again, and looks at him in that tuned-in way goldens have.

"So . . ." The kid looks at the forms I've got on the counter, like no one told him this was part of the deal. He looks at the sampler that the sister of the regional boss did for our office: "A MAN KNOWS ONLY AS MUCH AS HE'S SUFFERED." —ST. FRANCIS OF ASSISI. He has no answers whatsoever for the form. She's two, he thinks. Housebroken. Some shots. His dad handled all that stuff. She's spayed. Reason for surrender: she plays too rough.

She smashed this huge lamp, the kid says. Of one of those mariners with the pipe and the yellow bad-weather outfit. His dad made it in a ceramics class.

Rita looks over at me with bright interest. The kid adds, "And she's got this thing with her back legs, she limps pretty bad. The vet said she wouldn't get any better."

"What vet?" I ask. I'm not supposed to push too hard; it's no better if they abandon them on highways, but we get sixty dogs a day here, and if I can talk any of them back into their houses, great. "The vet couldn't do anything?"

"We don't have the money," the kid says.

I ask to see Rita's limp. The kid's vague, and Rita refuses to demonstrate. Her tail thumps the floor twice.

I explain the bottom of the form to the kid: when he signs it, he's giving us permission to have the dog put down if it comes to that. "She's a good dog," he says helpfully. "She'll probably get someone to like her."

So I do the animal shelter Joe Friday, which never works: "Maybe. But we get ten goldens per week. And everybody wants puppies."

"Okay, well, good luck," the kid says. He signs something on the line that looks like *Fleen.* Rita looks at him. He takes the leash, wrapping it around his forearm. At the door he says, "You be a good girl, now." Rita pants a little with a neutral expression, processing the information.

It used to be you would get owners all the time who were teary and broken up: they needed to know their dog was going to get a good home, you had to guarantee it, they needed to make their problem yours, so that they could say: Hey, when *I* left the dog, it was fine.

Their dog would always make a great pet for somebody, their dog was always great with kids, their dog always needed A Good Home and Plenty of Room to Run. Their dog, they were pretty sure, would always be the one we'd have no trouble placing in a nice family. And when they got to the part about signing the release form for euthanasia, only once did someone, a little girl, suggest that if it came to that, they should be called back, and they'd retrieve the dog. Her mother had asked me if I had any ideas, and the girl suggested that. Her mother said, I asked *him* if *he* had any ideas.

Now you get kids: the parents don't even bring the dogs in. Behind the kid with the golden/Lab mix there's a girl who's maybe seventeen or eighteen. Benetton top, Benetton skirt, straw blonde hair, tennis tan, and a Doberman puppy. Bizarre dog for a girl like that. Chews everything, she says. She holds the puppy like a baby. As if to cooperate, the dog twists and squirms around in her arms trying to get at the pen holder to show what it can do.

Puppies chew things, I tell her, and she rolls her eyes like she knows *that.* I tell her how many dogs come in every day. I lie. I say, We've had four Doberman puppies for weeks now. She says, "There're forms or something or I just leave him?" She slides him on his back gently across the counter. His paws are in the air and he looks a little bewildered.

"If I showed you how to make him stop chewing things, would you take him back?" I ask her. The Doberman has sprawled around and gotten to his feet, taller now than we are, nails clicking tentatively on the counter.

"No," she says. She signs the form, annoyed by a sweep of hair that keeps falling forward. "We're moving anyhow." She pats the dog on the muzzle as a good-bye and he nips at her, his feet slipping and sliding like a skater's. "God," she says. She's mad at me now, too, the way people get mad at those pictures that come in the mail of cats and dogs looking at you with their noses through the chain-link fences: *Help Skipper, who lived on leather for three weeks.*

When I come back from taking the Doberman downstairs there's a middle-aged guy at the counter in a wheelchair. An Irish setter circles back and forth around the chair, winding and unwinding the black nylon leash across the guy's chest. Somebody's put some time into grooming this dog, and when the sun hits that red coat just right he looks like a million dollars.

I'm not used to wheelchair people. The guy says, "I gotta get rid of the dog."

What do you say to a guy like that? Can't you take care of him? Too much trouble? The setter's got to be eight years old.

"Is he healthy?" I ask.

"She," he says. "She's in good shape."

"Landlord problem?" I say. The guy says nothing.

"What's her name?" I ask.

"We gotta have a discussion?" the guy says. I think, This is what wheelchair people are like. The setter whines and stands her front paws on the arm of the guy's chair.

"We got forms," I say. I put them on the counter, not so close that he doesn't have to reach. He starts to sit up higher and then leans back. "What's it say?" he says.

"Sex," I say.

"Female," he says.

Breed. Irish setter. Age, eleven.

Eleven! I can feel this dog on the back of my neck. On my forehead. I can just see myself selling this eleven-year-old dog to the families that come in looking. And how long has she been with him?

I walk back and forth behind the counter, hoist myself up, flex my legs.

The guy goes, like he hasn't noticed any of that, "She does tricks."

"Tricks?" I say.

"Ellie," he says. He mimes a gun with his forefinger and thumb and points it at her. "Ellie. Reach for the sky."

Ellie is all attention. Ellie sits, and then rears up, lifting her front paws as high as a dog can lift them, edging forward in little hops from the exertion.

"Reach for the sky, Ellie," he says.

Ellie holds it for a second longer, like those old poodles on *The*

Ed Sullivan Show, and then falls back down and wags her tail at having pulled it off.

"I need a Reason for Surrender," I say. "That's what we call it."

"Well, you're not going to get one," the guy says. He edges a wheel of his chair back and forth, turning him a little this way and that.

"Then I can't take the dog," I say.

"Then I'll just let her go when I get out the door," the guy says.

"If I were you I'd keep that dog," I say.

"If you were me you would've wheeled this thing off a bridge eleven years ago," the guy says. "If you were me you wouldn't be such a dick. If you were me you would've taken this dog, no questions asked."

We're at an impasse, this guy and me.

He lets go of Ellie's leash, and Ellie's covering all the corners of the office, sniffing. There's a woman in the waiting area behind him with a bullterrier puppy on her lap and the puppy's keeping a close eye on Ellie.

"Do you have any relatives or whatever who could take the dog?" I ask him.

The guy looks at me. "Do I sign something?" he says.

I can't help it, when I'm showing where to sign I can't keep the words back, I keep thinking of Ellie reaching for the sky: "It's better this way," I go. "We'll try and find her a home with someone equipped to handle her."

The guy doesn't come back at me. He signs the thing and hands me my pen and says, "Hey, Ellie. Hey, kid," and Ellie comes right over. He picks up her trailing leash and flops the end onto the counter where I can grab it, and then hugs her around the neck until she twists a little and pulls away.

"She doesn't know what's going on," I say.

He looks up at me, and I point, as if to say, Her.

The guy wheels the chair around and heads for the door. The woman with the bullterrier watches him go by with big eyes. I can't see his face, but it must be something. Ellie barks. There's no way to fix this.

I've got ASPCA pamphlets I've unboxed all over the counter. I've got impound forms to finish by today.

"Nobody's gonna want this dog," I call after him. I can't help it.

It's just me, now, at the counter. The woman stands up, holding the bullterrier against her chest, and stops, like she's not going to turn him over, like whatever her reasons, they may not be good enough.

ALICIA AND EMMETT WITH THE 17TH LANCERS AT BALACLAVA

Alicia and Emmett find themselves with the 17th Lancers at Balaclava. Emmett's a captain of one of the inner squadrons. He loves Alicia, has loved her since he met her in college. They have big decisions to make, things to work out, and they have no time for this. It's a gorgeous October day, crisp, blue, chilly, with the sun warming their backs. The entire Brigade has fanned out loosely around them in parade order, the only noise the light step of the horses' hooves on the soft grass, and the faint jingle of bits and accoutrements.

Alicia's mount takes a few mincing steps and then holds quietly steady. Its tail switches back and forth. She's waiting for the order Emmett holds in his hands. She's on a pearl charger, her back erect in the saddle, her scarlet-and-royal-blue tunic laced round and dazzlingly breasted with intricate gold braid, her furred pelisse lined with crimson silk, her brown hair swirling out from below her bearskin Hussar's cap, her thighs in tight cherry pants, gripping and controlling her mount.

Emmett has in his hand the fourth order of the day, for October 25th, 1854: *"Lord Raglan wishes the cavalry to advance rapidly to the front—follow the enemy and try and prevent the enemy from carrying away the guns. Troop Horse Artillery may accompany. French cavalry is on your left. Immediate."*

As an order, from where Emmett sits, it's alternately inchoate and nonsensical. What enemy? Follow where? There's no one in sight except the vast main force of Russians all the way down the end of the valley. But what difference does his bafflement make? What else in history does the Light Brigade do but charge?

And the order is almost beside the point. He can feel how much everyone around him is itching to *act.* They've been up since before dawn and they've been on and off their mounts like this for three and a half hours. They breakfasted on biscuits and hard-boiled eggs and water from their flasks. Earlier that morning from more or less this very spot, they watched the Heavy Brigade perform one of the great cavalry feats of all time, charging uphill—diagonally! through the ruins of a vineyard!—to break the *downhill* charge of a body of Russian cavalry four thousand strong. The Heavy Brigade—the Scots Greys, the Innskillings, and the 5th Dragoons, with the 4th Dragoons and the Royals in the second wave—had been able to muster less than five hundred troopers, after the morning's losses to dysentery and cholera.

After the Heavy Brigade's charge, the entire mass of Russian cavalry had broken and fled back over the Causeway Heights and down the North Valley to the east, passing, though some way off, right in front of the Light Brigade. Tactical situations like that—fleeting opportunities to turn breakthroughs into routs—were the reason units like the Light Brigade existed. The Brigade had remained, in its own eyes, shamefully inactive. It had been under orders not to move from its position, and its commanding officers had refused the initiative. Some of the men had wept. "My God, my God, what a chance we are losing!" the officer to Emmett's right had exclaimed, repeatedly slapping his leg with the flat of his sword.

Alicia's mount dawdles back and forth one horse's length in front of the center of the line. Her trumpeter waits half a horse length behind her and to her right. She looks over her shoulder at

Emmett. Her expression radiates the kind of poise that improves the manners of children and calms the hopelessly upset.

The captain of the next squadron over catches his eye and gestures with his chin toward Alicia. Emmett glances at his horse's withers, his white leather gloves at rest over his pommel, and then catches the captain's drift: it's Emmett's order to deliver. He surveys the front row of Lancers. He admires the precision of the line of square-topped Lancer caps. The gilded chin-chains glitter like jewelry. Each cap is loosely leashed to a shoulder loop with a gold cord. The jackets are dark blue with a plain white Prussian collar and white piping. The pants are gray with double white stripes down the seam. The lances are nine feet long with swallow-tailed pennons, white over red, and are at rest in leather lance buckets attached to the stirrups. Each of the Lancers seems to be looking at him.

He claps his calves on his charger's flanks and it trots forward at an angle. Alicia's mount turns and backsteps to meet him. He's impressed with her horsemanship.

He extends the written order, arm straight from the shoulder. Her face is set off like a cameo by the chin-strapped severity of her Hussar's cap. Her eyes regard him with composure. The crimson cloth-bag atop her bearskin cap ruffles in the wind. She lifts the note from his grip.

She reads it, her lips moving. They're painted a cool and delicate red. Her hair's thick and straight, sweeping to the base of her neck from under the cap and fanning out in the slight breeze. Her skin smells faintly of vanilla.

She turns to the east. The cloudless sky extends all the way down the valley. The valley is a grassy, undulating plain, five miles by two, a half mile north of the small town and harbor of Balaclava. The country is steppe, mostly bare and treeless. A mile or so back there was a small stream, with a bridge and a post house. The land ahead is as green and unmarked as a parade ground. The grass is firm and springy and smells slightly of thyme. The slope is gentle and downward. The place is absolutely made for a cavalry charge.

Ridges, busy with Russian infantry digging in and passing ammunition, extend like walls on both sides of the valley. Scrub growth lines a natural ditch along one side. It all leads like a sinister perspective drawing to the sprawl that fills the far end of the valley, every so often giving off glints of light: the main force of Russian infantry and cavalry, fronted by the Russian guns.

Alicia and Emmett have been married for four years. They have one boy, Oscar, who's three. Four days ago when Alicia was wrestling him into his onesie, she noticed lumps below his lymph nodes. She'd noticed them a few weeks earlier, and these were already bigger and more irregularly shaped. Their pediatrician hadn't returned their calls until after the long weekend, and then had heard her description and interrupted her to tell her to bring him in right away.

Emmett put in two years working with fabric at RISD before getting his Ph.D. in history. He told people he made Art Clothes. He got a lot of attention from his studio teachers for what they called his postcolonial pastiches but really all he was doing was collage-ing his favorite bits from Victorian costume. He left academia for jobs as a historical adviser and/or assistant costume designer for movies involving the nineteenth-century British Army. Every so often a director wanted the look of crimson jackets when the brigade wore blue, but for the most part he's handsomely paid to fly over to England and root around regimental mess and museum collections, and what could be better than that?

Alicia is pleasantly surprised by the movie money but otherwise finds that world of enthusiasts and curators and collectors and various other kinds of shut-ins to be both emasculated and childishly self-involved. Emmett finds her position hard to refute. On both sides of the Atlantic, archives teem with bachelors with bad teeth and embarrassed, furtive smiles who live with their moms. Every so often they leave their stuffy archives to hang around hobby shops, or, in bigger cities, Military Modeling shops, correcting each other on the year in which the Scots Greys changed the lining color of their sabretaches.

Emmett's got a monster break staring him in the face: the opportunity to be sole technical adviser for a seventy-million-dollar remake of *The Charge of the Light Brigade,* a payday in the high five figures. And it's not just the money. The Crimean campaign is what got him interested in the nineteenth-century British Army to begin with. This movie *cannot* be made without him; he'll hang himself from a showerhead if it is. But the people in Los Angeles are not going to delay his presentation; he's either on board this week or he's not. He's supposed to demonstrate what he knows, demonstrate that he'll be a pleasure to work with, and demonstrate, delicately, that he might have the occasional good *idea,* as well, all in his late-morning meeting and following lunch.

He really should be out there now, schmoozing. He *has* to be out there by Tuesday. Tomorrow, Monday, they hope to hear from the doctors about Oscar.

He and Alicia can consult by phone, Emmett has suggested. He can be back in New Jersey by Thursday morning. It's only a matter of dealing with the complications long-distance for a few days before being right back in person, ready to give his all to the crisis.

It was that way of putting it that may have exacerbated the problem.

One of the complications involves what Alicia calls his neck-deep wallowing in narcissism. A series of calm but humiliating talks on the subject at the kitchen table after Oscar's bedtime has sketched in the outlines of the problem. He almost always thinks about others only as they drift into view, while at the same time he pisses and moans about the way others lose track of him. About his own self-absorption he pretends to be as innocent as a horse. The inkling that others aren't spending their entire time thinking about his feelings rankles him.

His situation is to be distinguished from vanity, the two of them agree. He has no problems with vanity—someone who looks the way he does couldn't afford to—but Alicia has been dismayed in the recent months with how smoothly and relentlessly he's been able to relate everything that happens to others back to himself.

Oscar's a three-year-old, *their* three-year-old, who may be in a dire situation. Alicia is beside herself with worry. She really needs Emmett to demonstrate certain kinds of support right now, which Emmett seems incapable of demonstrating. When she tells him this, he flashes on Lord Cardigan's admonition to one of his subordinates in command of the second line, right before the Charge: "I expect your best support—mind, your best support." His subordinate, irritated at the implication, is reported to have loudly replied, "You shall have it, my lord."

The Light Brigade thing isn't the only project around, Alicia reminds him. There's also that other thing. By "that other thing," she means the planned remake of *Khartoum,* with Adam Sandler as Gordon.

There's some other kind of tang in the air, as well, a fresh, laundered smell. This is all a terrible mistake, but a glorious one. Of course the attack is intended for the eminently stormable Causeway Heights, where the Russians have carried, at the point of the bayonet, some redoubts and captured the British twelve-pound guns. But the Light Brigade can see only the massed army at the end of the valley, and the order is fatally vague. It's as if a dachshund, turned loose to sic a kitten that it didn't know was nearby, decided instead to go after what it *could* see: a bear flanked by wolves. Emmett trots along behind his wife and her trumpeter as she arranges the Brigade for its advance. The First Line will consist of the 13th Light Dragoons on the right and Emmett's 17th Lancers on the left. The 11th Hussars, brilliant as parakeets, are to be pulled back four hundred yards to form the Support Line. The Reserve, four hundred yards behind the 11th, is to be handled by the 8th Hussars and the 4th Light Dragoons.

She waits quietly in her saddle, her back to the enemy, while the troop officers dress and redress the lines to her instructions.

"There's not a lot I can do once we get the doctor's word, anyway," Emmett remarks, beside her. "We may not even have immediate decisions to make."

"It's not just about Oscar," Alicia tells him. She's drawn her saber and has it at Slope Swords, at rest against her shoulder, the regulation position when at the halt. "It's not even just about Oscar and me. It's about being able to focus on something other than what you want."

The trumpeter looks away, not wishing to eavesdrop. The front of his cap features a gilt plate with the Queen's arms over the regimental badge of a skull and crossbones, with OR GLORY inscribed beneath. His bugle is slung forward and his trumpet slung behind him.

"Do you know how much this means to me?" Emmett asks. He feels as though he hasn't made that clear. "It's not like I do this all the time."

"It *is* like you do this all the time," Alicia answers. She's weeping. She wipes her cheek and then examines the fingertips of her leather gloves.

The troop officers signal each regiment's readiness. Alicia brings her mount around, Emmett following. This entire week neither of them has been backing down, snapping miserably at each other while Oscar peered up at them from below. In the middle of the night he's been waking up with night terrors, the nightlight no help. The idiots commanding the Light Brigade were afterward compared to two pairs of scissors that went snip snip snip without doing each other any harm while chopping to pieces the poor devils between them. Alicia raises her sword. The trumpeter sounds the advance, repeating the four notes twice.

The lines step forward, accelerating smoothly into a trot. Ahead they flush the occasional hare. For a hundred yards there's only the quick thump of hooves on turf and the shake of equipment. From the ridges on their flanks there's complete silence, ominous and ceremonial. The Russians peering down at them are serenely puzzled as to what they could possibly be doing.

At first they cover the same ground they would have had the attack been on the Causeway Heights. The Russian battalions on the Heights form infantry squares, bristling hedgehogs of rifles enfilading outward, to prepare for the charge.

But the Brigade continues down the valley, trotting by in profile and in range.

It proceeds a few hundred yards unscathed, the Russians still at a loss. The trooper to Emmett's left has his eyes tightly closed but otherwise is sitting erect. Then from the north, the fire starts, and then from the south. The silence evaporates and the roar is total. Riders go down on all sides, spinning into each other, mounts slipping to their bellies.

"OSCAR SAD," Oscar now says as he wanders the house in the mornings after his waffle and apple slices. When he hears his parents fighting he makes what Alicia calls his Kabuki Face. His little lumps are visible when the light's right. At a stoplight this week he asked for an explanation of the red light. They told him it meant Stop.

"What about yellow?" he asked.

"Go slow," Alicia said. She teared up all the time now. While they waited for the news, it was like every single thing he said was impossibly poignant.

"What about green?"

"Go," Alicia said.

"What about purple?" His head was back against the headrest of his safety seat. He looked tired. He looked out his window, distracted.

"There is no purple light," Alicia said.

"Yeah there is," Oscar said.

"Then what's purple mean?" Emmett asked.

"Purple means Go Like Crazy," Oscar said.

Alicia's always been the better parent. And she was sacrificing right and left before Oscar even showed up. She got her degree in landscape architecture and walked away from an on-the-map firm in Providence when Emmett decided he was an academic. Then she left even the hole-in-the-wall firm in Vermont when he bailed on teaching at Middlebury. Now she gets whatever work she can, haggling patiently with suburbanites who want to do something half-Japanese with the area near the birdbath. She set up her drafting table and materials and piled the books she saved in the space adjoining the laundry room in the finished basement. With Oscar, most days she doesn't get down there.

THE BULLETS SOUND on the hard caps and saddlery like gravel flung at wood. The end of the valley is an unbroken white bank of gunsmoke and haze with the occasional flash of orange. Under such fire, the instinct for advancing cavalry is to quicken the pace, and then to charge, to get into close quarters where the horses' momentum and power can be brought to bear as soon as possible. The trooper to Emmett's left is lashed backward, his chin-chain spinning in the air where his head had just been. The air is a maelstrom. Each instant they survive seems inconceivable. In the roar one trooper, then two, then three shoot ahead.

"Steady, steady, the Seventeenth Lancers," Alicia calls without looking back, her voice hoarse.

The cannons gouge huge holes in the lines, men and horses in groups of two or three seeming to flash backward and disappear. Sticky mists bloom and pass, and a fleck of bone appears on Emmett's glove. Their lines close up as they continue. The concussions jolt them in their saddles, like someone giving them a rough shove. With the gaps filling in so reliably, the Light Brigade as a target is always equally dense, so every shot and shell has a field day. Halfway to the guns the First Line is only half as long as when it began. Emmett spurs his horse so that it's level with Alicia's. They're riding knee to knee.

"I never felt like I was sure I should be doing any one thing," Emmett tells her. "This is the first thing I was ever *sure* I should be doing."

A shell concusses thirty yards to their right and something windmills past in his peripheral vision. Alicia ducks her head and shakes it once to clear her eyesight. "So much for getting married," she says bitterly. "So much for having Oscar."

"You know what I mean," he says. Something incandescent from all the way down the valley helixes past his ear. There's a ringing and then the ringing goes away. The Russian fire from the front is now all-consuming. Officers can be heard as the men can no longer tolerate the pace: Close ranks! Close in! Back the left! Close ranks!

Come on! someone yells from the rear, and the back lines are all in a gallop, their gallop becoming headlong, forcing the forward lines to charge or be overwhelmed, and the last shouts audible are Close in! Close in! before the noise sweeps everything before it. Alicia and Emmett are at the apex, deafened, bloodthirsty, maddened by what they've been through, aiming for the gaps between the cannon mouths, so close they can see the gunners' expressions.

Grit in his teeth and soot in his eyes. Ten horses' lengths, six, two, and one gunner seems to have picked him out. He locks on Emmett's eyes. The entire battery fires.

"It's the doctor," Alicia says, holding out her Nokia. "You answer it."

He's been flattened, unhorsed, and he's on his back and elbows. The top of his head feels grated. His horse seems to have gone away. Alicia's on one hand and her knees. Her Hussar's cap is gone and her hair is splaying upward as if from static electricity. There's a spray pattern of darker blood on her cherry pants.

He takes the phone and puts a finger in his other ear to try and hear. The doctor's voice says something like *retro gooner.*

The second line is thundering over them. An officer getting to his feet a few yards down the line is poleaxed by a flash of chestnut. A trooper from the 11th vaults Alicia, wearing the wrong headgear: some incoherent mishmash of a French Dragoon's helmet and a shako, with a plume no less. The sky and smoke have gone monochromatic and the cacophony has morphed to include stirring theme music. The next guy flying past Alicia is Errol Flynn, his horse galloping impossibly fast, undercranked. Flynn's bareheaded and holding a lance. Color pours back into the world like seawater swamping a boat. John Gielgud's standing over him doing his prissy, citrus-eating squint. Gielgud's commander in chief's expeditionary cap is historically accurate and features a pleasing fan of crimson and white feathers. This is the Tony Richardson version.

Whatever you're about to hear, you'll recover from, he realizes about himself, still holding the phone.

After their fourth date, Alicia took him to see her great-aunt, dying of cancer. It was a three-hour drive. On the way, she explained how Rosalie was one of those relatives who saved you from your parents by demonstrating that not all adults were psychotic. And of course, the last few years Alicia'd been busy with school and neglected her. And now it was too late.

Rosalie was so bad off they'd let her come home. She was on a sofa that had been dragged onto the sunporch. She was on what he assumed was inadequate pain medication. She studied his face like that was one of the last things she could do for Alicia.

"Do you think she's as wonderful as I do?" she asked, with Alicia sitting there. He told her he did. And then when Alicia was laid low with strep he drove up to Rosalie's without her and without telling her, and sat there in the sunroom just keeping the woman company, his mind emptied of its own agenda.

There's some presence but the situation is treatable, seems to be the gist of what the doctor's saying. Alicia's on all fours, her attention on his expression, her pelisse in wrack and ruin across her back. There's a smudge on the end of her nose.

They're more or less at the very wheels of the guns, around which there's now pitched fighting. Russian cavalry has counterattacked and there's a lot of *Cut Three* and *Guard Four.* It's hard not to see it as derring-do. Alicia's got her back to it, waiting for his information. Behind her two horses are on their sides, washed with blood and spooning. Over them goes Oscar on a gray thoroughbred, his safety seat wedged between the saddle's pommel and cantle. The impact of the landing tips the seat, and out he tumbles. He lands in Errol Flynn's lap. Nigel Bruce—another Warner Brothers standby—lies beside Flynn, also mortally wounded. Broken lances crook up out of the ground in different directions and the Brigade's colors are planted just behind them, fluttering fiercely.

"What did he say?" Alicia calls into his face.

"He said he's never seen a couple as much in love as we are," Emmett calls back.

"What did he say about Oscar?*"* Alicia says with exasperation. Behind her Oscar's gotten to his feet, Flynn holding one hand and Bruce the other. He sees his father and sticks out his lower lip: the big boy who survives all bonks.

Alicia turns to follow Emmett's look and sees him. Above his proud little head sabers cut and parry. Someone turns with a lance and then claps a gauntleted hand to his breast and arches his back, as if miming *O! I am struck!*

Who had the right to give my boy this? Emmett's thinking. *Who says* any *presence—one fucking* particle *of presence—is acceptable?* He's flummoxed by the force of his feeling. A caisson's powder-tray detonates and the cannon barrel and carriage and wheels behind Oscar erupt outward, the blast wave sweeping the bodies like the wind over grass. Flynn and Bruce are rolled under and in an instant Oscar kites from their hands to his mother and father. Alicia has one hand up and Emmett has both. They're thinking not of their own bodies, but of his: luminous with the explosions powering it, intricate with its own history of neglect and care, and inexhaustible in what it's taught and what it teaches.

THE MORTALITY OF PARENTS

It's 1970. He's the glue that holds us together, the UN van pelted with rocks and bottles, the pro wrestling ref floored by the occasional dropkick but always gamely back on his feet and working to keep the eye-gouging to a minimum. Morning in and morning out, my father's up and has the coffee made and is reasonably ready for whatever we're about to, in our misery and impatience and bell-jar self-absorption, dish out.

Ours is not one of those families in which the tensions are played out in intricately subterranean gestures. My brother has thrown me across the living room so that my back impacted the wall above the sofa. To more fully demonstrate his dissatisfaction with the general drift of our family life, in our presence he's upended the dining room table, fully set, a massive Shaker cherry rectangle with big, cross-beamed legs. My mother has slung a just-filled humidifier across the length of the kitchen. The water reservoir's rubber-sealed cap ricocheted off the ceiling. I've been known to run full bore at the walls, all shoulders and elbows, the hero in a movie breaking down doors where no doors are evident. Our plaster is patched with football-sized ovals. The trim is scissored with scuff marks. Homicidal or suicidal exasperation is the norm.

As *Life* magazine reminds us every so often, it's a time of great uncertainty.

In each case, our attempts at self-expression are diverted by Shep into channels at least eventually more acceptable to the neighbors. He reasons, he pleads, he cajoles, he throws people around. The fact that we're still standing is incontrovertible evidence that he gets results.

I've put the leg of a serving table through the speaker on our console television from across the room during a football game. My mother has snapped an *oar*—a kid's oar from a plastic boat, but an oar nonetheless—around a cross-beam support in the basement when I ducked and wove while she was trying to apply a two-handed lesson. My brother has cleared our driveway from his second-story window with his turntable when the thing still made vocalists sound vaguely quaaluded after a third straight trip to the repair shop.

So there it is, the big broad granite slab perpendicular to our slippery little slope, dug in at the bottom of an increasingly steep drop: *What's going to happen when Shep dies?* We're going to go head-on smash into it sometime soon—he's fifty-nine and not the healthiest guy in the world in 1970—and none of us, including him, are anywhere in the neighborhood of being prepared. So what *is* going to happen? At all of fourteen years old I manage to think about it incessantly without enlightening myself on the matter. I don't know. I don't know because I don't want to know. In our family, we're either screaming or breaking things or cleaning up. Who has time for hypotheticals?

EVERYONE CALLS HIM SHEP. He's been Shep since the Dawn of Time. I apparently started calling him Shep when I was three, amusing visiting relatives and friends. My mother only became Ida when I was thirteen or so. He has his faults—for the sake of everyone concerned, in social situations, we don't get my mother started on his faults—but in 1970, for the fourteen years I've been alive and the ten I've been sentient, he's been for me the epitome of good—good being defined as patient and/or generous in his dispensation of care. Nowhere in my world do I know anyone as doggedly resourceful in his desire to do what he can for others.

Though my mother, when she overhears relatives marveling at how often her husband thinks of others, works to make clear that by "others," we all mean his two sons, me being one. By 1970 she's long been of the opinion that she gets a raw deal when it comes to conflicts with her sons, and as far as her sons are concerned, she's right; Shep's mode with her is an only slightly amended version of a position he's taken from the very beginning: *They're* just kids, but *you* should know better.

Our lives are divided into ongoing topics of contention. What do we fight about? Everything. My father has gone on record as believing we could fuck up a wet dream. Some subjects seem to roll out the ordnance more reliably than others, though. In ascending order of seriousness:

Number one: music. My mother inclines toward Jimmy Roselli and Lou Monte: singers so Italian they embarrass even other Italian singers. My father favors Nelson Eddy and Earl Wrightson: booming-voiced guys who sound as though they only sing in Mountie uniforms. Passing the stereo, they turn each other's music down, or off. My brother and I crack each other up regularly by making fun of both *oeuvres.* He favors vandalizing my mother's scungilli favorites—*Please, Mr. Columbus, turn-a da ship aroun'.* I get a bang out of replicating on car rides that basso-pretentious sound my father so enjoys: *Give me ten men that are stout-hearted men . . .*

Music generates the most benign of our free-for-alls. My father gives as good as he gets when it comes to heaping abuse on what he hears. He's caustic on the subject of Janis Joplin. He periodically suggests a saliva test for Joe Cocker. He refers to Jimi Hendrix only as "that banshee." But when he can make out the lyrics, and they're witty—as in the case of the Kinks or Randy Newman—every so often, from down below in the living room, our stuff can get a laugh.

Number two: drinking. Shep puts it away like he has a hollow leg, and the volume annoys my mother mostly because of the insulation it seems to provide. Maybe because he brushed by alcoholism so closely himself, and certainly because he's had so many good friends who've taken that easy slide into the pool (the best man at his wedding died of cirrhosis of the liver), his comedy is particularly blunt on the subject. Which, for Shep, is saying something. "She was a jug artist," he'll say. "He was always facedown in the sauce somewhere."

For spiff events, my mother drinks whiskey sours. When she thinks she's getting a cold, she may take the occasional shot of four-dollar brandy or rye. Her favorite drink is Thunderbird: wine of choice for winos, screw-topped and so cheap that it seems a bargain even to her. It smells so awful that I begin making fun of it when my age is still in the single digits. It tastes like something from a crankcase. "It's good enough for me," my mother always says in response.

Which brings us to number three: money. Money dictates our children-of-the-Depression parents' mantra, the bottom-line creed by which they live: *It's good enough for me.* Restaurants with linen napkins are too fancy, a big car or a new car is more than we need, vacations somewhere other than a dank knotty-pine cabin on Lake Champlain would be very nice if money meant absolutely nothing to us and was pouring in at an unprecedented rate. In Beloit, Wisconsin, years later, traveling on my own, I come across a marketing strategy apparently designed for my parents: a billboard that reads *Miller: Because Budweiser Is Just Too Darned Expensive.*

All expenses and all bills for whatever amount irk Ida. All charges of whatever size seem fair to Shep. Ida's expression will darken after having opened an electric bill of seventeen cents, while Shep's face will remain unperturbed watching a cashier ring up a wiffle bat for $21.95. Without waiting for birthdays or holidays, Shep spreads his money around like Diamond Jim Brady. He could spend twenty dollars on a trip to the dump. He buys the boys smallish things—four-dollar models, five-dollar albums—that the boys have agitated for, while Ida does her best to save, hating her role as the bad cop who always gets to suggest that the boys can wait. We're encouraged to hide gifts when arriving back home, but Ida checks all incoming packages like a customs agent. Fights follow. We sit up in our rooms enjoying our new whatevers while in the arena below the insults escalate in volume. Sometimes we go downstairs for a drink in the middle of it all. Nobody asks, but privately, we take Shep's side, while intuiting guiltily that Ida's probably right.

Then there are the topics that cause much more serious fights.

The Length of the Boys' Hair.

The Dean Martin Celebrity Roasts.

My brother's refusal to go to school.

Relatives.

My brother in general.

Me.

By 1970 my brother and I have put in a staggering thirty-one combined years with Shep and Ida in our household, and time with Shep and Ida in our household is the analog to spending time with Henny Youngman and Anna Magnani in Beirut. My brother and I don't have a lot of advanced training in this area, but even we can sense that as far as our parents' emotional lives go, there are compatibility and empathy issues that are not being properly addressed. Certain goals that are not being well met.

All of this would have sailed along with its own kind of stability—the way events sailed along from Shiloh to Antietam to Fredericksburg in 1862—but in August of 1970 my father had the first of his three heart attacks.

As far as my mother was concerned, his heart had always been the problem. His heart was too big, his heart was too good, his heart was the problem. His heart was evidently listening.

By the time I'm fourteen and my brother's seventeen, in 1970, we've provided my father with a string of unprecedented opportunities to confirm his status with relatives and friends as the biggest worrier they've ever known. At my brother's suggestion, I've taken a wagon down the steepest paved hill in a five-hundred-mile radius and landed on my face. We've both been caught jumping off the roof of our neighbors' house in an attempt to conceal that we'd been poking around the ground floor uninvited. Our summer fad of pelting passing cars with jawbreaker-sized rocks has backfired badly.

My father's response to our mulish and heroic refusal to acquire common sense is a darkly comic and highly obscene mixture of epithets and despairing interrogation that's often metrically pleasing—*What goes through your fucking head? Your brains stuck up your ass?*—and we can see, in the aftermath of one of our catastrophic exercises of free will, the physical toll it takes on him: for days afterward, he's exhausted, tentative in his steps, fractionally hesitant when lowering himself into a recliner. He's too old for this. He ages, while we watch.

Of course, in some ways he brings it on himself. We act up, he acts out. *He loves us, he loves us,* we think when the shouting subsides. We go to bed pleased, and entertained, besides.

Shep, don't get excited, Ida says, while he throws Tom Collins glasses against the side of the garage. At times like that—when the boys have shown yet again that they have the collective reasoning power of a squirrel—Ida placates, and assumes a long-view perspective, as if to suggest that we'll all chuckle over such shenanigans a few years down the road.

But Shep is a long way from Big Picture serenity. On the day of his first heart attack, he's in a chaise lounge in the backyard, recovering from the revelation that my brother and I have been running around the summer streets at three and four in the morning, potting streetlights with our BB gun, naked. The police have delivered this revelation in the middle of the night after having picked us up. We're without explanation as far as the naked part goes. Our MO is to leave our clothes on one corner or another and retrieve them on the way home.

The heart attack arrives long after the verbal abuse has subsided and all is relatively calm. My brother and I have gone to the beach. My mother is in the kitchen browning meat for a sauce.

All morning long, as far as Shep's concerned, he doesn't feel exactly right. Ida lends a sympathetic ear but her capacity for alarm is muffled by her sense of his slight hypochondria. A burning, parenthesis-shaped pain spreads beneath his sternum. Anxiety builds up, conjuring all sorts of scenarios. He resists jumping to conclusions.

When he leans forward, the pain lances upward to the base of his throat. This is cause for concern. He has trouble breathing. He calls Ida. The grease from the beef is making a racket in the bottom of the pan and he has to call her again.

He works at Avco Lycoming Industries, marketing helicopter engines, and so just as a basic business strategy always affects a formality with strangers whom he considers to be better educated. He tells the Emergency Room intern that he's "experiencing chest difficulties."

Blood is taken, an EKG is hooked up, and medication is fed into him intravenously before we get word down at the beach. Ida thinks to call a neighbor, who trots the five blocks to tell us, and then is nice enough to drive us to the hospital to boot. It's the same guy who found us on his roof.

When we come into the room, Ida's sitting there holding his hand, and he's chatting with the intern. He's saying, "Once you know it *is* your heart, there's a certain anxiety that takes over, and that affects the whole goddamn thing too, you know—" and then we interrupt. We take turns bending over and putting our hands behind his shoulders, the quasi hug for the bedridden.

He lies there for a while while we ask various questions and joke. Ida's eyes mist up every so often. My brother asks how he's feeling and he answers, "Not so good. I had a heart attack."

After his diagnosis, he's given stuff to stabilize his arrhythmia. In 1970 heart medicine is turning a corner from the Tertiary to the Quaternary, and tests are not as sophisticated as they are today. Certain predilections, certain hidden weaknesses, are missed. After a few days of observation, the little plastic bracelet is snipped off his wrist and he's sent home with medication. After a prudent interval, stress tests are administered. The problem of arterial blockage is addressed.

But Shep's heart, that big shaky flatbed trundling us down the hill, is not all right. It goes on about its business quietly, while we go on about ours. But its business involves preparing to blow up on Shep two more times.

As a family we resolve, with a minimum of discussion, to take it easy. No more battling of the sort that would only add to his strain. Israel and the Palestinians agree to be good. The Protestants and the Catholics decide to Just Try Peace in Northern Ireland.

Because we love him so much and because we cannot do without him, our resolution holds up for a month and a half. Opportunities for strife come and go daily, unpursued. In the den one evening after four hours of uneventful television watching, Shep expresses his gratitude. It's not the kind of thing that comes easily to him, and his family is genuinely touched.

In early October the party comes to an end. My brother is sent home from the shitty public high school he attends for having let his hair get too long—shoulder-length, in the back—and I come home from the same educational sinkhole two hours later in an equally black mood. My brother accuses me, even before I set a foot into my room, of having played his Elvin Bishop album. His tone is not interrogatory. I offer to let him kiss my ass. He throws me down the stairs.

This time Shep is in the hospital for four days longer than we expect. His face, when we visit, is gray. He talks hoarsely, when he talks at all. The intravenous seems to be pulling stuff out of him rather than putting stuff in. The three of us—Ida, my brother, and myself—are frozen with fear.

Between visits, our personal grooming habits decay. Our meals are cold cereal or tuna forked from the can at the kitchen table, our expressions ashen.

We were all raised Catholic. My mother prays. When my brother and I watch movies late into the night, she's audible in her bedroom next to the den, her smoker's voice quavering through the rosary. When I finally go to bed—school is temporarily out, as far as we're concerned, for the duration of the crisis—I open negotiations with God. Even at fourteen I feel the need to explain my previous lack of interest, and I do so by proposing that it be viewed not so much as hypocrisy as a desire not to bother Him over every petty little thing.

When I'm at my most honest, my formulations all express the same terror: *I can't live without him. I can't live without him. I can't live without him.*

Has God listened? Is He affected? In that early morning delirium before sleep, I'm oddly confident. Shep always did. Shep always was.

A specialist is consulted. It turns out that he doesn't like the look of things. We start bringing as gifts hefty biographies instead of magazines. Back home, nobody sleeps much. There's a lot of rendezvousing in the kitchen in the predawn hours. In the tossing and turning that goes on before that, I try to kick-start my sense of my own good fortune and gratitude. I make an effort to wax nostalgic about things my father taught me, without as much success as I would like. The problem is that I remember few Andy-and-Judge-Hardy-type sessions involving either me sitting still for patient instruction or him sitting still to give it. I am able to list for myself, though, some things I picked up, more or less incompletely, by keeping an eye on him:

How to build, and paint, monster models. How to go easy on the glue. How to enhance the effect of the blood by limiting its splatter. Before Shep, my monsters were like last-stage Ebola victims.

The isolating pleasures, in general, of all sorts of absorbed, small-detail work. Shep has the most appealing tuneless hum in the neighborhood. It sounds like the Bridgeport version of something Tibetan. The closest facsimile I've encountered is a shtick played entirely for comedy: W. C. Fields, as ever henpecked and harassed in a service capacity, keeps some barely restrained customer waiting while humming, just audibly, *Grubbing grubbing grubbing grubbing grubbing grubbing grubbing.* We watched it together, Shep and I. He hummed as he watched, and to my delight, never made the connection.

We want to bring in other specialists, at this specialist's suggestion. Shep is unimpressed with the idea. How much more poking and prodding do they need? Is this a convention? *This is good enough for me.*

Just before Halloween, it looks like he's finally going to be released. Somewhere in all the information and for their own private reasons the doctors have noted Progress. But on the morning of the big day, having shuffled over to the tiled bathroom rolling his IV stand beside him, his family's arrival an hour away, Shep knows something is wrong. His head is a helium balloon. His chest has been invaded by a plank. Sweat soaks his hospital gown before he becomes aware that he's sweating.

The nurses. The doctors. He needs reinforcements. He needs to sit. As far as whatever hope he's entertaining, the bottom falls out and fear's what's waiting there behind it, all the way down.

He tries the toilet but the lid's slippery, and he tumbles and folds up like a camp stool. I try to imagine his next moments. I try to imagine his next moments, alone on the floor of that actionably narrow bathroom, and something in me upheaves and rebels and inverts itself; something in me that's fundamentally cowardly refuses the engagement. Thirty years have passed and I'm still a timorous figure navigating a makeshift and narrow life. Thirty years have passed without my having addressed my ambition to shape myself into an admirable figure, in his image. My mother has lost the use of her personality. My brother's weeping has stabilized as a form of raging at himself and us. My own inventory—a meticulous examination of the barn door now that the barn is empty—reminds me that I didn't even do my best to love, whatever my best was. When exactly did their *It's good enough for me* become our *I need more*? Why did we let it happen?

Twenty-two years after my father hit the flush tank and then the tile, I fell in love and got married. My wife, a good woman, believes I'm a good man. My children, seven and four, repair my emotions every chance they get. They're both boys. They sprawl. They tumble. They raise hell. They love me. I can see it.

We had our luck and our luck ran out. We got the news when we arrived at the front desk of the hospital. My mother's knees stopped working before either of us could catch her. My brother swept his arms into the air and brought them down and cleared everything from the nurse's station counter in front of us. I gripped the counter with two hands like it was time to steer this lobby somewhere else and thought what I still think now, that all along my father was right: we could fuck up Paradise. We did. We have.

ASTOUNDING STORIES

He'd brought some books with him on the way out, but had lost the lot of them on the transfer to the smaller boat. One of the lifting pallets had upset and spilled the crate down the side of the ship. His almanac had been saved, for which he was thankful.

Among the losses had been his Simpson and his Eldredge; his *Osteology and Relationships of Chondrichthyans;* his *Boys' Book of Songs,* Balfour's *Development of Elasmobranch Fishes,* and, thrown in from his childhood, his Beadle's Boy's Library, including *Wide Awake Ned: The Boy Wizard.*

Above his head, interstellar space was impossibly black. That night he wrote in his almanac, *Velvet set with piercing bits of light.* There seemed to be, spread above him, some kind of galactic cloud arrangement. Stars arced up over one horizon and down the other. The water nearest the ice seemed disturbingly calm. Little wavelets lapped the prow of the nearest kayak. The cold was like a wind from the stars.

Thirty-three-year-old Roy Henry Tedford and his little pile of provisions were braced on the lee side of a talus slope on a speck of an island at somewhere around degree of longitude 146 and degree of latitude 58, seven hundred miles from Adélie Land on the

Antarctic Coast and four hundred from the nearest landfall on any official map: the unprepossessing dot of Macquarie Island to the east. It was a fine midsummer night in 1923.

His island, one of three ice-covered rocks huddled together in a quarter-mile chain, existed only on the hand-drawn chart that had brought him here, far from those few shipping lanes and fishing waters this far south. The chart was entitled, in Heuvelmans's barbed-wire handwriting alongside his approximation of the location, *The Islands of the Dead.* Under that Heuvelmans had printed in block letters the aboriginal word *Kadimakara,* or Animals of the Dreamtime.

Tedford's provisions included twenty-one pounds of hardtack, two tins of biscuit flour, a sack of sweets, a bag of dried fruit, a camp-stove, an oilskin wrap for his almanac, two small reading-lanterns, four jerry cans of kerosene, a waterproofed one-man tent, a bedroll, a spare coat and gloves, a spare set of Wellington boots, a knife, a small tool set, waterproofed and double-wrapped packets of matches, a box camera in a specially made mahogany case in an oilskin pouch, a revolver, and a Bland's .577 axite express. He'd fired the Bland's twice, and both times been knocked onto his back by the recoil. The sportsman in Melbourne who'd sold it to him had assured him that it was the closest thing to field artillery that a man could put to his shoulder.

He was now four hundred miles from sharing a wish, or a word, or a memory. If all went well, it might be two months before he again saw a friendly face. Until she'd stopped writing, his mother had informed him regularly that it took a powerful perversity of spirit to send an otherwise intelligent young man voluntarily into such a life.

His plan looked excellent on paper. He'd already left another kayak, with an accompanying supply depot, on the third or westernmost island, in the event bad weather or high seas prevented his return to this one.

He'd started as a student of J. H. Tate's in Adelaide. Tate had assured himself of volunteers for his fieldwork by making a keg of beer part of his collection kit, and had introduced Tedford to evolutionism and paleontology, enlivening the occasional dinner party by belting out, to the tune of "It's a Long Way to Tipperary":

It's a long way from Amphioxus,
It's a long way to us;
It's a long way from Amphioxus
To the meanest human cuss.
Farewell, fins and gill slits,
Welcome, teeth and hair—
It's a long long way from Amphioxus,
But we all came from there!

Tedford had been an eager acolyte for two years and then had watched his enthusiasm stall in the face of the remoteness of the sites, the lack of monetary support, and the meagerness of the finds. Three months for an old tooth, as old Tate used to put it. Tedford had taken a job as a clerk for the local land surveyor and his duties had exposed him to a panoply of local tales, whispered stories, and bizarre sightings. He'd found himself investigating each, in his free time, in search of animals known to local populations but not to the world at large. His mode was analysis, logical dissection, and reassembly, when it came to the stories. His tools were perseverance, an appetite for observation, a tolerance for extended discomfort, and his aunt's trust fund. He'd spent a winter month looking for bunyips, which he'd been told inhabited the deep waterholes and roamed the billabongs at night. He'd found only a few fossilized bones of some enormous marsupials. He'd been fascinated by the paringmal, the "birds taller than the mountains," but had uncovered them only in rock paintings. He'd spent a summer baking on a blistering hardpan awaiting the appearance of the legendary cadimurka.

All that knocking about had become focused on the day that a fisherman had shown him a tooth he'd dredged up with a deep-sea net. The thing had revealed itself to be a huge whitish triangle, thick as a scone, the root rough, the blade enamel-polished and edged with twenty or so serrations per centimeter. The heft had been remarkable: That single tooth had weighed nearly a pound.

Tedford had come across teeth like it before, in Miocene limestone beds. They belonged, Tate had assured him, to a creature science had identified as *Carcharodon Megalodon,* or Great Tooth, a recent ancestor of the great white shark, but nearly three times as large: a monster shark with a stout, oversized head and jaws within which a tall man could stand without stooping. But the tooth that Tedford held in his hand was *white,* which meant it came from an animal either quite recently extinct, or not extinct at all.

He'd written up the find in the *Tasmanian Journal of Natural Science.* The editor had accepted the piece but refused its inflammatory title.

A year later nearly to the day his eye had been caught by a newspaper account of the Warrnambool Sea Monster, christened for the home port of eleven fisherman and a boy in three tuna boats who had refused to go to sea for several days. They'd been at work at certain far-off fishing grounds that only they had discovered, which lay beside a shelf plunging down into very deep water, when an immense shark, of unbelievable proportions, had surfaced among them, taking nets, one of the boats, and a ship's dog back down with it. The boy in the boat that had capsized had called out, "Is that the fin of a great fish?" and then everything had gone topsy-turvy. Everyone had been saved from the vortex except the dog. They'd been unanimous that the beast had been something the like of which they'd never seen. In interviews conducted in the presence of both the local Fisheries Inspector and one B. Heuvelmans, dentist and naturalist, the men had been questioned very closely and had all agreed upon the details, even down to the creature's length, which seemed absurd: at least sixty-five feet. They'd agreed that it was at least the length of the wharf shed back at their bay. The account made clear that these were men used to the sea and to all sorts of weather and to all sorts of sharks, besides. They had seen whale sharks and basking sharks. They recounted the way the sea had boiled over from the thing's surfacing and its subsequent submersion. This was no whale, they'd insisted; they'd seen its terrible head. They'd agreed on everything: the size of its dorsal, the creatures's staggering width, its ghostly whitish color. What seemed most to their credit, in terms of their credibility, was their flat refusal to return to the sea for nearly a week, despite the loss of wages involved: a loss they could ill afford, as their wives, also present for the interviews, pointed out.

It had taken him a week to get away and when he'd finally gotten to Warrnambool no one would speak to him. The fishermen had tired of being the local sport, and had told him only that they wished that anyone else had seen the thing rather than them.

He'd no sooner been back at his desk when other stories had appeared. For a week, there'd been a story every morning, the relevance of which only he apprehended. A small boat had been swamped south of Tasmania in calm seas, its crew missing. A ninety-foot trawler had struck a reef in what was charted as deep water. A whale carcass, headless and bearing trenchlike gashes, had washed ashore near Hibbs Bay.

As soon as he could get away he took the early coach back to Warrnambool and looked up B. Heuvelmans, the dentist, who turned out to be an untidy cockatoo of a man holed up in a sanctuary at the rear of his house, where he'd built himself a laboratory. As he explained impatiently to Tedford, in the afternoons he retired there, unavailable to his patients' pain, and devoted to his entomological and zoological studies, many of which lined the walls. The room was oppressively dark and close. Dr. Heuvelmans was secretary to the local Scientific Society. Until recently he'd been studying a tiny but monstrous-looking insect found exclusively in a certain kind of dung, but since the fishermens' news, the Sea Monster story had entirely obsessed him. He sat in a rotating chair behind a broad table covered with books, maps, and diagrams, and suggested they do what they could to curtail Tedford's visit, which could hardly be agreeable to Tedford, and was inexpressibly irksome to his host. While he talked he chewed on the end of what he assured Tedford was a dentifricial root. He sported tiny, horn-rimmed sunglasses and a severely pointed beard.

He wanted no help and he was perfectly content to be considered a lunatic. His colleagues only confirmed his suspicion that one of the marvels of Nature was the resistance which the average human brain offered to the introduction of knowledge. When it came to ideas, his associates stuck to their ruts until forcibly ejected from them. Very well. That ejection would come about soon enough.

Had he information beyond that reported in the newspapers? Tedford wanted to know.

That information alone would have sufficed for him, Heuvelmans retorted; his interviews at least had demonstrated to his satisfaction that if he believed in the beast's existence he did so in good company. But in fact, he *did* have more. At first he would proceed no further upon that point, refusing all direct inquiry. The insect he'd been studying was apparently not eaten by birds because of a spectacularly malodorous or distasteful secretion, which began to rise faintly from the man's clothing the longer Tedford sat in the stuffy little room.

But the longer Tedford did sit, mildly refusing to stir, the more information the excitable Belgian brought forth. He talked of a fellow tooth-puller who'd befriended some aborigines up near Coward Springs and Bopeechee and who'd reported that they spoke of hidden islands to the southeast infused with the spirit of the deep upwellings, something terrible, something malevolent, something to be avoided. He'd reported that they had a word for *shark that devours the sea.* He displayed a piece of fisherman's slate—from a boat he said had gone entirely missing—on which was written "Please help us. Find us soon before we die."

Finally, when Tedford apparently seemed insufficiently impressed, he'd gone into a locked cabinet with a great flourish and had produced a tooth—white—identical to the tooth Tedford had been shown. The Warrnambool fisherman had pulled it from the tatters of their net-line, he said.

Moreover, the dentist said, working the dentifricial root around his back molars, he'd found the fishing grounds. And with them, the islands. Tedford had been unsuccessful at concealing his shock and excitement.

The job had taken him a couple of weeks, Heuvelmans had gone on, but on the whole he was quite set up by his overall ingenuity and success. He was traveling there in a matter of days, to positively identify the thing, if not catch it. Could Tedford accompany him? Not by a long chalk.

What they were talking about, Heuvelmans mused, after they'd both had sufficient time to ponder the brutality of his refusal, would be second only to the sperm whale as the largest predator the planet had ever produced. He then lapsed into silence with the look of a man peering into deep space.

When Tedford finally asked what sort of weapons he intended to bring, the man quoted Job: "He esteemeth iron as straw, and brass as rotten wood." And when his guest responded, "Am I to understand that you're proceeding unarmed?" Heuvelmans said only merrily, "He maketh the deep to boil like a pot."

Tedford had taken his leave intending to return the next day, and the next, and the next, but had returned the following morning to discover Heuvelmans already gone, on, as his housekeeper put it, "a sea-voyage." He never returned.

Tedford finally asked the housekeeper to notify him if there was any news, and two weeks after that the good woman wrote to say that part of the stern of the ship her master had contracted, the *Tonny,* had floated ashore on the Tasmanian coast.

He'd prevailed upon the housekeeper to give him access to the sanctuary—in order that he might help solve the mystery of the poor man's disappearance—and there discovered, in the course of tearing the entire place apart, the man's notes, a copy of the precious map: everything. On one of the three islands there was said to be a secret opening, a hidden entry to a sort of lagoon otherwise completely encircled by rock and ice. He was to look for light blue ice along the water level, under a half-dome overhang, to paddle up to that place, and to push through what he found. That would be his private gate into the unknown.

IT HAD REACHED the point at which his friends had noticed that the great majority of his expressions reflected discontent, and he'd started speaking openly about being crowded round by an oppressive world. Everything had been herded into a few narrow margins; everything had been boxed up and organized. What was zoology—or paleontology—but an obsessive reordering of the boxes? Finding what science insisted *wasn't* there—that was the real contribution.

He liked to believe that he was the sort of man who viewed the world with an unprejudiced eye and judged it in a reasonable way. In letters to those few undemanding correspondents who'd remained in touch, he described himself as suppliant before the mysteries of Nature.

He felt more frequently as though his only insight was his desire to be left alone. Passing mirrors, he noticed that his bearing was that of someone who'd seen his share of trouble and expected more on the way.

He didn't find himself to be particularly shy. When addressed he always responded. He had proposed to one woman and she had visibly recoiled and replied that their friendship had been so good and so pleasant that it would have been a pity to have spoiled it.

His mother, whose family had made a fortune in shipbuilding, was prone to remarks like, "I have upgraded my emeralds, down through the years."

His first memory was of beating on the fireplace hob with a spoon. Asked what he thought he was doing by his father, he replied, "I'm playing pretty music."

As a boy he'd felt his head to be full of pictures no one else could see. It was as if the air had been heavy-laden with strange thoughts and ideas. He'd grown up on an estate far outside of their little town with his brother Freddy as his closest and only friend. Freddy had been two years older. They'd trapped bandicoots and potoroos in the understory of eucalyptus stands, and Freddy had taught him how to avoid getting nipped by jew lizards and scaly-foots. They'd ridden each other everywhere on the handlebars of their shared bicycle, and worked together on chores. They couldn't have been more different in their parents' eyes: tall and fair Freddy, who'd announced at the age of fourteen that he'd been called upon to minister to lost souls in the interior, once he came of age, and the diminutive Roy, with a mat of brown hair he'd never fully wrestled into order and a tendency to break jars of preserves or homemade wine just from restlessness. Freddy had helped out at the local hospital while Roy had collected filthy old bones and left them lying around the house. Freddy's only failing, in fact, seemed to have been his inability to more fully transform his brother.

Until it all went smash the day before Roy's fourteenth birthday when Freddy, on an errand to the lumber mill, somehow had pitched into the circular saw and had been cut open from sternum to thigh. He'd lived for two days. His brother had visited him twice in the hospital, and each time Freddy had ignored him. Just before he had died, in Roy's presence, he had asked their mother if she could hear the angels singing. She had fallen to weeping again and had told him she couldn't. "What a beautiful city," he had responded. And then he had died.

Tedford's father had never mentioned the accident again. His mother had talked about it only with her sister and a close cousin. They'd had one other daughter, Mina, who had caught a chill and died at the age of seven.

His father had become the kind of man who disappeared the moment attention was directed elsewhere. He seemed to leave just for the sensation of motion. He had developed a way of lingering on a word, kneading it for its sadness. His mother had evolved the belief that Providence put such people as Freddy on earth to make everyone happy, and then to open everyone's eyes to certain virtues once they were gone.

Tedford had been found a month after the accident asleep in the road with a mouthful of raw onion, and a paring knife in his hand.

No one had ever talked to him about his brother's refusal to see him. And until his brother had died, he would have said that his life story had been the story of a nuisance.

DAWN CAME LIKE A SPLIT along the horizon. The first night had gone well, he thought, peering out of his tent flap. He'd even slept. While he pulled on his over-clothes the walls of the tent bucked and filled in the wind. His arms and back ached from the previous day's paddling. Cold damp air filled his sleeves and the back of his shirt.

The night before it had occurred to him, the moment he'd extinguished his reading-lantern, that for the next two months he would be as far from human aid as he would be on the moon. If he ran into serious mishap, only his own qualities would save him.

Old Tate had used to remark, often after having noted some particularly odd behavior on Tedford's part, that there were as many different kinds of men in the world as there were mothers to bear them and experiences to shape them, and in the same wind, each gave out a different tune. Tedford had slowly discovered himself to be unfit for life in the land-surveyor's office as he had gradually come to understand his inability to express to anyone else the awful resiliency the image of *Carcharodon Megalodon* had taken on in his psyche.

The creature inhabited dreams that did not even feature marine settings. He'd once pronounced its name in a church service. As far as *Carcharodon Megalodon* was concerned, he was still a caveman, squatting on his haunches and bewitched by the magic-conjuring representation he himself had drawn on the wall.

But if he was acting like a schoolboy, at least he'd resolved to address the problem, and see Life as it was, for its own sake, prepared to take the consequences. Lacing up his boots, he reasoned to himself that he wanted, in other words, to see the animal itself, and not his fear and delight in it.

Fifteen million years ago, such monsters had been the lords of creation, the lords of time; then they'd remained nearly unchanged throughout the ages, carrying on until there were only a few stragglers hanging on the very edge of annihilation. Life had gone on around them, leaving them behind. The monsters science knew about, and the ones it didn't. The formation of the northern ice caps and the extension of the southern during the Pleistocene had resulted in the drastic lowering of the sea level, exposing the continental shelves around Australia and Antarctica and trapping all sorts of marine life in the deep pockets of isolated water. Tedford was convinced that in a few of those deep pockets—adjacent to the cold, nutrient-rich bottom current that seemed to originate along the edge of Antarctica to flow north to all the other continents of the world—his quarry resided, surfacing every so often in the same remote feeding-zones.

What percentage of the sea's *surface* had been explored? (Never mind its abyssal depths.) And meanwhile, dunderheads who plowed back and forth across the same sea-lanes with their roaring engines announced with certainty that there was nothing unusual to see in the ocean. Outside of those narrow water-lanes, upon which everyone traveled, it was all darkness. He was in an unexplored area the size of Europe. He was in a region of astounding stories. And he had always lived for astounding stories.

His first day of searching came up a bust when a cresting wave swamped his kayak a few feet from camp. He spent the bulk of the afternoon shivering and beating his arms and having to disassemble and examine the camera for water damage. His second day was scotched when he slipped on an icy slope outside his tent and badly sprained an ankle. The third dawned gray and ominous and turned to an ice storm in the time it took him to outfit his kayak. The fourth dawned bright and clear and he lay in his tent, cold and wet, his ankle throbbing, unwilling to even believe that things were beginning to turn around.

He finally roused himself and hurried into his outer clothes and spent some time in the blinding sunlight chipping the glaze of ice off his kayak's control surfaces. He breakfasted on some dried fruit and tea. The sea was calm. He loaded the camera and rifle in their oilskin pouches into the storage basket on the kayak's prow, hung his compass around his neck, put his map-packet in his jacket pocket, settled into his seat, and shoved off from the ice with his paddle. His little tent seemed to be awaiting his return.

He traveled east along the lee side of the island. It was larger than he'd realized. He saw streaks of guano on some of the rocks but otherwise no sign of life. The paddling seemed to help the pain in his ankle, and the ice slipped by at a walking speed. Every so often he had to skirt what looked like submerged ice reefs.

The easternmost island unveiled itself through a torus-shaped mist. From what he could see in his bobbing little boat, it looked to be the largest of the three. The seas around it displayed more chop, perhaps from the open ocean beyond. He spent the remainder of the day circling it twice, each time more slowly. He saw no light blue ice, no half-dome overhang, no hidden entry. Upon completion of the second full circuit, he despaired, and immediately upbraided himself for his lack of pluck.

The sun was getting low. To the south, in the far distance, ice fields stretched from horizon to horizon, with peaks towering higher than mastheads.

He bobbed back and forth for a bit in the gathering swell, stymied, and then paddled a hundred yards or so offshore and began his circuit again, from a different perspective.

Halfway around on the northern side he spied a bit of yellow fifty feet up on an ice shelf. He considered various approaches to it for some minutes, trying to calm his excitement, paddling this way and that, and finally puzzled out what looked like a workable route. He lost another half hour trying to find a secure tie-up. When he finally began climbing, he had only an hour or so of sunlight left.

Even with his ankle, it was an easier climb than he'd hoped. At the top he came upon a recent encampment sheltered in the lee of a convex wall of ice-covered rock. There were meat tins and an old bottle. It looked as if the contents of a small leather bag had been burned. Only two notebooks and a stylographic pencil were left. The notebooks were empty.

He assumed all of this was Heuvelmans's work. Perhaps he'd had the ship he'd contracted wait some distance away while he'd made the rest of the journey alone.

But what to make of it? He crouched among the tins, feeling himself maddeningly unable to concentrate. It was only when he stood, aware that the light was failing at such a rate that he had to leave without delay, that he saw the rock cairn, arranged in an arrow-shape, pointing to the west, and the island from which he'd come.

He spent the evening in his bedroll listening to his tent walls buffet madly in the wind, and trying to devise a method of measuring the salinity of his little bay. The morning revealed the interior canvas to be tapestried with thin sheets of ice crystals in fantastic designs.

Sunrise was a prismatic band in the east, violet near the water and shading to golden above. He found it difficult to conceive that along that violet line, steamers ran, and men talked about the small affairs of life.

He'd secured a packet from Hobart on the southeastern coast of Tasmania for the trip across the south Indian Ocean. In spite of the steamships and railways and motor cars, the whole place had felt close to the end of the earth, especially at night. Tedford had prowled around in his sleeplessness, and in the last hours before dawn, the hills around the docks had emanated with layers of unearthly noises. He'd spent a little time in some pubs but had found a general state of disinterest in science to be the case among the fishermen and dockhands. His ship had left in the predawn darkness of his third day in the town, and he remembered thinking as it pulled away from its moorings that he was now up to his neck in the tureen.

Three mackintoshed figures had been walking the quay alongside his ship in a thin, cold rain. He'd thought of calling out to them a last word, and had dismissed the notion. He'd seen big ships and little ships on his way out of the harbor, some with their deck-lights burning and some in darkness except for the riding lights upon their mainstays. He'd been able to make out the names of a few of them as his ship's light had passed over their overhanging sterns or bows. Lighters and small craft had been crowded into their darker shadows. Near a steamship's funnel, a great lamp had illuminated some coaling basins and the sides of a wharf.

Once the sun was up, he had passed the time imagining that every wave had its twin, and singling one out and searching for its mate. The islands had revealed themselves only a few miles west of Heuvelmans's coordinates, and he'd arranged his pickup date, descended the ship's ladder into his heaving kayaks, at that point lashed together, had given the ship's mate a cheery wave, and had set off from the hull. He'd looked back only once, and the ship had disappeared by that point.

He opened a tin and made sure of his breakfast. While he ate he observed how the snow around his campsite organized itself into little crescents, as though its lee sides had been scooped out with tablespoons.

How he'd liked life, he wanted to think—every bit of it, the colored and the plain, the highlights and the low! He wondered whether the mere feel of things—common things, all sorts of things—gave anyone else the intensities of contentment that they provided him.

He thought he would start with the windward side before the breeze picked up. When he set off, a petrel winged past overhead, in a leisurely manner: the first sign of life. A half an hour later he noted, out to sea, the steampuff fountains blown into the air by the exhalations of whales.

Again he circled the entire island without finding anything. This time he repeated the circle even closer to the shore, however, his kayak often bumping and scraping on rocks. In a protected hollow, he found another arrow, this one hastily carved into the rock. It pointed the way into an unpromisingly narrow backwater, which, when he maneuvered it, opened a bit into an odd kind of anteroom. The water below him seemed to drop off into infinity. The wavelet sounds were excessively magnified in the enclosed space. Way below, he could make out thick schools of dull green fish, two to four feet long, which he assumed to be rock cod.

Before him was a wall of ice thirty feet high. He bumped and nudged his kayak back and forth. The wind played tricks down the natural chimney. He could see no opening, and he sat.

But in the late morning, when the sun cleared the opposite wall above him, it illuminated, through the ice, a ridge about ten feet high, in the middle of which a six-foot-wide fissure had opened. The ice in frozen cascade over the fissure turned a pearl blue.

He hacked at it and it came away in slabs which dunked themselves and swirled off in eddies. He kept low, poled his way in with his oar, and the mouth of a great blue cavern opened on his right hand.

When he passed clear of the cavern it was as though his vision was drowned in light. The sun rebounded everywhere off snow and ice. It took him minutes, shading his eyes, to get his bearings.

He was in an ice-walled bay, square in shape, perhaps four hundred yards across. The water seemed even deeper than it had before, and suffused with a strange cerulean light. There was no beach, no ledge. At their apex, the walls looked to be seventy feet high.

The atmosphere above them seemed to have achieved a state of perfect visibility. Away from the sun, in a deep purple sky, a single star was shining. The taste of the air was exhilarating.

He waited. He circled the bay. He felt a silent and growing desire for lunch. Schools of big fish roiled and turned everywhere he looked in the depths.

He'd wait all day, if necessary. He'd wait all night. His kayak drifted to and fro, his paddle shipped and dripping from the blade, while he double-checked his rifle and his lantern. He removed his camera from its case.

The fish-schools continued to circle and chase themselves about, every so often breaking the surface. He waited. Halfway through the afternoon the detonations of an ice fall boomed off to the west. The sun started to dip. The shadows in the little bay seemed to grow cooler. He suppered on some hardtack and a sip of water.

There was a great upwelling that he rode, like a liquid dome, and then calm. He put a hand on his camera and then his rifle's stock, as well. His pulse eventually steadied. A pale moon rose, not very high above the ice wall. While he watched, it acquired a halo. The temperature was dropping. His breath was pluming out before him.

He judged he'd been in the bay, floating, for six hours. His legs were stiff and his bum sore. When he rotated his foot, his ankle lanced and radiated with pain.

He'd been lucky with the weather, he knew. The South Pole was the Southern Hemisphere's brew vat of storms.

The darkness was now more complete. He switched on his lantern. As he swung it around, shadows became stones, or shards of ice. The water was as motionless as indigo glass, until he lifted his paddle and began to stroke with it, and every stroke sent more and more ripples across the shining surface.

As he paddled, he reiterated for himself what Tate had taught him regarding the cardinal features of Life: the will to live, the power to live, the intelligence to live, and the adaptiveness to overcome minor dangers. Life carried itself forward by its own momentum, while its mode was carved and shaped by its battle with its environment.

He sang a song his father had sung to him, while he paddled:

Over his head were the maple buds
And over the tree was the moon,

And over the moon were the starry studs
That dropped from the Angels' shoon.

He stopped and drifted once again, turning his bow so he could gaze at his wake. Freddy had always referred to him as Old Moony because of his daydreaming. Tedford carried in his almanac, back at his campsite, his membership card in the Melbourne Scientific Society and his only photograph of his brother: a murky rendering of a tall, sweet-looking boy with pale hair.

Above him the southern lights bloomed as green and pink curtains of a soap-bubble tenuousness. He could see the stars through them. The entire eastern sky was massed with auroral light. Draperies shimmered across it.

There in his bay, uplifted on the swell of the round earth, he could see how men had come to dream of Gardens of Eden and Ages of Gold. He wondered more things about *Carcharodon Megalodon* than he could have found out in a lifetime of observation; more than he had tools to measure. All that he could attend to now was a kind of dream noise, huge and muted, that the bay seemed to be generating, resonant on the very lowest frequencies. That, and a kind of emotional mirage of himself as the dying man taking his leave. He considered the picture as if from high on the ramparts of ice and found it to be oddly affecting. The cold was insistent and he felt his every fiber absorbed in it, his consciousness taken up in some sort of ecstasy of endeavor. The air felt alive with its innumerable infinitesimal crystallizations. His ankle throbbed.

He fancied he heard submarine sounds. Then, more distinctly, the stroke of something on the surface. His lantern revealed only the after-turbulence.

He paddled over. In the moonlight, splashes made silvery rings. He would have said he was moving through a pool of quicksilver.

The moon disappeared and left him in darkness. He glided

through it, close enough to whatever had surfaced to taste a mephitic odor upon the air.

For the first time he was frightened. He kept his lantern between his legs and shipped his paddle and pulled his Bland's to him by the stock. This thing was the very figure of the terrifying world around him, of the awfulness of Nature.

The surface of the bay began to undulate. His little craft rocked and bobbed accordingly, in the darkness. He was very near the end but he had not, and would not, lose good cheer. Things had come out against him, but he had no cause for complaint.

Why had his brother refused to see him? Why had his brother refused to see him? Tears sprang to his eyes, making what little light there was sparkle.

The moonlight reemerged like a curtain raised upon the bay. Above it, the stars appeared to rise and fall on a canopy inflated by wind. But there was no wind, and everything was perfectly still. Everything was silent. His heart started beating in his ears.

The water alone dipped and swirled. Just below the surface, shoals of fish panicked, scattering like handfuls of thrown darts.

He caught sight of a faint illumination in the depths. As it rose, it took the shape of a fish. The illumination was like phosphorescence, and the glimmer gave it obscure, wavering outlines.

There was a turbulence where the moon's reflection was concentrated and then a rush of water like a breaking wave as the shark surged forward and up. The body towered over Tedford's head. He lost sight of the ice wall behind it in the spray.

It was as if the bottom itself had heaved surfaceward. The run-up of its splash as it dove sent his kayak six or seven feet up the opposite wall, and he was barely able to keep his seat. He lost both his rifle and his lantern.

The backwash carried him to the middle of the bay. He was soaked, and shaking. Seawater and ice slurried around his legs. He experienced electric spikes of panic. His camera bobbed and tipped nearby in its oilskin pouch, and then sank.

A wake, a movement started circling him. The dorsal emerged, its little collar of foam at its base, and flexed and dripped, itself as tall as a man. The entire animal went by like a horrible parade. He estimated its length at fifty feet. Its thickness at twelve. It was a trolley car with fins.

It turned on its side, regarding him as well, its eye remarkable for its size and its blackness against the whiteness of the head, hobgoblin-like. It sank, dwindling away to darkness, and then, deep below, reemerged as a vast and gaping circle of teeth coming up out of the gloom.

Where would Tedford have taken his find, had he been able to bring it back? Who understood such a creature's importance? Who understood loss? Who understood separation? Who understood the terrors of inadequacy laid bare? The shark's jaws erupted on either side of Tedford's bow and stern, curtains of spray shattering outward, turning him topsy-turvy, spinning him to face the moon, leaving him with a flash of Jonah-thought, and arresting him an instant short of all for which he had hoped, and more.

SPENDING THE NIGHT WITH THE POOR

I was at the Plattsburgh Dance Studio for like thirty seconds before I realized it was a rip-off. I even went back outside like I'd dropped a mitten or something, but my mother was already gone. I could see her taillights two stoplights down. She was the only Isuzu in a pack of pickups with gun racks.

The facilities were terrible. It was in a warehouse. The wooden floor ran out at one point and whoever was on that side was supposed to dance on cement. I was like, No thank you, and wherever they wanted to arrange me, I made sure I ended up back on the good side.

The teacher was clearly unqualified. It was supposed to be a musical theater course, six weeks, and it turned out she hadn't been in anything. "She probably just owns the records," Crystal whispered while we stood there freezing. There was no heat. Ms. Adams—she stressed the "Ms."—gave us her Opening Day speech. It had to do with getting to Broadway one step at a time. I was embarrassed for her. When she finished, she looked disappointed that we didn't all cheer and carry her around the room on our shoulders. We just stood there warming our hands in our armpits.

She asked if there were questions. "Do we have any *heat*?" I asked, and Crystal gave me an elbow and I gave her one back. She loved it.

At the back of the room a *Threepenny Opera* poster was taped to a sawhorse. Pathetic.

"Is that a *Cats* sweatshirt?" I asked Ms. Adams. The way she said it was, you could see she didn't get it.

"You're terrible," Crystal said.

Crystal was the reason I stayed at all. Nobody asked, but I told my mother that night that it was horrible, and told her why. She said what she always said—Well, Give It a Little Time. I didn't argue. Not because I thought it would get better, but because of Crystal, and because what else did I have to do? Sit around staring at my brother?

Crystal was so poor. I knew most of the kids would be pretty low class, but it was either this or voice lessons and I really wanted to do this. Crystal was poor like in the movies. She carried her stuff in a plastic bag. She brought a little Tupperware thing of Coke instead of buying her drink from the machine. She was clueless about her hair; she had it up with a butterfly clip, like Pebbles. She wore blue eye shadow. And she was pretty anyway. She had a good smile and a mouth like Courtney Love's.

She *walked* to the school, every day. We met twice a week, after regular school: Mondays and Fridays. It was like a mile and a half. Her parents had one car and her dad needed it. She had two pairs of socks total, one gray rag, one a pair of guys' sweat socks with the stripes across the top. Her coat she got from a place called the Women's Exchange. Her older brother was retarded.

"So's mine," I told her.

He isn't, but he might as well be.

She said her father worked in an office. I didn't say anything.

That Friday we were helping each other stretch and she said, "So are you a little rich or way rich?" I told her my family wasn't exactly going bankrupt. It was a good way to put it. I told her what my dad did. I told her where we lived.

"Good for you," she said, like she meant it.

I told her I was going to keep ragging on her socks until she got new ones.

"Oh, *that's* funny," she said, meaning that they were rag socks.

But that next Monday she had different ones, and we didn't say anything about it. When we were getting ready to go I told her I was going to help her.

"Oh, yeah?" she said, yawning. She yawned so wide her eyes teared up. "How?"

I told her I'd been thinking about it all Sunday night.

"That's really great," she said. You could see she thought I was going to give her a Mounds bar or something.

I told her that since I was a foot taller I had a lot of clothes I'd outgrown or I wasn't using. Nothing was totally cheesy or worn out. Like this forest green top I completely loved but wouldn't fit me anymore. Or this wool skirt that was Catholic school–looking but okay.

"Please," she said, and we rolled our eyes and laughed.

There was more stuff, too. I named other things and even threw in some things I did want. I always do stuff like that and then regret it.

We were standing around the lobby of the building. It was cold from everyone coming and going, but at least it was out of the wind. I was wearing a man's wool overcoat I really loved and a fur-lined winter cap my mom called smart, but so what? When you got through all of that it was still just me.

We were just standing around waiting, looking at different things.

"Listen," she said. "Doesn't your mother want you to hang on to your stuff, or give it to a relative?"

"My mother doesn't care," I said. That wasn't really true. But I figured that later, when Crystal found out, she'd be even more grateful.

I didn't bring her anything on Friday, though. I had the stuff ready and I just left it in my room. While my mom drove me there, I thought, Why couldn't you just *bring* it?

"You are so stupid," I thought. I realized I'd said it out loud.

My mother turned to me. "What?" she said.

I was embarrassed. I was sitting there turning colors, probably.

"Why are you stupid?" she said.

"How do you know I wasn't talking about you?" I said.

She smiled. "The way you said it," she said.

I had no answer for that.

"Why are you stupid?" she asked again.

"Why do you think?" I finally said.

"Don't snap at me," she said. "All right? I don't need it."

When we got there I got out of the car and slammed the door. I saw her face when she drove off and I thought this was what always happened; I made everyone feel bad for no reason.

Crystal was waiting for me on the good end of the dance floor. She'd saved a space by spreading her stuff out. I was still mad. She saw how I looked, so she was all ears with Ms. Adams. She didn't say anything and neither did I.

We ended early because Ms. Adams had a dentist's appointment. She told us about the periodontal work she needed to have done, like we wanted to hear. Then she left. I felt like I'd just gotten there. Everyone else called their rides. My mother, of course, was still out. She hadn't even gotten home yet. I left a message on the machine. My brother was probably right there and didn't bother to pick up.

Crystal said she'd wait with me, which was nice of her, though all she had to look forward to was a walk home anyway. I told her we'd give her a ride when my mom came.

We talked about how much we hated the class. The ad said we would do Sondheim and stuff. So far we'd been working through the chorus of "Some Enchanted Evening." According to Ms. Bad Gums, that was so we could get to know our voices.

"I already know my voice," Crystal always said, like she didn't want to know it any better.

She shared some Hershey's Kisses, which looked pretty old. The foil was faded. She told me she liked my Danskin. I told her she had great calves. She said she worked out every night, watching TV. The conversation kind of hung there.

"Have you thought about doing something with your hair?" I asked.

"Have you thought about doing something with your mouth?" she said back, meaning I was a wiseass, which was what my mother and brother always said. "You bitch," I said, and she said, "It takes one to know one," which was true.

She showed me how to look back behind the vending machines where the money rolled and people couldn't get to it. We found fifty cents and got a Reese's. I had money but I hung on to it.

When my mother finally drove up it was totally dark. Two of the big lights were out in front of the building. She beeped the horn and we ran from the lobby to the car.

"Where were you?" I said, and she gave me one of her I'm-not-going-to-dignify-that-with-a-response looks.

"Who's this?" she said.

"Crystal," I said.

"*Crys*tal?" my mother said. She let it go at that.

"Can you take me to my dad's office instead?" Crystal asked.

"Sure," I said.

She gave my mother directions. She made zero small talk. I couldn't see her face.

We dropped her off. The office was a factory that made brake linings. I waved through the window. My mother pulled back into traffic.

"It's not such a horrible name," I said. I was sulking.

"It's a pretty horrible name," my mother said. "But it's only a name."

The next day I got the pile of clothes back together. It ended up filling a lawn bag. My mom came upstairs and asked what I was doing.

I told her. She sat on the bed. She watched for a little while. She said things like, "You want to get rid of *that*?"

"Is your friend going to take this the right way?" she said. "Did you tell her you were going to do this?"

I told her yes. She smiled. This was another one of her daughter's stupid ideas.

"Well, don't go crazy," she finally said. She got up and went downstairs.

Immediately my brother wandered into my room. I'm supposed to have privacy, but it's like a train station.

"Get out of here," I said. "I don't go in your room."

"What do you want from me?" he said. "Go in my room."

I didn't let him see what was in the bag.

He had my stuffed Snoopy from when I was little by the ears and he was pounding its forehead on the headboard. "Whaddaya doing?" he said. "Giving your clothes to the less fortunate?"

"None of your business," I said. Then I said, "Like you'd ever do anything for anybody."

"Why don't you do a telethon?" he said.

I got a book off my shelf and read until he left.

I complained about him to my mother and she reminded me he was going through a tough time. He had seven things he went out for his first year in high school and didn't get into any.

On Monday I told Crystal about him. I said, "Maybe we're both losers," meaning him and me.

"I doubt it," she said.

I'd left the bag of clothes home again. "I was going to bring the clothes this time," I finally said when we were getting ready to go.

"I should give *you* something," Crystal said.

"Oh, you don't have to do that," I said. What was she going to give me? Something she whittled?

She asked if I wanted to stay over Friday night.

"Sure," I said.

"Give me your number," she said, and I gave her a number.

I have like three friends, and they never call. They had to be practically dragged to my birthday party.

It was okay with my mother. "I am going to have a drink," she said, when I asked her what she thought. I told her it was Crystal, the girl she met. "I assumed," she said.

Later we ran it by my father, up in his study. Somebody on his team had totally screwed up a deposition, so he had to make another whole trip to someplace like Iowa. He asked who Crystal was. He said it was fine with him. "Spending the night with the poor," he said, and he gave me a hug.

"Very nice," my mother said to herself as we came back downstairs.

That Friday I loaded the lawn bag into the trunk. My mother would pick us up after the lessons and take us to Crystal's, and then pick me up Saturday afternoon after some errands.

Crystal was nervous in class. She was fidgety afterward, waiting for my mother. I was flattered.

My mother was right on time, which I told Crystal wouldn't happen in a million years. "How are you, Mrs. Gerwig?" she said when she got in the car.

"I'm fine, Crystal," my mom said. "How about you?"

Crystal said she was fine, too.

"It's nice of your parents to invite Lynn over," my mother told her once we pulled onto the highway.

"I so love the twilight this time of year, don't you?" Crystal said back. I almost lost it.

We got off at the Riverside exit. I didn't know anyone who lived down there, poor or not. All you could see from the highway was oil tanks.

Crystal gave directions while my mom turtled along like the whole thing was a trap. I kept hoping the houses wouldn't get any worse.

"Mom, the gas pedal. On the right," I said.

My mother just drove.

We were all quiet.

"Right here," Crystal said.

I peeped out of my window. What was I scared of? There weren't going to be enough cable channels?

On the way there I'd told myself that there wouldn't be anything so terrible about the house. I was wrong. It was a long white trailer. It had a yellow stripe. There were empty plastic buckets around the front porch. Something rusty was half buried in the yard. My mother pulled up so even the car wasn't too close to the curb. Her face was fine.

When she got out of the car Crystal's dad came out of the house. He looked like any other dad. He had on a Nirvana T-shirt. While they said hello I got the keys from my mom's hand and opened the trunk. I pulled out the bag and lugged it to the front door.

Her dad's name was Tom.

"Where you goin' with that?" her dad said.

"Lynn's givin' me some clothes," Crystal said. "The ones that don't fit her anymore."

My mother was wincing. Like Crystal and her father were blind.

I was still at the front door of the trailer. I could see people inside.

"It's just a lot of weird stuff, Dad," Crystal said.

"Hey, I don't care," Crystal's dad said. "If it's all right with Lynn's mother here," he said.

"It's fine with me," my mother said. After a second she crossed the yard to give me a hug. She looked at me. "You behave yourself," she said. She got back in the car and drove off.

"So what're we havin' for dinner?" Crystal's dad said.

"We should have hot dogs," Crystal said.

We all went in the house.

Her mother and her retarded brother were in the living room with the shades down, watching TV. I thought it was weird that her mother hadn't come out.

"Nice to meet you," I told them.

They were both fat, but not hugely fat. The brother had black hair combed sideways and his eyes were half closed. I couldn't tell if that was part of the way he was retarded or if he was just sleepy. His mother was sitting next to the biggest ashtray on earth. It was wider than the lamp table it was on.

Crystal said I should get the bag from the porch. She told them while I went to get it that I'd given her this huge bag of clothes. They were looking at me when I came back in.

"Merry Christmas!" I said, because I couldn't think of anything else. I put it on the rug in front of the TV.

The house smelled. There were dirty coffee cups on the windowsill. I had my hands flat against my thighs.

Her father poked in from the kitchen and said, "What's in the bag?" but then didn't wait to find out. He called he was starting dinner.

Her brother dug around in the bag. Her mother watched. I still didn't know his name. I was still standing by the front door. Crystal felt bad at the way things were going but I couldn't do anything to help her feel better.

"So what's in there?" she said, like everything was okay. It was horrible.

Her brother pulled out stuff I didn't even remember throwing in. Some things I could still wear, and a blue velvet dress.

"Oh," her mother said, when her brother held up the dress.

A *Penthouse* magazine was lying around in plain sight. The room was cold and everyone was bundled up. You could smell sweat. The kitchen was on one side and they had framed pictures of Crystal and her brother around the door leading to the other rooms. It was a longer trailer than it looked.

The kitchen was clean. We ate in there, watching the TV on the counter. I looked every so often at the floors and the ceiling, and Crystal caught me at it.

We had pound cake for dessert. Her father and brother got into a fight about how much her brother could have.

Afterward we hung out in Crystal's room. It was across from her mom and dad's. Her brother was going to sleep on the sofa. I thanked her parents for the very nice dinner, even though I hadn't seen her mother do anything. They said we should get ready for bed soon.

That was fine with me. It was about 7:30.

Her half of the room was neat. She had a throw rug, and her bed was made, with some books arranged big to small on a bookshelf in the headboard. Her brother's side was filthy. You could see that she'd tried to pick up. There were loose Oreos in some slippers under the dresser.

"You can sleep on my bed," Crystal said.

A poster of a muscle car flapped out from the ceiling over her brother's bed, like a sail. I told her I could sleep over there, but she said no.

I was still standing in the middle of the room. I didn't want to be there, and she knew it.

"Do you want to see some of my books, or play a game?" she said. "I got Clue."

"Okay," I said.

She didn't move. She sat on her brother's bed. I sat on hers. I smelled soap.

"Should we go to bed?" I finally said. She shrugged, looking down at my feet.

We brushed our teeth and got into our nightgowns. Even the water tasted weird. I was glad I brought my own towel. We called good night down the hall and got into bed. Then she had to get up to turn off the light. She got into bed again. The parking garage across the street lit up the whole room.

"Are you having an okay time?" she said, from her brother's bed.

"Yeah," I said. She shifted around on her back. They were watching some kind of travelogue in the living room and we both lay there, listening to it. I think she felt so bad she couldn't even ask them to turn it down.

"My cousin Katie has so much money," she said.

"Did you hear me?" she said.

"What am I supposed to say?" I said.

She sighed. It was like a bubble filling the house, pressing on my ears. I hated it there.

"I don't know why I say some things," she said. She started to cry.

"Are you crying?" I said. "What are you crying for?"

It just made her cry to herself. I hadn't asked very nicely.

"Why are you crying?" I said.

"Oh," she said, like she was going to answer, but she didn't.

We both lay there. I made a disgusted noise. I breathed in her smell on the pillow. She was quiet after that. The travelogue went off. I wondered if her brother had to stay up until her parents went to bed.

It was so bright in the room I could read my watch. When it was 11:30, I said, "I should go."

"What do you want from me?" she said, exactly the way my brother does.

I got up and got dressed without turning on the light. "I should use the phone," I said. She was still on her back.

I went out into the hall. The house was dark. The phone was in the kitchen. My mother answered on the second ring. I kept my voice down. I was worried she was going to make me explain, but she didn't. She said, "Are you all right?" Then she said my father would come.

It would take about a half hour. I had to wait. I hung up and went back into the bedroom and shut the door. "My father's coming," I said.

"Fine," Crystal said. She was sitting up. "You want the light on?"

"No," I said.

We sat there. I thought about the way I'd thought of her the night before. The night before I'd thought she needed beauty in her life.

"Take your clothes with you when you go," she said.

"This is totally me. I'm just being weird," I said.

I was going to quit the classes the next day by phone. If she tried to call me she'd find out the number I'd given her was fake. Like we said when a total dork asked for our number: I gave him my faux number. And she'd think I couldn't deal with her being so poor. She wouldn't realize it was everything else I couldn't deal with. I knew I deserved exactly what I got, all the rest of my life. And when I was stuck with her in her bedroom I didn't want her to deserve any more, either. But before that, for a little while, I wanted good things for her; I wanted to make her life a little better. I wanted to make her think, That Lynn—that Lynn's a nice girl. And wasn't that worth something?

DESCENT INTO PERPETUAL NIGHT

Impractical but Exciting Early Machines

When I was a boy I came across in my father's library an engraving of Father Gaspard Schott's design for what he termed an "aquatic corselet," composed of leather with four tiny panes of looking-glass, which let its passenger walk safely about the floor of the sea. It looked like a huge and inverted four-sided pail. In the engraving two bare feet tiptoed along a sandy bottom. According to the caption it had been published in 1664.

It was my first experience with what I came to understand as my near-constant state: that of being inarticulate with amazement. "Inarticulate is right," Mary, my first wife, and Elswyth, my second, and Miss Hollister, my present assistant, each remarked, upon being told that story. In the case of Miss Hollister, I congratulated her on having confirmed data that had apparently been obtained at great cost by earlier observers.

The Bathysphere in Its White Coat

My name is William S. Beebe and I am the head of the Department of Tropical Research for the New York Zoological Society. During 1927 and 1928 I considered various plans for cylinders that would be strong enough to sink deep into the ocean, but all of them, due to their flat ends, proved impractical. It soon occurred to me and others that there is nothing like a ball for the even distribution of pressure, and so the idea of a perfectly round chamber took form and grew. By 1929 Mr. Otis Barton at his own expense had developed and actually constructed a steel sphere large and strong enough for us to enter. The final design measured only four feet nine inches in diameter, but its walls were an inch and a quarter thick, and it weighed five thousand pounds. Any heavier would have been too heavy for the winches available in the Caribbean. Our dive would take place off one of the abyssal shelves a few miles from the Bermudan coast.

There were to be three windows: cylinders of fused quartz three inches thick fitted into steel projections resembling the mouths of stubby cannons, quartz being the strongest transparent substance known, and transmitting all wavelengths of light. The windows were eight inches wide. Because of the sphere's shape they turned in toward one another slightly, as if cross-eyed.

Opposite the windows was what was politely termed the door. It had a circular four-hundred-pound flanged lid that was lifted on and off with a block and tackle, and fitted with ten fist-sized bolts around the hole. It was fourteen inches wide.

A swivel at the top of the sphere held the lowering cable. Beside that the electric cable, carrying light and telephone wires, entered through what we called the stuffing box, formed of an inner brass and an outer stainless-steel gland between which the cable was sandwiched with layers of flax and oil packing and tightly bolted with hammered wrenches.

Below that, inside, oxygen tanks were bolted lengthwise to the walls, like benches. Trays in which powdered chemicals for absorbing moisture and carbon dioxide were exposed sat on brackets just above our heads. A crate-sized box of a searchlight occupied nearly all of one side. It had its own window.

One day I was drawing with my finger the shape of a deep-sea fish—*Bathytroctes*—on the stall in the gentlemen's room, when the appropriateness of the prefix struck me. I coined the name, *bathysphere.* The name stuck.

We painted the thing white, in the hope that it would attract sea life.

Corals and Fish Four Fathoms Down

When a previously impenetrable portion of a zone foreign to human presence suddenly becomes accessible, then every corner of man's mind susceptible to enthusiasm or to long-accumulated curiosity is aroused to the highest pitch. Those zones might be geographical, technical, historical, or emotional.

Our knowledge of deep-sea fauna was comparable to an African explorer's after he'd penetrated a mile into the continent's jungles, and seen two birds and a lizard. Were there rhinos? Lions? Elephants? How would he know?

Science had steamed about, lowered weights on a wire, and recorded the depth of the bottom. We'd dragged along tiny dredges and nets, and stared at whatever miserable and crushed specimens were slow enough to be caught by them. Because of the pressures recorded, the deepest any human being had made observations before the bathysphere had been a little beyond three hundred feet. We knew the ocean's depth in some places was likely to reach a mile and a half: eight thousand feet.

The Evolution of Human Diving

I was born in Brooklyn, New York, eighteen years after Darwin had published his *Origin of the Species* and six after he'd published *The Descent of Man.* Rutherford B. Hayes had just completed his first year in office. Colorado had just achieved statehood, and had chosen as its state bird the prairie lark finch, that gregarious ground feeder. A great cholera epidemic had just ended, and my mother had taken to calling me "Little Lucky." My luck had held, as it always would. In 1899 at the age of twenty-two I became the youngest curator of ornithology in the New York Zoological Society's history, and proceeded to make expeditions to Central and South America, the Orient, and the West Indies. After a while, as a joke, some of my coworkers back in New York had sold my desk.

Cruikshank's Idea of Life in a Bell

Miss Hollister believed I hadn't been doing my utmost to affect her parents' situation. I protested this interpretation more than once. I'd written a letter. I'd mentioned the situation to the head of the Society. I'd offered to telephone whomever she would wish. It wasn't clear to me how much more I could accomplish.

Her parents wished to emigrate but her father had run afoul of his government because of a petition he circulated to protest the requisitioning of a wetlands hatchery. The hatchery was in a valley south of Mainz.

"A petition?" I asked, during one of our first discussions on the subject.

"Apparently it identified the reason for the requisitioning as military maneuvers," she told me.

I tried to look sympathetic, not seeing the point.

"Strictly *verboten,* according to the Treaty of Versailles," she explained.

"Ah," I said.

This had been on the voyage down to Bermuda. She had been watching me double-check my figures for projected oxygen consumption.

"Hollister is German?" I had asked politely.

"Holitscher," she said.

"Ah," I said.

We had had a dalliance and this had complicated things. Waiting for me to respond further, her ears had colored with impatience and humiliation.

"Can you *help*?" she had asked again. She was much younger than I. She had a very American directness. This had been a partial cause of our dalliance.

The new government was by all accounts even less understanding than the old one. Her father was at that point in a prison in Darmstadt awaiting trial. His lawyer had been told that the charge might be sedition but his lawyer assumed that to be a scare tactic.

There seemed to be an unstated understanding that we would talk about this further. She wore shorts made from cut-off men's pants, and a floppy white hat against the sun. Sleeveless white shirts that billowed in breezes.

The Evolution of Human Diving

At the age of twenty-five I married Mary, my first wife, at sunrise at her family's plantation in Virginia. Her family had roots from the colonial days. Her grandfather was a Supreme Court judge. We went to Mexico for our honeymoon to obtain specimens for the Zoological Park. We published an account of our trip entitled *Two Bird Lovers in Mexico.* Mary wrote the final chapter and provided tips for female travelers in the tropics. Over the next seven years we traveled fifty-two thousand miles and visited twenty-two countries. A year after our return she fled to Nevada to begin the six-month residency requirement for divorce. Because of my celebrity as an author, it was very public. The front page of *The New York Times* carried her account of events under the headline *Naturalist Was Cruel.*

Fourteen years later, aboard a friend's yacht, I married Elswyth, my second wife. She was twenty-five years my junior. She was the surprisingly famous author of the play *Young Mister Disraeli*. She wanted only to stay in our farmhouse in Vermont and write; she detested the tropics and travel. I hated cold weather. She wrote a play about me called *Stranger in the Hills*.

A Diver Can Attract Fish with a Crowbar

When I first put on a diving helmet and climbed down the submerged ladder, I understood almost immediately that I had escaped from dry land etymology and entered an entirely new world. It was on a reef off Bermuda that I had named Almost Island: it was so shallow, and surrounded on all sides by abyssal depths dropping away into blue. Herring schooled above me like a tiny storm of silver comets. Parrotfish barged slowly along. Yellowtail floated about moving their jaws in an absentminded, adenoidal manner. A crinoid waved its orange ferns. The reef stretched up and up, alive with plumes and sea fans, brain coral and sharp-spined urchins. I stood amazed, vainly trying to catch the fish.

I found that what seemed to be a desert of animal life could be converted into a hectic oasis by a few strokes of a crowbar on the reef, fish rushing in from all directions to the source of the exposed food. I invented submarine slingshots and speared what I wished with barbed arrows of brass wire. I found branched arborescent growths into which I could climb.

One starlit night, when my eyes passed just below the level of the water, the illumination of the wavelets was like cold fire. From the bottom, the boat's keel was molten silver. Jellyfish and sea worms showed blue.

And I considered, hauling myself up the rope, sergeant majors and wrasse following me to the surface, the way the concrete intellectual returns from aviation have finally been superficial: the atmosphere itself being transparent, and our already having obtained knowledge of its upper reaches from our experience with heights such as lofty mountains. The same was true of our penetration of the tropical jungles: the new understandings and difficulties had arrived as a matter of degree, but not of kind.

"You're forty-nine years old," Elswyth remarked in a letter. "Isn't that a little too far along for Undersea Adventure?" "No," I wrote back.

All These Instruments Plus Two Men

By the spring of 1930 the sphere was nearing completion. In April I moved my field laboratory to Nonsuch Island, which had been donated by the Bermudans for oceanographic work. The pronoun "I," it should be noted, throughout should be considered as divided into four, four of us comprising the staff of the Department of Tropical Research: besides myself, John Tee-Van, General Associate, Gloria Hollister, Research Associate, and Jocelyn Crane, Technical Associate. For this trip Miss Hollister had brought a friend with her. Miss Crane would be helping with the charts for recording time, depths, and temperature. They'd been schoolmates. Miss Crane looked at me sharply at times when she fancied I wasn't paying attention.

We had a barge, a seagoing tug, and a seven-ton Arcturus winch. The barge was outfitted with twin boilers to drive the winches. A simple meter wheel measured the amount of cable paid out.

The distance between the generator and the bathysphere would cause a drop in voltage, necessitating the use of specially made ninety-volt lamps. The electric light circuit could also be used as an auxiliary signaling apparatus, in the case of a failure of the telephone lines.

In the trays we had calcium chloride (anhydrous porous, #8 mesh) for moisture, and soda lime (#4 mesh) for carbon dioxide.

The crew necessary for a descent turned out to consist of, besides our staff, a steersman for the barge, two men to tie the telephone line to the main cable, deckhands for paying out and hauling in, a generator hand, and a man at the meter wheel who also tied tape onto the cable at every hundred feet.

We made a trial submergence to one thousand feet with the bathysphere empty. It came up with the windows intact and only a quart of water at the bottom.

"Do you know anything at all about National Socialism?" Miss Hollister asked while we watched Mr. Tee Van work the pumps to empty it. She had her arms folded.

Spray whipped our faces as the tug dragged us about and then pulled us back to shore against the wind and the waves. We could attempt a descent as early as the next day if the weather permitted.

"Probably more than the next fellow," I told her.

"Then you understand some of my reasons for concern," she said.

I'd been hurt by her tone. Across the deck, Miss Crane was packing away the logbooks. One never had to justify concern for one's parents, I told her. The night of our rendezvous I'd talked about my parents. My father had been a dealer of paper, often away on business. I'd been an only child. We'd moved a few times and eventually settled in East Orange. We'd often visited the Museum of Natural History together on the elevated train. My father had wept at my first publication, a letter to the editor in *Harper's Young People's Magazine.* Miss Hollister had been greatly moved. We had been in my quarters on a steamer. I had invited her in. She had switched off the electric light after I had finished my account. The ship had wallowed a bit. She had eased me into my berth like someone attending an invalid. She had whispered her given name, Gloria, into my mouth. She had had a long face. Wispy blonde hair. Skeptical eyes. A long nose, and lips that were moist even after a day on the water.

"The German people have been through a terrible time," I told her.

She nodded and waited for me to continue. Mr. Tee Van stood about with his hands in his back pockets, waiting to ask a question. I excused myself and dealt with him.

She was still waiting after he went about his business. I said, "By which I mean we have to be wary of too easily judging the choices they made and why they made them."

She lowered her eyes as though she'd burst into tears, and I was swamped with helpless rage.

What I hadn't done was offer her father employment in our tiny Department. She believed it would make all the difference in terms of the possibility of an exit visa. Of course, we had no budget for it and he had no expertise for what we were doing. He barely spoke English. But this was in her mind a white lie that would save a man's life.

She was prone to hyperbole.

"Let me work on another letter," I told her. I myself was routinely accused of hyperbole. I had sympathy for those who suffered from it.

She raised her chin. I had to turn from her expression. Had I agreed to mention a job? Was I simply putting her off? I could see from her eyes that she couldn't tell.

She followed me, though I wasn't clear on where I was going.

"I realize that the very last thing we need are distractions," she said. Now she was weeping, though discreetly.

"Yes, yes," I said.

"And I want you to know how terrible I feel having to bring this up now," she said.

"Yes, yes," I said. "Please don't worry about that."

She stopped me with a hand on my arm. "Thank you," she said.

"Your father will be all right," I told her.

"Thank you," she said.

I didn't make it my practice to offer phantom positions as immigration aids. And I had no right to bandy about with the New York Zoological Society's reputation. As far as I could ascertain, her father's credentials were enthusiasm, a bookish background on spoonbills, and a willingness to break the law, and little else. But who knew? Perhaps the situation was as dire as she feared.

No one spoke to me about our little scene. It had never been clear to me how much information of a personal nature our little company had shared.

Each Nut Twisted into Its Numbered Place

The barge was anchored in the lee of the island. The next morning before the sun was fully up we settled down to watch sea and sky. Wind and barometer. We were looking for the absence of even the possibility of sudden squalls. It was June 6, 1930. Around five, a young gale blew itself out. The slender tips of the cedars beyond our veranda were motionless.

The sun rose on a calm, slowly heaving sea. We ran up the prearranged flag signal for those on the barge. The tug ferried us out to it and pulled us out to sea through Castle Roads. When we were eight miles offshore we had a mile of water beneath us. I stopped the barge and had it turned upwind and upswell.

A gull sideslipped back and forth above our mast. Everyone but me seemed to be ready. I looked around at the sea and sky, the barge, the tug. Miss Hollister.

"Here we go," Mr. Tee Van finally said.

Barton and I stood on a step-box and crawled painfully over the steel bolts, fell inside the sphere, and curled up on the cold hard bottom. The notion of cushions occurred to me, and I called for some through the opening. They took a few minutes to be fetched. Barton and I disentangled legs and got set. He grinned at me. The longer we were in the thing, the smaller it seemed to get.

I took up my position at my window. He put on the earphones.

Through the quartz I could see Miss Hollister arranging the other set over her ears. The four-hundred-pound door was hoisted and clanged into place, sliding and banging over the ten great bolts. The huge nuts were screwed on, each in its numbered place. Barton made a joke about Poe's "The Cask of Amontillado."

After the nuts were screwed down as tightly as humanly possible, the wrenches were hammered with sledgehammers to take up all possible slack. The sound threw us about. It made our eyes water.

We complained over the telephone. "Miss Hollister says it must be very hard," Barton shouted to me, when he was able. I could see her making a rueful expression. It didn't look like she could see us.

He tested the searchlight. He opened the valve on the first oxygen tank and verified the flow at two liters per minute. We began regulating our breathing. I peered out my window at an angle and could see Mr. Tee Van waiting for a signal from the captain. He got one. We felt ourselves tremble, lean over, and lift clear. We revolved, slowly, out on the beam until the barge came into view. Miss Hollister gave a small wave.

We began to swing with the roll of the ship. Barton said, "Miss Hollister wants to know why the Director is swearing so." I wasn't aware I had been.

She pointed out that my exercise in self-expression had already cost us several liters of oxygen.

We hardly noticed the impact on the surface until a froth of foam surged up over the glass and our chamber was dimmed to a pleasant green. The great hull of the barge came into view. Then the keel passed slowly upward, disappearing into the green water overhead.

A Quarter Mile Down

Word came down that we were at fifty feet. Then one hundred feet. The only change was a slight twilighting and chilling of the green. I knew we were sinking only by the upward passing of small motes of life in the water.

We passed what had been the greatest depth reached in a regulation suit by Navy divers. We passed the depth at which the *Lusitania* rested. We passed the point below which only dead men had sunk.

After so many deep-net hauls, and so much planning, to actually *be* where we were—! It was like an astronomer being allowed to visit Mars.

Barton gave an exclamation and I passed the flashlight over the floor and saw a slow trickle of water collecting. Maybe a pint. It was coming from the door. We watched it. I gave the signal to descend more quickly. As the pressure increased, the stream stopped. We turned the flashlight on the doorsill obsessively the rest of the way down, and saw no more water.

A tiny flaw formed on the rim of my outer window. It did not enlarge.

Barton, who had a lifelong fear of drowning, was unfazed by the flaw. He estimated the total pressure on the sphere would soon be six and a half million pounds. With any breach, there'd be no issue of drowning.

At one thousand feet Miss Hollister sent down word through Barton that a young herring gull was contenting itself flying about their stern. She knew I'd be interested to hear of one this far south. Barton shook his head to himself after passing the information on.

We reached a quarter mile down and were still alive.

We dangled in a hollow pea on a swaying cobweb a quarter of a mile below the deck of our ship.

We were the first human beings to look out on this strange illumination. It was an undefinable blue that worked on our optic nerves like a brilliance, and yet when I picked up my notebook, I could not tell the difference between blank page and print. The color seemed to pass materially through our eyes. The yellow of the searchlight when switched on banished it entirely; yet it returned instantly when the light switched off. It was an entirely new kind of mental reception of color impression.

I switched on a flashlight to mark the moment in my little observation-log. I felt a tremendous wave of emotion, an unnerved appreciation of what was superhuman about the situation. Here I was, privileged to sit and try to crystallize what I observed through wholly inadequate eyes. I wrote, "Am writing at the depth of a quarter of a mile. A luminous fish is outside my window." I could think of nothing else.

We attempted to pass some of our impressions up to Miss Hollister. Barton reported that she finally responded, with some frustration, that she couldn't understand us.

We told her that language was inadequate to the sensation. She answered back, "Evidently."

A Seascape from a Motion Picture Film

Over the next two months we attempted seven more dives.

We fastened the Tropical Research house flag of the Zoological Society and that of the Explorer's Club to the cable shackle, and tied a squid wrapped in cheesecloth beneath one of the observation windows. We also set out some hooks, attractively baited.

Three times before we were completely submerged, the horizon and barge appeared across the glass, instantly erased by a green and white smother. Air slipped upward like balloon pearls in its dry, mobile beauty. It formed vertical wakes of iridescence. The surface quilted above us with the undersides of wavelets. On one dive at four hundred feet, tens of thousands of sardines poured past our windows like elongated raindrops.

We conducted more systematic optical investigations. At fifty feet, a scarlet prawn I'd brought along as a color experiment was a deep, velvety black. On a marked spectrum, at one hundred and fifty feet, the orange vanished. At three hundred feet, the yellow. At three hundred and fifty, the green. At four hundred and fifty, the blue, with only violet remaining. At eight hundred feet, the violet evanesced, and only grayish-white remained inside the sphere. Outside remained the deepest blue-black imaginable.

Once, in a Central American jungle, I had had a mighty tree felled. Indians and convicts had worked for many days before its downfall had been accomplished, and after the wrack of branches, leaves, and debris had settled, a small, white moth had fluttered up from the very heart of the wreckage. In that way, life began appearing before us.

Strange, flat little crustaceans flashed like opals in the light. A transparent eel, vertebrae and body organs plainly visible, its eyes and filled stomach its only opacities, nosed our baited hook. A big leptocephalus undulated past like a ribbon of transparent gelatin.

We left the searchlight off. We kept descending. It was only by shutting my eyes and opening them again that I could realize the terrible slowness of the change from dark blue to blacker blue. The warm side of the spectrum was unthinkable. Speech was unthinkable.

Flashes of light sparked all around us. They vanished when we switched on the searchlight. At that point other fish and invertebrates swam up and down the shaft of the illumination like insects around a streetlight. Three myctophids. Pteropods. A big *Argyropelecus.*

Strange, ghostly, dark forms hovered in the distance, forms which never came nearer, but reappeared at darker depths. A great cloud of a body moved past us: pale, lighter than the surrounding water. It was maddening, as if astonishing discoveries were just outside the power of our eyes.

I heard Miss Hollister's voice through Barton's headphones. The sunbaked deck on which she sat with her notebook seemed hundreds of miles away.

"Miss Hollister asks me to tell you '*Darmstadt*,'" Barton said, mystified, an hour into our fourth dive. He had asked her to repeat the message.

"Why did she want me to tell you that?" he asked, after a few minutes had elapsed.

"Let's keep our minds on our work," I told him.

At twelve hundred feet, the fishes' iridescence seemed to dissolve into the water. I tied a handkerchief about my face below my eyes, to keep the quartz clear of breath. Barton and I kept as close to the eight-inch windows as we could, straining to see. On the seventh dive, at thirteen hundred feet we kept the electric light going for a full minute of descent and noted two zones of abundance with a wide interval of scanty, motelike life. The transitions were punctuated by milky arrow worms, with their swift darts and pauses.

At fourteen hundred feet we were sitting in absolute silence. I was aware of the cold even through the cushions. One leg was asleep. Barton's face reflected a faint bluish sheen. I marked time to a pulse-throb in my temples with my fingers on the icelike steel of the window-ledge.

How to explain to anyone the experience of such loneliness and isolation? How to articulate the pleasures of that sort of intensity?

The return was made in forty-three minutes, an average of a foot every two seconds. Twice during the ascent we were again aware of indefinite, huge bodies moving about in the distance. What they were we could only guess.

The Pallid Sail Fin

The night before our scheduled attempt at a half-mile dive, Miss Hollister asked if she could have a moment after our meeting on the next day's logistics. She produced a letter which had arrived by packet. Her father had asked that I read it, in order to demonstrate his facility with English.

Brötchen,

I kiss you from across the seas. I want to make quite certain that you're aware that I'm perfectly well. I'm sorry I was not allowed to write sooner. I have not been badly treated. The discomforts which one associates with prison life hardly trouble me at all. I have enough to eat in the mornings, with dry bread. (I am allowed a variety of extras such as jams as well.) The need to take one's bearings and come to terms with one's situation means that physical things lose their importance. This I find to be an enrichment of my experience, like a spiritual Turkish bath. My sole torment has been the fear that you were tormented by anxiety about me, and so not sleeping or eating properly. I hope this letter works to reassure us both.

You can imagine that I'm most particularly anxious to hear about your employer's news at the moment. If only I could provide something that might help. There is a redheaded thrush that sings in our prison yard. I cannot remember it from any of our ornithologies.

I am thinking of you, and your work, and your naturalist friends, and I am hoping you are having many adventures,

Your Father

"'Brötchen'?" I asked, once I'd finished. She looked away and began to weep.

"I didn't intend to pry," I told her.

"It isn't prying," she said. She crossed her arms and uncrossed them and came forward and put her head to my chest. She touched a hand to my arm, as if to steady me.

"I want to focus on tomorrow," she said, miserably. "I do." I heard steps in the passageway outside my door. The steps paused and then continued on their way.

"Oh, oh, oh," she wept. I could feel her face contorting through my shirt. I closed my own eyes, against the glare of the unshielded bulb on my desk.

"We'll do something about this," I finally promised. "I'll telephone Mr. Osborn."

Her entire body responded, startling me. It was what she'd been waiting for. Mr. Osborn had been a longtime supporter, had gotten me my first employment and introduced me to everyone I'd needed to meet. As President of the Society and the Museum of Natural History, his name would reverberate overseas.

Her relief and happiness seemed to distress her even more. She clung to me. She pulled me from the door. Her weight tipped us over onto my bunk.

I regained my balance, and hers. She wiped her face. She was able to look at me again. She pressed her hands to my cheeks as if cradling a single broken egg. "I need to show you how grateful I am," she said. She kept her voice low. "I need to show you," she whispered. And then she left.

The Wing Bolt Shoots like a Shell Across the Deck

The next morning we sent the sphere down empty for the half-mile test dive. It came up filled with water under tremendous pressure. With the deck cleared, two of us began to unscrew the giant wing bolt in the center of the door. There was a strange, high singing, a needle of steam, another, and another, and the bolt shot across the deck like a shell from a gun. Thirty feet away it sheared a five-inch notch out of the metal winch cover. A solid cylinder of water cannonaded out behind it with a roar for a good minute and a half.

The Shrubs of the Sea Are Animals

The trouble had been in the packing around the windows. The windows themselves were removed and double-checked and found to be in perfect condition. A coating of white lead was spread over the door flange and the window seals to make the junction of steel with steel as perfect as possible. We delayed only long enough to dry out the sphere and send it down again. This time it came up bone dry.

Three National Broadcasting men were along as well, their equipment arranged on the upper deck of the tug, out of the way of flying spray. It was to be the first time that radio engineers had traveled beyond the territorial waters of the United States to broadcast a program back to their home stations. They would be hooked directly into our telephone line.

"Congratulations on the beginning of your radio career," I teased Miss Hollister, while we waited for the second test dive.

"Thank you," she said. Miss Crane, beside her, sniffed. Miss Crane had even shorter hair, marcelled and black.

A Half Mile Down

The time finally arrived for us to clamber back aboard. Around us for miles all was calm. A waterspout twisted and coiled far out to sea. There was a clinking as I slithered through the opening, and I realized that pennies had tumbled from my pocket. In a perfect sphere every loose object constantly sought the bottom. I had my notebook and flashlight in an open pouch around my neck.

Barton and I provided the relevant assurances but otherwise were both silent during the descent, until an enormous luminous medusa seemed to envelop us at twelve hundred feet. It had firefly-like bands on its umbrella and lights at the base of each tentacle. A hundred feet later we saw an entire school illuminated from within with pale green light.

At seventeen hundred feet there was no hint of blue remaining. We had gotten below the level of humanly visible light. With the searchlight off, Barton's voice seemed now as unattached as something coming down the wire.

I had learned to encircle a light with my eyes and on one side or the other I began to be able to detect the body of the organism, and frequently, details of its outline and size. I found that even a momentary distraction, like an instrument check, diminished my visual powers for some minutes very considerably.

Occasionally the head of a fish would appear conspicuously against the surrounding black, illuminated by some unknown source of indirect light. Eyes especially stood out with no definite source of light visible. When teeth were silhouetted I knew it was from a luminous mucus which covered them.

Two lanternfish with pale green lights undulated past. Something else with widely spaced appendages. Here I began to become more inarticulate. Most of what I was looking at had no name; had never been seen by anyone.

The steel of the window-ledge was clammy. The quartz chilled the tip of my nose.

We were surrounded by a host of small unidentifiable organisms, most with what looked like legs. It was like being an entomologist in Hades.

At twelve hundred and fifty feet we encountered a vision to which I can give no name: a network of luminosity, delicate, with large meshes, aglow and in motion, waving slowly past. It seemed too diffuse and multivarious to be some sort of jellyfish, and too otherworldly to be anything else.

Farther down there were glowing explosions, inches wide. We pointed them out to one another and, after a few minutes of watching, speculated. Our wildest guesses were no help whatsoever.

At fifteen hundred feet Miss Hollister requested I take a turn on the earphones.

"I'm so happy for you," she told me.

"Yes, yes," I said.

"This is going out over the radio," she reminded me.

A large fish of an unpleasant white, like oversoaked flesh, something wholly unknown, swung suspended half out of the searchlight. It remained seemingly stationary, sinking with us, with only a slow waving of fins. I dragged Barton to my window to corroborate, and we did our best to describe the thing to Miss Hollister and the rest of America. It was over seven feet long. It had no lights or luminous tissue. A small eye. Long, filamented pectorals, and vertical fins that were huge and all the way back at the base of its tail.

"What will you call it?" Miss Hollister asked, when we'd finally stopped describing it. It still floated before us.

I called it *Bathyembryx istiophasma,* my fractured Greek way of saying, "Ghostly Sailor of the Abyss."

The Maw of the Saber-Toothed Viperfish

There seem to be three outstanding moments in the life of a bathysphere diver: the first flash of animal light, the discovery of a new species, and the onset of eternal darkness.

At 1:12 P.M. we felt an upward tug and came to rest, gently, at a depth of three thousand one hundred feet. We knew this to be as far as we could go; the cable on the winch was very near its end. A Roman candle of individual sparks burst beside our windows. We realized it to be an abyssal equivalent of the cephalopod's ink-screen.

Now and then my eyes peered into the distance, and I thought of all the lightless creatures forever invisible to me, even right here, before my windows.

I pronounced something suitably explorer-like for the benefit of those sitting around their hearths back home. Miss Hollister called for a check of our oxygen supply. It was fine, I assured her, without taking my eyes from the quartz.

We Emerge Again, with the Grace of Worms

There were days in my life when everything moved swiftly and emotions came hurtling along, one atop the other. From my earliest experiments, at the age of five, I felt at home submerged. It was an ancestral memory, spanning back hundreds of millions of years, from when I sang, *When you were a tadpole / And I was a fish—*

Billions of human beings have looked beneath the surface. Millions have descended to twenty feet. Hundreds to hundreds of feet. But only two to a half a mile.

Those Are Real Stars in the Heavens

Miss Hollister believed that I did what I did out of fellow feeling. That somewhere inside, her spark had reached mine. "I've never doubted your goodness," she said, the night we spent curled in my berth. "I hope you've found peace where you could," Elswyth wrote, when concluding her final letter. All those cups of water I absorbed and whirled about in my body were all steps leading toward a goal of final knowledge I'd never reach, and never could. My luck would hold, and maybe finally turn against me. When I died I'd find myself with the other fussbudgets and mote-counters arguing about phyla and condemned to the solution of problems, while the amateurs roamed at will in Elysian meadows, netting gorgeous, ghostly butterflies until the end of time. But I'd look up from my windowless carrel and remember my bathysphere, suspended in the blackness, a bubble of sanity and metal, with Miss Hollister's voice in my ear, saying, *Twenty-eight hundred feet,* saying, *Three thousand feet,* its breath and its warmth the most durable of illusions.

JOHN ASHCROFT:
MORE IMPORTANT THINGS THAN ME

Creative Self-doubt

When people have honest questions about where I stand or what I'm doing—in politics, it happens all the time—I've learned not to take it as an insult. In fact, I often find that their concerns mirror reservations I might have had on my own. Their honesty helps me clarify the situation. Nobody wins when anyone holds grudges.

Electability

Folks say, "Here's a fellow who doesn't spook moderates, who's actually electable." That word pops up a lot: electable. Paul Weyrich had some people over one night and we were lounging around out on his porch and he suggested that I was more than just presentable; I was a guy who could go on Jay Leno and play a couple of tunes with the Oak Ridge Boys.

Pessimists claim my only base is the profamily, religious vote. They say, "Where else can he go? The country club? The boardroom?" My answer is that those aren't the only places to look. My answer is that I'll take my chances with the American people. I served two terms as governor in a Democratic-leaning state, I had a national profile as a senator, and, yes, I have support among what the media calls the Religious Right. In my gubernatorial reelection

I carried 64 percent of the vote, the best showing of any Missouri governor since the Civil War.

My Principles

My principles are out there for everyone to peruse, and always have been. Whenever I get more than four people in a room, I tell them: You examine the record, and let me know if you find anything that's contradictory or troublesome. And if you think you do, you come back to me, and we'll clear it up on the spot.

In the Senate, I fought against national testing standards, activist judges, and the nomination of a pro-abortionist surgeon general.

I forced the first floor vote ever on term limits and had to fight my majority leader to do so. I wrote part of the welfare-reform law allowing states to deliver services through churches and private agencies.

I promoted the defunding of the NEA. The average guy who wants to go down and see Garth Brooks, he doesn't get a federal subsidy, but the silk-stocking crowd that wants to see a geometric ballet in Urdu, they get a break on their tickets.

When it comes to bills, I don't trim and I don't pork things up, whether the doors are closed on the session or not.

And I keep reiterating, wherever I go: It's against my religion to impose my religion on others.

Ethics

I tell people that I know about scandal. During my second term as governor, I had an overeager staffer who, when he heard about my boy's need for some books on Queen Elizabeth for a homework assignment, called the state librarian at home and got her to open the library after hours. The press got ahold of the story, like they get ahold of everything, and I quickly took responsibility. Around the house we call it Homeworkgate and joke that we learned from our mistake. A columnist for the *St. Louis Post-Dispatch* wrote about the whole thing that, "If a state ever had a less exciting governor than John Ashcroft, I never heard about it."

Turning Heads

I hear that I first started turning heads after the charges became public that Monica Lewinsky had turned the president's. Most everyone in my party maintained a code of silence in the early going. I did not. I said publicly in an address to the Conservative Political Action Conference that January, "Mr. President, if these allegations are true, you have disgraced yourself and the office of the presidency, and you should resign now."

That's what I said. It bears repeating: "Mr. President, if these allegations are true, you have disgraced yourself and the office of the presidency, and you should resign now."

Atlanta

If I've got one problem at this point in time, in perception terms, it's Atlanta. Atlanta was a nightmare. I dropped the ball there and I'm the first to admit it.

I was nervous. I started right in, once introduced, on principles, and what I stand for, and there was a point a paragraph or two into my notes when I realized that the silverware wasn't going to get any quieter, and flopsweat set in. I was fighting a losing battle with overdone filet mignon for everyone's attention.

It didn't help that Forbes was going on next and that he got about ten standing ovations for saying mostly the same things. *Steve Forbes.*

A nightmare. I get the shivers going back over it, I don't mind admitting.

"Shiver shiver shiver," Janet says, sometimes, late at night, lying next to me.

Ethics

It's fashionable, I guess, for people to talk down Jimmy Carter, but let me say this: Jimmy Carter was an unimpeachable straight-shooter who restored people's trust in the presidency. And don't think the American people couldn't use a little of that particular medicine right now.

The Transports of Love

Hollywood likes to showcase the tyranny of romantic infatuation—how two people might abandon their friends, family, and beliefs all in the name of an overpowering emotion—but my father didn't raise me that way. He wasn't a stoic and didn't despise emotion. He believed that delayed gratification was an essential practice for success in life. He always said, "Don't jeopardize the future because of the past."

A woman from a national magazine wrote that I had a Boy Scout's haircut and a choirboy's magnetic machismo. I wrote her a note explaining that I appreciated the joke, and that I didn't think magnetic machismo was what we needed in a president at that particular point.

Helpmate

Janet says that after God she puts family first, everything else second, and nothing third. During the campaign for the Senate she was asked if she minded being a helpmate. "No," she said. "The same way I don't mind being a math professor or writing textbooks."

Sex

Once in a diner, a fry cook said to me—I guess in an attempt to destroy his customer base—"I'll tell you one thing: I'm not getting any tonight." What I should have answered was something I thought as I drove away: that our country was affluent in sex, but bankrupt in love. Prostitutes have a sex life. Animals have a sex life. Human beings should have a *love* life.

The right results come first from working hard to make the right decision, and then working even harder to make the decision right.

Thrift

Missouri remains one of the cheapest places to buy gas in America. My staffers tease me because I've been known on drives home to run the tank down to near empty so I can save a few dollars by filling up on the other side of the Mississippi.

Why I Supported the Death Penalty as Governor

I was the ultimate appeal to correct error, not reward regret, emotion, or even religious conversion. Becoming a Christian removes us from *eternal* penalties.

Public Civility

The original rules of debate for the Constitutional Convention in 1787 did not allow conversation when another member spoke. No reading of any kind was permitted during debate, and no one was allowed to speak twice unless everyone else had spoken once.

Things to Work On

We're all works in progress. I know that I sometimes don't make a sufficiently forceful impression. I know that I can seem to people, as Janet likes to put it, too settled on my own road. There's a little motto painted onto the serape of a toy donkey on my desk: "We're all here to learn from one another." I look at that motto every day.

Recurring Dreams

Janet notes that I'm thrifty even with my dreams. I tend to have the same one for weeks running. They stay in my head. My most recent one features Barney Thomas, one of my father's oldest friends, who's sick now. My father called him The Judge when I was growing up.

R&R

I give visitors to my office copies of my ten-song tape, "The Gospel (Music) According to John," which I composed and produced myself.

Friendship

Harry Truman said, "If you want a friend in Washington, buy a dog."

Friendship

When I was state auditor of Missouri, I had seats on the fifty-yard line for Tigers games. When I lost reelection, I couldn't get into the end zone.

As the Seasons Change

Growing up I never imagined that I would one day need a man to work five days a week just to organize my schedule, let alone that I'd have an after-hours recording that goes like this: "Hello, I'm Andy Beach, scheduler for Attorney General of the United States John Ashcroft. If you'd like to request an appointment, please fax your request to the following number . . ."

Ambition

The presidency is like running the mile. You have to run the first few laps, and run them hard, before you know if you're really even in the race.

In 1998 Paul Gigot asked, in *The Wall Street Journal,* "Richard Nixon and Watergate helped make a president out of an obscure Democrat named Jimmy Carter. Can Bill Clinton and Monica Lewinsky do the same for an equally unknown Republican?"

The Judge

Two months ago he sent a letter I still haven't answered. Usually I'm a bear on correspondence. I haven't even finished reading it.

In the dream, he's as nice as can be. He quotes the first line of his letter: "So, John, the sawbones has come through with the bad news that apparently I've got the lung thing everyone's been worried about."

Moderation

Do we think a four-time murderer is only "moderately" dangerous?

Are drugs in a schoolyard only "moderately" a problem?

In combat, do we want our fellow soldiers to be "moderately" brave?

Are we so sure that "moderation" is always a good thing?

The Long View

Includes the understanding that the verdict of eternity stands above the verdict of history.

False Pride

I'm constantly on the lookout for it.

Losing to a Dead Man

My theory about elections is mirrored in what I hold about all of life. For every crucifixion, a resurrection is sure to follow—maybe not immediately, but the possibility is always there.

Melancholia

I became governor ten years ago. Twelve, I guess. Time flies.

The Hard Road

Like anyone else, there are weaknesses I've had to overcome to get to where I am today. A reporter once said that I speak like I'd rather be gigging fish on the Osage, and I dropped him a note telling him that that was because it was true: I would.

Secret Discouragements

Distractions don't seem to want to leave me in peace when my faith in myself is shaky or my defenses low. Janet calls them The Secret Discouragements. I think:

—In a February 1998 poll of registered Republicans in New Hampshire, 0 percent named me as their first choice for the nomination.

—Even John Kasich got 2 percent.

—I'm not a natural self-promoter.

—I don't like the way I look when I eat.

Unfinished Projects

The letter on my computer is entitled *Untitled.* So far it has the address and no date and two lines: *Dear Barney: It was terrible to hear about your terrible news.*

Always on Offense

During my first term as governor, Missouri landed both the Royals and the Cardinals in the World Series. There was speculation as to who I'd be rooting for. I rooted for both. My wife and I made a special hat the night before, half and half, red and blue, with bills on both sides. I flipped it around between innings to the team that was batting. An editorial the day after accused me of indecisiveness or double-dealing or both. But a letter-writer from Hannibal hit the nail on the head: there was another way of looking at it, he said. Governor Ashcroft is just always on offense. And he was right.

John Ashcroft in the Pocket of Big Tobacco

Who pays for years and years and years of government litigation? Who is it that foots the bill so the trial lawyers can pocket billions?

On Being Part of a Persecuted Minority

Most of those who criticize me for my religion haven't even taken the time to discover just what my religion is. The Assemblies of God is a Pentecostal denomination, so I know what it's like to be a part of a minority and mocked for one's beliefs. When the mockers come after me, I refer them to two bumper stickers distributed by AG pastor Fulton Buntain: "It's Never Too Late to Start Over Again," and "It's Always Too Soon to Quit."

On Pushing That Liberal Rock up the Hill

I used to tell my son when he got frustrated about his math scores: You know, there are times that maybe God will call us to do something that doesn't have an apparent success about it at the moment.

Learning About Values

My father was a pastor and a college president. I remember as a very young boy hearing his early morning prayers and tiptoeing downstairs to sit beside his knees, so that I was shielded by his body as he pleaded for my soul.

Learning About Values

The day before he died, in the presence of a small group of family and friends, he reminded me that the spirit of Washington is arrogance, and that the spirit of Christ, on the other hand, is humility.

Learning About Values

He was on the sofa, and struggled to get up to help family and friends pray over me. I said, "Dad, you don't have to struggle to stand and pray over me with all these friends." He said, "John, I'm not struggling to stand; I'm struggling to kneel." And he left that couch and came and knelt with me.

Why Should We Believe in the Resurrection?

After losing my first race for Congress, I was appointed state auditor. After losing the election to maintain that post, I was elected state attorney general. After losing the election as chairman of the Republican National Committee, I was offered the candidacy as U.S. senator. After losing the reelection campaign for U.S. senator, I was appointed attorney general of the United States.

Learning About Values

My role models are Jesus Christ, Abraham Lincoln, J. Robert Ashcroft, Barney Thomas, and Janet Ashcroft. With no apologies, and in that order.

Standards

No schoolteacher could have gotten away with the behavior that Bill Clinton did. No principal, no college president, no corporate president. That he wasn't forced to resign tells me that our standards for the presidency are lower than they are for virtually any other job in America. And that, to me, is a disaster.

Deception

How can we expect individuals to be faithful to us if they're not faithful to the people in their own families?

Government

Revival isn't something that comes from government. Government is not an agent of spirituality. But it can be a moral force. It's said you can't legislate morality. Well, I've got news for those who say that: *all* we should legislate is morality. And we certainly shouldn't legislate *im*morality.

What's in My Heart

Have I been the man I could be? No. What's in my heart? What do I spend my time thinking about? Could I at any moment make a clean breast of it to people; let them see, *so here's what I've been thinking*?

I get teased for starting every staff meeting with that phrase: "So here's what I've been thinking."

Having Good Memories

Is like having gold in your spiritual bank. Nothing can take the place of them. Nothing can diminish them. Nights I can't sleep, I remember floating on my back with Dad down the little stream behind our farm, the sun on our faces, the leaves spiraling overhead. When one of my colleagues from across the aisle is going on about this or that victimized minority, I remember my father and The Judge taking three straight Saturdays to help me with my soapbox racer. Their faces come back to me when I don't expect them, and when I do. Their faces are a gift I have to be strong enough to carry.

Mr. Perfect

Janet gets a kick out of it whenever a publication decides I'm Mr. Clean or Mr. Perfect or whatever they've decided to call me. She's happy for me but she always makes a wry little list of recent shortcomings to keep my head from swelling. "All well and good, Mr. Perfect," she said after the most recent article, in the *Southern Partisan,* "but you still haven't called Barney back."

Unfinished Projects

Dear Barney:

- Terrible to hear about your terrible news.
- Don't want to lecture an old lawyer on the law.
- Know full well that spirit of Christ is humility.

- Imagine how it felt to read you never thought you'd "find Bob Ashcroft's son in the pocket of Big Tobacco."
- Full slate.
- Sleeplessness.
- Wanting to write forever, feels like. Took stock, made notes, as way of preparing self.
- Really took stock.
- City on the Hill.

Dad's Twenty-One Life Lessons

4 Silence sometimes shouts.
5 Creative self-doubt fertilizes the field of creativity.
7 Never eat your seed corn.
8 When you've considered all your options, work to expand your options.
11 The lives of fathers and sons are intertwined; when one dies, the other is diminished.
12 A father should try to pass on not only his strengths, wisdom, and insight, but also how to handle weaknesses, failures, and insecurities.
13 When you have something important to say, write it down.
15 Little things mean a lot.
21 Saying good-bye is a way of beginning to say hello.

#22

When I was eight, my father took me to the sleepy Springfield airport, once a World War II training field. He was an amateur pilot. We walked up to a 1941 Piper Cub, climbed in, and took off. A few minutes later, he shouted over the engine noise:

"John, fly the plane for a while."

"What do I do?" I shouted back.

"Grab the stick and push it," he said. I did. We went into a sickening dive. He pulled us out. He had a good chuckle, and I had a good lesson: Actions had consequences. And when I put my hand to something, I could make a difference.

The Melancholy Truth

Each of us is required to exercise leadership, even if it's limited to our personal relationships.

Groundswells of Support

The Judge said when a politician claimed there was a public outcry for him to run for office that it meant that his mother and father thought it was a good idea. A groundswell of support meant that an aunt and uncle agreed.

My houses are filled with plaques and honorary pictures, keys to various cities: temporary acknowledgments of the offices I held, not indications of the man I am, or hope to be.

Flattery

Think about it: virtually any positive remark you could make about Jesus would be true.

The Long View

I try to adopt a forward-looking approach, focusing on what I might become, not on what others are saying about me today.

Attitude of Gratitude

My father didn't allow us to use the phrase, "I'm proud of . . ." "Say you're grateful for it," he always said. "Not proud."

God doesn't ask us to sacrifice our children to Him. He sacrificed His Son for us. Pride doesn't enter into it, here. Gratitude is the appropriate response.

Inner Reserves

Six weeks after my brother's funeral, my father had a massive heart attack.

What Family Is All About

My brother had lived in the same town and used to drop in on him every other day. My father told him he didn't need to feel as if he had to come by all the time. My brother answered that a phone wouldn't work for what he wanted, because sometimes he just wanted to lay eyes on him.

Good Fortune

The story of the Asian man who commissioned a work of art to represent good fortune, the artist free to choose any form or method of representing it. He chose three lines of calligraphy:

GRANDFATHER DIES
FATHER DIES
SON DIES

The wealthy Asian said, "How can this represent good fortune? Everyone dies!" The artist said, "The good fortune is in the sequence."

Gullibility

When someone promised my father something, he assumed that that person was telling the truth. Every so often someone would say to me, "Your father sure was gullible." But who'd want to be raised by a cynic? Believing in the best and giving others the benefit of the doubt may not be the most astute financial advice, but it's the only spiritual advice.

Despite Everything

Despite everything, I could hear sometimes in my father's voice the way a certain insecurity invaded his thoughts. A few times he said to me, "If I weren't a college president, I wonder if anyone would still care about my opinions."

Carrying the Ball

When people say pictures don't lie, they fail to realize that our favorite pictures try to suggest that our best moments are persistent moments. They're not. We might have looked like that for a second, but then our hair moved, our clothes wrinkled, our expressions got tired, our faces sagged back to normal.

Writing

There's something about being able to put writing down and pick it back up that makes it special. Maybe we have a struggle getting what we need to get out face-to-face, or on the telephone. Maybe the deliberate pace of writing allows us to express ourselves more clearly.

The Reason for Discipline

The very nature of Judeo-Christian culture is choice-driven.

Sunday School

When I was in Sunday school one of our songs went like this:

> *Be careful, little eyes, what you see;*
> *Oh, be careful, little eyes, what you see.*
> *For the Father up above is looking down in love;*
> *So be careful, little eyes, what you see.*

Punctuality

My father was never on time: he was always *early.* On time was not an option. If you weren't early, you were late. We were always the first to church, the first to school, the first to work.

More Important Things Than Me

Because of his ministries, he was never home in the summer. At Little League I'd look up and see all the other dads. As I got older I realized that the most important thing my father ever taught me was that there were more important things than me.

Road Trips

Once I was an appropriate age, I was regularly invited to go along on his ministry trips. Everyone talks today about getting involved in their children's worlds. My father invited me into *his.*

Hindsight

For a while, I thought he was ignoring me. It turned out that he was *building* me.

Respect

Once when I was twelve, I had just heard him address a group of college students, and he turned to me and said, "What do *you* think, John?" He asked my opinion. You know what that said to an adolescent boy?

When I traveled with him, he quizzed me about tensions or contradictions in any of the concepts he'd been dealing with. I wanted to be able to respond correctly, so I listened as if nothing else mattered.

Our Own Little Prisons

Do yourself a favor: the next time you're driving with someone and you see that faraway look in their eyes, and you wonder what's going on in their heads—*ask.*

Courtesy

Even in his latter, potentially lonelier years, my father was passionate about taking the pressure off people. He was always adamant about one part of his dinner invitations: "Come when you can and leave when you want to."

Discovery

I'm a fan of the discovery school of education. When education focuses exclusively on comprehension, a crucial spiritual element is lost. An educated person is someone who's become addicted to the thrill of discovery. If someone tells me they're feeling prematurely old, I tell them: buy a telescope, go visit a new culture, work through a college textbook.

Open Your Eyes

There's a spot on a twisting farm road near our place in Greene County where, at the right time of year, in the right weather, tarantulas make their crossing. Most drivers don't even notice, but I like to stop and watch, and I've been known to pick up one or two and take them home to Janet. I'll set one on the kitchen counter when I know she's coming. She'll scream loud enough to make me think it's all been worthwhile, but she doesn't appreciate it. She tells people that it's a family joke that I enjoy and she endures.

"Why would you do that?" someone might ask. That's the wrong question. We saw something new. We enlarged our lives.

Cookies

My father never let people leave without putting something in their hands. He developed a signature gift, a plaque he had produced for the sole purpose of giving away. The calligraphy read, *As long as he sought the Lord, God made him to prosper.* I've never been sorry for anything I've given away (whereas the same is not true for anything I've kept or purchased).

Once I was back in Missouri, I visited The Judge four days running. I said to him, "Is there anything I can do for you?" He said he could go for some chocolate chip cookies. I went back to the house and started assembling the ingredients.

"What are you doing?" Janet wanted to know.

I told her I was making cookies. It was something I wanted to do for myself. She watched for a while and then went about her business.

The stirring, the mixing, the baking, started paying me back. I started to process my prayers and work through my anger at the cigarettes that had shortened his life. I underbaked the cookies so they'd be good and moist. I made them small to stack in a Pringles can. I delivered them when he was asleep.

Generosity

Political liberals take the admonition to be generous in giving as an admonition directed toward the government. In actuality, it's the reverse. Real givers are people who enjoy giving away their *own* money. Beware the generosity of those who make a living giving away *other people's* money.

Staying on Message

All the good groups in the world, and a few bad ones, bring their causes, purposes, and bills to my office virtually every day, and if I don't happen to speak out on their particular concern at least once a week, I get asked, "What happened to you? Why are you silent? Don't you care?"

What some of these groups don't understand is the necessity of staying on message. Try to do everything and you end up doing nothing. It's like physics: if you don't concentrate your force, you don't penetrate the wall. Some issues have other senators as their champions, and I may stand behind them as a strong supporter. What each of us has to do is determine the primary emphasis of our calling. A good colleague of mine understands this: he says he has 365 titles but only two speeches. My father repeated the same things his entire life. Because he stayed so focused, it was impossible to be around him for any length of time and not know what he believed in.

Write It on Your Hand

Character is what you're made of when everything else that might hold you up evaporates on the spot.

Memories with Staying Power

Everyone was standing when I noticed my father lunging, swinging his arms, trying to lift himself out of the couch, one of those all-enveloping pieces of furniture that tends to bury you once you sit in it.

Good-byes

Back in Washington in our little one-and-a-half-room apartment, in an alley just off Second Street, Janet and I had just fallen asleep when we heard a rattling of the iron bars on the door. She thought it was someone trying to break in. I said, "No. It's my dad." The next morning we heard the news.

Good-byes

I was told that in the Emergency Room, he finally said to the doctors, "Boys, you better just quit. You're hurting more than helping."

Everyone who knew him joked about his good-byes. He waved like a person stranded on an island. Fifty, a hundred yards down the road, you'd look back, and he'd still be waving, his arms going like he was helping to park a jet.

Good-byes

As a boy, on days when there were no Little League games, I'd get a bat and a dinged-up softball and go into a field by myself and play All-Time Home Run Derby. It was always the same six guys in a round-robin: Mel Ott, Ernie Banks, Eddie Matthews, Ted Williams, Jimmy Foxx, and Mickey Mantle. I'd bat for each, and after each swat I'd have to troop after the ball and find it. "What're you doing?" Janet finally said, after having watched me from the kitchen window for about twenty minutes.

Hellos

I stood there in the field, holding my softball like an apple. Somewhere I'd lost my bat. Janet was wiping her hands on a dishtowel as she walked across the alfalfa stubble. There were apple trees and behind them a beautiful twilight, with our farm spreading out around us. A contrail made a quiet little line across the sky. I was attorney general of the United States. My father was sitting on my bed. He was telling me that things don't *happen;* they're *made* to happen. He had his palm to my face. He had only my welfare in mind. This was the only world we knew. This was the world that was swept away.

MESSIAH

Right off we'll talk about it: people are (were) wrong about Macon. Macon this, Macon that, Macon's what's wrong with college football today. What Macon *is* is the best Corvair to run the football for State since God knows who, and some class-A studs have hauled leather there, Pops can tell you.

Pops says, "It's like, you wanna back the Ferrari out of the garage, you gotta break some eggs."

Pops is one of the trainers. He handles ankles.

Macon I met on a recruiting visit. I was ass-kicker at defensive back, all-everything in Ohio, he was a fullback phenom from Jersey, one of those guys who scored nine thousand times a minute. We were flown in by the same alumnus. We were taken to the same restaurant. We were favored with the same jerky grins. We were told to stand in the middle of our prime rib and we were cheered by the crowd. Ever have a crowd cheer you in a restaurant?

Once we'd hunkered back to our meat I said my name and stuck my hand out. He looked at my hand and said, "Messiah." I said, "I beg your pardon?" and he said, "That's right, you *beg* my pardon."

We were both scout teamers at first. Scout team being Coach's idea of a way of using the freshmen, drop-goobers, and general nose-pickers that infest a major college bench. What the scout team does is impersonate the upcoming opponent in practice and get its tiny brains beat out in the process. Neither Macon nor I intended to be on that little ride too long, but, like Pops says, "Caligula, he had to start somewhere."

It is something to see, trust me: every week two thousand or so come to see it.

So here's Macon, little Wilber Macon out of New Jersey of all places, having sewn MESSIAH on his back where his uppercase humble name should be and taking all sorts of radical verbal and physical abuse from the starters in pileups for his presumption in such matters, here's Macon coming back to the huddle with blood dripping from his nostrils like he's some sort of bull and then turning all sorts of savage, absolute maniac, and this being practice. Real officials work these practices—State saves money in all sorts of places, but football is not one of them—and they were throwing flags at Macon like they were hoping they'd stick. Coach would take him out and talk to him, arm around his shoulder in the August heat, gruff but kind from the stands, but in your ear it was something like, "Meat, you don't start producing out there and we are going to collectively plant your ass like an azalea and tamp down the soil."

So back in comes Macon, who goes wide on a sweep and tears through a linebacker and pops into the secondary expecting a big gain. You could see his eyes, big-gain eyes. Except Charlie Hall, starting monster man, cut his feet out from under him so that he went down like something hinged. Coach held his clipboard out for a flunky to take and then announced we'd run that play again. Not a radical nice thing to do, since the element of surprise was somewhat gone. Macon got stuffed big-time, and the sound he made when hit was like the sound of someone beating a rug.

Which is where this starts to sound like *The Sports Book for Teens*: Macon, stung, pissed, lets fly on his final carry, coming out of his crouch like a psycho, a speedboat flipping, a ski jumper losing it, and is through a gap in the line before the hogs are up and set. It was terrifying, talent. We had seen a vision and some of us had to look away. Some of us saw but could not see. You could hear the whoosh of his breath on the sidelines and he lowered his helmet and stuck Jimmy Ford, as in starting weakside corner Gator Bowl MVP Jimmy Ford, such a shot that they heard the crack up in the practice towers. Jimmy let out what we call the dog yelp and went airborne with his face mask in pieces tumbling after. Macon kept going until he decided he wanted to stop. He carried Charlie Hall into the end zone and dropped the ball on his head.

So he started. He was, I wasn't. "Specimen under the bridge," Pops said. Testing jokes were big that year. Everyone was pissing into bottles.

He not only started, he messed around at length with senior girls. He'd been on campus all of five weeks; they'd been on campus all of one. I couldn't find the student center. He had three different girls in three different dorms waiting up with the lights on, their hands on themselves, waiting for him to walk through that door.

This he told me.

The day he became a starter he took one girl into her room and slapped her face over and over and over. The resident assistant came to the door and asked her if she was all right and she said she was. She was not, but she said she was. I saw the swelling.

We opened against South Carolina. Dirty program, ugly uniforms, skaggy cheerleaders. They'd had another one of their nine-and-two-but-we-got-our-ass-kicked-by-the-good-team-in-the-bowl-game seasons, so they were underdogs, and deserved to be. I hoped we won big. I hoped to get in.

We were home. I lay in my bed from ten P.M. Friday night to seven A.M. Saturday morning, and I did not unclench my fists. My roommate lay there on his side whispering, "You fucker, you fucker, you fucker," for that same amount of time, his consonants sounding like the wind.

We got taped early. I got Pops. He handled my ankles and wrists like they were already broken and gone and he was going to miracle-ize them. I remember him pressing tape along my heel. I remember him aligning tape with my Achilles tendon. He squeezed and molded tape to my arches and instep, and I believe I jumped higher and ran faster as a result.

I remember my locker, the steps of getting into the game uniform. I remember the cleats and the bright red rug. I remember the officials checking our pads. I remember the quiet before the tunnel. I remember the tunnel. I remember the run down that dark and hot and altogether soothing corridor into the light with the noise building until you hit cool air and nuthouse. We could not hear ourselves scream or touch pads and that was the way we wanted it. In the sunlight on that turf we were deaf but could hear, were blind but could see. We wanted a part of whoever was nearby, South Carolina, the Seattle Seahawks, mad dogs. We were a natural disaster that moved in stages, a moment of misanthropy so pure we could have dashed babies around on the ground and then just gone on to the next thing.

We only mildly calmed down the whole first half. There were about sixty of us Denizens of the Depth Chart, as Pops called us, and we roamed and lined the sidelines, making treaties, breaking alliances, watching the game. Adding to the circus of TV cables, condenser dishes, Mini-cams, yard markers, drink and aid stations, whatever. We got in the way.

Some hotshot we'd seen all week on the films fumbled the opening kickoff and we scored right off. Our defense kept hitting like animals and by the half it was 26–0. Macon didn't see much of the ball. In the second half they came out and scored on some kind of half-assed reverse and the game ended that way, 26–7. So there was that clear locker-room division afterward: the studs hunched over, spent, blue in spots and dripping, just really spent, and content, more content than we would ever be. Content to be there, content the hurting was over, content to have all that quality of stop. They sat there pulling at clammy tape like they were underwater and did not talk unless spoken to and sometimes not then. The rest of us bobbed back and forth like idiots in our fresh uniforms, wanting to go out on the town, show who we were or rather who we associated with, hurt people who weren't dressed as we were. We all listened to Coach. No one in fresh uniforms gave interviews.

I took to following Macon, when I found him. Hazardous hobby, Pops said, and Pops knew. Macon, the first night, took me to bars where he sat alone, took me to the video store, took me to the 7-Eleven. Did he notice me? He did not let on, and I was good. The second night he took me to a girls' freshman dorm called Sweetwater and I watched him through a second-floor window dry hump a girl who under no circumstances appeared to want to be dry humped.

Did I do anything? I did not.

I followed him more. This I told Pops.

Pops said, "It is definitively true that we as a country are producing a lesser breed of cat."

Pops said, "Do you have a girlfriend?"

I said, "Are you named after Louis Armstrong?"

Pops said Armstrong could not hit. Armstrong could not stick. This we laughed at. I would not, I realized, tell him that I wanted to see what Macon did when I followed him.

And did Macon know? What about the night he maneuvered the girl over to the window, got her there when it could not have been easy and could not have been necessary? What about the night I lost him crossing the quad and found him again standing under the streetlight, hands bouncing in jacket pockets?

What about the night he had the girl under the arch by the wrist and let her go, so that she walked and then ran past me, where I was waiting?

And how did I get to start? Macon made me a spot.

IN PRACTICE after our second game, Macon found the strong-side corner strung out and exposed after having absorbed the block from the guard, and Macon put the crown of his helmet into the earhole of our strong-side corner's helmet so that the strong-side corner's head went one way and his body went another. The strong-side corner's name was Jeff Voight. The cheerleaders turned away as a group. I myself thought he was dead. I thought, "He's dead, and I'm starting." Someone orbiting the earth would have known it was his neck. This was confirmed very slowly by eleven medical staffers who finally removed him the way you'd pick up a finished jigsaw puzzle. While this was happening Macon was ranging up and down the sideline waiting, and my adrenaline was heading around the block, my college career about to begin.

So this Jeff Voight had a big scare but is now all right. He had, as well, a lot of friends on the defense and they were all now intensely interested in Macon in practice, and the hitting went from absurd to a little out of hand. They rode him in pileups. While people untangled, they pulled hair from his calves. They poked fingers through his face mask, searching for eyes.

The head terrorizer of this group was our weakside linebacker, Billy Jeter, who'd been Jeff Voight's best friend. Mr. Jeter and I took Macon down on a swing pass, and Mr. Jeter got up by standing on Macon's ankles. Macon said, and I quote: "Next play, motherfucker, you get yours."

This was like Ruth calling his shot. Who knew the play would send him in Jeter's direction, and who knew if sent whether he could truly and permanently hurt Jeter? But both of these came to pass, Macon revving up, getting a nice start on a pitch, coming out all helmet and knees, and clawing up one side of Jeter and down the other. Jeter had both hands on his chest like a grandmother in distress and he was right to do so because he had a cracked sternum and his football career was now over.

This, maybe, Macon did for us.

So here is how I played, as a starter in week three for State in 1989: well. I was mesmerized out there at first, reacting too late to the snap and flow, but got it in gear for part two and started hitting, and things, as Pops said, turned out all right. People were much bigger at this level, so that I was frequently trampled and not infrequently felt like something in the spin cycle when I tangled with the big meat inside, but they were no meaner than I was, nor more willing to hurt, and this for me seemed a kind of grace.

We won games we were supposed to win. We lost one we were supposed to lose. While that was happening Coach took off his watch and jumped up and down on it on the sidelines. Charlie Hall behind me said, "There's Coach killing time again," and the goobers on the bench laughed and slapped their pads like members of the team.

Claudia was my ethical dilemma. Claudia was my moral choice. Claudia was in my Many Faces of Man class and she had only been kind, to me and to most others. When the professor had said, "Mr. Proekopp, you aren't with us, are you?" Claudia had said, "Is the idea here that the football players can't keep up?"

Claudia I could have wanted to go out with. Claudia I introduced to Macon, at a mixer. She liked him. I followed them around the party. I followed them home. At her door he kissed her sweetly good night. At his door he whistled and hooted. I knew he would see her again.

In practice his eyes were unreadable in the heavy shadow under the helmet. Our big game was this week: conference rival and interstate matchup. Every day I went home trailing equipment behind me, watching Macon disappear in his direction, thinking, *Tonight?* Monday and Wednesday I sat next to Claudia and talked about everything that would not help. Thursday night he led me out and around the campus, the full tour, Macon the director of nighttime admissions, always fifty yards ahead, slowing down faintly at points of particular interest. When we got to Claudia's he went inside without hesitation. From the base of a tree I watched her fourth-floor window. But the light was a yellow blank, and they appeared in the lobby, came out, and started walking. We walked everywhere. I trailed, the tail of the kite. By a doughnut shop they kissed and I rubbed the glass of a bookstore window with my cheek. They passed a park and sat beside a series of bike racks. They ended in the arboretum.

In the darkness I lost them. I blundered along. I left the path. I did not call her name. I stepped on glass which crunched underfoot. By a tree I found her, kneeling. Her arms were behind her. Her head was back and her pants were open, though there was only a white triangle of belly in that light. Macon was behind her. Macon was holding her that way. Macon had convinced her to be silent.

Even with her head back she could see me. I could not tell what her eyes intended to communicate. I could not tell how long they had been there like that. I could tell she was not going anywhere. I could tell they could both see something in my face that I could not.

PIANO STARTS HERE

We were trying to see a dog that could've been dead already and we weren't getting anywhere, Susan said. We were standing outside her veterinarian's office in a four A.M. drizzle. My hair felt like wet old clothes on my neck. Susan's breath ghosted the glass. She had asked to be let in, and the boy inside had not yet responded. He gazed at us vacantly, his mop handle teetering, running water shifting and realigning his image on the pane. Susan spread a hand across it, as if to push through. She had twice explained that her dog was in there and that the doctor had given her permission to come down so late. The boy seemed to have trouble focusing.

Doppleresque trucks rushed and whined on the interstate in the distance. The boy palmed the door handle with an appealing gentleness. He puffed his cheeks like a bugler and turned the latch. The door swung outward.

"Audrey," Susan said, once inside. "A beagle mix. She hasn't come out of the anesthetic."

The boy did not respond. He led us through a second door. Susan's boots made amphibious sounds on the tile.

Audrey was still on the table. She had been brought in earlier unable to stand on her hind legs. Cortisone had been no help. The decision had been made to operate, and they had found a lesion impinging on the spinal cord. The recommendation was to let her go. That was the veterinarian's phrase. Susan was taking the night to think it over.

Audrey had not revived from the anesthetic and was not a good bet to do so. She lay on her side with her midsection shaved and bandaged. One paw hung from the table.

"I came in and checked earlier," the boy said. "She hasn't moved."

Susan gave him a wan smile. "Audie-feeber," she said. "Old Audrey-feen." She sounded like the loser on a quiz show. She squatted near the dog and put her fingers against its nose. "Here we got our big numbers tomorrow and where will you be?"

OUR RECITAL in Adult Music was the next afternoon at three.

We had signed up together eleven weeks previous. Susan had kept her distance from me, and that was something I hoped to change. Friends scoffed and remained casual about the possibilities, musical or romantic. They admitted that they themselves rarely did that which was in their best interests, whether because of the kids or work or general laziness. Around me they seemed both distracted and skeptical, as if always aware of neglected parallel tracks of richer possibility.

Susan and I showed zero aptitude for the instrument. I had no ability. Susan flustered and grew frustrated and banged the keys like someone losing an argument. For us the keyboards stretched limitless in each direction, and the keys lay in quiet and narrow rows as individual as grains of rice. We had both, it turned out (Susan saw nothing interesting in the coincidence), abandoned the instrument in childhood, spurning the loneliness of solitary application to music, I theorized, for yet another sort. We had sat imprisoned with stereotypic piano teachers in dark parlors, reinventing simple exercises, sweating and hesitant, imagining a world of joy and laughter beyond our windows while our hands produced a series of remorseless sounds.

The patterns returned to our adult lives in the singsong cadences of nonachievement: *Every Good Boy Deserves Favor. All Cows Eat Grass. Big Dogs Fight All Cats.* We behaved as true believers trusting that refusing to confront the catastrophe might yet reverse it.

Susan and Audrey arrived at the North Adams Congregational Church hall that first day in my company, though she specified for the benefit of our instructor that we were not attached. She taught fourth- and fifth-level high-school history, she said, and for what? Her last group's PSATs were so low, she said, she'd recommended to one kid, when he had asked where he should go to school, the University of Mars. She was getting burned-out, in other words.

"Well, let's see what happens," she said, and cracked her knuckles theatrically. Audrey laid a chin on the piano bench.

We stood ready at that point to commit ourselves to eleven weeks of Adult Music and become part of a group seemingly already dispirited by a lack of adults. Mrs. Proekopp, our instructor, assured us she'd add younger people if necessary to fill out the class. She gestured as evidence toward a tiny child waiting wide-eyed with her mother by the front door.

The church hall had been rented for the occasion, and Mrs. Proekopp had not put herself out. Upright pianos were arranged back-to-back on the maroon linoleum, and the effect was that of a dismal and half-realized Busby Berkeley number.

Mrs. Proekopp had speculated right off the bat that the dog would naturally be a disruption and in the future would be better off and no doubt happier at home, and Susan had suggested that she would be the judge of that, thank you, and when the dog disturbed anyone they would let her know. Audrey had yawned.

The few other students had looked on with interest. Susan believed in serious rudeness when people in her opinion refused to see or speak clearly.

"We need something, I guess," she allowed that first day.

"You never know what you can do until you try," I told her, settling into the piano beside hers. Audrey shot me a look.

"Then you do," Susan said. "That's the problem." She lifted the index card with her name penciled on it from the fallboard. "Makes me feel like a kid again," she said, and played four notes, *plink plank plonk plunk,* and squinted at the music sheet.

I watched her hands rehearsing and re-rehearsing their intended patterns above the keyboard, her brow furrowed in puzzlement. She stared at the music like someone facing crisis in an exotic land trying to read the instructions on the emergency gear.

Her problem, she said, was that she didn't like what she'd done with herself and she didn't like what she was doing. "*One* problem, anyway," she added. The situation demanded change.

There, on the first day of Getting Acquainted with Our Instruments, even basic techniques remained blandly elusive. The exercises drifted serenely around my attempts to order them. Susan at one point compared the effect to that of a system created by random generation. We did not improve. Audrey lay under the piano bench, dreamily twitching.

The second day the tiny girl in the doorway, Mary Alice, was admitted to the group, and Susan told her, by way of explaining me, "He thinks he's in love with me." Mary Alice looked uncertain as to how to handle the information. After a moment or two she regarded me unsympathetically. I suggested by my expression that I didn't need the sympathy of children.

At the break we sniffed coffee in Styrofoam cups and lingered near the doughnuts. Mrs. Proekopp kept a wary eye on Audrey, who nosed the air around the tray experimentally.

"There's a difference between believing in things and refusing to see," Susan said. "You've got that love-at-first-sight thing going in your head right now; I can see it. Forget it. You and me, we're not made for each other. We're just not."

I suggested that it wasn't something that needed deciding right then.

"It's *been* decided," Susan said. "Smell the coffee, pal."

"It isn't a wholly rational process," I said. She made a squeaking noise with her lips.

"You're something," she said. "Your mouth's writing checks your behind can't cash." We drifted back to our pianos. I did a little fingering and the doughnut grease left filmy fingerprints on the ebony keys.

BETWEEN SESSIONS we met coincidentally in a garage. Her tired orange Opel hatchback balked in the cold, she reported. Desmond, her mechanic, told her to just leave the checkbook.

I was sitting in a red plastic chair in the waiting room, waiting for my own bad news. In the garage area proper, dog dishes spotted the cement floor.

"For the rats," Susan explained. "This place is Rat Motel." I pulled up my feet.

In the Pan Tree across the street we sat in the window so we could watch our cars slowly come apart. Susan slurped her Constant Comment and watched Desmond poke disinterestedly under the Opel's hood. Audrey remained upright and stoic in the backseat, resembling at that distance the mysterious figures in the windows of suspense movies.

"You don't know me," she said. "We never dated. I have B.O. I'm always pissed off at something. I'm not your dream girl." She looked away, and I was encouraged. "All this interest is sad, you know?"

I asked about a piece of hers in the *Advocate* entitled "Jazz Giants Snub the Berkshires." Her thesis had been that they had no place to play, so it was inevitable. We talked about the older greats: Jelly Roll Morton, Art Tatum, Fatha Hines, Willie the Lion Smith. I was frequently pretending to appreciations I didn't have. She tried to make comprehensible Tatum's sixteenth-note runs at up-tempo. We considered ways of improving articulation. We had very little idea what we were talking about.

The garage lights went on across the street. "There you go, Desmond," she called to the window. "He's given up going by feel," she said to me. People in the restaurant were looking.

"Want to go to the Blind Pig?" I asked. "For a drink?"

"I don't know," Susan sighed. She made binoculars with her hands and looked at me through them. "What am I doing? What are you doing?"

"You're teaching and writing for the *Advocate,*" I said. "That could be exciting."

She nodded, her eyes on the garage. "They got me covering a guy who does gun-rack art," she said.

I folded the paper around my pumpkin muffins. I asked if she remembered the little girl, Amanda, from the last Fourth of July. Once it had gotten dark Amanda had wandered over and stood next to us petting Audrey while the fireworks boomed and popped over our heads. Her mouth had been open and the lights warmed our faces. Susan spoke quietly with her. Someone took us for a family. Amanda leaned back, her palm leaving Audrey and patting air. Look at the noise! she said. Look at the noise! Susan had lifted her up, as if for a closer look. I thought then that we were both happy. I thought, *She's usually unhappy, and I'm usually unhappy.* I called her after that, tried to shop where she shopped.

"I remember her," Susan said. "Beautiful girl."

The cars still weren't ready an hour later, so we walked the strip to the Artery Arcade. From the benches in front of the Zayres we could see over the Department of Motor Vehicles to Mount Greylock. Susan rubbed her eyes industrially with her fingertips. She said, "I'm thirty-three already. Billy DeBerg was sixteen years ago."

"Billy DeBerg?" I asked. She did not elaborate.

There was an immense and distant crash, as though someone had dropped a carton of bedpans.

"Fat," she said sadly, as if that followed.

"You're very beautiful," I said. This kind of talk did not come easily to me and I tried to list specifics.

"Right here," she said. With two fingers and a thumb she pinched her hip and twisted it. "Miss Cushions."

I had no comeback for that. Audrey deflected some of the awkwardness by scratching herself. Susan told some Audrey stories. The dog ate the spines of books, and at the age of eleven still urinated with joy when Susan came back from school.

"*Don't* you?" she asked. Audrey's tail thumped. We sat with her unperturbed silence as our model. The world seemed to be rewarding restraint only incrementally, but I refused on my part to push things. I had the patience of a coral reef.

MRS. PROEKOPP informed us two weeks later that she wasn't pleased with our progress and could not believe, after hearing my hands skitter like frightened crabs across the keyboard, that I had been diligent in my practicing.

"Come now," she said, looking over her glasses at me. "Do you think you would sound like that if you practiced?"

I looked helplessly at my hands.

"Listen," she said. "Mary Alice, play the piece." Mary Alice straightened up and her tiny frame hunched forward. She peered at the music and began. Her version was not very good, but it was a resounding improvement. She appeared to be five to seven years old.

Mrs. Proekopp was not one to tread lightly on a point. "Did yours sound like that?" she asked, unnecessarily. "Class? Did his sound like that?" Around me neutral murmurs, blank looks. "Susan," she said, "has he been practicing?"

"It doesn't sound like it," Susan said.

"Class," Mrs. Proekopp concluded, with an excess of élan, "we are not going to get anywhere"—she thumped my shoulder for emphasis—"not anywhere, if we do not p-r-a-c-t-i-c-e."

On the chalkboard, as we entered the hall every afternoon, were separate lists for each student which our instructor had entitled WHAT WE NEED TO WORK ON. By week three Susan and I were not on the board. We attributed this to a lack of space.

"Have you thought there might be other girls out there looking for you?" she said during one session, looking at her hands.

"I like *you,*" I said. She bared her teeth at the music book.

"I DON'T KNOW what to do with you two," Mrs. Proekopp said. Mrs. Bunteen, an elderly widow from Adams, looked on, the lights glazing her glasses. "Neither of you seem able to accomplish the smallest things with a keyboard."

"You're being too hard," I said, in Susan's defense.

"Prove it," she said. She believed herself to be, she confided, a whiz at motivation.

The room was silent. I realized I had the opportunity at that point to play for the two of us, to redeem weeks of performance with one flourish and show up the instructor. I began without taking a breath and my fingers spilled around with a palsied urgency. Mrs. Proekopp granted me a short grace period and then walked around the piano to bring an ear closer to the atrocities. Slowly and clearly she called out the missed notes like a public autopsy: B flat. G flat. B flat. B flat. At a tricky bridge I stopped, some fingers still trembling. I imagined for my hands the most grotesque punishments.

Mrs. Proekopp had by that time been reduced to grim little noises. Susan and I had been doing daily violence to the "Minuet in G" for two weeks. Mrs. Bunteen had begun to master the piece in six days. Mary Alice in three. Mrs. Proekopp crossed to the doughnut table and pulled a sheaf of dittoed pages from her satchel, which she divided between Susan and me.

"Here," she said. "Take these home."

Susan leafed through the first few, pale. Centered on the page before her was a small cartoon figure of a smiling quarter note. *Hi there,* he was saying. *I'm B flat.*

SHE AGREED TO DINNER, at her place, after practice—circling the wagons, she called it. We sat on the living room sofa, Audrey snoring on one end, and looked out on the erratically shingled roof next door. We had a lot of California wine. *Mr. Smith Goes to Washington* was on cable. On the jacket of an album I pulled from behind her stereo, Art Tatum was making a thumbs-up sign and grinning, under the title *Piano Starts Here.*

She apologized for the cork in the wine and said we should have more because of it. She laughed at the movie and made fun of a woman in a commercial who worried about feminine protection. During a Miller Lite ad she asked unexpectedly about football pads. "I never figured out where the pads went, exactly," she said. The knees, I said. The thighs, the hips, the tailbone. She made a face and said I wasn't being too specific.

So I traced the outline of a knee pad around her knee. I traced the broader shape of the thigh pad. I showed her where on the hips.

She was looking at me, serious. My hands described around her head the narrowed globe of the helmet, my fingers outlining the full cage of the face mask.

Audrey sighed and turned onto her back. The commercial ended. Susan put her glass down and her legs flexed and resettled like beautiful animals. She relaxed, a little sadder, I thought. A frazzled Jimmy Stewart filibustered on the floor of the Senate. His head was lowered in close-up, and he examined letters in his hand. He mentioned lost causes. Claude Rains, sitting nearby, looked uncomfortable.

I woke in the darkness disoriented. I was on the sofa. Susan poked a coverlet under my chin like a bib, her frizzed hair silhouetted against the lamplight from her bedroom. I could hear Audrey lapping water faintly in the distance.

"My Boy Senator," she said. "We sure bring a lot to the party, don't we?"

AROUND WEEK EIGHT of our lessons Audrey began to have difficulty rising after any time at all off her feet, and Susan worried about her getting old and stiffening up. Mrs. Proekopp posted her recital decisions. I was paired with Mary Alice—five-year-old Mary Alice—in a duet. If it was an effort to hide me, it could only have been spectacularly unsuccessful.

Mary Alice was no happier with the arrangement and in fact claimed equal humiliation. We resolved to make the best of it and huddled in one corner of the hall to schedule extra practice sessions, miserable Mary Alice in her MOZART sweatshirt trying distractedly to remember which days her mother could provide a ride, which days her father could pick her up. On the third emergency meeting she pounded the keys with startling force, crying, "No No No No No *No*," and asked herself, as though I wasn't there, "What am I gonna *do*?"

THINGS GOT WORSE. Susan's improvement was imperceptible, and my fingers moved like sinkers as we hurtled toward our recital. She called and said something was wrong, Audrey wasn't getting up, she couldn't reach the vet, and when I went over, there was Audrey pained and sheepish over an inability to rise, pulling herself slightly this way and that in the hopes of lessening Susan's distress. The operation was authorized. Audrey was passed from arm to arm in the veterinarian's office and seemed bemused when I last saw her, before the doors shut us out.

WE STOOD AT THE GREYLOCK Animal Hospital before Audrey, packaged like an animal coming apart, and the boy with the mop said he had a lot of cleaning to do, and turned away. The four A.M. stillness amplified sounds. He went through the cabinets and poured Janitor in a Drum quietly into a clean yellow bucket, hushing the sound by easing the liquid down the tilted edge as though drawing a beer. The smell filled the air around us. On the far side of the room, the animals in their holding cages were quiet. Their nails made occasional and light sounds on the metal screens of the doors.

The boy's mop slid across the floor in even strokes, renewing the shine. The tile gleamed in streaks. We all listened to Audrey breathing. The boy worked around in the sterilizer, organizing the instruments. They glittered and clashed musically in the drawers. He wiped the counter and then his hands and left the room.

Audrey's bandage looked unwieldy and impractical. Her exhalations were a quiet rasp. Her muzzle trembled. Susan ran her hand over the ribs. A drop from the nose ran onto the stainless steel. Her whiskers moved briefly, and she smelled of the anesthesia and the medicated bandage.

Susan lifted her hand. The dog seemed dead, but I wondered if there was some check we could do. She asked, finally, for the collar, and the license jingled weakly when I took it off. The boy went back in when we left, and behind us there was the flat sliding sound of Audrey being pulled from the table. I wondered if he should move her before the vet looked at her, just to be sure. I kept the thought to myself. In the car Susan's only words had to do with whether I needed a lift to the recital, and I rode beside her all the way back with an overwhelming sense of what I could and couldn't do.

By the time of the recital it was raining. Susan's Opel, a sad mustard color in that weather, broke down, and she had to walk the last four blocks. She sat beside me in the wings of the makeshift stage with her hair dripping. The collar of her new black blouse was floppy and soaked. The recital crowd was small and uncertainly enthusiastic, as if the rain might have changed everything.

Susan was represented in the audience by Desmond, who looked apologetic, and an old boyfriend. The boyfriend's name was Kevin, and he looked more uncomfortable than I was. He looked at me with the unalloyed hatred of someone with no chance considering someone else in very much the same position.

Introduced, I walked to my piano, bowing unsteadily beside Mary Alice, her brown hair jumbled into an oversized pink bow. We sat down to our minuet. Unhappy Kevin two rows back seemed to wish the piano would detonate. Mary Alice's parents projected sympathy.

Mary Alice stretched with a child's grace to reach the pedals, her polished black shoes gently toeing the brass. She could not look at me. She waited for the sound of my opening chord to begin.

MY PIANO had not improved. Mary Alice's had not improved, and Susan's had perhaps deteriorated. We would work in concert with our instruments to order the sounds and give what we had to the music. Over the seats and before the mingy floor-to-ceiling divider I could see in the maroon linoleum wet with tracked-in rain an oscillating image of Susan coming to love me, of our raising wondrous children in a sunroomed house, with a Steinway and their growing young arms displaying a heartening gift for the instrument.

Susan would be unaware of the gift the future held for her: her life as a stirring solo across the harmonic map by Fatha Hines. Her life performed with the left-handed abandon of Oscar Peterson. Her life joined in mine and mine finding meaning in hers, if only I would have—and I knew I did—if only I would have the patience to wait.

BATTING AGAINST CASTRO

In 1951 you couldn't get us to talk politics. Ballplayers then would just as soon talk bed-wetting as talk politics. Tweener Jordan brought up the H-bomb one seventh inning, sitting there tarring up his useless Louisville Slugger at the end of a Bataan Death March of a road trip when it was one hundred and four on the field and about nine of us in a row had just been tied in knots by Maglie and it looked like we weren't going to get anyone on base in the next five weeks except for those hit by pitches, at which point someone down the end of the bench told Tweener to put a lid on it, and he did, and that was the end of the H-bomb as far as the Philadelphia Phillies were concerned.

I was one or two frosties shy of outweighing my bat and wasn't exactly known as Mr. Heavy Hitter; in fact, me and Charley Caddell, another Pinemaster from the Phabulous Phillies, were known far and wide as such banjo hitters that they called us—right to our faces, right during a game, like confidence or bucking up a teammate was for noolies and nosedroops—Flatt and Scruggs. Pick us a tune, boys, they'd say, our own teammates, when it came time for the eighth and ninth spots in the order to save the day. And Charley and I would grab our lumber and shoot each other looks like we were the Splinter himself, misunderstood by everybody, and up we'd go to the plate against your basic Newcombe or Erskine cannon volleys. Less knowledgeable fans would cheer. The organist would pump through the motions and the twenty-seven thousand who did show up (PHILS WHACKED IN TWI-NIGHTER; SLUMP CONTINUES; LOCALS SEEK TO SALVAGE LAST GAME OF HOME STAND) wouldn't say boo. Our runners aboard would stand there like they were watching furniture movers. One guy in our dugout would clap. A pigeon would set down in right field and gook around. Newcombe or Erskine would look in at us like litter was blowing across their line of sight. They'd paint the corners with a few unhittable ones just to let us know what a mismatch this was. Then Charley would dink one to second. It wouldn't make a sound in the glove. I'd strike out. And the fans would cuff their kids or scratch their rears and cheer. It was like they were celebrating just how bad we could be.

I'd always come off the field looking at my bat, trademark up, like I couldn't figure out what happened. You'd think by that point I would've. I tended to be hitting about .143.

Whenever we were way down, in the 12–2 range, Charley played them up, our sixth- or seventh- or, worse, ninth-inning Waterloos—tipped his cap and did some minor posing—and for his trouble got showered with whatever the box seats didn't feel like finishing: peanuts, beer, the occasional hot-dog bun. On what was the last straw before this whole Cuba thing, after we'd gone down one-two and killed a bases-loaded rally for the second time that day, the boxes around the dugout got so bad that Charley went back out and took a curtain call, like he'd clubbed a round-tripper. The fans howled for parts of his body. The Dodgers across the way laughed and pointed. In the time it took Charley to lift his cap and wave, someone caught him in the mouth with a metal whistle from a Cracker Jack box and chipped a tooth.

"You stay on the pine," Skip said to him while he sat there trying to wiggle the ivory in question. "I'm tired of your antics." Skip was our third-year manager who'd been through it all, seen it all, and lost most of the games along the way.

"What's the hoo-ha?" Charley wanted to know. "We're down eleven–nothing."

Skip said that Charley reminded him of Dummy Hoy, the deaf-mute who played for Cincinnati all those years ago. Skip was always saying things like that. The first time he saw me shagging flies he said I was the picture of Skeeter Scalzi.

"Dummy Hoy batted .287 lifetime," Charley said. "I'll take that anytime."

The thing was, we were both good glove men. And this was the Phillies. If you could do anything right, you were worth at least a spot on the pine. After Robin Roberts, our big gun on the mound, it was Katie bar the door.

"We're twenty-three games back," Skip said. "This isn't the time for bush-league stunts."

It was late in the season, and Charley was still holding that tooth and in no mood for a gospel from Skip. He let fly with something in the abusive range, and I'm ashamed to say that I became a disruptive influence on the bench and backed him up.

Quicker than you could say Wally Pipp, we were on our way to Allentown for some Double-A discipline.

Our ride out there was not what you'd call high-spirited. The Allentown bus ground gears and did ten, tops. It really worked over those switchbacks on the hills, to maximize the dust coming through the windows. Or you could shut the windows and bake muffins.

Charley was across the aisle, sorting through the paper. He'd looked homicidal from the bus station on.

"We work on our hitting, he's got to bring us back," I said. "Who else has he got?" Philadelphia's major-league franchise was at that point in pretty bad shape, with a lot of kids filling gaps left by the hospital patients.

Charley mentioned an activity involving Skip's mother. It colored the ears of the woman sitting in front of us.

It was then I suggested the winter leagues, Mexico or Cuba.

"How about Guam?" Charley said. "How about the Yukon?" He hawked out the window.

Here was my thinking: The season was almost over in Allentown, which was also, by the way, in the cellar. We probably weren't going back up afterward. That meant that starting October, we either cooled our heels playing pepper in Pennsylvania, or we played winter ball. I was for Door Number Two.

Charley and me, we had to do something about our self-esteem. It got so I'd wince just to see my name in the sports pages—before I knew what it was about, just to see my name. Charley's full name was Charles Owen Caddell, and he carried a handsome suitcase around the National League that had his initials, C.O.C., in big letters near the handle. When asked what they stood for, he always said, "Can o' Corn."

Skip we didn't go to for fatherly support. Skip tended to be hard on the nonregulars, who he referred to as "you egg-sucking noodle-hanging gutter trash."

Older ballplayers talked about what it was like to lose it: the way your teammates would start giving you the look, the way you could see in their eyes, "Three years ago he'd make that play," or "He's lost a step going to the hole; the quickness isn't there." The difference was, Charley and me, we'd seen that look since we were twelve.

So Cuba seemed like the savvy move: a little seasoning, a little time in the sun, some señoritas, drinks with hats, maybe a curveball Charley *could* hit, a heater I could do more than foul off.

Charley took some convincing. He'd sit there in the Allentown dugout, riding the pine even in Allentown, whistling air through his chipped tooth and making faces at me. This Cuba thing was stupid, he'd say. He knew a guy played for the Athletics went down to Mexico or someplace, drank a cup of water with bugs in it that would've turned Dr. Salk's face white, and went belly-up between games of a doubleheader. "Shipped home in a box they had to *seal,*" Charley said. He'd tell that story, and his tooth would whistle for emphasis.

But really what other choice did we have? Between us we had the money to get down there, and I knew a guy on the Pirates who was able to swing the connections. I finished the year batting .143 in the bigs and .167 in Allentown. Charley hit his weight and pulled off three errors in an inning his last game. When we left, our Allentown manager said, "Boys, I hope you hit the bigs again. Because we sure can't use you around here."

So down we went on the train and then the slow boat, accompanied the whole way by a catcher from the Yankees' system, a big bird from Minnesota named Ericksson. Ericksson was out of Triple A and apparently had a fan club there because he was so fat. I guess it had gotten so he couldn't field bunts. He said the Yankee brass was paying for this. They thought of it as a fat farm.

"The thing is, I'm not fat," he said. We were pulling out of some skeeter-and-water stop in central Florida. One guy sat on the train platform with his chin on his chest, asleep or dead. "That's the thing. What I am is big boned." He held up an arm and squeezed it the way you'd test a melon.

"I like having you in the window seat," Charley said, his Allentown hat over his eyes. "Makes the whole trip shady."

Ericksson went on to talk about feet. This shortened the feel of the trip considerably. Ericksson speculated that the smallest feet in the history of the major leagues belonged to Art Herring, who wore a size three. Myril Hoag, apparently, wore one size four and one size four and a half.

We'd signed a deal with the Cienfuegos club: seven hundred a month and two-fifty for expenses. We also got a place on the beach, supposedly, and a woman to do the cleaning, though we had to pay her bus fare back and forth. It sounded a lot better than the Mexican League, which had teams with names like Coatzacoalcos. Forget the Mexican League, Charley'd said when I brought it up. Once I guess he'd heard some retreads from that circuit talking about the Scorpions, and he'd said, "They have a team with that name?" and they'd said no.

When Ericksson finished with feet he wanted to talk politics. Not only the whole Korean thing—truce negotiations, we're on a thirty-one-hour train ride with someone who wants to talk truce negotiations—but this whole thing with Cuba and other Latin American countries and Kremlin expansionism. Ericksson could get going on Kremlin expansionism.

"Charley's not much on politics," I said, trying to turn off the spigot.

"You can talk politics if you want," Charley said from under his hat. "Talk politics. I got a degree. I can keep up. I got a B.S. from Schenectady." The B.S. stood for "Boots and Shoes," meaning he worked in a factory.

So there we were in Cuba. Standing on the dock, peering into the sun, dragging our big duffel bags like dogs that wouldn't cooperate.

We're standing there sweating on our bags and wondering where the team rep who's supposed to meet us is, and a riot breaks out a block and a half away. We thought it was a block party at first. This skinny guy in a pleated white shirt and one of those cigar-ad pointed beards was racketing away at the crowd, which was yelling and carrying on. He was over six feet. He looked strong, wiry, but in terms of heft somewhere between flyweight and poster child. He was scoring big with some points he was making holding up a bolt of cloth. He said something that got them all going, and up he went onto their shoulders, and they paraded him around past the store-fronts, everybody shouting, "Cas*tro*! Cas*tro*! Cas*tro*!" which Charley and me figured was the guy's name. We were still sitting there in the sun like idiots. They circled around past us and stopped. They got quiet, and we looked at each other. The man of the hour gave us his fearsome *bandido* look. He was tall. He was skinny. He was just a kid. He didn't look happy to see us.

He looked about ready to say something that was not a welcome when the *policia* waded in, swinging clubs like they were getting paid by the concussion. Which is when the riot started. The team rep showed up. We got hustled out of there.

We'd arrived, it turned out, a few weeks into the season. Cienfuegos was a game down in the loss column to its big rival, Marianao. Charley called it Marianne.

Cuba took more than a little getting used to. There was the heat: One team we played had a stadium that sat in a kind of natural bowl that held in the sun and dust. The dust floated around you like a golden fog. It glittered. Water streamed down your face and back. Your glove dripped. One of our guys had trouble finding the plate, and while I stood there creeping in on the infield dirt, sweat actually puddled around my feet.

There were the fans: One night they pelted each other and the field with live snakes. They sang, endlessly. Every team in the *Liga de Baseball Cubana* had its own slogan, to be chanted during rallies, during seventh-inning stretches, or just when the crowd felt bored. The Elefantes' was *"El paso del elefante es lento pero aplastante."* Neither of us knew Spanish, and by game two we knew our slogan by heart.

"What *is* that?" Charley finally asked Ericksson, who *habla*'d okay. "What are they saying?"

"The Elephant passes slowly," Ericksson said, "but it squashes."

There were the pranks: As the outsiders, Charley and me expected the standards—the shaving-cream-in-the-shoe, the multiple hotfoot—but even so never got tired of the bird-spider-in-the-cap, or the crushed-chilies-in-the-water-fountain. Many's the time, after such good-natured ribbing from our Latino teammates, we'd still be holding our ribs, toying with our bats, and wishing we could identify the particular jokester in question.

There was the travel: The bus trips to the other side of the island that seemed to take short careers. I figured Cuba, when I figured it at all, to be about the size of Long Island, but I was not close. During one of those trips Ericksson, the only guy still in a good mood, leaned over his seat back and gave me the bad news: if you laid Cuba over the eastern United States, he said, it'd stretch from New York to Chicago. Or something like that.

And from New York to Chicago the neighborhood would go right down the toilet, Charley said, next to me.

Sometimes we'd leave right after a game, I mean without showering, and that meant no matter how many open windows you were able to manage you smelled bad feet and armpit all the way back. On the mountain roads and switchbacks we counted roadside crosses and smashed guardrails on the hairpin turns. One time Charley, his head out the window to get any kind of air, looked way down into an arroyo and kept looking. I asked him what he could see down there. He said a glove and some bats.

And finally there was what Ericksson called a Real Lack of Perspective. He was talking, of course, about that famous South of the Border hotheadedness we'd all seen even in the bigs. In our first series against Marianao after Charley and I joined the team (the two of us went two for twenty-six, and we got swept; so much for gringos to the rescue), an argument at home plate—not about whether the guy was out, but about whether the tag had been too hard—brought out both managers, both benches, a blind batboy who felt around everyone's legs for the discarded lumber, a drunk who'd been sleeping under the stands, reporters, a photographer, a would-be beauty queen, the radio announcers, and a large number of interested spectators. I forget how it came out.

After we dropped a doubleheader in Havana our manager had a pot broken over his head. The pot held a plant, which he kept and replanted. After a win at home our starting third baseman was shot in the foot. We asked our manager, mostly through sign language, why. He said he didn't know why they picked the foot.

But it was more than that, too: On days off we'd sit in our hammocks and look out our floor-to-ceiling windows and screened patios and smell our garden with its flowers with the colors from Mars and the breeze with the sea in it. We'd feel like DiMaggio in his penthouse, as big league as big league could get. We'd fish on the coral reefs for yellowtail and mackerel, for shrimp and rock lobster. We'd cook it ourselves. Ericksson started eating over, and he did great things with coconut and lime and beer.

And our hitting began to improve.

One for five, one for four, two for five, two for five with two doubles: the box scores were looking up and up, Spanish or not. One night we went to an American restaurant in Havana, and on the place on the check for comments I wrote, *I went 3 for 5 today.*

Cienfuegos went on a little streak: nine wins in a row, fourteen out of fifteen. We caught and passed Marianao. Even Ericksson was slimming down. He pounced on bunts and stomped around home plate like a man killing bees before gunning runners out. We were on a winner.

Which is why politics, like it always does, had to stick its nose in. The president of our tropical paradise, who reminded Charley more of Akim Tamiroff than Harry Truman, was a guy named Batista who was not well liked. This we could tell because when we said his name our teammates would repeat it and then spit on the ground or our feet. We decided to go easy on the political side of things and keep mum on the subject of our opinions, which we mostly didn't have. Ericksson threatened periodically to get us all into trouble or, worse, a discussion, except his Spanish didn't always hold up, and the first time he tried to talk politics everyone agreed with what he was saying and then brought him a bedpan.

Neither of us, as I said before, was much for the front of the newspaper, but you didn't have to be Mr. News to see that Cuba was about as bad as it got in terms of who was running what: The payoffs got to the point where we figured that guys getting sworn in for public office put their hands out instead of up. We paid off local mailmen to get our mail. We paid off traffic cops to get through intersections. It didn't seem like the kind of thing that could go on forever, especially since most Cubans didn't get expense money.

So this Batista wasn't doing a good job, and it looked like your run-of-the-mill Cuban was hot about that. He kept most of the money for himself and his pals. If you were on the outs and needed food or medicine, it was your hard luck. And according to some of our teammates, when you went to jail—for whatever, for spitting on the sidewalk—bad things happened to you. Relatives wrote you off.

So there were a lot of *demonstraciones* that winter, and driving around town in cabs we always seemed to run into them, which meant trips out to eat or to pick up the paper might run half the day. It was the only nonfinable excuse for showing up late to the ballpark.

But then the demonstrations started at the games, in the stands. And guess who'd usually be leading them, in his little pleated shirt and orange-and-black Marianao cap? We'd be two or three innings in, and the crowd out along the third-base line would get up like the chorus in a Busby Berkeley musical and start singing and swaying back and forth, their arms in the air. They were not singing the team slogan. The first time it happened Batista himself was in the stands, surrounded by like forty bodyguards. He had his arms crossed and was staring over at Castro, who had *his* arms crossed and was staring back. Charley was at the plate, and I was on deck.

Charley walked over to me, bat still on his shoulder. I'm not sure anybody had called time. The pitcher was watching the crowd, too. "Now what is this?" Charley wanted to know.

I told him it could have been a religious thing, or somebody's birthday. He looked at me. "I mean like a national hero's, or something," I said.

He was still peering over at Castro's side of the crowd, swinging his bat to keep limber, experimenting with that chipped-tooth whistle. "What're they saying?" he asked.

"It's in Spanish," I said.

Charley shook his head and then shot a look over to Batista on the first-base side. "Akim's gonna love this," he said. But Batista sat there like this happened all the time. The umpire straightened every inch of clothing behind his chest protector and then had enough and signaled play to resume, so Charley got back into the batter's box, dug in, set himself, and unloaded big-time on the next pitch and put it on a line without meaning to into the crowd on the third-base side. A whole side of the stands ducked, and a couple of people flailed and went down like they were shot. You could see people standing over them.

Castro, in the meantime, stood in the middle of this with his arms still folded, like Peary at the Pole, or Admiral Whoever taking grapeshot across the bow. You had to give him credit.

Charley stepped out of the box and surveyed the damage, cringing a little. Behind him I could see Batista, his hands together over his head, shaking them in congratulation.

"Wouldn't you know it," Charley said, a little rueful. "I finally get a hold of one and zing it foul."

"I hope nobody's dead over there," I said. I could see somebody holding up a hat and looking down, like that was all that was left. Castro was still staring out over the field.

"Wouldn't that be our luck," Charley said, but he did look worried.

Charley ended up doubling, which the third-base side booed, and then stealing third, which they booed more. While he stood on the bag brushing himself off and feeling quite the pepperpot, Castro stood up and caught him flush on the back of the head with what looked like a burrito of some sort. Mashed beans flew.

The crowd loved it. Castro sat back down, accepting congratulations all around. Charley, when he recovered, made a move like he was going into the stands, but no one in the stadium went for the bluff. So he just stood there with his hands on his hips, the splattered third baseman pointing him out to the crowd and laughing. He stood there on third and waited for me to bring him home so he could spike the catcher to death. He had onions and ground meat on his cap.

That particular Cold War crisis ended with my lining out, a rocket, to short.

In the dugout afterward I told Charley it had been that same guy, Castro, from our first day on the dock. He said that that figured and that he wanted to work on his bat control so he could kill the guy with a line drive if he ever saw him in the stands again.

This Castro came up a lot. There was a guy on the team, a light-hitting left fielder named Rafa, who used to lecture us in Spanish, very worked up. Big supporter of Castro. You could see he was upset about something. Ericksson and I would nod, like we'd given what he was on about some serious thought, and were just about to weigh in on that very subject. I'd usually end the meetings by giving him a thumbs-up and heading out onto the field. Ericksson knew it was about politics, so he was interested. Charley had no patience for it on good days and hearing this guy bring up Castro didn't help. Every so often he'd call across our lockers, "He wants to know if you want to meet his sister."

Finally Rafa took to bringing an interpreter, and he'd find us at dinners, waiting for buses, taking warm-ups, and up would come the two of them, Rafa and his interpreter, like this was sports day at the UN. Rafa would rattle on while we went about our business, and then his interpreter would take over. His interpreter said things like, "This is not your tropical playground." He said things like, "The government of the United States will come to understand the Cuban people's right to self-determination." He said things like, "The people will rise up and crush the octopus of the north."

"He means the Yankees, Ericksson," Charley said.

Ericksson meanwhile had that big Nordic brow all furrowed, ready to talk politics.

You could see Rafa thought he was getting through. He went off on a real rip, and when he finished the interpreter said only, "The poverty of the people in our Cuba is very bad."

Ericksson hunkered down and said, "And the people think Batista's the problem?"

"Lack of money's the problem," Charley said. The interpreter gave him the kind of look the hotel porter gives you when you show up with seventeen bags. Charley made a face back at him as if to say, Am I right or wrong?

"The poverty is very bad," the interpreter said again. He was stubborn. He didn't have to tell us: On one road trip we saw a town, like a used-car lot, of whole families, big families, living in abandoned cars. Somebody had a cradle thing worked out for a baby in an overturned fender.

"What do you want from us?" Charley asked.

"You are supporting the corrupt system," the interpreter said. Rafa hadn't spoken and started talking excitedly, probably asking what'd just been said.

Charley took some cuts and snorted. "Guy's probably been changing everything Rafa wanted to say," he said.

We started joking that poor Rafa'd only been trying to talk about how to hit a curve. They both gave up on us, and walked off. Ericksson followed them.

"Dag Hammarskjöld," Charley said, watching him go. When he saw my face he said, "I read the papers."

But this Castro guy set the tone for the other ballparks. The demonstrations continued more or less the same way (without the burrito) for the last two weeks of the season, and with three games left we found ourselves with a two-game lead on Marianao, and we finished the season guess where against guess who.

This was a big deal to the fans because Marianao had no imports, no Americans, on their team. Even though they had about seven guys with big-league talent, to the Cubans this was David and Goliath stuff. Big America vs. Little Cuba, and our poor Rafa found himself playing for Big America.

So we lost the first two games, by ridiculous scores, scores like 18–5 and 16–1. The kind of scores where you're playing out the string after the third inning. Marianao was charged up and we weren't. Most of the Cuban guys on our team, as you'd figure, were a little confused. They were all trying—money was involved here—but the focus wasn't exactly there. In the first game we came unraveled after Rafa dropped a pop-up and in the second we were just wiped out by a fat forty-five-year-old pitcher that people said, when he had his control and some sleep the night before, was unbeatable.

Castro and Batista were at both games. During the seventh-inning stretch of the second game, with Marianao now tied for first place, Castro led the third-base side in a Spanish version of "Take Me Out to the Ball Game."

They jeered us—Ericksson, Charley, and me—every time we came up. And the more we let it get to us, the worse we did. Ericksson was pressing, I was pressing, Charley was pressing. So we let each other down. But what made it worse was with every roar after one of our strikeouts, with every stadium-shaking celebration after a ball went through our legs, we felt like we were letting America down, like the poor guy on the infantry charge who can't even hold up the flag, dragging it along the ground. It got to us.

When Charley was up, I could hear him talking to himself: "The kid can still hit. Ball was in on him, but he got that bat head out in front."

When I was up, I could hear the chatter from Charley: "Gotta have this one. This is where we need you, big guy."

On Friday Charley made the last out. On Saturday I did. On Saturday night we went to the local bar that seemed the safest and got paralyzed. Ericksson stayed home, resting up for the rubber match.

Our Cuban skipper had a clubhouse meeting before the last game. It was hard to have a clear-the-air meeting when some of the teammates didn't understand the language and were half paralyzed with hangovers besides, but they went on with it anyway, pointing at us every so often. I got the feeling the suggestion was that the Americans be benched for the sake of morale.

To our Cuban skipper's credit, and because he was more contrary than anything else, he penciled us in.

Just to stick it in Marianao's ear, he penciled us into the 1-2-3 spots in the order.

The game started around three in the afternoon. It was one of the worst hangovers I'd ever had. I walked out into the Cuban sun, the first to carry the hopes of Cienfuegos and America to the plate, and decided that as a punishment I'd been struck blind. The crowd chanted, "The Elephant passes slowly, but it squashes." I struck out, though I have only the umpire's say-so on that.

Charley struck out too. Back on the bench he squinted like someone looking into car headlights. "It was a good pitch," he said. "I mean it sounded like a good pitch. I didn't see it."

But Ericksson, champion of clean living, stroked one out. It put the lid on some of the celebrating in the stands. We were a little too hungover to go real crazy when he got back to the dugout, but I think he understood.

Everybody, in fact, was hitting but us. A couple guys behind Ericksson, including Rafa, put together some doubles, and we had a

3–0 lead which stood up all the way to the bottom of the inning, when Marianao batted around and through its lineup and our starter and went into the top of the second leading 6–3.

Our guys kept hitting, and so did their guys. At the end of seven we'd gone through four pitchers and Marianao five, Charley and I were regaining use of our limbs, and the score was Cuba 11, Land of the Free 9. We got another run on a passed ball. In the ninth we came up one run down with the sun setting in our eyes over the center-field fence and yours truly leading off. The crowd was howling like something I'd never heard before. Castro had everybody up on the third-base side and pointing at me. Their arms moved together like they were working some kind of hex. Marianao's pitcher—by now the sixth—was the forty-five-year-old fat guy who'd worked the day before. The bags under his eyes were bigger than mine. He snapped off three nasty curves, and I beat one into the ground and ran down the first-base line with the jeering following me the whole way.

He broke one off on Charley, too, and Charley grounded to first. The noise was solid, a wall. Everyone was waving Cuban flags.

I leaned close to Charley's ear in the dugout. "You gotta lay off those," I said.

"I never noticed anything wrong with my ability to pull the ball on an outside pitch," he said.

"Then you're the only one in Cuba who hasn't," I said.

But in the middle of this local party with two strikes on him Ericksson hit his second dinger, probably the first time he'd had two in a game since Pony League. He took his time on his home-run trot, all slimmed-down two-hundred-sixty pounds of him, and at the end he did a somersault and landed on home plate with both feet.

For the Marianao crowd it was like the Marines had landed. When the ball left his bat the crowd noise got higher and higher pitched and then just stopped and strangled. You could hear Ericksson breathing hard as he came back to the bench. You could hear the pop of the umpire's new ball in the pitcher's glove.

"The Elephant passes slowly, but it squashes," Charley sang, from his end of the bench.

That sent us into extra innings, a lot of extra innings. It got dark. Nobody scored. Charley struck out with the bases loaded in the sixteenth, and when he came back to the bench someone had poured beer on the dugout roof and it was dripping through onto his head. He sat there under it. He said, "I deserve it," and I said, "Yes, you do."

The Marianao skipper overmanaged and ran out of pitchers. He had an outfielder come in and fling a few, and the poor guy walked our eighth and ninth hitters with pitches in the dirt, off the backstop, into the seats. I was up. There was a conference on the mound that included some fans and a vendor. Then there was a roar, and I followed everyone's eyes and saw Castro up and moving through the seats to the field. Someone threw him a glove.

He crossed to the mound, and the Marianao skipper watched him come and then handed him the ball when he got there like his relief ace had just come in from the pen. Castro took the outfielder's hat for himself, but that was about it for a uniform. The tails of his pleated shirt hung out. His pants looked like Rudolph Valentino's. He was wearing dress shoes.

I turned to the ump. "Is this an exhibition at this point?" I said. He said something in Spanish that I assumed was "You're in a world of trouble now."

The crowd, which had screamed itself out hours ago, got its second wind. Hurricanes, dust devils, sandstorms in the Sahara—I don't know what the sound was like. When you opened your mouth it came and took your words away.

I looked over at Batista, who was sitting on his hands. How long was this guy going to last if he couldn't even police the national pastime?

Castro toed the rubber, worked the ball in his hand, and stared at me like he hated everyone I'd ever been associated with.

He was right-handed. He fussed with his cap. He had a windmill delivery. I figured, Let him have his fun, and he wound up and cut loose with a fastball behind my head.

The crowd reacted like he'd struck me out. I got out of the dirt and did the pro brush-off, taking time with all parts of my uniform. Then I stood in again, and he broke a pretty fair curve in by my knees, and down I went again.

What was I supposed to do? Take one for the team? Take one for the country? Get a hit, and never leave the stadium alive? He came back with his fastball high, and I thought, Enough of this, and tomahawked it foul. We glared at each other. He came back with a change-up—had this guy pitched somewhere, for somebody?—again way inside, and I thought, Forget it, and took it on the hip. The umpire waved me to first, and the crowd screamed about it like we were cheating.

I stood on first. The bases were now loaded for Charley. You could see the Marianao skipper wanted Castro off the mound, but what could he do?

Charley steps to the plate, and it's like the fans had been holding back on the real noisemaking up to this point. There are trumpets, cowbells, police whistles, sirens, and the godawful noise of someone by the foul pole banging two frying pans together. The attention seems to unnerve Charley. I'm trying to give him the old thumbs-up from first, but he's locked in on Castro, frozen in his stance. The end of his bat's making little circles in the air. Castro gave it the old windmill and whipped a curve past his chin. Charley bailed out and stood in again. The next pitch was a curve, too, which fooled him completely. He'd been waiting on the fastball. He started to swing, realized it was a curve breaking in on him, and ducked away to save his life. The ball hit his bat anyway. It dribbled out toward Castro. Charley gaped at it and then took off for first. I took off for second. The crowd shrieked. Ten thousand people, one shriek. All Castro had to do was gun it to first and they were out of the inning. He threw it into right field.

Pandemonium. Our eighth and ninth hitters scored. The ball skipped away from the right fielder. I kept running. The catcher'd gone down to first to back up the throw. I rounded third like Man o' War, Charley not far behind me, the fans spilling out onto the field and coming at us like a wave we were beating to shore. One kid's face was a flash of spite under a Yankee hat. A woman with long scars on her neck was grabbing for my arm. And there was Castro blocking the plate, dress shoes wide apart, Valentino pants crouched and ready, his face scared and full of hate like I was the entire North American continent bearing down on him.

KRAKATAU

I was twelve years old when I figured out that the look my brother would get around his eyes probably meant that there was a physiological basis for what was wrong with him. Six years later as a college freshman I was flipping through Gardner's *Art Through the Ages,* fifth edition, and was shocked to come across that same look, Donnie's eyes, peering out at me from Géricault's *Madwoman.* The madwoman in question was elderly, wrapped in some kind of cloak. She wore a white bonnet. Her eyes looked away from the painter as if just piecing together the outlines of another conspiracy. She'd outsmarted the world, and was going to outsmart this painter. I recognized the hatred, the sheer animosity for *everything,* unconcealed. Red lines rimmed her eyelids in a way that did not resemble eyestrain or fatigue. It was as if the mind behind the eyes was soaking in anguish. The next morning my Intro to Art History professor flashed a slide of the painting, ten feet wide, on the screen in front of us. A gum-chewing class went silent. "How'd you like to wake up to that in the morning?" the professor joked.

That night I called my father. He and my mother and Donnie still lived in the house Donnie and I grew up in, two hours away. I was in the little public phone booth in the dorm. It was lined with cork, and the cork was scribbled over with phone numbers and ballpoint drawings of dicks.

Donnie answered. “How ya doin’,” he said.

“I’m all right,” I said. “How about you?”

He snorted.

Some kid opened the door to the booth like I wasn’t in there and poked his head in. “Who *you* talkin’ to?” he said.

“No one,” I said. “Get outta here.”

The kid made a face and shut me back in.

“Who was that?” Donnie asked.

“Some asshole,” I said. I didn’t say anything else. Donnie sniffed in like he was doing a line of something.

“You wanna talk to Daddy?” he said. He was four years older but he still used words like that.

“Yeah, put him on,” I said. You couldn’t talk to him for five minutes? I thought to myself.

He put his hand over the receiver. Things went on on the other end, muffled. “Hey there,” my father finally said.

“Hey,” I said back. There was some dead air.

“What’s up?” my father said.

“Not much,” I said. I’d planned on my father being alone. I don’t know why. My brother never went out. “Just callin’.”

I was rubbing my knuckles hard over the cork next to the phone’s coin box. Pieces were scrolling off as if from an eraser. “How’s the money holding out?” my father said. Donnie made a comment behind him.

“Is he standing right next to you?” I asked.

“Yeah. Why?” my father said, instantly more alert. When I was little and I wanted his attention, I just mentioned a problem with Donnie. By college it had gotten to the point that hashing over worries about my brother was pretty much it in terms of contact with my parents.

"I wanted to ask you something," I said.

"Is there something I should know about?" he said. Donnie was always doing things that we kept from him because he got so upset.

"Nothin' big. Maybe I should call back," I said.

"Awright. I'll see you," he said. It was a code we'd worked before.

"Short call," I heard Donnie say before my father hung up.

WHEN MY FATHER called back, we went over the physiological thing again. I'd run this by him before. We thought drug therapy might be a possible way out.

I could see the blowups coming in Donnie's eyes. I could see the redness. And I usually didn't stop whatever I was doing to help them come on.

THE PROBLEM was that Donnie had had drug therapy, back in the Dawn of Time, in 1969. Who knew anything? Various combinations of doctors tried various combinations of drugs. Most of the drugs had humiliating side effects. My brother became a master at lying to the doctors about what he'd taken and what he'd squirreled away, further confusing the issue. He came out eight months later as one of the Yale–New Haven Institute's complete failures—"We throw up our hands with him," the resident told my parents—and with a loathing even for Bufferin.

"IN GÉRICAULT'S PAINTINGS, suffering and death, battle frenzy, and madness amount to nature itself, for nature in the end is formless and destructive."

But really: how helpful are we going to find art history prose as an interpretive model?

• • •

WE CALLED THE POLICE six times on him. After high school I was home only a few weeks a year—the World Traveler, my father called me, caustically—yet I'd been home four of the six times we had to call the police. My father mentioned the coincidence.

WHILE MY BROTHER was in a holding pen in New Orleans I received my B.S. from Swarthmore in geological engineering. While he was touring youth hostels on the East Coast on my father's dole, keeping to himself, a dour man in his late twenties surrounded by happy groups of much younger Europeans, I was getting my Ph.D. in geology from Johns Hopkins. He had a scramble of fine black hair that he almost never combed. He wore pastel polyester tank tops long after even Kmart shoppers had abandoned them. He had a little gut which he accentuated by tucking in his shirts and wearing too-tight pants without belts. While he was giving night school a shot in Florida I was mapping the geology of Mount Rainier. The fall he spent going through his old things at my parents' house and getting his baseball card collection sorted out, I spent crawling around ancient volcanoes in equatorial East Africa. The third time my parents had to call the police on him, I was in a little boat in the Sunda Strait, getting my first look at Krakatau.

WHAT WERE MY PARENTS supposed to do? They never went to college, and just wanted their sons comfortable and reasonably happy. A steady job in a stable business would have been nice. Instead, one son disappeared into the academic ionosphere: I had to literally write down *postdoctoral fellow* so my mother could pull it out of her wallet and say it for people. She asked me to. They had a copy of

Volcanoes of the World around the house, with my name listed among the fourteen junior authors contributing. My mother would say, "Here's his book." And their older son dropped out of high school because, as he put it, he was "being stared at." If I was hard to explain, my brother was impossible to explain. For relatives, the etiquette was to ask about the younger one and then move on to the older one. I was never around and always doing well. He was always around and never doing well. Yes, doctors had seen him, and yes, he was clearly disturbed, but no one had a diagnosis, and as far as their ability to present him as a coherent story went, he operated in that maddening middle ground: too disturbed to function and not disturbed enough to be put away.

THE FIRST TIME we called the police because he threw me down the stairs. I was twelve, and he'd dropped out of high school the month before. We'd been arguing about sports, matching feats of memory by reciting NFL championship scores ("1963, 14–10; 1964, 27–0; 1965, 23–13"), and he'd heard the contempt in my voice. He'd been livid, and my father's mediation attempts had consisted of stepping between us and shouting for my brother to go upstairs. He had, finally, shouting abuse the whole time about my privileged and protected status, and for once I thought I wasn't going to back down and went up after him, as homicidal as he was. At the top of the stairs I jabbed a finger in his chest. Shouting was going on. I watched his face move into some new area of energy. He lifted me up. My feet kicked above the risers like a toddler's, and then he threw me. I caught the banister with my hands and landed on my elbow and side. The stairs were carpeted. I got up, unhurt. "Play with pain," he shouted down the stairs at me. "Play with pain."

"You're gonna kill them both," I screamed up at him, pulling out the ultimate weapon, his guilt. I said it so they could hear. "They're gonna kill *me,*" he screamed back.

MY MOTHER, FATHER, AND I sat around the kitchen table after the police had taken him away. The policeman had been awkward and embarrassed and stood around Donnie's room while Donnie packed a little blue duffel in silence. We could hear the creaks in the floorboards above us as the policeman shifted his weight from foot to foot. The routine was that the police would drive him to the bus station and tell him he couldn't come back for a while. Then the police would come back and talk to us. While we waited for that, my mother would outline the fatal mistakes my father had made raising my brother.

We were three coconspirators each operating with a different plan. My mother's theory was that special treatment was his undoing. My father's theory was that explosions could be avoided if everyone did their utmost to work around him. My theory was that something cyclical and inexorable was going on, and that one way or another, sooner or later, he had to go off.

THAT NIGHT my father had taken as much abuse as he was able to. He shouted at both of us, "You can't treat him like a normal human being; you can't keep baiting him." He said, "It's like having a dog on a chain. You don't keep sticking fingers in his mouth." Then he said to me, "And your situation doesn't help."

WHAT MY FATHER MEANT was that just by being alive I made my brother's life harder. In Donnie's eyes I was proof that whatever had happened to him—genetically, environmentally, whatever—hadn't been inevitable. One of his consolations had always been that something in the alchemy of the parenting he'd received had been so lethal that he had had to turn out the way he did. But I was the problem with that theory, because if that was true, then why wasn't the kid (he called me the kid) affected?

Whatever I achieved threw the mess he'd made of his life into sharper relief. He went to Catholic school and it ruined him; I went to Catholic school and got good grades. He was always shy and turned out to need hospitalization; I was always shy and turned out to be bookish.

At one point in Pompano Beach, he took a job as a dishwasher at a Bob's Big Boy. My mother's first response when she heard was to congratulate him. Her second was to remark that she thought they had machines for that now. That same day he went into work and the day manager was chatting him up. The day manager asked if he had any brothers or sisters. The day manager asked what his brother did. "He's a rocket scientist," Donnie said, up to his elbows in suds, thirty-eight years old.

MY THESIS ADVISER at Johns Hopkins always ate Fudgsicles while he looked over my work. All the charts and text he handled turned up with chocolate thumbprints. Slurping away, flipping through the data, he liked to ask, "What is it with you and Krakatoa, anyway?" He meant why was I so driven. He intentionally pronounced it the wrong way. He liked to think of himself as puckish.

The founder of the Smithsonian, James Smithson, explained his institute's interest in the subject this way: "A high interest attaches itself to volcanoes, and their ejections. They cease to be local phenomena; they become principal elements in the history of our globe; they connect its present with its former condition; and we have good grounds for supposing that in their flames are to be read its future destinies."

I quoted Smithson to my adviser as an answer. He shrugged and took out his Fudgsicle and said, "You can talk to someone like me now or talk to a shrink later."

PICTURES CAME INTO MY HEAD periodically of what my brother must have gone through, on the road. He told me, occasionally, as well. When he traveled the country, he stayed at youth hostels because they were so much cheaper, but he paid a price for it: he was pathological about his privacy, and there he had none. In Maine an older woman asked him about his hair. It was falling out. At Gettysburg some teenaged Germans took him out, got him drunk, and asked if he was attracted to one of the prettier girls in the group. Assuming that some sort of positive sexual fantasy was finally about to happen to him, he said yes, at which point they all laughed. He said he woke up the next morning near the site of Pickett's charge. A middle-aged couple with a video camera stood nearby, filming him alongside the stone wall.

THE LAST TIME I was home he was on the road. We'd timed it that way. I spent one late night going through a family album that my mother was putting together in a spasm of masochism and love. Looking back over pictures of my brother developing year by year, his expressions progressively more closed off and miserable, brought back to me powerfully the first time I saw the sequence of photos tracking the birth of Paricutin, the Mexican volcano that grew from a tiny vent cone in a farmer's field.

THE POSTDOCTORAL FELLOWSHIP involved part-time work for SEAN, the Scientific Event Alert Network, which was designed to keep the geological and geophysical communities in touch about active volcanoes throughout the world. I compiled and cross-referenced known data about older eruptions so that it could be manipulated for studies of recent and expected volcanism. Which was where all my work on Krakatau came in.

My thesis adviser had been the first to point out that I'd developed what people in the field call a bias. I had a heightened appreciation for the value of eyewitness accounts. I always leaned toward the catastrophists' viewpoint, that while the ordinary eruptions needed to be documented, the complete cataclysms had the real answers; they were the ones that had to be milked for all they could yield. "What do we have here?" my adviser would say wearily as he picked up another new batch of text. "More screamers?" "Screamer" was his term for Krakatau eyewitnesses. He called their rough calculations, made under what geologists would laconically call stressful situations, "Fay Wray calculations."

AND YET, OFTEN enough for me, working backward from a dispassionate scientific measurement—the tidal gauges at Jakarta, say—I'd be able to corroborate one more eyewitness account.

IN MY DUMPY carrel at the Grad Library I had narrowed the actual subject of my thesis down to the precise causes of the Krakatau tsunamis that swamped Java and Sumatra. This was a reasonably controversial topic. There were all sorts of wave-forming mechanisms, all of which could have operated to some extent at Krakatau. The problem was to understand which mechanism was the dominant one. The expectation was not so much that I would find a solution to the problem as add something intelligent to the debate.

The first two years I worked eighteen-plus hours a day. I never got home, almost never talked to my family. Crises came and went;

what did I care? I combed everything: the Library of Congress, the National Archives, the U.S. Geological Survey, the Smithsonian Library, the British Museum, the Royal Society of London, the Royal Institute for the Tropics, the Volcanological Survey of Indonesia, the *Bulletin Volcanologique.* I needed more help than anyone else on earth. And I turned out to possess the height of scientific naïveté. I believed everyone I read. Everyone sounded so reasonable. Everyone's figures looked so unassailable. I was a straw in the wind. I labored through Verbeek's original monograph from 1885 as well as later papers by Wharton, Yokoyama, and Latter. At one point my adviser told me with exasperation, "Hey, know what? It's not likely that everyone's right." I incorporated this into my text. I wrote, "Nevertheless, it is safe to assume that all of these contradictory theories cannot be accurate."

I uncovered a few things. I turned up a few photographs of the devastation from as early as 1886. I tracked down some math errors in the computations of the airwaves. Then, in 1983, the centennial year of the eruption, everything I'd done was surpassed, the dugout canoe swamped by the *Queen Mary*: the Smithsonian published *Krakatau 1883: The Volcanic Eruption and Its Effects,* providing me with 456 phone-book-sized pages to pore over. It would have been my fantasy book, if I hadn't already sunk two years into a thesis.

EVERYTHING HAD TO BE RETOOLED. My new topic became this baggy, reactive thing that just got me through, something along the lines of This Big New Book: Is It Almost Completely the Last Word? The answer was yes.

I had a Career Crisis. My personal hygiene suffered. I stared openmouthed out windows. I sat around inert most mornings, working my way through tepid coffee and caramels for breakfast. I faced for the first time the stunning possibility that everything I touched was not going to turn to gold.

My mother called to see how I was doing. I put on a brave front. She called back the next day and said, "I told your brother you weren't doing so well."

"What'd he say?" I asked.

"Nothing," she said.

"I'm worried I'm gonna end up like him," I joked.

We heard a click on the line. "Uh-oh," my mother said.

A WEEK LATER my brother sent me *Krakatoa: East of Java.* He'd taped it off a Disaster Film Festival and mailed it in a box wrapped in all directions with duct tape. Maximilian Schell, Rossano Brazzi, Brian Keith: that kind of movie. What my brother remembered was that the second half of the film—the eruption itself, and the tidal waves that followed—was the really unendurable part, and always had been for me, ever since I sat through its sorry cheesiness with him when I was thirteen years old.

He didn't include a note with it, and he didn't have to: it was exactly his sense of humor, with the aggression directed everywhere at once.

Even my brother, in other words, had seen through the schematic of my private metaphor and knew the answer to my adviser's question: Why is he obsessed with volcanoes? Because they go off, regardless of what anyone can do. And because, when they do go off, it's no one's fault. Volcanology: the science of standing around and cataloging the devastation.

MY FATHER DISCOURAGED my brother from visiting me, wherever I was. He did it for my benefit, and my brother's. He was the Peacemaker, he thought; if he wasn't around, anything could happen. My brother didn't particularly enjoy visiting me—anything new in my life seemed to cause him to take stock of his—but he had few places to go. Occasionally he'd call, with my father in the room, and drop a hint. My father would hear the hint and intervene in the background. The excuse he always came up with—I was too busy, I had all this work, this was a bad time for me to be receiving visitors—could not have helped my brother. But if he wanted to keep us apart, what else could he say? My brother was too busy?

"This isn't the greatest time anyway," I'd say. "What about around Thanksgiving? What're you doing around Thanksgiving?"

Knowing full well that the tiniest lack of enthusiasm would destroy whatever chance there was that he'd work up the courage to visit.

DONNIE WAS SIXTEEN when we went through family counseling. He'd been out of high school two months, and had had three jobs: landscaping, freight handling for UPS, and working construction. The construction work was for an uncle who owned a company. We'd had our first incident involving the police. That was how my father referred to it. I was twelve. I had relatively little to do during the sessions. I conceived of the time as an opportunity to prove to this psychiatrist that it wasn't all my parents' fault, what had happened. I acted normal.

Donnie called my father the Mediator. The shrink asked what he meant by that. Donnie said, "Mediator. You know. Zookeeper. What the fuck." It was the "What the fuck" that broke my heart.

EVEN THEN I had a mouth on me, as my mother would say. Christmas Eve we watched the Roddy McDowall/David Hartman version of *Miracle on 34th Street,* a version my brother hadn't seen but insisted was the best one. It was on for four minutes before it was clear to everyone in the room that it was terrible. Which made my brother all the more adamant in his position. The holidays were hard on him. We'd given up on the family counseling a few weeks before, as if to get ready for Christmas.

In the movie Sebastian Cabot did a lot of eye-twinkle stuff, whatever the situation. I made relentless fun of it. I mimicked Cabot's accent and asked if Santa came from England, stuff like that. I was rolling. Even my father was snickering. Roddy McDowall launched into something on the Spirit of Christmas and I said it sounded like he was more interested in getting to know some of the elves. Donnie took the footstool in front of him and smashed the TV tube. That was the second time we had to call the police.

They took him to the Bridgeport bus station, 8:30 at night on Christmas Eve. The two cops who came to the house wanted to leave him with us, but he wouldn't calm down. One cop told him, "If you don't lighten up we're gonna have to get you out of here and *keep* you out of here," so Donnie started in on what he was going to do to each one of us as soon as the cop took off: "First I'm gonna break *his* fucking neck, and then *her* fucking neck, and then *his* fucking neck." Stuff like that. It was raining, and when they led him out, he had on a New York Jets windbreaker and no hat.

My father drove down to the bus station a half hour later to see if he was still there. The roads were frozen and it took him an hour to get back. My mother vacuumed up the glass from the picture tube. Then she sat in her bedroom with the little TV, flipping back and forth from *A Christmas Carol* to the Mass at St. Peter's.

When my father got back he made some tea and wandered the house. I remembered the nuns talking about the capacities of Christ's love and thought, What kind of reptile *are* you? I was filled with wonder at myself.

I finally went to midnight Mass, alone. My mother just waved me off when I asked if she wanted to go. I found myself once I got there running through a fractured catechism, over and over:—Who loves us?—We love us.—Who does this to us?—We do this to ourselves.—Whose victims are we?—We are our own victims.

THE NEXT MORNING I was supposed to come downstairs and open presents.

Around noon we gathered in front of the tree with our coffee. I suppose we were hoping Donnie was going to come back. I opened the smallest present in my pile, a Minnesota Viking coffee mug, and said, "That's great, thanks," and my parents' faces were so desolate that we quit right there.

He called from the bus station on the twenty-seventh. He opened one or two of his presents a week after that. The rest stayed where they were even after the tree came down. Some of them my mother gave, the next year, to our cousins. We never put tags on our presents; we just told each other who they belonged to.

THE THIRD TIME they had to call the police I was fourteen thousand miles away, fulfilling my dream, standing on what was left of Krakatau. I brought back pieces of pumice for everybody. Donnie had called my mother's sisters whores, and she'd slapped him, and he'd knocked her to the kitchen floor. When he was going full tilt he tried everything verbally until something clicked. He was thirty-four then and she was sixty. My father left his eggs frying at the stove and started wrestling with him. He was sixty-three. My brother let him wrestle.

• • •

FROM PAGE FIVE of my thesis: "Early theories explaining the size of the Krakatau explosion held that millions of tons of rock had unfortunately formed a kind of plug, so that pressure-relieving venting was not allowed, making the final detonations all the more cataclysmic. But in fact the opposite might also have been true: gas fluxing of the conduits and the release of pressure through massive cracks may have hastened the catastrophe, since once the vents were opened, the eruption might have grown, as deeper and hotter layers of magma were tapped, leading to the exhaustion of the reservoir, and following that, the collapse of its roof."

My adviser had written in the margin: "Anything new here?"

I HAD THREE REASONS for my own passivity: selfishness, cowardice, and resentment.

AS DONNIE GOT OLDER the anger inside him was not decreasing but increasing. His rage was driven by humiliation, and year by year he felt his situation—forty-one and living at home, unemployed, forty-two and living at home, unemployed—to be more and more humiliating. The friends-and-family question, "So what are you up to?"—fraught when he was eighteen—was, when he was forty, suffused with subtextual insult. His violence was more serious. His threats were more pointed. He defined himself more and more as a misfit, and more and more he seemed to think that the gesture that was going to be necessary to redeem such a life, with each passing day, needed to be grander, more radical.

HE WAS FORTY-TWO. I was thirty-eight, two hours away, mostly out of contact, and all of my failures with him were focused in one weekend that summer, when, despite everything, he visited. We spent two days circling each other, watching sports and old movies and making fun of what we saw. His last night there he told me about some of his fantasies. One of them ended with, "They'd *think* they knew what happened, but how could they *prove* it? How could they *prove* anything?" My stomach dropped out.

It was late. I'd turned off the TV. I could see his eyes in the dark.

"Listen," I said. "You've gotta see somebody."

"Don't you think I know that?" he said.

AFTER TWO LATE MOVIES he fell asleep facedown on the sofa. I went to my office and called Psychological Services at the university. The guy on call gave me a referral number.

"I don't think you understand," I told him. "This isn't a kind of wait-and-see situation."

"Are you saying he should be picked up, for his own good?" the guy said. There was a buzzing on the line while he waited for my answer.

"No," I said.

THE NEXT MORNING my brother was leaving. I stood by my parents' car while he settled into the driver's seat. I told him I had the name of a guy he should talk to. "Thanks," he said.

"You want the name?" I said.

"Sure," he said. I could see his eyes, see a blowup coming on again. This was excruciating for him.

I fumbled around in my pockets. "I don't have a pencil," I said. "You gonna remember?"

"Sure," he said. I told him the name. He nodded, put the car in gear, said good-bye, and backed out of the driveway.

• • •

I WARNED MY PARENTS. Which, I thought to myself, would help my conscience later.

WHY DIDN'T I HELP? Why did I stand aside, peering down the rails toward the future site of the train wreck? Because even if he didn't know it, all along, he was the lucky one. Because he was the black sheep, he was the squeaky wheel, he was the engine that generated love from my parents.

I KEPT HOPING that my worst feelings had been left behind in childhood, and that only analysis, diagnosis, remained.

Volcanoes, volcanoes, volcanoes. In a crucial way he didn't resemble volcanoes at all. Most volcanoes look like oceans. Because they're *under* oceans. Nothing happening for hundreds of years. Something destructive surfacing only very very rarely: who did that *really* sound like?

The first record of explosions came months early, May 20 at 10:55 A.M., when the director of the Observatory at Batavia, now Jakarta, noticed vibrations and the banging of loose windows in his house. Explosions brought lighter articles down from the shelves at Anjer. There was this homey little description from the captain of the German warship *Elisabeth,* in the Sunda Strait: "We saw from the island a white cumulus cloud rising fast. After half an hour, it reached a height of 11,000 m. and started to spread, like an umbrella." Or this, from the same ship's Marine chaplain, now seventeen nautical miles away: "It was convoluted like a giant coral stock, resembling a club or cauliflower head, except that everything was in imposing gigantic internal motion, driven by enormous pressure from beneath. Slowly it became clear that the top of the entire continuously growing phenomenon was beginning to lean towards us."

OR THIS, from a telegraph master on the Java Coast: "I remained at the office the whole morning and then went for a meal, intending to return at two. I met another man near the beach, and we remained there for a few minutes. Krakatau was already in eruption, and we plainly heard the rumbling in the distance. I observed an alternate rising and falling of the sea, and asked my companion whether the tide was ebbing or flowing. He remarked that it seemed to be getting unusually dark."

OR THIS, from the captain of the Irish steamer *Charles Bal*: "At 2:30 we noticed some agitation about the point of Krakatau, clouds or something being propelled from the NE point with great velocity. At 3:00 we heard all around and above us the sounds of a mighty artillery barrage, getting evermore furious and alarming; and the matter, whatever it was, was being propelled with even more velocity to the NE. It looked like a blinding rain, a furious moiling squall. By 4:00 the explosions had joined to form a continuous roar, and darkness had spread across the sky."

AND HERE'S what I imagine, from the eyewitnesses who spent those last minutes standing around with their hands in their pockets on the Java Coast and Sumatra, from Lampong Bay to Sebesi and all the other islands in the strait:

Some made out an enormous wave in the distance like a mountain rushing onward, followed by others that seemed greater still.

Some made out a dark black object rising through the gloom, traveling toward the shore like a low range of hills, but they knew there were no hills in that part of the strait.

Some made out a dark line swelling the curve of the horizon, thickening as they watched.

Some heard the roar of the first wave, and the cry, "A flood is coming."

Some heard the rushing wind driven before the immense dark wall.

Some heard a whipsawing noise and saw the great black thing a long way off, a cliff of water, trees and houses disappearing beneath it. They felt it through the earth as they ran for sloping ground. They made for the steepest ravines. There was a great crush. Those below climbed the backs of those above. The marks where this took place are still visible. Some of those who washed off must have dragged others down with them. Some must have felt those above giving way, and let go.

But this is the only account hand-copied and tacked to my bulletin board, the testimony of a Dutch pilot caught on shore near Anjer, a city now gone: "The moment of greatest anguish was not the actual destruction of the wave. The worst part by far was afterwards, when I knew I was saved, and the receding flood carried back past me the bodies of friends and neighbors and family. And I remembered clawing past other arms and legs as you might fight through a bramble. And I thought, 'The world is our relentless adversary, rarely outwitted, never tiring.' And I thought, 'I would give all these people's lives, once more, to see something so beautiful again.'"

WON'T GET FOOLED AGAIN

We were the great group for things going wrong. Cancellations, electrical failures, bad weather, broken-down vans, missed dates, slashed thumbs, broken noses, sprained knees, bugger-all equipment, beggary, rookery, penury, and out-and-out thuggery: all just a part of that tag-along high-speed death march that called itself The Detours/The High Numbers/The Who.

We'd come on with sticking plasters, bleeding. We had fistfights onstage. Every five minutes someone was quitting the band.

For the first fifteen years we owed money because of everything we smashed up, and everything we needed. From the beginning we traveled with a small bungalow's worth of Marshall cabinets and amps, and four or five Rickenbackers for Pete, and always a triple kit of red sparkle Premier drums with a big crate of spare skins and sticks besides, because our drummer was the most physically destructive mild-mannered middle-class boy in the Western Hemisphere.

By 1965 we had the world's loudest gear onstage, and we'd scream like victims of the Inquisition and not hear our voices. Staying in key was an act of faith. It was like when you listened to something with earphones and sang along out of tune because there was no way to tell. We always had someone in the house who could signal us visually as to how we were doing. More than once Keith and I got a few bars into one song and realized that Pete and Roger were having a go at another.

In pubs and rooming houses we were the Little Hooligans' Circus, because there all we had was each other, and we hated each other. With Moonie it was always, "A bottle of brandy!" and when it came along, "Fuck me, I've fucking knocked it over! Let's have another, all right, hey? Fucking brandy, eh?" and he'd pour some on Roger and Roger'd knock him on his Middlesex behind. One night Roger went for some of his chips and Keith stuck a fork in his hand.

ALL SCHEDULES disintegrated. All alliances were temporary. Eventually our manager, who was equal parts long-suffering and insufferable, negotiated a truce. A certain amount of pride had to be swallowed on each side. We promised to behave and Roger promised not to hit us.

FIGHTS WITH the paying customers started from all sorts of things, usually after we came offstage. They didn't last long. Roger only had to punch you once and that was it. A girl got knocked flat by a mike stand in one, and we were all hauled in front of a magistrate.

Keith would go up to anyone around the bandstand and say, "Have you got anything in the upward direction, hey?" At Reading he gulped down some poor sod's purple hearts—twenty-four of them—at once. The guy complained to me afterward that he'd planned them to last three weeks.

We had this kid called Pill Brian who used to come down on his scooter to our shows. He'd come down and say, "I've got these today," and we'd take all of what he had. "This one's for rheumatism," he'd finally say, and Keith'd say, "Yeah, I'll have that."

We played night in, night out for cellars full of kids out of their brains and getting off on R&B. The unstable fell over in various directions and you'd see clearings appear in the packed-in heads. Strangers traded hand jobs along the walls while keeping track of the show. It was like Imperial Rome. When the clubs were raided it sounded like hailstorms when everyone emptied the pills from their pockets onto the dance floor. The cops went round frisking people, and it was like they were walking on gravel: *crunch crunch crunch.*

POOR ROGER couldn't do the pills because of his voice, and because he drove the van. So he'd be stuck stone sober driving this bunch of pilled-up louts about. He hated it.

WHEN PETE FIRST STARTED writing, his songs were other people's songs badly remembered. He was knocked out by the Kinks' "You Really Got Me" when he first heard it, and went home and tried to remember it and couldn't, and came up with "I Can't Explain" instead.

Ours was a weird kind of enraged, what's-the-use protest rock. "My Generation" was a song that said, "We don't have to be shit because you say we're shit. We can be shit because *we* say we're shit."

I WAS THE LEAST POPULAR one, the immobile one onstage, stolid Johnny. Fans called me The Ox. I had much to be quiet about. I was hopeless for Keith's girlfriend, Kim. I'd met her ten minutes after he had. She was sweet to me, nothing more. I hung about and watched her cook. I rubbed myself against banisters and gateposts after she'd gone by.

"You're a mate," Keith'd say to me when I'd offer to phone her, let her know he'd be back late or not at all.

"Oh, *shit,*" she'd always say, and even that was worth hearing.

Pete and I knew about unrequited longing. As a boy I had nothing going for me, and Pete was a nose on a stick.

He grew up with parents who came out of the end of the war with big ideas and left him behind. We met in school, when we were eleven: I remember this willow switch with a wicked great hooter behind me in line sneering, "Entwhistle: what kind of posh name is that?"

We spent all our time ducking school at his house since no one was there. He didn't have much music at home except his Dad honking away on a clarinet in the back room. They didn't have much of a record player and they had Chiswick's shittiest radio. He had a strange relationship with his mother. She was beautiful and his Dad was good-looking so who knew what they made of him. He always said, "I fail to interest them." He was very self-pitying, even then.

His parents split and left him with his grandmother, who was insane. She walked naked in the streets and things like that. He said his first musical experience was in the Sea Scouts, on a boat ride. A brutal summer day and he was lying in the gunwale sweltering and dropping in and out of heatstroke while the outboard motor kept making these funny noises. The *noises,* he said, got inside his skull and took it over while he lay there in his swoon. By the time he'd gone up the river and back again, he'd had to be carried out of the boat. He'd been so transported by the sound.

After *Tommy* came out he said to a BBC interviewer, "Where did '*See me, feel me, touch me*' come from? It came from a four-and-a-half-year-old in a fucking unlocked bedroom in a house with a madwoman. *That's* where it came from."

• • •

WE MET ROGER when we were thirteen. He beat up a friend of ours and Pete shouted that he was a dirty fighter because he'd kicked the boy when he was down. Roger came over to us and said, "Who called me a dirty fighter?" And Pete said, "*I* didn't." And Roger said, "Yes you did." And he took off his belt and whipped Pete across the face with the buckle. We should've taken it as a sign.

Every time he came up to us in the corridor at school we thought, "Oh my God, what's he going to do now?" He was a horrible, horrible boy. A real kind of spiv. And then one day he stopped us and said, "I hear you play the guitar."

He was the balls of the band when we started out. He ran things the way he wanted. If you argued with him you got a bunch of fives.

He was a shit singer at first, but nobody needed a singer in those days anyway. What was needed was somebody who could fight, and that was Roger.

We listened to records and copied what we could. We rehearsed together in the front room of Pete's house. He had a good guitar that he'd paid for himself with a paper route. Our rehearsals never went well. None of us had much talent. A month or so of that and his grandmother came in shouting, "Turn that bloody racket down!" And Pete said, "I'll do better than that," and smashed his guitar against the wall. A hideous big cuckoo clock pitched from a nail from the impact. He bashed it to smithereens with the remnants of his guitar while we stood there. The little wooden cuckoo ended up atop my foot. He said, "Now will you *fucking get out of my life*?" and she stomped out.

The three of us stood about looking at the wreckage, and Roger said, "What now?" When Pete didn't answer, I said, "Another paper route, I think."

Someone at Philips offered a record deal if we dropped our drummer, because he was too old: thirty-six. Keith was there and said, "I can do better than him." At his audition he broke the drum pedal and high hat and put a hole in the skin. "I'm hired, aren't I?"

he asked when he finished, and saw us all looking at him. We met Kim a year later in the Disc A Go Go in Bournemouth.

Nights he wasn't home I phoned her, but couldn't bring myself to speak. *"Oooohhh,"* I'd say, holding the receiver to my chest. *"Owwwwww. Uuunnnrrh."*

"Sod off," she'd say, after a moment, and hang up.

NO ONE REMEMBERS where the name came from. Maybe a guy who'd been a friend of Pete's. *The Who:* it made people think twice, and worked well on posters because it was so short and printed up big.

PETE'S NORMAL STATE when awake was also frustration, and back then it was particularly hard. There were a lot of brilliant young players around. Beck was around; Roger first saw him in a band called the Triads or the Tridents or something and came back and said there was this incredible young guitar player. Clapton was around. Page. So Pete was morose that he couldn't manage all that flash stuff. So he just started getting into feedback. And he expressed himself—as he put it—physically. I always thought of it as making up visually for what he couldn't play. He got the windmill bit from watching Keith Richards warm up backstage.

CHARLIE WATTS said that the first time he came to hear us, he looked at our drummer and thought, *My God, that guy's not doing the same number.* All those mad fills. Then he realized that our Keith had left the backbeat behind. Charlie'd been sitting there going, "This is rubbish," until it hit him that Keith was another lead instrument. One night at a club, everyone else passed out, Charlie said, "It's exhilarating hearing you lot trash numbers everyone else does so faithfully." I don't think I ever told the rest of the band. If you couldn't stay awake, you missed praise from the Rolling Stones: that's the way I looked at it.

FROM THE BEGINNING, we had just these massive, massive amps. People came just to see *them.* One atop another on both sides of us, like an ogre's steamer trunks. At small clubs Pete had to turn some sideways to fit them all onstage. People like the T-Bones, and Clapton and the Yardbirds, had only these little Vox AC30s. Doctors issued warnings about our concerts in the local papers. Word got around that outdoors at Croydon, we'd surpassed 120 decibels.

Even so, the big power chord sound that Pete got wasn't only his amps. He also used hugely thick strings, and hit them so hard that he shattered picks and tore the skin from his fingerprints. Really, the sound came from us playing as a three-piece band, but trying everything we could to sound like more. In any number, Keith or I might take over the lead while Pete bashed out the chords.

A journalist for the NME saw us on one of those Maximum R&B Tuesday night shows at the Marquee. He said we sounded like someone chainsawing a dustbin in half. It was one of our favorite notices.

OUR FIRST TIME on *Ready Steady Go!* the producers never knew what hit them. We took over the show by blocking anyone who wanted to get in who wasn't our sort. We nicked their tickets and filled the place with our audience, all mods. No one else could get past Roger. He shoved someone from BBC security who tried to intervene down two flights of stairs and the poor sod never came back. The Hollies, who were on before us, didn't know *what* was going on. They found themselves surrounded by all these step-dancing geeks all dressed alike. The geeks seemed to be singing our lyrics to Hollies songs. Then for our first number the director had the genius idea of putting Keith and his whole kit on a rostrum with wheels, and having everyone push it this way and that through the crowd. Pandemonium. Geeks were knocked hither and yon. The BBC's big old cameras could barely roll out of the way in time. Between numbers our crowd kept swaying and singing, like at a football match. You couldn't hear Roger announcing the next song. Mods then wore all these old college scarves and at the end they tossed them all onstage. The four of us just held our poses after the last note, festooned.

I WANTED MY SONGS to be like songs no one else was writing. My bandmates didn't agree on anything except the notion that my songs were inferior. Keith was the nicest about it. He said, "What do you give a toss what *we* think?"

But the truth was I was trying something different, dark, in a childrens' book sort of way. "Silas Stingy"; "Dr. Jekyll and Mr. Hyde." They weren't autobiographical; God knew, I wasn't one for *opening up*. What was I, a can of beans? Kids responded when the singles came out; kids loved "Boris the Spider." Keith and Roger came round a bit when they saw that, and we talked about releasing a kids' rock album, but it never happened. The songs all ended up as B-sides.

I wrote two about Kim, though nobody knew it: for a year or so our concerts always opened with one—"Heaven and Hell," about the perils of mortal misbehavior. Its position on the playlist didn't mean the group was any more enthusiastic about my writing. Everyone just thought it was a good song to tune up to. It featured a lot of open strings.

The other was "Smash Your Head Against the Wall."

• • •

OUR BIGGEST HITS involved Pete's mock-baroque bits, like the pseudo-flamenco thing he used to kick off "Pinball Wizard."

I always admired his handling of his songwriting. He said what he wanted to say and ignored or patronized our suggestions about ways he might improve. He told us during one depression, "I'm sulking because you don't worship me for making your lives financially viable."

A JOURNALIST doing a behind-the-scenes piece wrote long harrowing accounts about Keith and Roger and Pete, and then when it came to me, the article said only, "Entwhistle was never around—permanently asleep, apparently."

Oh, he was a miserable bastard, that John Entwhistle. Who else wrote horror songs for children? Dressed all in black and kept to himself and then moped about when people left him to his own devices? "Why haven't they come and coaxed me out?" he said to himself. Sold himself as his best friend's best friend when all he was thinking was, *He'll never know how lucky he is.* Angry about most things and frightened about everything. Guilty of all he saw in others, and maestro of a self-pity as vast and chilly as the North Sea—

THERE'S A CERTAIN *attack* a bass guitarist gets in his style when he's miserable. All great bass guitarists are miserable.

THE ROCK GODS did four things for us: they sent us Keith, kept me miserable, gave Roger his ego, and put the idea in Pete's head of writing for Roger as an alter-ego. Pete would no more expose himself directly than *I* would—his own family never really got to know him—but when it came to Roger, he got, in his songs, the braggadocio, the grandiosity, the aggression, the flash, the emptiness. We all kept waiting for Roger to go, "Hey, *wait* one minute . . ."

Pete wrote his best about characters he could see from the outside. When he got introspective, it turned into melodramatic dross. If you want my opinion.

By 1966 he was writing for Roger's voice—for those things in Roger that he thought he was lacking. He didn't have one of the most crucial things Roger had: that *conviction.* Which was why he was no good in fights. He also certainly didn't have Roger's magnetism. Or his looks. All he had was talent. He *hoped.* He was this angry nose with a guitar.

What he was trying to do was to get himself halfway to Roger, and drag Roger halfway to him. They resented the way they used each other, but they never stopped taking full advantage of it.

WHEN PEOPLE THOUGHT about The Who they thought about Pete and Keith, playing music and tearing into controlled substances as though they had only twenty-four hours to live. From the very first there were nights when they didn't remember who they were, walked offstage and into the audience, got into fights and got the daylights beat out of them. In Birmingham two security people were sent to hospital trying to protect them. By our first U.S. tour of '68, the only bandmember who *could* fight, Roger, would be sitting with me in the dressing room sipping carbonated water and wondering where they'd gone to.

I'd phone up Kim and let her know where Keith could be retrieved in the morning.

They'd married in March of 1966 at the registry office in Brent, in Middlesex. It rained the entire day. Our manager's idea was to keep the marriage a secret at the time.

They had a daughter, Mandy, that July.

He was a lunatic for the clubs, before and after Mandy. There were nights I worked through the playlist thinking this was the night I'd phone Kim and finally explain myself. I'd watch Pete pinoning around in his white boiler suit, Roger in his buckskin fringes swinging his mike like a lasso, Keith in his cartoon T-shirts, spinning and pinwheeling his drumsticks into the light—*Substitute: me for him; substitute: my coke for gin; substitute: you for my mom—at least I'll get my washing done*—and I'd funnel all motion into two hands, not moving my feet twelve inches the entire show, all in black so that I'd disappear even sometimes when lit.

ONSTAGE WE WERE the musical version of a row in a moving van. But what was the alternative? We were never one of those Serious bands, all dignity and sobriety and "minor sevenths" this and "atonal chord progression" that in interviews, that pillaged mediocre classical music and traveled with a Philharmonic in tow. We were a gang of louts you wouldn't trust round your back garden, never mind your mum's china. We were best booked into rough places. Anywhere else, we didn't fit in, and we weren't happy, anyway. We performed *Tommy* at the Metropolitan Opera House in New York, and Keith screamed over Pete's big finish, "It's like playing to a fucking *oil* painting—" And the crowd cheered, like it had been saluted.

ONE NIGHT in the rear of a club, lying on his back buried in Skol and Carlsberg bottles, Keith told me that every morning he went home, he and the missus smashed up the flat with fights. It was terrible for little Mandy. "What should I do?" he asked. I didn't say, *You can't go on like this,* or *Stop what you're doing, for fuck's sake.*

"She's a great woman," I managed instead. "She is, she *is,*" he agreed with a moan. In Tottenham he took a hammer to all nine pieces of his kit at the end of "Magic Bus." Roger threw his microphone off into the seats. Pete toppled a stack of amps and bounced his Rickenbacker on the debris. By that point if we waited too long to lose our tempers, we'd start to hear during the breaks, "Throw something! Smash something!"

Because what did that kind of music come down to, in the first place? What was the audience at a concert saying, if not, *You stand there so we can know ourselves*?

Of course, the crashing irony was that all of our songs had always been about pathetic little wimps: *Can you see the real me? Can you? Can you?* But we were *presenting* pathetic wimps with anthemic power: my hair-raisingly overamped bass, Keith's Hammer of Thor drumming, Roger's Valkyrie voice, Pete's power chords. At times I thought *Quadrophenia* was the best thing Wagner ever wrote. Here it was the story of a sad little mixed-up kid and every track on it sounded like a war cry, like something designed to terrorize the natives.

Rage in the service of self-pity was what we'd *always* been about. It was what *rock* had always been about.

I GOT MARRIED. A lovely woman, at the Acton Congregational Church, a year after Keith and Kim. I was going to be a homebody and not hang out and about anymore. It wasn't good for me.

Recently my wife turned up an old battered and juice-stained appointment book from 1970, and after a few pages I couldn't bear to read any more: 9/12, Munster, Germany, 9/13, Offenbach, Germany, 9/16, Rotterdam, Netherlands, 9/17, Amsterdam, Netherlands, 9/18, Rotterdam, Netherlands, 9/20, Copenhagen, Denmark, 9/21, Aarhus, Denmark . . .

• • •

IT WAS A MATTER of being bored with who we were, with being selfish fuck-ups each and every night and each and every gig. For all our arrogance. Keith took to traveling with a hatchet and chopping hotel rooms to bits: televisions, chairs, dressers, cupboard doors, beds: the lot of it.

His version of himself was Moonie the amiable idiot, the genial twit, the victim of his own practical jokes. He broke his collarbone, knocked out his front teeth, gave himself three or four concussions. But he was only playing the same game as the rest of us. Look at photographs of us next to Roger: it's like three frightening goons with Jesus of Nazareth. During a backstage squabble, Pete shouted, "I don't know who's worse: Mr. God's Gift to Hammersmith or the rest of us with our Self-Hatred badges."

"I vote for the Wooden Indian," Keith called from the floor. He liked calling me the Wooden Indian when he was in his cups.

"I've done it again, haven't I, Wooden Indian?" he'd say in those wee hours when he was back in Kim's shithouse. She finally moved out, though she kept track of him through friends. I finally phoned. We chatted and I didn't even mention if she needed anything, etc. I phoned back a few weeks later and she was out. She went on holiday. The holiday extended itself. Years trooped up my chest and down again. Round about this time, Pete helped his friend Eric Clapton take the great love of his life, Patti Harrison, away from her husband, George. I didn't talk to him for a month. About the same as George.

"YOU LOVE ME or not, Ox?" Moonie would say when he'd been the cause of particular unpleasantness: when there was a mess to be cleaned, or so forth. So when he died, why would we have done the right thing? Why would we have acted adequately? When had we acted adequately our entire lives?

He came apart step-by-step, over years. Cry for help? He started *his* when he was ten. The man broke his wife's nose with his head. He burst into tears at stoplights. He was arrested for disorderly conduct in a mortuary. He paid New York cabbies to blockade each end of a side street so he could throw all of his hotel furniture into the street. In Boston in '76 we kicked off "Substitute" and I looked back and there was no one behind the drum kit. He'd pitched over onto his face. He was ambulanced to the hospital. The crowd rolled forward in murderous little wavelets until it finally sank in that Pete and Roger were promising a make-up concert at the end of the tour.

He had no direction, no nothing. "Why don't I ever, like, pick up a bloody *book*?" he asked me once. I gave him back the old Entwhistle silence. He used to tell us he was the best Keith Moon–type drummer in the world. Alcohol, downers, uppers, painkillers, horse tranquilizers, anything you could fit in a capsule or pour down your throat. "Fuck-all drank all my maple syrup," Pete complained one morning on an American tour. In one recording session he just lay on his tom-toms, and when I asked if he was okay he said, "God, it's hard." Roger asked me to talk to him. "He might listen to you," he said. "His old lady's worried to death." She's talked to *you* about it? I remember thinking.

He was the original Madman who had to outdo everyone else in rock. And imagine what kind of degenerate one had to be to outdo everyone else in rock. Eventually it got so bad that even he had to go for the cure. He started calling each of us each night to say good night and that he loved us. You'd pick up the phone and only know who it was because he was crying so hard. A week into that his girlfriend found him dead in his apartment from an overdose of Heminevrin, the drug they gave him for his other addictions. When I heard I thought: we must've saved his life thirty times, getting him up and walking around, getting him to a hospital. I thought of him saying, "John, let's throw it over and join the Beach Boys." I thought of the nights I'd gotten him on his feet and he'd slurred some version of, "John, you're me only friend."

I asked if anyone had contacted Kim. The police had. After a few drunken nights I went over but she only talked to me through a crack in the door.

"I can't *face* anyone right now, John," she said. I could hear Mandy wailing in another part of the house.

"We're thinking of you," I told her. I hung my head and clasped my hands before me, like the undertaker. Still all in black. "Let us know if there's anything that would help."

"Poor Keith," she said.

The three of us remaining filled the airwaves with talk of how The Who couldn't go on without him. Then we went on without him.

Eleven boys and girls were trampled to death in Cincinnati before a show a year later. We'd insisted on festival seating instead of reserved—we didn't want *our* fans having to sit in numbered rows, unable to move about or dance or shove their way to the front. So naturally when the doors opened there were stampedes. In this case too few doors were opened. We were backstage and knew of a commotion but how many gigs had we played *without* commotions?

What we said to the press, scribbled out and read by Pete in a stupefying hangover at the next tour site, was: "It seems that everyone wants us to shed the theatrical tear and say 'I'm sorry.' Whereas what we have to do is go on." Even Kenny Jones, our new drummer, seemed a little stunned by the heartlessness of it all.

We should have stopped the tour. We knew it. Everyone with whom we dealt was a cretin. Lawyers, managers, promoters, fans. And we sat atop the pile: the emperors of stupidity.

Imagine being as drunk as you've ever been, seven, twelve, fifteen nights in a row. Imagine not knowing which pills are doing what. Imagine each day when you come round you're reminded how much depends on you, how many responsibilities you have for the next few weeks. Imagine something terrible happens. And your head feels like there's been a heavy heavy rain and this is now the runoff, and you're in a big easy chair in a haze listening to the details on the radio and your manager is keeping after you about the way the first three weeks of a tour pay for the fares and expenses, and the next two the road managers and managers, and three preteens in braids and microhalters like Pippi Longstockings from Weimar apparently grew up listening to your music, and are bouncing on their hands and knees on the bed in your suite while your manager keeps repeating himself through the closed door.

We were told after the show how many had died. For one second, our guard dropped. Then it was up again. Everywhere we went journalists asked the same question: "Anything to say about Cincinnati?" And how could it not start to seem false, anything we said? "Oh, we were deeply moved, the terrible tragedy, the loss of life, arrgghh—"

It was like the crowds had out-Moonied us. They'd finally out-Moonied us.

We'd only become who we were because of him. He'd been the missing part. He'd made the rest of us work to capacity. With him in his bicycle saddle bashing away for dear life, all the bad parts and the wrong parts became this awesome and distorted energy. The day he'd met us it was like we'd recognized each other. We hadn't *liked* each other, but we'd known that everyone in the room was pissed off with the way everything was, and with the alternatives. We'd looked around at one another and known right then that we would make it. And we'd had a sense, even as bollocks-stupid as we were, of what making it would mean: of the bodies we'd leave behind.

One thing no one ever seemed to understand: When Pete smashed his guitar, it was because he was *pissed off.* When Keith threw his snare out into the front row, same thing. And why *did* I never move? Why did I *stand* there in the midst of all of this mayhem, like a bloody statue? It was my way of making my mark and erasing my mark, simultaneously. There's nothing like it for exaltation and nothing like it for rank, flat-out failure. You're working as hard as you can to get one fucking song across—to get some livable part of *you* across—and it's never really perfect, it's never really acceptable, it's never even really *right,* is it?

CLIMB ABOARD THE MIGHTY FLEA

I am Oberleutnant Heini Opitz of Test-Commando 16 and this is not a war story. It's the story of a lunatic revolution—the inmates with Bedlam's keys—and the boys all call me Pitz. We fly (Fly? Ride!) the Messerschmitt 163, the first manned rocket-powered aircraft, the first aircraft in the world to exceed a thousand kilometers an hour in level flight, and in statistical terms the most dangerous aircraft ever built in a series. We sit in these squat fireworks with wings and are skyrocketed upward eight thousand meters in under a minute to bring down the Allied bombers. Mostly we bring down ourselves. (We move at such speeds that they can barely touch us with their defensive fire, and we have little more success shooting at them.) The emblem of our fighter wing is an escutcheon depicting a jet-propelled silhouette of a flea, bracketed by the inscription *Like a flea—but oho!* We strap ourselves in and lock down the canopies and plug our helmets' R/T leads into the radios and give our thumbs up, and before we ignite the witches' cauldrons behind our rear ends, we shout as loudly as we can into our masks, "Climb aboard the mighty flea!"

Our field controllers know to pull away their earphones at the last minute. It's a tradition. We've been doing it for weeks.

On our nose shields we have a little emblem of Baron Munchausen riding his cannonball.

We are all good Germans but we've stopped caring about the war. They'll bomb Leipzig flat or they won't; either way we'll be tearing their engines out by the roots with our cannons. If anything ever goes right. Either way we go up and come down, skidding and bouncing and exploding across our grassy airstrip. Either way we lose two pilots and four aircraft per week. Either way sense has long since abandoned us.

Our aircraft's designation is Komet, which suggests that someone in Aircraft Development at Messerschmitt A.G. still has some wit: sorties, and careers, with the thing tend to be nasty, brutish, and short. Wörndl—who received his certificate in philosophy from Heidelberg—says they should have named it the Hobbes.

DIFFIDENCE, TIMOROUSNESS, and timidity. Bad hygiene. Paltry thoughts. Stupidity. The inability to *think.* As a boy in Aschau I was a real one-legged duck. I was prim. I lacked the masculine touches. I hoarded recipes.

I imagined girls as the way out. I did at the age of twelve induce one to touch me, but she only did so with a stick. Afterward she reported the incident to her friends.

Wörndl became my friend out of pity, he says. He called me Baby Bird when he first watched me dismount from the step of the train car at the Bad Zwischenahn station. Apparently there was something insufficiently masculine about the care I was taking to avoid the mud with my shoes. He called Ziegler Toffee and myself Baby Bird when announcing himself as our ride to the airfield. He was my rank and I raised my arm as if to give him the back of my hand and he pushed me down. There was no passenger door on the truck and when trying to find my posting orders at the main gate I fell out of the seat.

His bunk was below mine and when I set my kit on his blanket for a moment while emptying my duffel, he pitched it out the window.

I pitched the rest of my duffel after it, and he laughed.

He had a boxer's flattened nose and wide ears and an exaggeratedly wide head. "You know what they say about big ears," I said, apropos of nothing, and he laughed again, while going about his business.

Gradually I learned about him from the other fellows.

No one is sure why he's still an Oberleutnant. He's at least three years older than everyone else. He told us one night in the mess that he was involved in rocket development back when it was so secret that people would joke that documents were stamped *To Be Burned Before Reading.*

Every unit needs a certain number of matter-of-fact, heavy-lidded types who never complain. The day after I arrived he put a Stummel-Habichts glider into the ground on a low-level loop right in front of all the assembled trainees. We ran to the wreckage to discover him shaking the shattered wooden pieces of the glider from his shoulders the way a dog shakes water from its fur. Our commanding officer said about him that he combined maximum sturdiness with absolute dependability.

"Are you a bed wetter, Baby Bird?" he said to me that night during a quiet moment before lights out. I pitched my duffel out the window again, and again he laughed.

The next morning he asked if I wanted to help test the very latest thing in Home Air Defense. First he led me to the aircraft hangars, completely swathed in camouflage netting. Squatting out of the sunlight in the comparative gloom of the hangar door was an A prototype, as graceful as a young bat.

He opened a hinged hatch like an icebox door in the fuselage and we peered in at a maze of pipes that resembled a refrigeration unit. This, I was told, was the engine. Two thousand horsepower.

The test he was talking about was at the engine hangar at the far end of the airfield. He called it the Poison Kitchen. When we arrived, I was introduced to two of our engineers, Eli and Otto. Otto poured a thimbleful of white liquid into a saucer on the floor. I had a sense from his face that this was standard treatment for the new arrivals. Then Eli, leaning away, held his arm at head height and squeezed an eyedropper over the saucer. The saucer blew up with a surprisingly loud bang. A piece of it rattled off the far window.

"Your aircraft carries a ton of each of these in its wing tanks," Otto said.

Wörndl made bogeyman noises.

Otto poured a little more of his liquid into another saucer. "Touch it," he said.

I rested my fingertip on its surface, held my hand up, and the tip was white, and burned like a horrible sunburn.

"I'd put it in my mouth if I were you," Wörndl said offhandedly.

I did, and the burning stopped. It was explained that my saliva neutralized the effect.

"Completely eats through anything organic," Wörndl said.

But when the first engines were fired! There was never anything like it. The noise was colossal, sheeting against the eardrums even when you covered your ears. I shouted in Wörndl's face and heard no trace of what I said. The hangar had instantly become a wash-house, steaming and roaring and fire-spitting, with billowing clouds swirling and colliding. The engine shut off with a bang and the silence seemed to oscillate. Wörndl led me like a child over to the cockpit and front half of an A prototype with the engine exposed on a mount behind it. The engine exhaust was aimed out a huge aperture in the opposite wall. The entire thing was bolted and cabled to the floor. He gestured me up the short steel ladder and into the cockpit. He followed me up the ladder rungs, and settled me in. When Otto called out "Ready!" he showed me which button to punch. The hangar bellowed and the cockpit bucked and thrummed so my teeth rattled. Wörndl had to hold the ladder with both hands. I could see the walls shaking. The plates that held the stay wires quivered. He gestured for me to push the thrust lever forward, and the increased sound and power cleared away all before it. I screamed; I braced myself; I shrieked with laughter. For two and a half minutes I was Thor controlling the thunder and the lightning. After a muffled bang and the end of the ride I was still shrieking and laughing. Wörndl and Otto had to pull me out of the cockpit by my armpits.

What does a man have the right to do to feel better about himself? From that instant onward I've been an acolyte or a high priest, and I've loved our 163 A's and B's no matter what they did or will do to us.

AS IS OFTEN the case when learning something lethal, our training began innocuously: serene flights in gentle gliders. We progressed through a series of shortening wingspans, and with each lost inch, the landing speed rose. It was useful training, we were told, since the A had a landing speed of over a hundred miles per hour, while the fully loaded B touched down at around a hundred and thirty-seven. To add to the entertainment value, those landings were accomplished without a real undercarriage. The wheels were jettisoned on takeoff. Only a skid cushioned the impact on touchdown. Flight trials at Peenemünde had already taken their toll of vertebrae.

And of course the rocket pilot enjoyed no second chance if he muffed his approach; he couldn't just open the engine up and go round again. He had to bring it in on the first approach and touch down with enough sliding space to decelerate to a standstill before running out of airfield. Flipping the craft, given the fuel, was fatal.

So? we said to ourselves. Everyone knew that learning to fly meant little more than learning to land.

But pilots are taught to land by flying *alongside* instructors. There was no room for two in these things. So we'd have to be *told,* rather than shown.

"Does the landing," Ziegler asked in a classroom session, "have to be *perfect*?"

"No," Wörndl shrugged. "You could die, instead."

There were other complications as well, he remarked. A perfectly acceptable takeoff or landing could provoke the engine into exploding. Or it might explode without provocation. Constant experimentation had been conducted with the aim of eliminating that possibility, without success.

The A and B's cockpits also periodically filled with steam, almost completely obscuring the pilot's view.

By October of 1944 everything bad that could have happened to our brain-dead but still staggering little war machine of a Reich had already happened. Kursk, Stalingrad, Normandy, the firebombing of everything from Berlin to the most inoffensive and lonely hayrick. My hometown of Aschau had its cathedral so obliterated by a night raid, my sister wrote, that the next morning no one could find the *site.* Our bunch came together from Fighter Geschwaders in lost causes all over Europe, from the Ukraine to France to Africa to Italy to the Dalmatian Coast. We had each volunteered for our own reasons. We took as the most ominous sign of all, however, the revelation that Fighter Command had spared nothing when it came to our mess. Items that had long since been hoarded as precious holiday treats were apparently for us a matter of course, every day: creamed rice with fruit preserves, omelettes with kidneys, macaroni with goulash, toast with real white bread. When we asked why we rated such a table, we were told "Altitude diet." It seemed clear that this was a kind of in-joke. "'Altitude' as in, the afterlife," Wörndl explained.

That first breakfast after our commanding officer spoke, Wörndl welcomed us to what he called, with some pride, a program of flight-testing more lethal than any in the history of aviation. But what followed seemed no more hazardous than a lazy drift down a stream: hours on the gliders, followed by towed flights with the A, with the rocket fuel replaced by water ballast. We cast off the tow cables, got whatever feel of the aircraft we could while we lost altitude, and tried to hit the house-sized touchdown cross painted on the field. Landing approach—flaps down—a little right rudder—a gentle bank—level off—stick back slightly—and the thump and the slither. What could have been easier? On my first such landing, after a lengthy slide along the grass, my wing dropped almost tenderly, and I came to a gentle, spinning standstill.

I threw up down my front at my debriefing. Too much rich food, Ziegler suggested.

For excitement we stood a hundred meters from the rocket-testing apertures while the rockets were going. We ground the heels of our palms into our ears and marveled like idiots on parade at the hot waves of air pounding our stomachs and chests. One hundred meters away, and it was like a jolt from a strong man's forearm. While the old hands looked over every so often with unreadable expressions, we competed at how far we could advance, step-by-step, before the heat became too intense.

ON A SATURDAY afternoon two weeks later, a locomotive pulled a solitary, sealed freight car along the airfield branchline and came to a hissing halt beside the largest of our hangars. It was the arrival of the first B, the Komet. The seals were broken and the doors pushed back in a frenzy. It was like we were outside the Pharaoh's Tomb. The thing was wheeled out on a dolly into the cold November sunlight. Unlike the A, there was nothing slender or ballerina-like about the silhouette. This had a look of overpowered stubbiness, like a sawed-off wrestler in a crouch. We circled it, running our palms along it and asking questions of each other, as if we each understood different parts of the machine. Ziegler lay with his cheek on the Perspex canopy. The fuselage was a light alloy with a Dural stressed skin but the wings were single-spar wooden units with a plywood and fabric covering. The construction seemed fantastic, absurd, for something designed to attain such speeds.

Otto and Eli explained everything as the thing was safely rolled into its resting place, like a wheelbarrow with outrageously large wings. The entire rocket motor weighed a little over 300 pounds. The total fuel supply of 336 gallons was consumed in four minutes. The entire engine assembly was attached to the airframe by four bolts and could be removed and replaced in an hour. A climb to altitude that took thirty minutes in a conventional fighter took less than one in our rocket.

Wörndl was the first to go up, late that very afternoon. Otto and Eli were still hovering around and worrying various parts of the ship while he climbed the ladder and strapped himself in and banged the canopy shut. They backed off, as did we all. There was a sharp crack, and a shimmer of heat from the rear and a firehose of flame shot out, and Wörndl was already halfway down the runway and up, his undercarriage falling away and wildly leaping off the runway and into the weeds. The B stood on its tail and shot straight upward, and its engine cut out prematurely. It started falling backward. While we all shouted for him not to do it, he brought the fully loaded thing around in a bank, and onto the grass at what had to be one hundred and fifty kilometers per hour. It went all the way to the end of the field and blundered heavily through a few shallow depressions without exploding.

By then, he'd thrown open the canopy, jumped out, and started running. He stopped at the hangars. The firefighting crew was still arcing water from a good distance away onto the smoking rocket.

It was explained to us the next morning, by Wörndl, that in the event of trouble, we should never do what he did; as a strategy it was almost certainly fatal.

"What *should* we do?" someone asked.

"Bail out," Wörndl said.

"At *two hundred meters*?" we asked.

He shrugged. "I'm not going to pretend we have a solution to this problem if we don't," he said.

The trainees drew lots to see who would go first. Short straw went to a boy I knew only as Herbert who'd transferred in from the Africa Korps. His last name, Ziegler whispered, was Glogner. Glogner climbed into the cockpit the next morning with the sun in his eyes, squinting and grinning while Wörndl helped him, from the ladder, with his various snap-fasteners and connections. It was cold. We could see our breath. We stood around joking and steaming like a clutch of small dragons. Wörndl shut the canopy and cleared away the ladder, Glogner started his engine, and off he went with a roar down the grassy field, white with frost, while we cheered as if at a football match. He left the ground and the undercarriage dropped away, hit the grass, and rebounded upward into the belly of the aircraft. Glogner must have realized what had happened because he pulled the nose up and banked, just as Wörndl had done. He brought the thing around creditably but his wing clipped one of the flak towers on the airfield boundary. He hit the grass at an angle, bounced, and skidded eighty meters or so before ending up on his nose. Again, no explosion. We all rushed to him behind the racing fire tender and ambulance.

When we arrived the stretcher-bearers were kneeling with their backs to the cockpit, weeping and tearing up grass. We fought one another for a view, and shouted and argued over what we were seeing. Some caught on sooner than others. The cockpit was filled with a black-and-red-and-yellow soup. The yellow looked like chicken fat.

The fuel cells had shattered and the fuel had poured into the cockpit. Those who understood explained it to those who still didn't: Glogner had been dissolved alive.

OUR *ESPRIT DE CORPS* was affected by this turn of events. Seven of the fourteen remaining trainees requested transfer, which was immediately granted. We were told their replacements would arrive within the week.

In the meantime the seven of us remaining went on with our straw-drawing.

A boy named Uhlhorn was the next winner and went off and returned without incident. When we swarmed him afterward he pronounced the whole thing a piece of cake. As did our next winner, a near-midget named Bamm. That night we celebrated our first full day without a disaster. The next day we began with one: a sour Bavarian whom no one liked named Hauff came in too high to touch down anywhere near the landing cross and was thrown from the cockpit when the Komet hit. The Komet bounced, splintered, turned over, and blew up. Hauff jackknifed and tumbled nearly as far as the Komet and broke his neck and both legs.

The next Komet exploded on the flight line. When we reached the spot, there was only a blackened and steaming stain. Medical personnel found a bone fragment, and brought it in on a stretcher.

My turn came next. "Come come come, Baby Bird," Uhlhorn said as I held up my straw. "Your one-six-three-B is steaming and ready to blow. We need to put you in it or it will blow up for no reason."

"I don't think we've worked out all of the problems with this aircraft," I muttered to Wörndl as we walked to my Komet. The fueling trucks had topped off the tanks and were backing away. The mechanic's face was red and streaming tears from the fumes.

"In engineering the phrase for a machine like this is 'still technically immature,'" he answered.

I climbed the ladder. He helped with my seat harness and R/T lead.

"Hold the stick steady after you punch the ignition and keep your eyes on the pressure indicator," he said. If on takeoff you lose pressure, pull the throttle back and let her just roll. If she doesn't stop before the perimeter, jump for it."

"Jump for it," I said.

"Jump for it," he repeated. Otherwise I was to keep the stick steady and not push her after I was airborne. I was to drop the wheels when about ten meters off the ground. When my airspeed hit eight hundred I was to pull back on the stick and just let her climb until the rocket gave out on me. Was all that clear? It was.

He mentioned that from inside with the canopy closed, the engine would sound uncannily like an abandoned fox terrier. Apparently his parents had made a stab at an unprofitable kennel before the war.

"Here's to you, Pitz," he said. "Broken neck and legs!"

He saw my face and explained that, after Hauff, that would be his standard good-luck cry.

To trust is to honor, I thought, as he backed away, and I swung the canopy closed and slid the lock.

Otto, Eli, Wörndl; they were all the kind of men I wanted to be. They worked with their hands to retool the world. They'd taken this marvel of design—a child's riding toy that was presently the fastest thing on earth—and prepared it to be ready for me, in this place and at this time. Here, Pitz, they were saying with their expressions, and with their bearing. You take it.

My palms were sticky inside my gloves. I could smell the sheepskin. I trimmed the tail slightly heavy, opened the fuel cocks, engaged the starter motor, and eased the control to full thrust. The thing bolted like a wild horse. Landscape jerked, unreeled, and started ribboning by. The jolting and juddering ceased, my cheeks flattened, and I was up and tore forward like an arrow from a bow. I was on my back with only a few strands of cirrus above me. Blue and blue. My mind was washed clean. There was a jerk and a swinging, suspended in midair. I registered that the fuel was exhausted. Silence descended like a soft curtain.

I filled my radio with a blizzard of static from shrieking. *This* is Heini Opitz, I shouted to myself in my little box. Not that poultry-legged dumpling from Aschau—!

The speed started to fall away. I glanced at my altimeter. I dropped a wing and saw a lake and some farmland. On the horizon, the sun. On my headset I could hear Flight Control still asking why I'd been shouting. I started my wide turns. It took forty minutes to descend. I kept her steady as I lost altitude, let down the landing skid at three hundred meters, and put her down like a bag of stones just past the landing cross. The shoulder harness straps gave me welts from the concussion. But she held together, and stopped.

SO LIKE PENGUINS we sit huddled in the snow and ice at Brandis outside of Leipzig. Our little group is intended primarily for the protection of the immense Leuna synthetic fuel plants. Our success has been limited. That's the way our commanding officer chooses to phrase it in his communiqués. We've flown a dozen interception missions. As far as anyone can tell, no one has hit an enemy aircraft with any kind of ordnance, though Bamm has inadvertently almost torn the tail off a B-17 on a dive through the formation. Five of us still have not fired our guns. It's January and we're fond of telling ourselves that our casualty rate will be one hundred percent before the year is out. Wörndl predicts the same by midsummer.

Most days we're fogged in and can't see the wind sock at the top of its ten-meter pole. The bombers go by overhead and we play skat. After yet another snowfall, Wörndl sculpted a reclining Aphrodite near the mess. He surpassed himself with the care he lavished upon certain details. We christened her Mrs. Wörndl.

As a boy I was thought to handle free time badly. I spent my unsupervised summer days with a stick shearing smaller branches off the birch trees outside of town. I redirected streams. I cooked a mouse.

Bamm has his kit all packed and is perpetually trying to conceive a way of organizing a trip to Berlin on the sly. We play pranks on one another. We explore the varieties of depression. We experiment with irritating behaviors. We watch our moods deteriorate. Ziegler, a big redheaded Frisian, appoints himself Morale Officer and drinks himself into a stupor with two bottles of plum brandy. He claims to be conducting a test. In December he became the first to perform a forward loop in a Komet, though not voluntarily. Each night he informs whoever will listen that his fiancée lives too far away, and that brandy *consoles* him.

We are all insomniacs. We are, as a group, a picturesque compendium of physical tics.

The subject of the day for armchair strategists is The Problem of Pilots. The Komets are cheap and easy to produce. Hundreds can be had in a matter of months. That leaves the question of who will fly them. Recruits appear in our midst regularly. After each new crash, most put in for reassignment. Which leaves our group not so much growing by leaps and bounds as just barely replenishing itself.

But this isn't about winning the war. This is about our doing what we want to do. If others don't want to do it with us, the hell with them.

Otherwise, are things so bad? The rocket motors, tested and tested again, now give a good account of themselves. Or at least don't explode so frequently. We've all become adept at picking up the slightest off-note in the rocket's roar. The fuel stinks so dreadfully at altitude that tears pour down our cheeks, even through our goggles, but the steam problem has been solved.

Ziegler has taken to weeping in his sleep. Uhlhorn and Bamm have taken to carrying his cot out into the latrine and leaving him there.

We're strafed by a pair of silver Mustangs sweeping in low over the forest, but no one's hurt, and otherwise we're left alone.

We're instructed to entertain a delegation of visiting Japanese, come to view the wonder weapon. Wörndl takes up his Komet and roars it around at tree level, pelting along like some kind of insane flying reptile at full throttle just ten meters above the field. "Wasn't that something!" he shouts at the Japanese after he lands and is presented to them. Still deafened, they smile politely, bow from the waist, and remain silent.

ON SUNDAY, the 24th of January, church bells are ringing and the sky is a brilliant blue, and our dozen new 163 B's are lined wingtip to wingtip in the early-morning sun, resplendent in their fresh varnish. No breakfast today. We all stand outside with our hands in our pockets, watching the bombers come on. They're so high they're only specks at the ends of vapor trails that extend back for miles.

We're going up in staggered pairs and Uhlhorn and Ziegler are first. I'm to help Uhlhorn while Wörndl assists Ziegler. Uhlhorn's in too much of a hurry and I work to slow his rush through the pretakeoff procedures. He's not a complete loss by any means, but so Austrian he might have fallen out of Franz-Joseph's waistcoat, and forever gesticulating and talking sixteen to the dozen when you want him to just sit still. Across the runway, Wörndl is leaning into Ziegler's cockpit with the self-assurance of a baker sliding loaves into an oven.

Finally Uhlhorn's ready, I pull away the ladder, he goggles his eyes and gives me a thumbs-up through the Perspex, his rocket fires, and off he goes. Ziegler follows.

Bamm and Wörndl are the next pair. I'm in the final one with a new boy named Rösle.

Otto helps me into my seat. The shipping tag is still on the control stick. "Has anyone flown this one yet?" I ask him. "No," Otto says, absorbed in my harness buckles. "But Eli said he saw a test run of the engine."

I make a face at him through the Perspex and give him the thumbs-up. "Climb aboard the mighty flea!" Rösle shouts over our R/T. I test my controls for free play and punch the starter button. Again the rush and the bouncing, again the upward sweep and the arrowing, again my war whoops and shrieks.

Still high above, the bomber stream begins to change course slightly. Arcing toward them, the first contrails from our Komets. It looks to be forty or so B-17s in five echelons. Now they're the size of match heads. Now coffee beans. Now crickets, spreading all around me, and the air is filled with lariating tracers and I hear thunks on my wings and fuselage. Rösle half-turns in my peripheral vision, and, standing on his wingtip, flashes away to my left. I try to use my cannon but my principal—only—advantage—speed—is lost when jockeying around for the proper firing angle. The air seems dirty and filled with debris. I bank and sweep over one, then two Fortresses and I'm out of the formation and the air is clear again. I fire my cannon off into space. My engine cuts out.

The Komet seems to brake hard in midair, and I'm thrown forward against my harness. There's still more than enough momentum and speed for one more pass through the formation. A Thunderbolt spins by, hoping to provide the bomber stream with some protection. I pass him like he's a dray horse. I close distance to the trailing B-17s, depress the trigger, and my cannons jam. I curse God and creation and scream frustration for the next sixty minutes all the way down to the airfield.

Still ranting, I approach slightly high and overshoot the landing cross and hurtle along the frozen grass. The perimeter thrums toward me. I pull the canopy release and unbuckle the harness.

There's blinding white light from the floor and heat sears upward, and I jerk up my knees and plant my feet on the seat and jump. Maybe I land on my head or possibly all fours. The Komet blows up seventy meters or so farther down the runway.

The ambulance drivers rush up and take inventory. My face is stinging. I'm told my eyebrows and eyelashes are gone, along with a good third of my hair. Someone smears something on my cheeks and neck and I'm carried off to a bed.

WHEN I WAKE there's an impromptu celebration and meeting around my bunk. It transpires that Wörndl's Komet caught fire right above the field. He had to bail out forty meters from the treetops and his parachute caught the upper branches of a big pine, insuring he only cracked his ankle. He tells everyone that it was like jumping off a church steeple with an umbrella.

Uhlhorn had his motor cut out when he was hardly a thousand meters from the formation. Ziegler's cockpit filled with steam on his first pass. Rösle's Komet flipped on landing just before the perimeter. It didn't explode and he was pulled from it just conscious, but pints of the fuel had run over his back while he hung there, and when they tore off the flight suit, the skin underneath was a jelly. He was on enough painkillers to last until April.

The entire thing was witnessed by eighteen new trainees who arrived just after we'd taken off. Many of them, it's clear, now deeply regret their daring. Seven have already left.

But up in the thicket of the bomber stream, while the rest of us were wasting time and fishtailing about to no great effect, Wörndl's cannons tore the wing off one Fortress and the tail off another. Both were confirmed.

"This was a high-altitude interception that took *less than five minutes* from when we first spotted them," he reminds us. His big ears are red from the sheer love of our enterprise. He's commandeered my chair and slung his temporary cast onto my bed to keep his ankle elevated. "Who'd return to a Bf 109 now? And take a half hour to get upstairs? If we're unhappy where we are, our Komets can have us somewhere else. Faster than we can say, 'somewhere else.'"

"Somewhere else," Ziegler says, standing with his arm on the windowsill. "But, I'm still here," he smiles, when we all look at him.

AROUND NOON there's a short snowfall. The airfield is lightly covered. Cumulus clouds have arrived. I'm instructed to rest my face.

I've received a letter from my sister. *Do you remember the way you hoarded candies?* she writes. *The way we all joked you'd end up a landlord, or a miser alone in his room?*

The Komets are back on the line, topped up and ready to go. No one imagines the Americans are going to waste weather like this this afternoon. Uhlhorn, Bamm, Ziegler, and some of the new arrivals have a snow-fight. Wörndl and I visit Rösle, who's asleep on his belly with his mouth open. The dressings on his back are soaked through.

Wörndl gazes at his face for longer than seems necessary. "When we write our squadron history, every chapter's going to be entitled 'Our Numbers Dwindle,'" he finally remarks.

As if under a far-off pot, Leipzig's air-raid sirens begin to howl.

We step outside. The burned part of my face feels slapped in the sunlight. Wörndl leans on an oaken stick the medical orderly has dug up for him. At the operations post, we struggle into our flight suits, and then I walk with him, at his pace, to the starting line.

Ziegler, Bamm, Uhlhorn, four of the less-new trainees, and our CO are already aboard their rides and at Immediate Readiness, all of them listening intently to situation reports over the R/T. Wörndl and I climb our ladders into adjacent aircraft. We settle in, strap in, and plug in.

The regional spotter sounds as though he's calling a close finish at the racetrack. They're coming directly toward us. Leipzig or Berlin. Leipzig or Berlin. They're changing course. No. Back on course. Leipzig.

Our sky is a washed bowl. The occasional cumulus has moved off to the west. Over Leipzig and the Leuna Works there's a browner haze.

High above to the north, finally, a phalanx of contrails. I think of drypainting: someone dragging a dry white paintbrush across the clear dome of the sky.

Voices volley through the R/T. Three hundred planes. No, five hundred. No, more.

Slightly behind and below them, silken threads, just visible: the fighter escorts.

There's a stunned lull in our earphones. Wörndl calls me on the R/T. I can see his eyes through his canopy. He hasn't lowered his goggles yet.

"You've got a lot more luck than sense, Pitz," he says. He seems to mean it as a compliment. His voice rattles and pops in my ear.

"My mother says the same thing," I answer. He laughs.

It occurs to me that we missed celebrating his birthday on Friday. It's our custom to celebrate birthdays on the anniversaries of days on which someone should have died. Wörndl, for example, has six, all clustered in the winter.

Eli and Otto and our ground crew members move from aircraft to aircraft performing final checks. The ground crew members peer worriedly at us, as always, torn in their allegiances between aircraft and pilot.

I'm not interested in love, or wealth, or fame, or wisdom, or in being longed for, or in being admired for my perspicacity, or for my sage and considered advice. I'm not interested in my family's admiration, or in politics. I'm not interested in alcohol. I'm not interested in killing. I'm not interested in me.

See if you can understand: I'm not interested in what drives you. I'm not interested, as Wörndl is, in philosophy. He had a phrase for what I want. He called it "being the perfect expression of my own instrumentality."

On my left, engines are roaring. Thumbs-up are moving down the line. Wörndl slams shut his canopy. I slide shut mine. "Climb aboard the mighty flea!" he shouts in my earphones. "Climb aboard the mighty flea!" I shout in his. Out on the grass before us, someone's Komet is already slingshotting away toward the perimeter fence. Whoops and Red Indian yells are starting to fill the R/T.

In the future, the short future, those of us who survive this day of the Komet's greatest success will be eradicated by accidents, collisions, and Allied fighters dawdling over our airfield, waiting for the helplessness of our landing approaches, having finally puzzled out our Achilles' heels. One day Mustangs, one day Lightnings, one day Thunderbolts. There will be requests for volunteers for ramming attacks. There will be, in the evenings, the misery-inducing spectacle of the mess: puddles of spilled wine under dirty glasses. Empty seats. Tobacco smoke still in the air.

That group will have found itself well on the other side of anxiety. The far shore. That group will climb into their B's as though they were rowboats on a lake. That group will finish what rations are delivered in those final days and deliver itself to St. Immolation.

This group is hurtling upward, wingtip to wingtip, to engage the biggest bomber stream any of us has ever seen. The roar beneath us will never stop. We reach that part of the sky that turns from turquoise to green to dark blue—*fifteen thousand meters up*—before our engines stop and we tip and falter and prepare to fall onto the bombers' heads. We bank and dive like swallows. My cockpit is clear of fumes but still I'm weeping. There's Wörndl, a good thousand meters below me, drawing helixes from the contrails of his spiraling wingtips. There's Ziegler, right behind him, rocking from side to side like a boomerang from hell. Flights of Thunderbolts, sluggish specks, struggle upward to meet us. No one's speaking. Our ears are on the slipstream. Our thumbs are on the cannon triggers. Our hearts are in the dive. We have become the inexplicable. We have become the unbelievable. We are our own descendants, the children we have always wanted to be.